STEAM

STEAM

by Jay B. Laws

Boston: Alyson Publications, Inc.

To Alan, first and always,
And in memory of Danny and Mark,
Two of many, now sorely missed.
Hold the elevator, boys...

Acknowledgments

Many friends contributed time, energy, and support while I worked on this book. First and always, my partner, Alan, who pulled me from the quicksand more than a few times and set me back upon the proper path. A big thank-you to Larry G., who insisted I join the computer age and put up with all my questions and constant need for printed-out drafts. To Dennis B., the most psychically gifted individual I've ever been privileged to know, for his uncanny suggestions and tips. To the gang at San Francisco Suites — Robert, Isabel, Pete, among others — for providing a work environment that nurtured friendship as well as my writing; quite a bonus. Lastly, one more thank-you to Richard Labonté at A Different Light Bookstore in San Francisco and Sasha Alyson for sponsoring the contest that made my dream come true.

Contents

Part 3: Disco inferno

After: After words : 396

Before

IIIII ... love to love you, baaaby...
—Donna Summer

The fall from grace

1

Life a winding parade down Main Street, music blasting off grandly colored floats, men and women dancing, baton twirlers twirling: a huge multicolored family.

How brightly the sunshine lit upon our faces.

But the darkness, you see, had already crept in on cat feet. Crouched in the corner. Waiting.

2

Before: New York City, June 1982, 2:30 a.m.

For David Walker, the first horror began here, in this other city in an earlier time.

David inserted the key to his apartment and threw open the door with an unexpected bang. Three or four vodka tonics sloshed in his belly. Two joints. A line of coke at the party before he and the gang went out dancing. He was weaving as he stood at the door.

Nothing prepared him for catching the young burglar inside his apartment.

A startled moment spun out between them. Each eyed the other with eyes huge as saucers.

David took in the rifled drawers, the smashed mirrors, and winking broken glass. Overturned furniture. And most of all: the long serrated edge of the knife in the thief's hand — David's knife, taken from its resting place beside the stove — as the teenager swiveled in shocked surprise and stabbed the air in his direction.

He launched himself out of the doorjamb, arms pinwheeling. He ran. His drunken mind flipped into panic as he ran heedlessly down the carpeted hallway, flying toward the stairwell as he heard the thief scramble after him.

"Hey!" the punk shouted. "Get back here!"

David burst through the stairwell door and made a decision that would haunt him for the rest of his life: He ran up the one flight of stairs to the rooftop, not down to the lobby and street below, where he might have found help. Too late. He knew it even as he took the stairs two at a time. Screams undulated out of him.

Forty seconds had passed since he had slipped the key into his apartment door and startled the burglar.

Reflex drove him forward. All that mattered were the footfalls banging up the stairs behind him in chase. A machine gun sound. A killing sound.

He burst upon the rooftop, lungs hitching for air, his screams unabated. Moments before he had been an ordinary young man coming home from a night of dancing and overindulging with his friends. Now, he screamed for his life. Would no one hear him on this hot summer night? Wasn't there anyone with windows flung wide for a breeze to catch his cries?

He stumbled across the gravel-and-tar roof until he stood by a ledge. Cautiously, he peered over. Four stories up. The nearest building too far to jump. Wait! The fire escape! He spun around.

His heart caught in his throat. The burglar was advancing.

"Shut up!" the kid screamed. The knife slashed a jagged path across the air. He was scared by this man in front of him who would not be quiet. "Shut up! I'm warning you!" He stole two steps.

In this world that had been irrevocably reduced to confrontation, there was no room for grays. And David, spinning, saw two choices: Stand there and get hacked to pieces — or jump.

Up over the edge he scrambled. Still railing against a night silent and unforgiving. No conscious thought about what would happen next. His life distilled into a single impulse: Get away.

"Hey!" the punk cried. "Where the fuck you going?"

David slid over the edge, buttons on his shirt popping against the rough ridge, his feet swinging. He kicked at the building for a ledge to rest upon, a foothold. Suddenly he imagined that knife plunging into the back of one of his hands.

And let go.

Air rushed out of him.

The universe sank.

Dimly aware of his body striking ground.

Darkness engulfed him. And darkness was enough.

1

Devil's gun

We did not dream it
We had no warning
That one day all too soon, across the land:
A fog
Sun paled to autumn shadow
And we: at war.

1

Alas, Flint

1

The razor bit a clear red line across his wrist.

Flesh parted. Candy-red blood, a surprising quantity of it, trickled down between the fingers of his left hand and splashed into the swirling water of the hot tub.

And it don't hurt one bit — ain't that a killer?

Flint switched the razor to his left hand and laid bare his right wrist. He tried to focus on an appropriate vein, but hey, who was he kidding here: A vein is a vein. Slash the goddamn thing and get this over with. The razor's edge gleamed in the dim light before arching downward across the exposed dark flesh. Again, the candy blood.

And Flint thought, *None of this is real.*

2

Of course, in the hours preceding this momentous event, Flint had made damn sure he would feel no pain. He had started the day with a full bottle of Johnny Walker Red, tooted a line for courage, and then puffed a joint to calm his nerves. Ralph and Will had come by his flat about eight that night, threatening to tear down the door or call the police. Flint had sat in his easy chair, lights out, listening to their pounding and demands. He knew what they wanted to tell him. His answering machine was jammmed with their frantic messages.

Flint what's wrong why aren't you answering was it bad news huh Flint what did the doctor say—

After about twenty minutes, they gave up and left. Maybe they figured he was down at the Eagle, or the Powertool. The usual hangout.

Not tonight, buddy boys. He was checking out, toot-a-loo, arrivederchi, catch you next time.

He packed a gym bag. A towel. The last of the Johnny Walker Red. Two joints. Half a gram of coke. Razor blades.

He swept the apartment with a final appraisal. He hadn't done so bad. A black leather sofa. Two original Nigels on the wall. Stocked bar. Waterbed big enough to sleep six comfortably, and, oh baby, how it had slept six, a dozen nights' worth. Monogrammed towels, big as a door, fluffy the way he remembered being dried off as a kid with his momma, the initials L.F.S., Larry Frank Stone, "Flint" Stone to his friends, har har. A record selection four shelves high, every Donna Summer Diana Ross Barbra Streisand Aretha Franklin Gloria Gaynor ever printed, including the cream of the disco hits, new wave, you name it, he owned it. His customers had to have *some*thing to listen to while they sucked cock.

Yeah, he thought, for an old black fart he could have done a lot worse.

He was thirty-eight, light-skinned for a black man originally from Atlanta, hair flecked with gray. Six foot two. A baseball player in his youth, perhaps a sports career if he'd really wanted it. But no. He had hightailed it to San Francisco, a horny young man with two hundred dollars in his pocket, and he had built himself an empire.

He'd had a good time. He couldn't ask for better than that.

Flint scooped up the gym bag, threw on his Calvin Klein leather jacket, and left his apartment without a backward glance. He navigated two narrow flights of stairs, hanging onto the railing for dear life. He wasn't about to end his life as a twisted heap at the bottom of a staircase, no way. He opened the front door and walked out into the night.

Low clouds pregnant with rain floated soggily across the sky. A storm on the horizon. As if on cue, a fine mist cooled his face as he locked the front door to his apartment building on Folsom Street. He welcomed it. A dozen memories of himself as a young man, running zigzag trails through flash storms and sudden showers as he loped toward protective awnings and trees — a lifetime of memories shifted through his mind. For just a moment, anger at his predicament welled. He tasted it in the back of his throat. It was unfair: to be so completely reminded of life as his task lay before him...

But in the end he smiled and lifted his eyes to the heavens. That such a small pleasure as this could be given to him now was enormously comforting.

You takes what you can in life, and right now the treasure chest, she emmmpty.

Flint walked down a block to Harrison and turned left. A few men were out on this Saturday night, but not many. Streets unnaturally quiet, as though everyone had elected to stay inside and wait out the storm. Even traffic was light. The low clouds seemed to sag against his shoulders.

He rounded the corner at Roberts Alley and headed down the block. Completely deserted. Just a handful of years ago Roberts Alley was one hoppin' street. The few straight families who lived there used to regularly complain about all the cruising in the street, the quick sex between parked cars and on unlit front porches. Flint had complained, too — he didn't want guys out on the streets.

He wanted them in his bathhouse.

That's what the Caverns was all about: convenient hot sex. If they got it out on the street for free, he'd have no business.

Of course, he had no business anyway, now. The city shut him down in 1987. Unsafe sexual practices, and all that bullshit. He still bristled when he thought about it. Wasn't he the one who had single-handedly taped AIDS-awareness posters on the walls? Given away rubbers in a basket beside the lockers? Laid out stacks of literature at the snack bar in the rec room? He'd bent over backwards, "Yah-suh"-ing the city at every new demand until he was up to his eyeballs in regulations. And still they shut him down, along with all the other clubs.

He'd fought it, you bet. The other club owners banded together and took it to court, but meanwhile the doors stayed shut and daily Flint watched his tiny fortune get eaten away. Then—

Then he'd gotten sick, and now he was here. You live by the cock, you go out by the cock. Something like that.

Out of his reverie Flint looked up to find himself standing directly in front of the Caverns. It was a big brick building three stories high. Its upper-floor windows were boarded up, blind to the surrounding bland neighborhood. Up three steps, the shiny black doors with a sign beside it, in neat printed letters: CAVERNS.

End of the road.

He pulled out his set of keys and swept up the steps. He steadied the door with one hand and was about to insert the key when

What the fuck?

the door popped open.

Flint whirled drunkenly, as if expecting an intruder to be standing at a distance, watching and laughing at his distress.

Somebody got inside somebody got hold of the key who could have done this?

And as he stepped inside, closing the front door behind him and sealing out the last night he would ever know, he was right about one thing.

He was not alone.

3

A sudden cloudburst let go its treasure chest of rain right as Flint locked the door behind him.

Just made it, he thought. He chuckled as the absurdity struck him. Made it from — what? To — what?

Home sweet home.

He lit a reefer and punched up lights for the basement. This front entryway was dark, but, shit, he could walk this stretch blindfolded. Lots of guys had gotten lost within these winding halls and twisting staircases. This building wasn't called the Caverns for nothing. The whole interior had been specifically designed to create the look and feel of an underground cave. Flint had seen a Hercules movie once about an underground maze and a Minotaur, and he'd decided that was some cool shit, that spooky place where the Minotaur could ravish you if you were caught. He had recreated such a world here. A thousand miles from the glass and chrome of his competitors, it had been an instant hit going strong for over ten years.

He went into his office and popped one of his favorite disco tapes into the cassette player. Cranked up the speakers. Soon he heard the familiar croon of Donna Summer's "Love to Love You" over the speakers. He smiled. Just like the old days.

Flint crossed the length of hallway, swaying, one hand outstretched as if to touch the dark, the joint squeezed between two fingers. He did not want to grace these rooms and hallways with even one sweet parting glance, so he walked right past the snack bar and TV room, the rows upon rows of cubicles where men used to play. He felt as neglected and outdated as a dinosaur, and about as pretty.

The music began to lift his spirits. This place had been too quiet, echoey the way a gymnasium never knows true quiet, with a hum of activity just this side of hearing.

The ghosts that must walk these halls, Flint thought as he tossed away the reefer. All the hundreds of men who had come here to suck and fuck and play. All that male energy. Where did it go? Right into the walls, probably. Storing up all that energy like a great big battery.

Of course, he soberly reminded himself, a few ghosts did walk these very halls, yes indeedy. Let us not forget the five (or was it six?) men who said hasta la bye-bye in here. Two by sleeping pills. One heart attack. The others, speed or heroin overdose — he couldn't remember all the details. At the time he hadn't understood why they chose the Caverns as the place to off themselves. Why didn't they just fucking stay home? Leave a tidy note and be done with it.

Now, as Flint stumbled down the spiral staircase to the basement, he understood their motive, because tonight, he embraced it as well.

They liked it here. They had a good time here. Fun. Why not come to a place that served you well, that made you remember happier times? Shoot, isn't that why I'm here?

He walked into the shower area. The air was heavy, vaporous in the low light. He knelt beside the jacuzzi and flipped the switch. Jet streams churned the water. To his left were the showers, a row of seven nozzles. Directly in front of him, the steamroom. Oh, the fun he'd had in *there*. On his right, a hallway that led to rooms with chains and a sling, for men who had a particular itch to scratch.

Yes, sir, I'm gonna be in fine company in here. Maybe they'll come say hello when I cross to the other side. They won't care that I've got purple spots popping out on my skin, and lungs all congested with shit. Hell, maybe we'll throw ourselves a party. This is for the best, going out in style on my own terms.

He opened his gym bag and snorted two spoonfuls from his little vial. He'd paid for it; he might as well use it up.

Flint yanked off his Calvin Klein jacket and hundred-dollar shoes. Popped the buttons on his silk shirt designed by somebody fancy in New York. Whispered out of his pants. Threw them all into a pile beside the hot tub and slid into the lukewarm water. That was fine by him; he didn't want the water up to full temperature. He'd read that slashing wrists in a tub of water was an easy exit. Supposedly it felt like just melting away.

And so Flint, with the doctor's words ringing in his ears — *I'm sorry, Mr. Stone, but our biopsy definitely shows Kaposi sarcoma* — hesitated only briefly before cutting first the left, and then the right, wrist.

The water churned red. He melted.

The disco retrospective was up to another Donna Summer hit, this time singing "I Feel Love" in 1977 (or was it 1978?), before Jesus came knocking at her door.

Let's face it, he thought dreamily, head resting on the outer rim of the tub, slashed wrists somewhere underwater. *I'm a child of the seventies. Nothing's ever been the same since then.*

At least he'd had his golden years. Nothing wrong with a candy store. You eat too many sweets, you floss. These young kids coming up — they'd missed it all. They wrinkled their cute smug noses at the very idea of patronizing a bathhouse. Playing in the orgy room. Sniffing poppers. Taking a hot load down the throat or up the ass.

At least he'd had fifteen years. These kids were still wetting their beds when he was down on his knees, taking care of a man. Growing up in Atlanta had been no bed of roses, and he'd plugged a girl or two as a teen to keep his suspicious friends at bay — but moving to San Francisco had ignited that spark that was his truest self, and he had embraced the city and his new lifestyle with all the fever of youth.

He played hardball, but he played to have fun. What was that dippy French song all the drag queens loved to sing? "No Regrets."

Flint glanced groggily at his surroundings. The very best had come to play within these walls. This was his crowning achievement. Top of the world, Ma.

And now here he was, center stage in the hot tub, Flint Stone, ole har-de-har-har himself, presently offing himself.

He sank into crimson waters.

4

Suddenly, awake.

He thinks he must have dozed. Nodded off. Because everything is different, now. The air around him is bloated with moisture. The lights, dim.

The steamroom breathes with a mechanical hiss. It sits in front of him, ten feet away. The generator that runs it is old-fashioned and loud. Its steamy sigh wafts over him.

Had he turned it on? He can't remember. He thinks no, he had no reason to, but his head spins and he's not sure of anything.

His homemade disco tape has rewound and started over again. Gloria Gaynor, "Never Can Say Good-bye." Below the music, like a slumbering giant, the hiss and gasp of steam.

Flint looks down at himself. The swirling water is candy red, sticky. He studies it with cool detachment. Did all that come out of two little cuts? He lifts his eyes to glance about the room and blinks.

The steamroom door swings open on silent hinges. A cloud of steam rolls out and up, running along the water-spotted ceiling in billowy tendrils. The sharp tang of eucalyptus fills the room.

He smiles. Calm. Almost as though he expected such a thing. The door opened by itself — ain't that a killer? He is not the least bit frightened when the voice speaks to him.

(Come to me, Flint)

Who's there?

he answers, unaware that he said nothing aloud.

(I am here to make you king)

King?

(This shall be your palace. We will fill it, you and I)

I don't understand.

(Isn't that what you want?)

Yes, but—

I'm dead, Flint thinks all at once. *I must be dead.* And he hears a chuckle, as though the voice has heard his thoughts and confusion.

(I shall reward you, Flint. You have paved the way for me. All you have to do ... All that is required...)

Yes? Yes?

(Come to me)

Steam billows out toward him. Flint sits up. He moves. He can move! The knowledge sweeps through him. It isn't too late, then. With hardly an effort he glides through the water and steps up and out of the hot tub. *A second chance.* That thought propels him forward, even as he hears that laugh again, reverberating up through his soul. The steam pouring out of the room reaches for him, urging him forward. Tingling against his body. He has but one thought: a second chance.

And as he stands at the entrance of that yawning dark mouth, steam touching his skin with a hot damp kiss, Flint glances behind him, and chokes back a scream.

His body floats in the jacuzzi, faceup, swimming in the bubbly red water.

Flint takes a backward step.

The laugh, fiendish and high-pitched with excitement.

As the steamroom door whispers shut.

5

Outside, the great Pacific storm lashes San Francisco. Lightning rips and shreds the purple sky.

It begins.

The comic-book storm

1

The darkness rode the wings of a Pacific storm, and only a few saw — or sensed — its arrival.

2

A low fog erased twilight on that Saturday night. It rolled in like a living gray smudge upon the horizon, blanketing all of the city west of Twin Peaks that faced the Pacific. From there, it quickly whipped across the panoramic slopes of Twin Peaks and spilled into the Castro district. Lights flipped on early downtown and in the Marina, as if nightfall had caught the city by surprise. Even the normally fog-free belt south of Market was not exempt that day. Whole chunks of the city all but disappeared. The world fell gauzy white, gray.

In the Castro, streets that had earlier hummed with activity began to empty as temperatures plummeted and a chilling wind whistled down Market Street. Men and women caught unprepared for the cold dashed home for jackets and sweaters or ducked into bars to warm up. Customers in these bars peered out of tinted glass windows with mounting alarm; never had the fog seemed so ... suffocating. Everywhere men hurried helter-skelter with hands buried in zippered jackets and chins tucked against the damp wind.

High clouds gave way to the storm that had traversed the entire Pacific. Thunderheads boiled purple and black, gaining strength as they collided with land. Heat lightning lit the sky in crazy negatives. The wind shrieked with a banshee cry, rattling Victorian homes.

By nine-thirty the first drops of rain began to fall. And then it seemed a giant took a knife and ripped open the pregnant bellies of the clouds, for all at once rain descended in torrents. Half of San Francisco would sit up and watch, wild-eyed with a mixture of dread and delight, the storm's pounding of the city.

David Walker thought he knew about storms, and their darkness. They held no fascination for him.

That's why now, in his two-bedroom flat on Noe Street, he wasn't sitting by the sliding glass doors for the spectacular view. All of the apartments on his side of Noe Street (that's pronounced No-*e*, as he used to correct all his New York friends) sported gracious views of the Castro and the steep sparkling slopes of Twin Peaks. In the mornings, blurry with sleep, he usually perched on the couch with his candy-sweet coffee. And sometimes — especially during the long summer twilights — he would come home from his days of running errands, plop onto the couch, and simply watch twilight paint the city.

But he was not at the window now.

Tonight, he sat at his desk. Not in an office, but in a chunk of his bedroom, a tiny corner sandwiched between closet and dresser, where he had set up a desk, typewriter, books. Here, he wanted no distracting view. Here, the wall was bare, mutable, for the cinema of his mind.

Tap. Tap. Tap. Purr of electric typewriter.

Tonight, each sentence was a wild effort, all of it clumsy and clichéd. The trash can beside the desk was stuffed high with paper snowballs, a sentence or two typed on each crumpled page.

Tap. Tap. Tap. Purr.

Tonight's story should have been a quickie. He'd labored on it for three days, and still it was a piece of crap, all loose threads with no central thrust and — sin of sins — no climax. He remembered that scene in *Julia* where Jane Fonda, as Lillian Helman, tossed her typewriter out the window in frustration. No writer would *ever* do that, he had thought smugly at the time.

Tonight, if someone had handed him an axe, he would have chopped his Smith Corona into baby food.

David rubbed his eyes. The clock on his desk read 11:45. One more cup of coffee? He was already jittery, still wired from his afternoon visit with Eddie at the hospital. Even so, he debated the coffee. It'd give him another hour of writing — maybe. Or another hour of staring at the blank wall in front of him where he should see his short story projected upon a mental screen, but where instead it was Eddie he saw, Eddie with his full-moon eyes and tubes sticking out of places David didn't dream existed, Eddie his roommate and old college chum who now weighed one hundred and thirty-two pounds soaking wet, shrinking away to nothing in a hospital bed.

David Walker knew about real horror, oh yes indeed.

He reread the paragraph it had taken him thirty minutes to write:

Hank knew if anyone could teach him how to be with a man, it would be Rob, the swarthy Italian hero of his own stories. But Rob would only visit at night, lights out. In the morning, all that would be left of him were little black curls of hair on the sheets. He

He *what?* David thought miserably, and then added "and who cares."

Porn. That was his problem. Years ago, in New York, it had been a pretty good racket, an unexpected meal ticket to augment rent and waiting tables while he labored over his sci-fi novels. He had discovered, once he relaxed about it and simply went with the flow, that by tapping into his own sexual fantasies and experiences, he could crank out three or four stories a month. In traditional stories, sex — if it was even included at all — lasted a paragraph or two, perhaps a page, as an interlude between the *real* action. The secret to writing porn was inverting that process. Take that sexy paragraph and pull it inside out, stretch it until the whole story reveals itself using sex as its canvas. Spice the sex with an exotic locale, or danger, with the first sexual encounter no later than the bottom of the first page, and end the story with an orgy of unsurpassed pleasure for the host character. Mail it out, get busy on something else, and see what trickled in.

Somewhere along the way — long before his move from New York back to San Francisco — all the fun had gone out of writing porn. Actually, he knew the where and when, though it had happened as a whimper and not a bang. Like air escaping from a balloon, leaving him flat and deflated and worst of all scared.

That night in his New York hospital room, six months after his accident, the night he read "1100 And Counting" on the front page of the *New York Native* and learned about an enemy far worse than an army of Anita Bryants and John Briggses.

And just like that, before he could say abracadabra, the fear had settled into the pit of his stomach, an uninvited house guest. Don't mind me, Davie ole boy, the fear seemed to say. We're going to be pals for a long time, I say a *loo*ng time, so better just get used to me. I'll give you a tweak whenever you catch a cold and make you wonder if it's The Big One. I'll feed on your guilt and spit on your worry and just kick up my feet and laugh and laugh, because I've got all the time in the world buddy boy, but you? Well, who knows how long it'll take before the pounds begin to slide right off of ya and you wake up in pools of sweat with your heart hammering to beat the devil, who knows how long, that's the great question. *I* know how long — but I ain't telling.

His life, in that instant, surgically divided into a "Before" and an "After." The new sickness (and his accident, which somehow swirled together) had swept aside the Before part of him; he, a misbehaving child, his toys snatched away.

Little by little, as the days turned into years and news of the "plague" grew into out-and-out war, as friends and acquaintances and strangers succumbed into the bottomless well of statistics, his work became a mockery of the life he saw around him. In this world where men searched for love through phones and video and pornography, the desire to write about sexual adventures paled and grew hollow. Perversely enough, the need for his stories was never greater. And so David kept at it, even after he moved back to San Francisco to finish his recuperation. His concentration was shot for attempting something as heavyweight as a novel; he just didn't have the energy any more. What else could he do? He had to pay rent. He had to put his life back together. So he stuck with the porno, trying sexy new angles, different themes, rehashed dialogue. What the hell; the editors loved him, even though his writing flew on automatic pilot.

Then he would have one of his nights, like now, where he sat at his desk writing of cocks and sweat and desire but his mind stayed on Eddie, sick for the past eight months and going fast now, Eddie who wanted to see one more Christmas but who would probably never even see Halloween.

Yes, David knew the horror.

This stuff ate at his insides day by day, a bite at a time. The horror of monsters from outer space that he wrote about in his many unfinished science fiction novels couldn't hold a candle to the quiet horror that was his "After" life.

Tap tap tap. Purr.

He snapped off the typewriter and wrenched himself away from his desk. No good. It was just no good, tonight. Too many haunted faces.

He stood up and stretched, his cramped muscles flaring. His hip, where he had broken it (along with just about every other bone in his body), thudded dully. He was of modest height, five foot ten, and lanky, with short black hair so shiny it often looked blue, like something out of a Superman comic book. A wide strong forehead showcased his almond-shaped green eyes — a writer's eyes that regarded the world around him with intense scrutiny. David pumped iron at one of the local gay gyms, and his body, at thirty-one, still retained its wiry definition. A kind smile, quiet conversation over a glass of wine, and he had a bed partner, if he so desired. He did not so desire, not like in the Before days. Sex with the VCR was just fine, thank you very much. The need for real contact with another man was slipping away, one more quiet casualty in the Great War. After a while he did not even notice.

He lurched stiffly down the hallway to the living room. His lower back screamed, his hip a pounding drumroll. God, he was going to pay for his writing session tonight. Up half the night, tossing and turning, if he wasn't careful.

Lured by orange flashes and rumbling thunder, he stood by the sliding glass doors fronting his living room and looked out at his unobstructed view of Twin Peaks. He'd forgotten about the storm building all day (though it probably accounted for some of the soreness in his joints; his mended bones had become a regular weather station).

And what a view, tonight.

He rolled himself a joint from the tray he kept tucked under the couch and watched the mad display of fireworks over the city. Thunder and lightning was a rarity in San Francisco — usually storms had to move inland first and clash with warmer currents of air. David smiled. Tomorrow, many bleary-eyed people would stumble to work, exhausted but happy, to swap stories about watching the storm and its handiwork.

Mammoth bolts of lightning crisscrossed the sky. Twice, as he watched, the radio and TV tower up on Twin Peaks flashed like a skeletal Christmas tree as it was zapped by lightning. The very fabric of the night sky seemed torn.

This was better than struggling over his porno story, a hundred times better.

Even so, as he watched the sky and finished his joint, senses blurring pleasantly, a quiet unease wormed into his gut. It was not new, this unease; it had nipped at him all this long unsettling day, hounding him. Even Eddie had felt it, uncharacteristically restless, unable to do more than pick at his hospital food.

Suddenly unease gelled into outright fear. It felt as if something was being set into motion. This storm, only a diversion. Or a warning. Or both.

And under this thought, with a flash of perfectly clear understanding: *I am here.*

David spun around. Had there been a voice? He dropped the remainder of the joint into an ashtray. Enough of that, ole buddy, when you start hearing voices at midnight. Enough.

But it wasn't enough, apparently. It was just the beginning.

In his bedroom, the typewriter whirled abruptly into life. Each key striking paper was a machine-gun shot in the preternaturally quiet apartment: tap tap tap tap tap tap! An explosion of artillery. Then, nothing.

He sat where he was, frozen. His legs would not move. Hadn't he shut off the typewriter? Of course he had, a reflex action from years of practice.

That alien voice, inside him and yet outside too: *Take a look, Davey.*

The typewriter was humming with electricity as he forced himself to walk into his bedroom. Seeing it, hearing it on when he knew he'd shut it off — his bowels froze into a greasy block of ice. He inched himself closer, sober now with fright, heart pounding. In what would be his last burst of understanding for that night,

David saw his life divided yet again into a new Before and After.

Several inches below where he had finished typing, these words blazed in capital letters:

I HAVE A ROOM PREPARED FOR YOU.

4

"Hey! Wake up!"

A rough hand shook Bobby awake. "What the—"

The room exploded with blue light. Bobby saw Mick in that instant, sitting beside him on the bed. A wild grin danced on his face.

"You've got to see this, Bobby! It's incredible!"

Thunder rumbled through the room.

"This better be good," Bobby groused, but he was smiling. He scooted against Mick and followed his glance out the window.

"Watch," Mick whispered.

They did not wait long.

A bolt of lightning whipped across the sky. Viewed from their window, downtown San Francisco flashed as an electric blue negative. Lightning discharged across the sky like a giant appliance cord spewing electrical sparks from its chewed-off end.

Then: gone. Utter darkness, the imprint of the blue city visible long after the flash, and booming thunder.

"Mickey, this is great!" Bobby planted a kiss on Mick's neck. "This is worth waking up for."

"I haven't seen anything like this in years. Not since coming to San Francisco, anyway. You should have seen the storms we got in Denver. Now *those* were beauts!"

They hugged each other and watched. Mick was sandy-haired and blue-eyed, outlandishly handsome, with a wide Nordic face crowned by hair that tended to curl. Bobby was shorter, more compact, dark, of Italian descent, with a crew cut. At twenty-eight, he was older than Mick by three years.

"Too bad we can only see downtown from here," Mick said. "I'll bet the view of Twin Peaks is phenomenal."

"What's the matter; you don't like my place?"

"The apartment's okay," Mick said. "It's the man who lives here I love." He pushed Bobby onto the bed and traced a line across his luxuriantly furry chest, stopping once and then again at each nipple. Each squeeze reverberated through Bobby as delicious tingles.

Bobby lived in an upstairs loft south of Market on Tehama Street. His first friend in San Francisco had lived there for eight years, paying pittance compared to present-day rent. But the friend moved back to Seattle last January, and Bobby had gotten first dibs. Sure, the neighborhood attracted a mixed bag of characters, Asians and Saudi Arabians and Chinese, gays and lesbians, yuppies who acted as if the area was their new oyster. Blue-collar families. Shipping and crating businesses. So it wasn't Pacific Heights. He could do a lot worse.

Rain pelted the window. The building creaked and groaned against the wind. Suddenly the room lit up in a brilliant flash. Giant cymbals of thunder crashed overhead.

"Jesus! That one was right over us!" Bobby sat up.

"Where are you going?"

"I want to see if it hit anything." He padded to the window on bare feet and peered outside, searching the rooftops. He perched at the window and waited, watching thunderheads march across the horizon. He half expected a tongue of flame to pop out of any of the neighboring houses at any moment.

"Maybe it'll hit *my* lightning rod."

"What?" Bobby glanced over at Mick sprawled across the bed, sheets kicked back, his erection stabbing the air. Bobby felt a keen excitement. "Better put that away or you'll electrocute us both."

"But what a way to go, huh?"

Bobby wagged a finger. "Wait until I get my hands on you."

Mick folded his hands behind his head. He opened his legs. "Come and get me."

As Bobby turned away from the lightning and the rain, from his search for fire-damaged rooftops, he glanced into the alley below his window — and froze.

A man was down there.

He stood in the shadows, draped in blankets or something free-flowing and loose, so that none of his body was visible, not even his feet. The blanket fluttered voluminously in the rain-driven wind, billowing in all directions at once.

Bobby stared at the figure on the street. *A bum. He's a bum.*

Almost every night transients made their home in the nooks and crannies of the buildings across the street. A dark front porch, an abandoned car, an indentation in a wall — these were the new homes for the homeless. Their numbers continued to increase, every year it seemed. And with Canon Kip dining hall just blocks away, he had adjusted to the sight of men and women camping out near his doorstep. As long as they left him alone and didn't piss in his doorway, he didn't care what they did.

But there was something about the way he just stood there...

The man in the street raised his head. A flash of lightning, then darkness.

Bobby took a startled step backward.

"What is it, Bobby?"

He blinked his eyes. He still saw it.

Mick raised onto his elbows.

"Stay," Bobby ordered. He softened. "It's nothing, really. There's a bum across the street. He startled me."

And he moved away from the window and onto the bed, where he scooped Mick's young hard cock into his mouth, banishing all images of rain-soaked transients from his mind.

But he remembered him as he tried to fall asleep much later, Mick curled beside him like a glove. As lightning lit the room with electric flashes, Bobby saw him quite clearly, the man with a Cheshire Cat grin and not much else, twin rows of white teeth stretched into an awful leer, floating on a sea of black.

3

Over the ledge

1

I t took less than one week for David's life to fall apart.

2

And it started with the dream:

David charging up the staircase two steps at a time, arms outstretched in ready anticipation to throw open the rooftop door, flying toward freedom. He ran, yet made no progress. His feet sank into a marshy goo that should have been the staircase. Raising each leg required wild effort — the gummy stuff dragged each foot down. Only he had to run. He had to get away.

A growl from behind.

Deep throated. Gargantuan. It was the sound of a dragon awakening to discover a thief traipsing over its gold. David trembled with childlike terror.

Don't look back, he told himself. *Don't look back, or he'll catch me—*

He ran. The door that opened onto the roof of the New York building swam tantalizingly just out of reach. With gritted teeth David slogged up the stairs and threw his weight against the steel-plated door. It screamed open. He stumbled across the gravel roof, pushed by the momentum of his dash.

A noise in the doorway. David whirled around.

The warm summer night, the twinkling lights of New York skyscrapers, the crunch of gravel beneath his feet, his racing heart: the moment, culled from memory, in a freeze-frame of agonizing detail.

He faced the doorway. It was empty. David stared in shock. Where was the boy with the knife? Who had followed him out the door?

Suddenly a blast of humid air slammed into him. It packed the punch of a quarterback, yet had no physical shape. He was enveloped and pitched backward, a voice so close to his ears it might have originated inside his own head.

(Coming to get you I'm coming to get you COMING—!)

David shrieked. His butt collided with the ledge wall of the roof, pitching him up and over. Skyscrapers. A swollen June moon. Black carpet sky. He saw it all in agonizing detail as the tornado wind hurled him over the roof in a backwards somersault. His feet kicked against the velvet sky.

And then he was falling.

No! David shouted. *Feet first, not head first!*

Four stories' worth of tumbling. Down he fell. His hands stretched out beyond his head in a futile attempt to catch himself when he landed. He saw the concrete hungry to embrace him, to break his bones in a dozen different places—

No!

Not concrete, this time. Not a sidewalk.

A mouth.

Hideously huge, blotting out the landscape as he rushed toward it. The dragon mouth slid open with a snarl, twin rows of fangs gleaming in the moonlight. Nothing perched above it: no crown of hair nor pair of eyes to watch his descent. Only the mouth of the beast, jaws fully extended, ready to take him with a gulp.

Like a fish drawn into a shark's mouth, he fell.

And David slammed awake with a gasp, nearly catapulting himself out of bed.

3

"Cute."

David looked. "Where?"

Jack gestured toward a man on a Nautilus machine. "There. The blond."

"Oh. Him." David had noticed him a couple of times, a handsome man always absorbed in grueling marathon workouts.

"He works downtown," Jack said, wiping his brow with a hand towel. He was ten minutes ahead of David on the exercise bike and coaxing up quite a lather. "Near me, in fact. Comes here on his lunch hour, and sometimes even returns after work. What a body."

David nodded. "I thought you didn't care for blonds."

"When they look like that — hey—" And both laughed.

It was true. The man across the weight room was model material, every inch of him. Muscular, but in proportion to his average height. The sort of curly blond hair David would kill for, if he himself had been a blond. Jack, his buddy pedaling beside him, was somewhat similar in looks, but brown haired, less sharply drawn, average. They'd flirted casually for several weeks but never taken it beyond the boundary of this gym, content to talk and cruise and occasionally eye each other with lingering glances.

"What's his name?" David asked.

Jack shrugged. "Mike. Mick. Begins with an M."

The man in question strode across the floor and bent to the water fountain. He seemed unaware of the heads that turned to follow his progress.

David cocked his head, recognizing the opening notes to a familiar song. The steady barrage of music over the loudspeakers ("Music to pump by," Jack had once quipped) had taken a decided nostalgic turn. The current offering was vintage Sylvester, "You Make Me Feel Mighty Real."

"You're too young to enjoy this," David chided. "Probably in diapers when this was popular."

Jack ignored the dig, pedaling furiously.

David rolled his eyes.

A few of the older men stopped working out. One man danced a little jig and smiled unabashedly. The mood in the gym subtly changed. One by one the crowd stopped what they were doing to listen.

Men stood around with enchanted grins on their faces, weights and weight machines momentarily forgotten. David was grinning as well. This old song cuts us right to the quick, he thought, and an unexpected wave of bittersweet nostalgia lapped over him. It helps us remember carefree times.

Oh, you make me feel mighty real

The music swept over the men, and they drank it in. They swayed with the beat. Fingers snapped. Toes danced to the rhythm. Lips silently mouthed the words.

David surveyed the room, and thought, *We'd do almost anything to have it all back, wouldn't we? Even though we're fighting pot bellies and bags under our eyes, receding hairlines and gray hair at the temples. What we wouldn't do to recapture some of that light that was our youth.*

It made him happy and a little sad to watch, how everyone brightened at this old song. Nautilus machines were temporarily abandoned. Free weights rested in their racks. Beside him, Jack had slowed to a crawl on his exercise bike. His own legs had stopped pedaling, becoming lax. Actually, it *was* rather nice, wasn't it, to just listen to the music. Hitch a ride on this nostalgic surf, and skim this wave forever—

An icepick jab of pain suddenly gouged him right between his eyes. David winced, hissing between his teeth.

"Hey. You okay?"

He glanced at Jack. His eyes refused to open past slits; the lights in the gym were too bright. *What the hell happened?* He managed a feeble nod.

"What's wrong?"

David shrugged. He blinked a few times, his eyes readjusting to the light. Moving his head hurt too much, as though a sinus headache had decided to fluff up a few pillows and stay a while. "That was strange, wasn't it?"

Jack wrinkled his brow. "What?"

"The way everyone stopped just now." He looked at Jack's blank expression. "You know. To listen to that Sylvester song. Everybody loves that old disco."

Now Jack's face was an empty chalkboard, clean as on the first day of school. "What Sylvester song?"

"The one we just—" The words stumbled on his tongue. The flesh on his arms crawled. —*listened to. Didn't you listen?*

The latest hit from the Pet Shop Boys pounded over the speakers. Barbells hoisted above heads with grunts of exertion. Pockets of conversation resumed in midsentence. Men stretched before mirrors, dipped to the water fountain, patted each other on the back. The blond he and Jack had cruised gazed at his reflection in a mirror as he sweated through curls. Beside him, Jack pedaled and pedaled.

David clenched the handlebars of his bike. Sweat trickled down his sore forehead and stung his eyes. He pedaled too, but felt himself suspended in midair, like a cartoon character who bicycles off a cliff and pedals the air to get back to land. No, he wasn't falling — yet. Soon, though. That inevitable clutch in his stomach, his bowels, recognized free-fall. And if he stared between his feet, what would he see? Concrete — or the mouth?

Jack wore a dreamy smile on his young face. "You're right. What you said about that old music? I wish it'd come back. I could listen to music like that all the time."

And he broke into a frozen grin that chilled David into gooseflesh.

4

The elevator door whispered open. David stepped out into the hospital lobby and crossed over to the nurses' station. Several men and women were clustered there, reading patient charts, preparing medicine trays for the afternoon rounds. He recognized most of their faces by now (he was never any good with names, try as he might). Except for Bessie, the head nurse, who glanced up from her patient chart and greeted him with a smile.

"Afternoon to ya, Mr. Walker," she said. Her wide round face broke into a huge Pepsodent grin.

"Hi, Bessie."

"How's the writing coming?"

"Same old story," he answered. "Some days it's pure inspiration; other days it's just another job." He bit back the urge to tell her that he hadn't stepped near his typewriter in several days. How in the mocking silence of night he both feared and anticipated hearing the typewriter purr into a life of its own, with another cryptic message. He was going to give it a try later that night.

"Honey, I knows what you mean," Bessie said with a peculiar sigh. Her eyes darkened as she hoisted herself up from her chair and waddled around the counter that divided the station.

Uh-oh, David thought as he watched her approach. *She's got something to tell me. And she wants to do it up close. Personal.* As if to brace himself first, he suddenly blurted, "How is he?"

No pretenses now. She frowned. "He's taken a turn."

"For the worse?"

She nodded. "For the worse."

David hung his head.

"Cheer up," Bessie said in that honey voice which made her so popular on the ward. She punched him lightly on the arm. "It ain't gonna do you no good if you turn blue every time Eddie has a bad day. You listening to me?"

"Yes." He grinned reluctantly. She reminded him of that black actress who had once been Maude's maid on that old TV sitcom. Bessie was wide as a door, busty, her kind face crowned by a salt-and-pepper Afro.

"Now go and give him a hello," she said. "He's expecting you."

"I will. Thanks."

He walked away from her and started down the long hallway. Quiet for this time of afternoon, he noticed. A lot of people liked to visit patients in the early evening, after dinner, but Eddie had specifically encouraged him to visit in the late afternoons. That was the toughest chunk of the day, the three-to-six-o'clock slump. Too easy to start feeling sorry for yourself, Eddie had told him, when all you can do is lie in bed and watch the sunlight drain out of your room.

And now he's taken another turn for the worse, David thought morosely. He hoisted his gym bag to his left shoulder. His footsteps echoed down the hallway.

He did not glance into any of the rooms. Too depressing, life inside hospital walls. Muted conversation and laughter floated out into the hallway. Phil Donahue on the tube. One man coughing his guts out. But what pained him the most was the funereal silence blanketing several of the rooms he passed, where — if his glance strayed into any of them — he saw only the legs and feet of the men, motionless, in bed. Waiting.

He could not halt the twinge of fear that reached up and knocked on his door:

This could be you one day oh yes you just might very well end up right here in these hallowed rooms waiting for your ticket to expire.

David shook the thought away. Yeah, his ticket might be drawn for this merry-go-round; the days of exemptions had passed. But until such time, he was determined to go about the business of living. Wasn't he the Miracle Kid? That's what the doctors in New York had dubbed him — the Miracle Kid who survived the fall. He'd awakened in head-to-toe bandages, his eyesight dimmed to no more than pinpoints for a week after, because of delayed shock. Eight broken ribs. Broken pelvis, broken hip, punctured lungs, internal bleeding. The irony of it all: The drugs and alcohol in his system had undoubtedly saved his life. His body had been so loose, so rubbery from the drugs that he had simply accordioned up when he hit the ground.

Oh, yes, David knew hospital walls all too well. He'd spent the better part of '82 and the first half of '83 in intense physical therapy. Slowly, his bones had mended. His only residual scar was in his abdomen, where surgeons had opened him up to take care of internal bleeding.

Maybe it *was* false hope, but he wanted to believe he'd been spared for a reason. Surely he'd not gone through such a grueling recovery only to have his life snatched away, like Eddie, because of a tiny virus. Being surrounded by illness, he sometimes felt as though he were holding his breath, as though he could somehow escape the whole terrible epidemic by not breathing.

Room 203.

David sucked in his breath — and would have denied doing so, if someone had accused him of it — threw on his best happy face, and entered the room with a quick knock on the door.

5

A fever burned merrily behind Eddie's eyes. His gaunt face glowed with its heat. Not that Eddie noticed: He was doped to the gills, floating on a cloud of morphine. He wouldn't have flinched even if the entire hospital caught fire. As it was, his brown eyes flickered with only vague recognition as David pulled up a chair and sat beside the bed.

He's so pale, David thought uncomfortably. *His skin's the color of paper.*

A couple of days ago Eddie had appeared to improve. A new drug the doctors tried had restored some color to Eddie's cheeks. He'd sat up in bed and they'd played gin rummy and laughed at "Wheel of Fortune." Chatted about the possibility of his coming home. They both knew it would never happen, but it cheered Eddie to think about it, so where was the harm?

Now Eddie looked like a tiny broken bird, his head too big for his withered body, his arms the size of broomsticks. His head lolled gently from side to side to express his pleasure in David's company.

David filled the room with his voice. He talked about Saturday night's storm. His lack of progress on his porno story. The bustling excitement in the Castro as Halloween dawned closer. Sometimes

Eddie would start to speak, or he'd nod, or his eyes would go blank and he'd drift away. It wasn't necessary for him to answer; David knew Eddie liked to hear him talk.

Eventually, though, a long pause spun out into silence, and in that silence he gingerly tucked one of Eddie's fragile hands into his own. At first Eddie seemed not to notice, but after a few moments he felt a reciprocal squeeze.

Sometimes it was better like this, in the silence that said, simply, *I'm here for you,* than any of his inane conversation. Oh, how he hurt to see Eddie like this! It made his gut ache. Eddie had been the one to coax him out of New York and back home to San Francisco. Eddie, who had helped him piece together a new life while he finished his recovery. Now, he was the one doing the hand holding. They were old college chums, friends for over twelve years. And friends stuck by each other.

He gave Eddie's hand a final squeeze.

"I'm going now, Eds," David whispered. He returned Eddie's hand to the drawn-up sheets. "Rest well. I'll be back tomorrow."

Eddie's head rolled in his direction. A purposeful light suddenly blazed behind fever-swelled eyes. His throat muscles worked.

"I'll be better. Soon."

"I know you will," David said, pleased by this effort to speak.

"He told me so."

"Who? Dr. Allen?"

Eddie shook his head. The fire was dimming from his eyes as quickly as it had appeared, replaced by a wet purple glow.

"Who told you you'd get better?"

"The man, Davey. The man in the steam."

6

Why am I here? What in the world am I thinking of?

He had to laugh about it. What else could he do? Here he was, at the Goodwill store south of Market, fondling polyester shirts.

After leaving the hospital, David had been seized by a desire to reclaim his life in the face of Eddie's illness — and on the spur of the moment he'd decided to go shopping. Halloween was only weeks away, after all.

Never mind, he told himself as he rode the Muni underground bus to Montgomery Street. Never mind that I haven't gone out on Halloween in three years. What do I need a costume for?

Still, it gave this wholly unexpected trip a purpose, and softened the idea that he was acting compulsively. He chastised himself for the writing he was neglecting but strode happily through the dilapidated stretch of city to the Goodwill at Sixth and Howard.

Once inside the building, he drifted toward the racks of men's clothing. On rare days a bargain could be had with a little patience and a sharp eye. But his fingers brushed past the few leftover Calvin Kleins, Pierre Cardins, Christopher Hayeses — shirts that ordinarily would have rung his bargain-alert button. He wanted bright colors. Prints. Something deliberately spring or summery, in contrast to the dreadful dull weather outside.

His thoughts skipped along merry tracks. He hummed a song he had played that morning off an old K-Tel Disco Fire album found in the back of his records.

He's a pistol-packin' Boogie Man
Come to pump us full of love

David smiled secretly. He would have been mortified with embarrassment, had anyone known he was humming such a song.

His gun is loaded
It's pointed at our heads
Those better be love bullets, baby
Or it looks like we're all dead

Now he stood next to rows of polyester shirts — big bright shirts with wild landscapes and catch-can patterns, shirts he'd worn oh so many moons ago unbuttoned to the navel, sleeves rolled up just so. Here was one, a blue moonscape-and-star design. Not bad. And another, whimsically Hawaiian with pineapples and palm trees.

All I need now is a gold chain around my neck, a pair of 501s, and I'm all set.

He chuckled. This was pre-Clone, midseventies look. Even with the nostalgia craze lately for fifties and sixties outfits, he could hardly consider this apparel trend-setting, even if it *was* (he obstinately reminded himself) for Halloween.

He heard tittering beside him, and looked over. Two queens had elbowed up next to him and were poring over the polyester prints with a zeal bordering on the orgiastic.

"It's perfect for Rhoda!" one of the men insisted. He laid the shirt against the other's chest, checking the fit. "A yellow scarf, a floppy hat, and you're perfect!"

"Pants," the other thin one cried. "We need pants for Mary."

Off they skipped to the adjacent rack of women's clothes.

David glanced around. Peppered among the Spanish women in housedresses and clusters of down-on-their-luck families were a dozen or more gay men. It shouldn't have been odd, their presence — but so many of them? At five in the afternoon, on a weekday? Half of the men were in business suits, as if they'd left their offices in haste to elbow their way to a Macy's White Flower Day Sale.

Had they been in the store when he'd walked in? Had he not noticed, in his own preoccupation?

That song wound through his head, pesky:

Those better be love bullets, baby
Or it looks like we're all dead.

Okay, he told himself. Nothing strange about this. It's almost Halloween, remember? Time is short. Weekends too crowded. Why *not* come on down, and browse? I did.

The rationalization should have soothed him, but it didn't. It gave him a queer sensation that began to multiply his doubts.

Two men dressing as Mary Richards and Rhoda Morganstern. His own thoughts filled with disco music. And what was this? Several newcomers were drifting toward the racks.

Next thing you know they'll be snatching up the leisure suits.

Odd. So odd. He felt removed and yet a part of it, whatever this urge was. He watched as the gay men around him wiped sweat from their foreheads with the backs of their hands and then slammed through the racks of acrylic shirts and pants with rapid-fire determination. Like an alcoholic stealing a concealed bottle from the underwear drawer: same whiff of shame and guilt, same inability to control the compulsion.

David was horrified. Is that how he had looked, moments ago?

He threw his shirts back onto the racks (where a fiftyish man in a pin-striped suit scrambled to look at them) and beat a hasty retreat from the store. He burst gratefully out onto the sidewalk and leaned against a wall, catching his breath.

Had he escaped something? It felt as if he had.

An early-evening breeze was cool against his clammy skin. Rain in the air. His forehead thrummed with that awful headache right between his eyes. Gingerly, he fingered the flesh above the bridge of his nose. It was tender to his touch, slightly swollen.

He sighed wearily. God, he was a mess.

This little jaunt to the Goodwill meant he now had to fight rush-hour commuters on his ride back to Castro Street. The last thing his headache needed was a trip home in a crowded cattle car.

Steeling himself for the brisk walk back to Market Street, he let his gaze wander over the building tops to the east. The darkening sky was the color of plums. The hairs on the back of his neck suddenly prickled; he had the feeling that eyes were boring into him. Yes. Someone was watching him. As simple and as strange as that: He was being watched. Something was near, beyond those buildings and many streets down.

Disco music wound through his head like an endless reel-to-reel tape.

Unaccountably spooked, David hoisted his gym bag and fled.

7

At first, he dismissed it as a pimple.

It felt like a pimple, even though the emerging lump didn't have the familiar trademarks of a blemish.

*Some*thing pushed against the skin of his forehead. It thrust up and out, bruising the skin above the bridge of his nose in a hard dime-sized knot.

Had he struck himself, somehow? At the gym, perhaps?

Scratched himself last night and torn the skin? Broken a blood vessel?

No, no to all that. Yet here it was, this mysterious pimple that bruised his skin up and out. No wonder he had such a stupefying headache.

Why, oh, why, out of all the places on his body, did he have to have this fucking lump right between his eyes?

8

A deadline is a deadline is a deadline.

David paced and cursed and paced some more before he literally threw himself into his chair, flipped on the switch to the Smith-Corona, and began to type. He didn't care what the words looked like, or if the sentences made for smooth reading. He began to fill the page. He had a deadline, and he had to write.

And when no cryptic messages appeared unbidden beneath his fingers, he sighed with relief and got to work.

This story should have been finished and mailed south to L.A. days ago. An editor at *Torso* magazine wanted him to write a kinky story for the April issue. Anything at all. He had tried all the angles. An exhibitionist who gets more than he bargained for. A pair of old lovers seduced by an antique mirror that reflects their image at twenty, not sixty. A stripper who gets the surprise of his life while working a birthday party.

All began with promise, and all fizzled after two or three pages. Now he had lost the luxury of being creative. Time weighed against him. He had to crank something out, anything at all, and mail it off by week's end. With an editor making housecalls, you don't blow the chance, even if your friend lies dying in a hospital and your head feels like it's swelling up to explode. David bent over the typewriter.

And gave up after an hour. Dry. He was dry. Distracted. What had Eddie meant, the man in the steam would make him better?

He ran his fingers through his hair with a desultory gesture and forced himself to stand. His knees let out a shriek of pain. Might have to pop a few Tylenol if he expected Mr. Sandman to come pay a visit tonight.

His fingers lightly brushed against the pimple between his eyes. What he felt there caused him to rush into the bathroom and switch on the lights.

He stepped up to the mirror.

All illusions of a harmless bump shattered in that instant.

No pimple, this thing between his eyes.

A battle, on his forehead. Two forces, one pushing out, the other pushing in. The lump was now the size of a quarter. The tight uncomfortable pressure was its only characteristic indicative of a blemish. There, the resemblance ended. He saw that clearly, here beneath the glare of his bathroom light. The lump was an odd grab bag of colors: bluish black, like a bruise. A tinge of pink that graduated to blood red as the mound peaked at its center. Puffed and raw. Nothing indicated the lump was drawing to a head, which would have at least meant eventual draining of the infection (if that's what it was) and cleansing.

A cold wind blew through him.

What he stared at was the betrayal of his own body. Something was going terribly wrong. What else could account for that hallucination at the gym, for feeling watched when he was clearly alone, and for hearing music that wouldn't leave his head? What else, except a free-fall into death's waiting jaws?

Maybe he wasn't the Miracle Kid after all.

Maybe his ticket *had* been punched.

He wheeled away from the mirror. Tears stung his eyes. All of it unraveling, his health, his life. Sink or swim time, boys; sink or swim.

Sink. Sank. Sunk. In this underwater world of his misery, David thrashed.

4

Miggy and Jack, respectively

1

It was a wild kick, stupendous in its high arc and magnificent in its distance, but it bore home with terrible accuracy. Miggy and Kevin stood slack-jawed with disbelief as the football bounced against the brick building and crashed to rest in a shadowy pile of rubbish and winking glass.

Miggy whistled through his teeth. "Now you've done it," he said.

"You told me to!" Kevin shot back. His face, Miggy noticed, was a bunch of runny colors, like cheese on a pizza. "You told me to kick it hard, and I did!"

Both boys surveyed the damage.

Oh, the building was fine — after all, what harm could come to a brick building from a little football? But the football itself — ahh, there was the rub. It sat atop its pile of trash like a toy long abandoned, and seeing it there gave Miggy a funny pain in his chest.

"Get it," Miggy said.

"You get it," Kevin countered.

"You kicked it!"

"You told me to!"

Back and forth they went. The cloudy twilight dimmed as they fought, throwing long plum-colored shadows up and down their quiet street. The streetlight at the end of the block had thrown out its pool of light long before they even began this game of punt and catch. They were killing time before each was summoned home for supper. Shadows ripened into black. Soon it'd be too dark to see much of anything.

Finally Miggy said, "We'll both get it."

It seemed the fairest solution. They were buddies, after all. Not exactly best friends, but neighbors and good companions, playing with each other often.

They marched across the street. As they neared the fearsome building their footsteps grew tinier and tinier. Kevin's mouth opened and closed with an expression identical to Miggy's pet goldfish. It was hard to breathe, up this close. After all, this place was off-limits.

"Can you see it?" Kevin whispered.

Miggy squinted. The dark was swallowing up everything. The football — his *prize* football, autographed by Joe Montana himself — did not lend itself to being seen across twenty-five feet of rubble-strewn parking lot. Thirty minutes ago there would have been enough light in the sky, but now everything was lumpy shadows.

They peered anxiously through the wall of chain-link fence that partitioned off the parking lot. Suddenly Miggy tugged on Kevin's arm.

"There." He pointed across the expanse to a pile of cardboard boxes and splintered wood. A crescent-shaped shadow stuck its nose out of one of the boxes. "How we gonna get it?"

"Climb the fence?" Kevin asked — although his tone of voice clearly indicated he hoped Miggy would nix the idea.

Miggy grabbed onto the chain-link fence and tested it for strength. It was blotched with rust in many of its hexagonal circles, but certainly sturdy enough to support his eighty-pound frame. Shoot. A piece of cake. The only tough part climbing over the top and avoiding the wire teeth of its ridge.

"Don't!" Kevin gasped, when he realized what Miggy was about to do.

"It's easy, Kev. We climb up and over, get the football, and climb back. It'll take five minutes."

Kevin was wearing his goldfish expression again, jaw opening and closing wordlessly, button eyes in a round face. He was only a year and a half younger than Miggy, but, good grief, what a baby sometimes! Miggy grew impatient with Kevin's fumbling for an answer and was about to climb without him when Kevin broke through his fright and whispered, "We aren't supposed to."

"What about my football?"

"We'll get in trouble."

Miggy chewed the inside of his cheek. His young face looked suddenly thoughtful. "What do you think this place was?"

Kevin was not as surprised by the question as it would first appear. This building at the end of their block had been off-limits to them for as long as they could remember — long before the police came and actually shut it down. Both sets of parents refused to speak of the place, but both parents promised red fannies if the boys were ever caught trespassing on the property.

"Some kind of club," Kevin answered, after some thought.

"A *secret* club," Miggy added.

"For witches," Kevin chimed in.

"Witches are *women,* dummy." Miggy rolled his eyes. Jeeze, what a moron. "Warlocks are men, and that's all I ever saw coming out of there."

Kevin's eyes had gone wide again. "Do you think they're any left inside?"

"Naw."

But each fell silent. Up this close, in the dark, the huge building seemed perfectly suited for housing all kinds of mischief. They had always treated the place as something haunted and to be avoided (not least because neither wanted a red behind). It gave both boys a certain notoriety at school each relished — after all, how many kids could boast of a haunted house at the end of their block?

Now the fuel of all their whisperings about the building burned brightly in their anxious faces. Miggy's stomach felt squishy at the thought of his prize football spending the whole night in this wicked parking lot.

"Five minutes," Miggy said, his voice perilously close to pleading. Then he hastily added: "No one'll know. It'll be our secret."

Kevin looked all cheesy again. "Well..."

Down the block a front door popped open. A rectangle of light spilled out.

"Kevin Ashley!" trumpeted a woman's voice. "Supper!"

An expression of infinite gratitude swept Kevin's young face. Already he stepped away from the chain-link fence.

"I'm sorry, Miguel," he said, torn with loyalty but programmed to automatically obey his mother's command.

"Five minutes," Miggy pleaded, though he saw it was hopeless.

Kevin was already lost to the shadows, stepping away. "I'll help ya, honest I will," he promised breathlessly. "Tomorrow, right after school." He turned on his heel and bolted down the street.

"'Fraidy cat!" Miggy shouted. "Little two-faced 'fraidy cat!" His hands balled into fists at each side. He was crying a little — tears squeaked out of each corner of his eyes. He watched Kevin run all the way home and heard the slap of his front door open and close.

2

Miggy turned stubbornly and looked at the fence and beyond. He wiped his eyes with the tail end of his Forty-Niner sweatshirt. Five minutes. Up and over. A cinch, really, if he just wouldn't be afraid.

But now that he stood all by himself, fear bloomed in his belly like a delicate black flower. Graveyard dark surrounded him. To his left, the front of this warehouse building stared down at him with shuttered windows. If only his football hadn't landed in the fenced-off parking lot. If only it had bounced against the front door, or for that matter landed in the empty lot to the immediate left of the building, where the charred remains of a house's foundation stuck out of the ground. Both places were just as frightening to retrieve his football, but at least he wouldn't have to struggle up and over a fence.

Just then a voice at the opposite end of the block called out: "Miggy! Come wash up! Supper!"

Indecision warred across his troubled face. That was Mom. Dinner. He had to hurry home. But his football, his personally autographed by Joe Montana football that Dad had presented to him not three weeks earlier — how could he abandon it? He'd never get another one, never. Only because of lucky timing had his father gotten the autograph in the first place.

He hooked his fingers through the chain-link fence. Quite suddenly he was scrambling up its side. He flew up as though driven by a cannon blast. The late hour, his hot panic, and shame in disobeying his mother's call to supper propelled him up the chain links with a sound like toneless wind chimes. He clattered to the top, breathless not from exertion, but fright.

He swung his left leg up and over the top, hooking his toes into a link on the other side. Straddled the top as the fence swayed under his weight. Careful to avoid the ragged edge of exposed wire as he hoisted over to the other side. His sweatshirt caught on one of the wire's teeth, and in his panic to loosen himself, he ripped the sleeve and gave his right forearm a nasty scratch.

He clambered down to the other side and dropped to the parking lot. His forearm sparked with pain. A deep regret blossomed in him. He should have just run home and told his parents what happened, punishment or no, and let Dad decide what to do about retrieving the football. Now he had a ripped shirt and a stinging slash on his arm for his troubles, not to mention each minute ticking away that he did not answer his call to dinner.

A dark wind tousled his hair and blew into his heart, urging him forward. Miggy sprinted across the hateful parking lot, his feet bouncing back into the air almost before touching the asphalt. He'd held a pet canary in his hands once — it had belonged to his oldest brother Tomas — and he remembered how terribly hard its heart had beat against its tiny chest, surely going to burst. His own heart beat so forcefully he was dizzy with the pounding of it against his ribs.

He beelined for the lumpy shadows that housed his football. He meant to scoop it into his hands and run back to the fence without stopping, but fright swooped down on him like a net fallen from the sky. His foot caught a tangled mass of sprouting weeds and sent him sprawling with a terrified cry. He fell heavily, his left arm thrown out to break his crash landing. More shooting stars of pain.

Trembling, Miggy pushed himself to his knees — and saw the glow of amber light that leaked around the back corners of the pile of rubbish. He froze, in equal parts terror and wonder at the sight of it.

He urged himself closer, step by step. He snatched his prize football from its resting place. That was better, having the ball in his hands; it quieted his pounding heart a little, and he caught his breath.

He leaned around the pile of rubbish and saw that the glow radiated out from a rectangular basement window at ground level.

By all rights he should have been quaking with fear — this was the forbidden place of goblins and warlocks, after all — but a curious desire held him rooted to the spot. The light had a campfire's flicker but none of the warmth to go with it. He was reminded of a field trip he'd taken with classmates to the Exploratorium, and a laser light show.

A sudden gust of wind walked and talked around him. Surely it couldn't be the light, which seemed to whisper

(Come ... play ... come ... play...)

with every flicker from the other side of the basement glass. His death grip on his football loosened slightly. He was vaguely aware of his pee-pee a hard pencil in his pants. His lips parted in a wordless O.

From down the block, furious, his father's voice rang out:

"Miguel Samuel Garza come home at once!"

Miggy wrenched away from the building. "Daddy!"

And it was Miggy's father who heard the terrible screams cut off in midsqueal, like a door slammed shut upon his son.

3

Later that same night, in his Natoma Street apartment, Jack Martin popped a tape into his VCR and pushed play. He kicked off his gym shorts and settled, naked, onto his couch.

Tonight Jack was in the mood for an old film — a film where men still gobbled up every ounce of cum as it shot into hungry mouths. And fucking, prerubber style. He owned a collection of over two dozen porno tapes. Collecting the tapes had become a hobby of sorts, born out of necessity: His libido ran miles ahead of his ability to land dates. This way, watching the tapes, he had a different man to play with every night, no strings attached.

He'd love some real company — sure (he'd been trying to have a date with David Walker for weeks) — but over the years he'd happily discovered that watching men have sex was almost as much fun as the real thing.

Tonight's offering was *Falconhead*, a surreal classic he'd stumbled across at Superstar Video months back. An eerie film about men who became enslaved through the power of a magical mirror, and the true owner of the mirror, a huge muscular man with the head of a falcon. Jack hadn't watched the movie in a while, but he remembered several particularly sexy scenes. He fast-forwarded to one now. Two men stood in a steamy netherworld of Hollywood oranges and reds, with steam piped in around their feet.

Jack settled back and stroked himself into a full erection. He closed his eyes and allowed David Walker to briefly flirt across his vision, followed closely by the blond he'd ogled at the gym the other day.

My oh my, what a three-way *that* would be! He opened his eyes and saw that the two men in the showers had vanished. The screen was a gauzy white cloud.

Hey — where'd the men go?

He could still hear the movie's soundtrack, a kind of saxophone-blues-and-harp combination, but he may as well have been staring at the inside of a cloud. He kept expecting a close-up of a hard dick to appear, or a hand roaming up a thigh. *Some*thing. Not this blank white screen. He picked up the remote and thumbed fast forward. The screen remained obstinately white.

What gives?

He put down the remote. Clouds began to thin as a picture formed on the TV. The steam rolled back to reveal a chamber of some sort with a row of shower nozzles and a bubbling jacuzzi center stage. But the two men from the film were gone.

I don't remember this, Jack thought. But he was intrigued. This is what he loved about old films, rediscovering scenes he might have skipped on first viewing but which he could now settle back and enjoy.

Only this huge room upon his television screen didn't look like a scene in the movie. *Falconhead* had been shot in 16mm, transferred to videotape.

The picture didn't even resemble video any more.

It looked real.

Jack felt his breath catch in his throat. He was staring into another world, directly through his TV. Swirling steam buffeted against the inside glass of the television screen.

Warring emotions gave way to a strange erotic fascination. Though the room was empty, it seemed strangely full, pregnant with energy. It beckoned and repelled like a beautiful lover who may yet fly into a jealous rage if its needs are not met. This information seeped into him as though through his pores, reaching him not through conscious thought at all. Yes, it waited, this place, but so too a tank of gasoline, waiting for the match to ignite it.

His erection bounced to his ever-quickening heartbeat. Despite his anxiety, Jack was a rock in his own hand, indescribably turned on.

Before any real fear could settle into him the voice floated out, a whispering chant:

(Be)

(Be the)

(Be the)

(Be the first)

(Jack)

(Be the first)

Jack wiped his brow with the back of his arm. Hot. His apartment was too hot. Perspiration broke out over the full length of his naked body. Fucking hell, *what* is going on?

He glanced to his living room window and stared with numbed disbelief. The window had fogged over.

Runners of water dribbled down the inside of the glass. It puddled along the windowsill and dripped onto the hardwood floor.

Jack shot out of the couch. He snatched the remote and clicked the off button. Nothing happened. The picture on the TV stubbornly remained. "God damn it!" he shouted. "Go away!"

(Be)

(Be the)

(Be the first)

"Shut up!" Jack raged. "Just shut up, whatever you are!" He spun around. His apartment was steaming over, somehow becoming the image that filled his TV screen. Yes: A match to gasoline, that's what this was. Truer than the erotic tug, the dark sensuality that encouraged him to

(Be the first)

Heart pounding, he sprinted over to the mass of electrical cords plugged into the wall socket. If he couldn't shut the TV off, then by god he'd pull the plug.

(No!)

The voice bit into him.

It was like being jabbed in the neck with a hypodermic needle. It grabbed him on the back of his neck and tugged him back toward the front of the TV set. Sharp needles of pain shot through him. Whimpering, he faced the television screen, terrified of the pain if he moved.

(Look who I'll give you)

said the voice, and eased its grip.

On the television, a man floated out of the steam.

Jack's eyes widened. The blond. The man from the gym, Mick or Mike. He was fondling himself in slow concentric circles. A surprised "Ohh" sighed out of Jack's mouth at the sight of his fantasy, this beautiful man. The blond tilted back his head and moaned lustily. Steam geysered up around him, and he vanished.

(Anyone you want, Jack. Anyone at all)

The pressure on his neck let go.

Jack tore his gaze away from the TV. He swept the room for a weapon. He would be hypnotized, drugged, if he kept looking at the screen. Atop a bookshelf not two feet away sat a hardbound collection of bibles. Family heirlooms, inherited years ago.

The TV was beginning to glow. Warm purplish light infused the screen and pressed against its confines.

(Jack)

(Come Jack)

(Be the)

Jack lunged for the bookcase. He instinctively snatched one of the bibles. And before the voice could stop him, he hurled the book at the TV screen. It exploded with a blinding flash of sparks and shattered glass. In the ensuing commotion Jack heard a trumpeting roar fill his ears, and his last thought before being thrown across the living room was *Is that a lion?*

But then he was slammed against the far wall, stars winking across his field of vision, as a dark shape flew on top of him.

4

He awoke later, life still in him.

Jack put a hand to his neck and withdrew it, sticky with blood. His vision swam. Not much time. Dawn, soon.

He staggered to his knees and crawled toward the bookshelf. He slammed into it and fell heavily back onto the floor as bibles and books dropped like miniature bombs around him. He reached for one of the bibles, picked it up — and immediately dropped it. Something foreign inside him yelped with pain, burning. Doggedly, he again picked up the bible, this time prepared for the pain. It cut a bright clear path for him to follow. He opened the book, and with trembling fingers began to rip handfuls of pages from the bible.

The rumor mill

1

It was the talk of the gym.

2

Are you sure?

Sure I'm sure.

The guy who always wore red shorts? *He's* the one that's missing?

The very same.

No!

I swear!

What happened?

Police think he invited someone over. They watched porno.

Porno? They put that in the papers?

Yeah.

How embarrassing. Imagine having everyone know you bit the big one while watching smut.

3

He just disappeared.

Like that other kid.

Jack wasn't a kid.

No, no. A real kid. A boy. Been missing for a couple of days. Parents frantic. Read it in the *Examiner*.

Christ. Both South of Market?

He was a nice guy. Jack.

Friendly sort.

Especially in the steamroom.

Maybe with *you,* sweetheart, but not me.

Forgive me, Miss Pollyanna White Gloves. God forbid I insinuate you diddle in the jacuzzi.

Oh well. He won't be the first face to disappear from this gym. Honey, I lost track years ago. Too many faces just gone with the—

Are you going to spot me on these lifts, or impersonate Scarlett O'Hara all afternoon?

Pity, though.

Yeah.

4

I wonder.

What?

Why'd he do it?

What? Break his TV?

Bible pages. Why'd he tape them all over his apartment?

Probably a bad acid trip.

Nobody does acid any more.

Oh yeah? Nobody chases murderers away with pages torn from a bible, either.

5

And in the streets, a new kind of chatter, not heard in many a while:

6

Great shirt.

Thanks.

New?

Yes. But.

What?

I bought it at the Salvation Army.

No! Really! You bought it there? Why?

'Cause Macy's doesn't carry these shirts any more, you ninny.

Flashy.

Yeah. I swore I'd never wear polyester again, but this design was too wild to pass up.

Everything comes back in style, given time. Look at flattops. Gold chains.

That's fifties. You forget that it's "in" to hate the seventies. Pretend they never existed.

You mean pretend you weren't out sucking and fucking all night?

All night? Try ten years.

So what's with the polyester? Is this the new you?

Who knows? Maybe I'll start a trend.

7

Anyone know where I can score some coke?

I thought you gave that up.

I did. Two years ago.

So why spoil the honeymoon?

Dunno. Bet it'd be a lot of fun, though. To do it after all this time. Maybe even throw a party.

I know a guy who can help you out.

How much?

Hey: Blow is blow. They don't give it away for free, comprende?

Hook me up with him, would ya? I could sure use a toot for the tea dance.

8

Have you heard?

What?

They're starting nostalgia night at one of the corner bars in the Castro.

I don't know. What's all this looking backward shit? I *like* the new songs. Though I must admit I pulled out some of my old twelve-inch disco singles the other day and listened to a few. Got stoned out of my gourd — you can't appreciate that music without being stoned. It was fun. Sweet. Made me feel young again.

9

Around David, the voices flapped on bat wings.

In the gym. In the Castro, as he walked the streets. Shopping at Cala Foods. The talk pierced the heavy curtain of pain which enveloped him and settled like bricks, one atop the other, inside him. He was too mired in the quicksand of his failing health to give these whisperings and gossip much attention.

But at night, in bed, waiting for the merciful blanket of sleep, David sifted through these voices. He decided he must be hearing wrong, must be getting the tail end of conversations related to a wholly different subject. For how could a neighborhood, almost overnight, become so obsessed with its past that an intervening decade meant nothing?

He tossed in bed, his mended bones aching, his forehead a misery. Delusions, and more delusions. The clock beside his bed ticked and ticked, holding negotiations with the enemy. Deep in his heart, he knew: He had to grab onto a ledge, stop this tumbling down, down. For this hole housed more than emptiness as its bottom. It held something savage.

Flytrap

1

It stands alone on a street corner, shiny and cool and inviting, shrouded in fog. Mick cannot see it yet, not completely anyway; it calls to him as a prize from a half-remembered (yet fiercely yearned for) dream. His fingertips touch cool glass. There is no light overhead. His erection is rock hard beneath 501 jeans — now why is that? Is it because of the voice? Or the ringing?

Yes. The ringing awakens the desire. The—

2

telephone woke them from their doze. Mick's eyes flew open. Bobby rolled over onto his side and scooped up the receiver. "Hello?" Mick waited, his heart beating fast. He did not know why.

"Hello? Who is this?" Bobby sat up against the headboard, his expression moving from sleepy puzzlement to annoyance.

Mick looked at Bobby and simultaneously glanced past him at the gaudy five-inch crucifix on the nightstand beside the bed. A present from Bobby's grandma.

"Don't you ever call this number again." Bobby slammed the receiver down. "Fucking nerve. Calling so late."

"Who was it?"

"Didn't even have the decency to breathe hard. Silence. Just silence. The creep."

Mick glanced at his watch. "Oh, Christ. It's almost eleven-thirty." He propped himself up on elbows.

"Don't go."

"Have to."

"No, you don't." Bobby trailed a hand across Mick's chest. "Stay with me and I'll give you dessert..." He pushed back the sheet and was delighted to find Mick with a hard-on. He squeezed it. "Where did *this* come from?"

Mick shrugged. "Sweet dreams, I guess."

"All the more reason to stay." Bobby rolled Mick's cock up and down with his hand.

Mick brushed him away. "Honey, I've got a long day waiting for me at the office—"

Bobby's hand shot away. "Oh, the hell with your office. That's not why you're leaving."

So *that's* it, Mick thought, swinging his legs over the side of the bed. Our one and only argument, round fifty-four. "It's time for me to go home."

"As always."

"I don't have any work clothes here! Give me a break!" He faced Bobby, and softened. He didn't want the night to end on an argument, not after the wonderful dinner together, and the sex that had left them so contented they had dozed. He touched his lover on the thigh. "You know I have to be at my desk by eight a.m."

Bobby bit his lip. "Maybe you should bring over some of your suits so we won't have to go through this."

"Maybe I should."

Bobby's face lit up. "You mean that?"

Mick shrugged. "Why not? It's about time, don't you think?"

Bobby laughed delightedly, and they kissed.

They'd met five months earlier, in June. At the I-Beam of all places, dancing their little tushies off at the Sunday tea dance. While on the dance floor with friends, Bobby had spotted Mick and elbowed himself and his partner closer, so that they danced side by side. An immediate attraction had leapt between them, canceling all doubt or fear. Sure, it sounded corny whenever they related their how-they-met story to their friends, but to Bobby and Mick it was love — and lust — at first sight. They had edged closer and closer to each other, so that eventually both of their dance partners shrugged good-naturedly and walked off the dance floor, leaving them to themselves. And for Bobby, whenever he thought of that first night, he always remembered it as Mick dancing in front of him, shirt off, sweat flinging from his wavy blond curls, and that sweet come-hither grin.

"You've already got a toothbrush here and some shirts and pants," Bobby said. "And you're closer to downtown from here anyway. Might as well take advantage of it." A pause, then: "I won't crowd you, you know. You're free to do whatever you want."

"You too," Mick said quickly. He scooted off the bed in search of his clothes. They were a scattered pile on the floor. If he didn't hurry, he'd miss his eleven-fifty bus.

Bobby watched him dress. It still gave him an absurd amount of pleasure to watch the play and pull of his lover's gym-toned muscles as he moved about the bedroom. Mick naked was like a blond Nordic statue with a spray of freckles on his cheeks and shoulders. Lean, yet tightly muscled, with a bubble butt the equal of Michelangelo's David. It was in moments such as these that he congratulated himself on such a fine catch. "You want me to call you a cab?"

"I only have a few dollars on me."

"I'll lend you the money."

Mick buttoned his shirt. "The bus stop is only a couple blocks down. I'll be home in no time."

"Don't be silly. You were right; it's late. You should be in bed."

"I can use the fresh air."

Bobby shook his head, exasperated. "Won't even spring for a cab. You don't expect much out of life, do you?"

"Nope." Mick flashed a smile. "That way I'm rarely surprised."

"Sounds boring."

"Comfortable is more like it. That's the sort of guy I am. Receptionist by day, lover by night." Dressed now, he sat beside Bobby and favored him with a lingering kiss. They snuggled.

Bobby glanced at his alarm clock and patted Mick on the arm. "All right Mr. Comfortable, go catch your bus. And button up. It's a cold night."

"*Every* night in San Francisco is a cold night."

"Just get home quickly." Bobby's face clouded.

"What's the matter?"

"Nothing." But for some reason his thoughts had folded back to last Saturday night's storm. "And steer clear of any bums."

"Why?" Mick's eyes fell upon the gaudy crucifix beside the bed. Mischievously, he scooped it from the nightstand. "Is there a full moon tonight? Maybe I should take this with me to ward off evil spirits."

"Don't make fun." Bobby nibbled at his lip, a nervous gesture.

What's he so worried about? Mick thought. The joke ruined, he replaced the crucifix.

"Mick, did you read the paper today?"

"Only had time for the 'Daily Punch.' Why?"

"There's been a couple of disappearances."

"So what else is new?"

"In the neighborhood, Mickey. A gay man."

Mick grimaced. "What happened?"

"No one knows. It's really weird. The guy taped pages from a bible all over his windows and front door."

Mick wrinkled his nose. "Yuck. Shades of *The Omen*. So what happened?"

Bobby shrugged. "The place was ransacked. Pages taped everywhere. And the guy — vanished."

"Do they think he was murdered?"

"They don't know, exactly. But he's definitely disappeared."

"Oh, swell." Mick ran his fingers through his sandy hair. "You're determined to keep me here tonight, aren't you? Now I'll watch every shadow."

"Maybe you should."

Mick glanced at his watch. Better hurry. He gave Bobby a final quick kiss. "Relax. I'll be okay. Besides," he said with a sly smile, pulling out a whistle and key chain, "anybody gives me shit, I blow this."

3

A fine mist hung in the air as Mick walked the two blocks to his bus stop. Cold tonight. Ever since Saturday's storm he could feel the chill drawing strength as the days tumbled toward an early winter. Just one week ago the days had glowed sunny and warm, an Indian summer. And now — well, welcome to San Francisco, where the weather changed according to the daily whims of high and low pressure systems flowing in off the Pacific. He thought Denver had been bad, the weather spinning on a dime as each new norther blew in, dumping rain or snow. But San Francisco took the cake.

Only a handful of lights glowed from the surrounding apartments as he walked by. This was no time to be out on the streets, waiting for the 19 Polk that was sure to be off schedule, as usual. Maybe he should have stayed with Bobby. No; he'd wanted some fresh air, and if that meant waiting for the bus in this goddamned mist, well, he'd made his bed and now he'd have to lie in it.

He walked to his usual bus stop and looked around. No sign of the 19 Polk. Maybe he'd just missed one, and would have to wait half an hour. That was a depressing thought. He brushed damp hair out of his eyes and glanced at the threatening sky. At this rate, he was going to get rather wet if the mist held up, and the drizzle showed no signs of slacking.

Almost as an afterthought Mick spun on his heels and glanced down the street in the opposite direction. Three blocks away stood another bus stop for the 19 Polk.

Something fluttered inside him.

That bus stop had a protective green awning with a bench inside. Beside it stood an old-fashioned phone booth. The overhead street-light had either burned out or been the victim of a teenager's vandalism. It offered protection from the drizzle, but it sure was dark. Too dark for a sleepy bus driver to see him? Probably not, not if he flagged the bus down.

A sudden escalation in the wind and drizzle tipped the scales in favor of a decision. Mick started walking. Why not go stand there? He could stay under the awning, out of this drizzle, and keep reasonably dry.

But as he walked toward the bus stop the strangest feeling crept over him. His ears buzzed. His chest and shoulders began to shake with muscle spasms. Mick halted in his tracks. Was he shivering from the cold? The wind and rain? No. Something else was at work here, like an ancient nerve or an obsolete organ triggering danger signals to his body and brain. His forehead beaded with cool sweat. There was something primitive about this rush of adrenalin pumping through him, something so deeply buried that it remained hidden, unconscious.

He glanced at the bus stop. His eyes shifted from the army-green awning structure to the phone booth. He stared at it, his breath and pulse quickening. His feet moved below him.

The phone booth.

That was the source of his whatever this was, this fight-or-flight panic. Oddly, the booth looked familiar. Something shrouded and half-remembered skirted the corners of his thoughts. He shrugged it away and forced himself to walk. It wasn't wise to have such spooky thoughts, not when he was alone on a dark, wind-swept street. This was the hour when good men sleep and bad men awaken — best to keep thoughts light. Right now, all he wanted was his bed. His electric blanket. His English muffin in the morning, strawberry jam only, with a cup of French roast.

He arrived.

Calmer, now. That flight-or-fight sensation a dull undercurrent. Perhaps it *was* just the cold. Nothing unusual about this bus stop. Besides, another five minutes, with any luck, and he'd be bouncing his way up Polk Street to his studio apartment on Clay.

The protective awning housed a bench, but when Mick sat down on it he was immediately assaulted by the stench of stale urine and cheap wine. He sprang away, wrinkling his nose in disgust. This was home for some of the guys who wandered the streets — but did they have to piss in their own living rooms?

He moved away from the foul-smelling bench and stood at the edge of the awning, where he was still protected from the drizzle. This was better. He could spot the bus from down the street with enough warning to flag the driver.

Idly, Mick stared into the dark phone booth on his left.

And was not the least bit surprised when the public phone, which had hung rightfully silent, began to ring.

4

Bobby paces the floor.

Half a dozen times he has gone to the bedroom window and peered out onto the misty street below. Mick is not there, of course. The alley is empty. Mick is riding the 19 Polk by now. He has to be.

But that is not why Bobby paces. He can't explain this free-floating panic racing through him, the cold hand of dread squeezing his intestines. His forehead tingles with a maddening itch right between his eyes. Twice he has pulled on his sweats with the intention of retrieving Mick. And once he made it to the door before looking down at himself and laughing nervously, thinking, *Mick is gone already. Call him in thirty minutes if you want, to make sure he's okay. Otherwise go to bed.*

Instead, Bobby stands at the window again, thinking of the man with no face.

It was the rain — the storm — the streetlight — a million things. No one could look like that, with that terrible grin.

He crosses to the bed and sits with his back against the headboard. Curses himself for this bizarre anxiety, knowing sleep will be difficult tonight. Perhaps a shot of bourbon will calm the nerves. Or a joint, if he has anything left besides seeds and stems.

He checks the alarm clock. Yes, Mick is surely on his way home. Should he call him later? No. Too pushy, like checking up on him. Mick's a big boy.

His glance slides past the clock and settles upon the crucifix. Impulsively, he scoops it into his hand.

And almost drops it as the cross hums into life. His hand feels as if he has shoved his fingers into an electrical socket. A tingling current shoots down his arm as the crucifix glows, in rapid succession, red blue green gold yellow white. A halo of white light.

With a startled gasp Bobby drops the cross onto the bed. Instantly, the light snuffs out. His arm tingles with the phantom energy. And he thinks, not for the first and certainly not for the last time, *Oh, Mick, what's happening to you!*

5

By the third ring, amusement had given way to curiosity.

By the fifth ring, irritation.

He answered on the sixth.

"How would you like a real man tonight?" asked a man's voice.

Mick shuddered with relief. Oh, so *that's* what this is: a dirty phone call. The low-pitched siren of his anxiety let go its wailing as the tension ran out of him.

"Sorry, guy," Mick said. "My dance card's been filled. I'm not interested."

"You're talking to me, aren't you?" the man at the other end of the line whispered. "Feeling that stir of excitement in your cock. All I want is a good time. You do, too."

Mick frowned. What was that accent? Spanish? Something European. He rather liked it. Who knows? Had this guy randomly called his apartment while he was in bed watching Johnny Carson or some late movie, this whole conversation would be exciting. Hell, no need to be jealous of a voice, right? It could be fun to get off that way, two voices over the phone. But standing at this dark bus stop, in the mist, cold and damp — this was just the wrong time, wrong place.

"Listen," he said, glancing down the street for his bus, "I think I should tell you where you're calling. I'm not some guy in bed who wants to get his rocks off."

"I know where I am calling."

"No. See: I'm not at home. You've dialed a pay phone."

A humorless laugh. "I know that."

Mick gulped. "You do?"

"Of course."

"How?"

"I can see you."

What? A chill ran through him. Immediately, he scanned the tall silent buildings across the street. Dozens upon dozens of dark windows looked down upon him.

"Don't be frightened."

"I'm not!" Mick said, too loudly. Then: "You can really see me?"

"Oh, yes."

His legs turned to jelly. God, this was weird. "How can you see? ... I mean ... Fuck, why am I even talking to you!"

"Because I want you to, my friend."

Mick looked around. No one; there was no one. No bus in sight. And somewhere, in any one of the windows, in any one of the buildings, a man studied him. A man who saw the surprise and dawning fear magnified on his face.

"Where are you?" Mick asked, swallowing hard.

"That shouldn't concern you."

Why am I talking to him? he thought crazily. *Hang up. Just hang up and wait for the bus or get the hell out of here.*

"I'll tell you anything you want to know," the man said.

"Oh yeah? Then what's that accent in your voice? You sound — I don't know — European."

"Very good. I am Turkish."

"Really?" That was a new one on him.

"You may call me ... Victor. This is all you need to know. Except to remember I can see your every move. And I *can* see you, oh so clearly."

Mick bristled. "What do you want from me?"

"I thought that was clear."

"The only reason I'm talking to you is because the goddamned bus won't come. You're passing time, that's all. So don't get any ideas. Understand?" The urge to hang up rose in him. This Victor guy was too strange, even if all this sex talk was kind of arousing.

"Listen to me," Victor said, his voice dropping to a husky growl. "We are strangers, you and I. And so we have freedom. Understand? Sometimes it is — how do you say this — *easier* with a stranger. So let us see what we can teach each other."

"No."

"No. No. It is time you put yes into your life, am I right?"

"I'm fine the way I am, thank you."

"Don't be cross. I know I excite you. Oh, don't deny it. I can see your hard-on through your pants."

Mick looked down at himself. Sure enough, his penis had swelled against his blue jeans. He stared at it as if witnessing the betrayal of a friend. His cheeks flushed. Damn it, this guy *did* have a sexy voice. He had the kind of voice that could convince you of anything. You had to be careful with a voice like that.

And a new thought struck him: Hadn't he fantasized about this very sort of conversation? Wasn't he the one who had almost called one of those phone sex numbers half a dozen times, always thinking better of it at the last minute? Well, here was such a call, a gift from heaven brought right to his door. It wouldn't go any farther than this because he had no intention of cheating on Bobby. But for now ... couldn't he just enjoy this?

"Why don't you show yourself to me?" Victor purred. "Go ahead. I dare you."

"No."

"Come on; let me see how big you are."

Mick couldn't catch his breath. He was suddenly dizzy with excitement. He looked up and down the rain-washed street. The buildings across the street appeared utterly deserted. But this man had to be hiding out in one of the apartments, right? For if he wasn't across the street, how could he see him? Alone. Still alone. Oh, what the hell. His hand brushed across his erection, stopped, and squeezed.

"Ahh, that's nice. You are very handsome, my friend. A diamond in a sea of coal. So al! ... American. Blond hair. Freckles. You should listen to your dick. It tells you to come to me."

A car drove by. Mick shook free of the spell. "I can't do this."

"Of course you can," the dark voice urged. "In fact, my young friend, I think *you* will be the one. I have need of someone with your attributes. I have much I will teach you, when you decide to come to me. We will be good for each other, yes?"

"Oh, sure. You know so much about me, is that it?"

A soft chuckle. "This is not the first time I've seen you."

"What?"

"I have watched you for several days now. You come from the arms of someone else. The scent of sex is upon you. But you crave more. I can give you want you want. But first, you must prove yourself."

"You're crazy." Mick's legs began to tremble and would not stop. He had to lean against the cool glass of the booth to steady himself.

"So why haven't you hung up?"

Mick stammered a protest.

"You don't because you know I speak the truth," Victor interrupted. "I know more than I should, and it intrigues you."

What was that sound in the background? He had confused it with the drizzle around him. Now he realized it originated on the other end of the phone. Drip. Drip. Drip. Water hitting water. Mick went hot and cold. And a sudden certainty flashed across the horizon of his consciousness:

Hang up just hang up he's tricking me—

"If you come to me, I will give you a gift. You have never known the passion we could share. Would you like that?"

"...No..."

"Ahh, but I think you *do*. I think we have found each other. I was right from the very beginning, the first time I noticed you."

"I told you," Mick snapped, trying to regain the upper hand. "I already have a boyfriend."

"A pale excuse, my friend. What you search for you have found in me. Perhaps you were not even aware of your search, and yet — here you are."

He was about to respond when all at once, like an angel of mercy, he saw the 19 Polk round the corner several blocks down. Relief flooded through him. The cold night, the long day of work for him tomorrow: It all snapped back. Priorities lined up like so many dominoes. He found his voice as this new strength surged through him.

"Yeah? Well here I go. My bus is coming."

"Wait for another one."

"No."

"Then you'll be back."

"Don't count on it."

"Oh, but I *will*. We have unfinished business, you and I. This is just the beginning."

Mick sucked in a deep breath. "As far as I'm concerned, we're finished right here and now. You'll have to play out your fantasies on someone else!" Before the hypnotic voice could respond, he hurled the phone into the receiver. He stepped away, his breath ragged. It had taken all his effort, every bit. If the bus hadn't shown up...

And in his ears, like a phantom connection, he heard the drip, drip of water in some unimaginable place, and a laugh as chilling as some deep bottomless lake.

7

Free-fall

H e thought the pain couldn't get any worse, but he was wrong.

2

At first he ignored the tingling and the dull ache. He willed the bump to go away. When it swelled to the size of a quarter, and refused to come to a head, David dug around in his bathroom cabinets and discovered a leftover tube of pancake makeup. Carefully, he dabbed it on. Touching the spot gave him a queer light-headed sensation, as if he'd smoked some grass and then performed fifty jumping jacks. His heartbeat wobbled. Lights flickered inside his head.

So he left it alone, and took to wearing a Giants baseball cap with the brim tugged down to cover his forehead. He received startled looks from passersby on the streets, and at the gym, men stared with surreptitious sideways glances. There were too many mirrors at the gym, too many ways to catch sight of his misshapen forehead, so reluctantly David gave up on his workouts.

He gave up on the sauna as well, though he hadn't expected to. He thought the steamroom's heat might urge the bump to come to a head, which would release the terrible pressure. It was worth a try.

So after showering in the downstairs locker room, David padded across the wet floor to the sauna. He reached for the door handle and swung the door wide.

That's as far as he got.

A wave of frigid air rolled out — or so it felt to him, the way his teeth began to chatter and his skin to prickle. He took a faltering backward step and stared into the swirling darkness.

"Hey!" shouted a man from inside. "You're letting out all the heat!"

An image reared across the frozen landscape of David's thoughts: the giant mouth in his nightmare, teeth bared.

"You coming or going?" shouted another irritated man.

David commanded himself to stretch out his arm and shut the door. This time its solid wood frame was vaguely leathery to his touch, cool and unpleasant. He slammed the door shut as a wave of nausea rolled over him. He stumbled away and fell gratefully into a nearby lawn chair provided for those who overindulge in the jacuzzi or sauna. And as he waited for the world to right itself he may have heard it, the whistle of air past his ears as he continued to fall.

3

For two days David stayed home. Every time he met his reflection in the mirror a voice would rise in him and whisper: *Go to a doctor.*

But he couldn't. He was afraid.

He called in sick at Uncle Charlie's, the Castro restaurant where he worked part-time as a waiter. He checked on Eddie, who remained stable and showed hopeful signs of improvement, but he could not bring himself to visit.

A new twist had been added.

When he touched the bump, he saw things.

He discovered the change one night as he resolutely examined the bruise in the bathroom mirror. The swelling had now grown beyond the size of a quarter and was presently rectangular, a two-inch lump that followed a vein across his forehead. Gingerly, he explored the rose-colored fringe of the swelling. He traced the puffy outline with his forefinger, but when he touched the center

4

an airless hut
a black face
"Kahmaal"

5

David startled awake. The images scattered, replaced by his reflection in the mirror. *What happened?*

His face was a white sheet, his eyes full moons.

Leave it alone, he admonished himself. *Don't touch it any more.*

He retreated from the bathroom and went into the living room to smoke a joint. The marijuana should have calmed his nerves, but it only added to his restlessness. He got up from the couch to scrounge for supper. The cabinets were abysmally empty. He opened his last can of soup. His forehead throbbed like a rotten tooth, daring his fingers to probe and touch the way a tongue returns ceaselessly to probe the hole where an extracted tooth has been.

He flipped on the TV for distraction and listened to Mary Hart ooze praise for some TV star he had never heard of before. He was almost finished with his bowl of chunky chicken vegetable when a fierce itch suddenly stabbed him between the eyes. Without thinking he reached up

6

rolling, rocking
ocean
chains
something palmed into his hand, a chunk of ice
drowning

7

He thrashed awake.
On the living room floor.
Naked.
Clothes were scattered about the room as though torn off in a frenzy. Buttons littered the carpet. Sweat sluiced off his torso. Groaning, David rolled over onto his back. It wasn't *all* sweat running off of him: He smelled water. Chlorine-scented

Ocean?

No; that was from his vision, or whatever fit he'd just had. Miles and miles of ocean, and a stone pushed into his hand.

He sniffed himself. Chlorine. A graham-cracker gym smell. And *naked.* He couldn't get past that one, discovering himself shorn of all clothing, thrashing on the floor as though coming up for air. He'd never blacked out before in his life. Well. Except for his fall.

All the strangeness, the terrible confusion of the past week, peaked in him.

So this is what it's like to lose your mind, David thought, and before he could stop himself, he wept over his bizarre malady.

8

"David Walker, please."
"Speaking."
"David? This is Bessie Watson, at Davies Hospital."
"Yes? What's happened? How's Eddie?"
"He's asking for you."
"Oh god. Is it time?"
"You'd better come."
"I'm — I'm not feeling well. I'm sick."
"Shame."
"Is he bad, Bessie?"
"You'd better come see for yourself."

9

"Jesus!"
An amused chuckle from Eddie. "What's the matter?"

David pulled up a chair beside the hospital bed. "You. You're what's the matter. Whatever it is they're giving you — I want double."

Eddie beamed. He had reason to, today. He was sitting up for the first time in a week, the head of his bed raised behind him. High color flamed on his cheeks. Brown eyes clear. He was *here,* today. Not a doped-up shell. "What's with the third eye?"

David bowed his head self-consciously. He tried to wave the question away. "I'd rather talk about *you.*"

Eddie's smile faltered for just a moment. "Okay." He hesitated. "I like the cap. Looks good on you."

"Thanks. You look terrific." It relieved David. He couldn't get over how vibrant Eddie looked. Oh, he was still a bag of bones, and pockmarked by half a dozen purplish lesions. But a light had turned on inside him, and its glow shone through every gesture and smile. "So what's the secret? Did an orderly slip extra vitamins into your tomato juice?"

Eddie sighed contentedly. His hands played beneath the crisp white sheets. "I don't care — how long — it lasts," he said in short gasps (it was the longest sentence David had heard him string together in weeks). "I just want to" — his eyes rolled — "enjoy it."

Bessie had been right, after all. Eddie's particular roller coaster would have many dips and turns, with an occasional rest at the top. He didn't want to speculate on when Eddie would take his next plunge off this amazing high. Better to enjoy this hiatus while they could.

Eddie was ravenously interested in everything outside his hospital room. Hollywood gossip. Liz Smith. Any new books or movies causing a sensation. The entire time he talked he fiddled with something underneath the sheets and smiled as though he'd won a special prize.

Then Eddie asked, "Anything new in the Castro?"

"No," he answered, adding, "More like everything old."

His friend stared at him quizzically.

"Nostalgia seems to be the latest fad," David said. He amended to himself, *Unless I'm hearing things.*

"People want before," Eddie said simply.

An apt comment. But mentioning this to Eddie suddenly gave him a peculiar feeling.

"And so do I," Eddie beamed. "Hey, if I keep improving, I'll be out in no time." He flexed one of his broomstick arms. "Maybe even pump iron again."

It was the funny pasted-on smile on Eddie's face that rang an alarm inside him. A suspicion rose in him, but having no firm ground to light upon, it buzzed and flitted, joining the larger pack of oddities that continued to pile up in his brain.

Like now: the flexing of Eddie's left arm, a muscle-man pose, and that baby-grand smile of satisfaction. Pump iron again? Eddie? Never.

But the gleaming fire just then in Eddie's eyes, as he looked at his arm. A sort of adoring infatuation. What did he see, exactly?

His head began to throb. The Tylenol he'd taken was beginning to wear off. His bump ached to be massaged, but he couldn't bring himself to touch it. Where would he wake up, if he did? In the room next door, surrounded by doctors?

Feigning playfulness, David grabbed Eddie's left foot and massaged it. "Gotta go now, Eds," he said. "I'm not feeling so great. You need anything before I go?"

A shake of head. "I'm fine."

He looked it, too. That self-satisfied grin: like a student who knew all the answers to what was supposed to be a pop quiz. Suspicions buzzed, with nowhere to land. David stood up.

"See you tomorrow, then," he said.

"'Kay." Eddie closed his eyes and sighed. Their conversation had tuckered him out. The sight pleased David in some vague way he could not explain — it struck him as more natural than this unexpected burst of energy.

As he started out of the room the question sprang to his lips. He felt a need to say it, to air it between them: Eddie's "man in the steam."

David faced the bed. He opened his mouth to speak, but Eddie beat him to it.

"You're a — good — pal," Eddie sighed. "Thanks for coming today."

David beamed. "You're worth it."

He walked out of the room, and put the question to sleep. For now.

10

Eddie dreamed his dreams.

And in moments of wakefulness, as the sun slipped from his room with a lingering sigh, Eddie reached under the covers and withdrew his prize.

He wasn't quite sure what it meant, this prize of his. Only that it filled him with indescribable longing. He had awakened the morning before to find it on the dresser beside his bed, a tiny puddle of water next to it.

A ticket.

Admit One, it said.

Promises in the dark

Eddie looked at the ceiling.

1

After so many weeks in here, lying flat on his back, it had begun to take on the appearance of some great chapel wall. Here a patch of plaster, a dark line running three quarters across the ceiling, looked like a road map. A river. No; the canals of Mars. Timeless. This patchwork design of plaster and tiny sparkle flakes had been here to greet him and — just as surely — would remain, mute, ready for the next restless patient to stare at, months after he was gone.

Of course, at this time of night only shadows danced on the ceiling and walls of his room. There were no maps to chart in this darkness, and Eddie thought that was okay, he thought that was just okeydokey. Life inside room 203 had narrowed down into one of those kaleidoscopic toys where every twist of the handle created a slightly new design, a new angle to shift through and explore. He was growing less and less aware of the turn of seasons outside his hospital window (although he hoped to see Christmas, even if he couldn't put into words exactly *why* it was important for him). He counted on David for news and current events, but for the most part his seasons were now the ebb and flow of nurses and orderlies into his room, the daytime chats with his doctors, and any special treat his lunch would bring. That is, if he had an appetite.

He flicked his tongue over fever-dried lips. What time was it? And why was he awake? An odd expectancy rippled through him. Ever since he'd discovered that ticket beside his bed, he'd felt alert and alive, better than he'd felt in weeks.

Eddie stretched under the white hospital sheets and abruptly discovered why he'd awakened.

He had a hard-on.

What a sense of power flushed through him! This was better than his shots of morphine to take away the pain, better than the best cocaine he'd once stuffed up his nose oh so many lifetimes ago. This was a gift from his old life, a gift of his maleness, and he welcomed it and the electric charge it gave him.

How had it happened? Hadn't he been dreaming? Yes. That was it. He'd dreamt of

Caverns

that place. That bathhouse south of Market. The old homestead, as he used to call it.

He had been too busy as a lawyer to cultivate boyfriends. Sure, he always managed to meet guys at the social rallies, the volunteer groups, the Harvey Milk meetings. But it was tricky (no pun intended) having sex with these men. Bad politics. Easy to hurt feelings, trample on toes. Much better to leave the rallies, the meetings, with a shrug of the shoulders: Why, I'd love to go home with you but duty calls, the time is late, and I'd better get my forty winks, ha ha. But let's do lunch, huh? Ah, yes. Better to leave with no hard feelings, no stepped-upon toes, and hightail it out of there. Sometimes he actually convinced himself he *was* driving straight home, back to his apartment on Noe Street where David would most likely be holed up in his bedroom, tap-tapping away on his latest story.

Yes, Eddie would convince himself, better to go home and sleep. But once behind the wheel of his Audi, his dick would entertain other ideas. He'd think of the Caverns, of the twisting hallways and dim lights, of the men who sat jerking off in private rooms, doors open, in invitation; or better yet, the steamroom. No pretenses. No exchange of business cards, no phony promises of a call the following Saturday night. With a bit of luck, he could be in and out in just over an hour, hard-on satisfied for the night through the effortless exchange of man lust. Home in bed before midnight.

The Caverns.

An apt name, if ever there was one. Even an old regular like himself had gotten lost in there on several occasions. The place gave the illusion of an underground cave, a playground deep inside a mountain, like something out of a Tolkein book. Not for the claustrophobic, not by any means, but one humdinger of a sex palace.

With trembling joy, Eddie reached between his legs and grasped his erection. God, how good that felt! Like wrapping his hand around a lightning bolt. He shut his eyes and remembered how it had been once, walking those hallways with a towel wrapped around his middle. The Caverns had its own scent, too, rich and musky and humid, a gym smell of man sweat and jism. Ripe. Underneath all other smells was the scent of eucalyptus leaves from the steamroom, clean and sweet. The memory surged in him, so startlingly clear he could almost—

A soundless cry caught in his throat.

Hooked to his intravenous tubes, Eddie gagged on the cloying scent of eucalyptus leaves, its fragrance too rich for his oxygen-poor body.

What the—?

Stronger now. As if dipping into an artery of memory, he drank. Why, he could even hear, ever so dimly, the mechanical hiss of the steamroom, storing up and squirting out steam in regulated jets.

Beads of sweat popped onto his forehead.

Hot in here. Hot, but oh so wonderful to relive this again (if that was what was happening — he was too excited to stop and sort it all out). How many nights had he sat in the steamroom, holding court, as men circulated in and out, hard-ons swinging in the steam scant inches from his face, his lips? How many men had he taken, tasted, tossed aside?

Eddie squeezed his eyes shut, remembering, reliving, afraid to move an ounce of himself for fear of breaking the spell. Yes, he could hear the jets of steam quite clearly, a rhythmic whoosh and hiss. Eucalyptus stung his nostrils. There was another smell, he noticed, not quite masked by the eucalyptus, and for a brief instant he panicked. This was the stink of rotting things, of mildew and damp and mold, of things that never see the light of day. He opened his eyes in panic, his heart hammering, his cherished erection going limp in his hand.

Something was happening on the ceiling.

Shadows tossed and whirled, running together, solidifying. Dust motes, like tiny pinpoint stars, swirled in a lazy clockwise direction. This was no road map forming on his ceiling. No charted tour of the canals of Mars. A growing black shape, darker than the midnight darkness of his room, was attaching itself to the ceiling. As he lay flat in his bed, he watched what appeared to be a bird spread its enormous wings across the entire length of ceiling. No, not a bird

A bat oh my god is that a giant bat?

but something that flew, something with wings. Eddie began to whimper.

And then, within the blink of an eye, the wings (if there had ever *been* any wings, he wasn't sure any more) folded into the black shape floating on the ceiling, and what was once only shadow became a man. He beheld his guest.

A black man, his skin the color of polished coal, floated effortlessly above him. Hair salted with gray crowned a face that was vaguely familiar, as though they'd been acquaintances from years past. A darker shadow fluttered behind the man like a cape, rippling in the invisible currents that webbed him to the ceiling. He was naked, and as Eddie watched, transfixed, the shadow man began to fondle himself, one hand cupping balls while the other stroked his penis into a full enormous erection.

He was there and he was not there; one instant the figure floated above him, and in the next moment he saw only a swatch of shadow, and two blinking eyes.

"Who are you?" Eddie croaked. All his spit was gone. But a cartoon name rose to match the face in front of him, dissolving before his mind could form it. Wait a minute. The manager. Wasn't he the owner of—?

(Talk to me like this. I can hear you)

a voice whispered back, inside and yet outside of his mind.

What do you want from me?

(I bring you a gift)

A gift?

(Behold)

The shadowy figure lifted an arm, and Eddie found himself staring into the steamroom of the Caverns. Five men, slick and naked, were sprawled across the split-level wooden benches. One man squatted in front of another, taking the man into his mouth while the man stroked his hair. Two other men sat facing each other, their hands on each other's hard nipples, toying and squeezing. Another man looked across the void and stared directly into Eddie's astonished eyes, his legs spread open in invitation, an erection bouncing in his hand.

Eddie moaned. His penis surged back into life. He both absolutely believed and totally rejected what his eyes beheld. Suddenly he remembered what he had forgotten, what the morphine had almost hidden from him: This was not the shadow man's first visit here. *He* was the one who had brought the ticket.

And then he saw something that filled him with such longing, his heart wanted to burst.

The door to the steamroom opened, and in walked Eddie. This was not the Eddie reduced to a bundle of tubes and lesions and bones, gaunt flesh giving him the appearance of a modern-day concentration camp survivor. The man who walked into the steamroom was his old self, all one hundred and sixty-two pounds, tanned from his business trips to Palm Springs, ready for action. The other men greeted him with warm smiles and beckoned him closer. Hands swarmed over the naked contours of his body, hands that caressed and squeezed and welcomed, and oh how good that felt, this was heaven boy, this must be heaven, and for an instant the Eddie who lay in bed watching actually *felt* hands touching him, urging him into their circle.

A quiet voice floated down to him.

(Do you like what you see?)

Oh yes! Yes!

(We can give you this. Sex the way you enjoy it. Sex as you have never known it could be, forever and ever)

But I'm sick. I — I can't—

(Not if you come to him. With him, you shall live. Would you like that?)

Yes!

The shadowy arm lowered. The steamroom and all its occupants vanished.

Bring it back! Oh please—

(What will you do for me?)

Anything! Whatever you want!

A chuckle, like the grinding of glass between teeth.

(Then open yourself to me)

And Eddie did.

2

In the stillness of his room, David lay awake.

He couldn't sleep. The pressure above his eyes was agony. It pulsed in synchronistic rhythm to his heartbeat. It was like enduring a terrible sinus headache and being forced to stand head bowed, with all the blood rushing between his eyes. A migraine's vehemence without the sharp stabs of pain. This was like giving birth to death.

"What is happening to me?" David moaned.

He was afraid. That was the bottom line. He knew what would happen. One look at his misshapen forehead and off he'd be whisked into a hospital room. And like Eddie, he would never again breathe crisp October air. He'd be examined, poked. Doctors with heads bowed, tsk-tsking.

I'm sorry, Mr. Walker, but you have a tumor the size of a baseball in your head. Guess you aren't the Miracle Kid after all. Guess your ticket's been punched, and nothing we can do but sit back and watch it eat you up, one bite at a time. But don't worry: We'll keep you here as long as it takes, I say as looong *as it takes.*

These thoughts were boulders in his head, gathering momentum as they knocked and bounced and tumbled on top of each other, hurrying toward a pit that housed his total despair.

Not only that, crazy images flickered across the screen of his mind. Bright flares of disjointed images, like an acid trip out of his youth. Staring into a campfire. A net raining out of the sky. Standing on a vast, high cliff, an ocean wind upon his face, with something hidden in his hand.

How much time passed in this state he did not know. He could not bring himself to call 911 and request an ambulance, even though he knew he was very sick. He lay perfectly still in his agony, sheets thrown back to cool the sweat dripping off of him. He flushed hot and cold, hot and cold. Night sweats. Dear god.

In desperation David tried to rein in his thoughts, but the boulders crashed and tumbled over the calm landscape he attempted to conjure for himself. He thought of Eddie's vibrant health and for some reason the boulders crashed through that, too: Something about it rang false.

Something about *every*thing rang false, lately. It was all around him.

Images swooped and capered in the dark of his bedroom. He knew he was delirious, and that whatever had gotten hold of him might very well kill him, if he didn't get some immediate help. But he could not have climbed out of bed to dial 911 even if his life depended upon it — as he suspected it did. No. He gave in to the seasick nausea and prayed for a respite from its stormy waters.

Soon enough, it came, announcing itself with a smell.

Chlorine.

The odor cut through David's haze of pain. He sniffed the air and winced as the chlorine burned the tender cavities of his nostrils. Instinctively, his whole body tensed.

He gasped. That's all he had time for.

A blast of wet air cascaded over him.

And the creature pounced.

Quite suddenly he was pinned to the bed. Hot breath snorted across his neck and face — the breath of a mad bull. He was smashed against the mattress by a weight that was more a pressure than a physical form, like the repelling ends of two magnets. But the voice that barked over him, the menacing growls and gnashing of teeth: That much of it was real.

No time to think. No time to even conceive what was happening. He was suddenly fighting for his life.

Rabid dog snarls issued out of the opaque darkness just above his face. His head whipped side to side, but he couldn't get away from the terrible gnashing. It flooded over him with startling, suffocating ferociousness. His fingers raked the air, his legs bucked and kicked. There was no moving the force on top of him.

One thought lit a blazing trail:

Oh, god, it's killing me—!

In the winking starlight before his eyes, as consciousness ebbed, a voice insinuated itself into his ear: *Release me.*

The snarling presence growled at this exchange. It gobbled the air above David's lips, suffocating him. In desperation he summoned himself, all of his strength and fight. The tendons in his neck stood out like bridge posts. His brow furrowed. Above his eyes, that stabbing pain pushed and pushed, like something demanding to be born.

Release me—

He shrieked with pain. Something warm sprang free with a zippering wet explosion above his eyes. Sparks blew across his vision.

He heard a frustrated howl of rage — and the presence, the creature, the whatever it was — leapt off him. No longer crushed against his mattress, David greedily gulped air into his lungs, happy to be breathing again.

A lamp overturned in the darkness. Books crashed onto the carpet amid the flapping of loose papers. The room shook as if it housed a whirlwind.

Stunned to find himself free of the suffocating weight, David sprang into a sitting position, hiccupping for air. Hands flew to his forehead before remembering he ought not touch — and snapped back in reflex, but not before they were painted with his blood.

Where is it? he thought wildly. *Where has it gone?*

He sensed the presence in the room. Sensed it hating him, yet keeping its distance. What caused it to retreat? His cry — or his blood?

"Go away!" David shouted into the darkness.

A snarling wind spun papers about the room — and then it was gone. The sharp odor of chlorine hung in the air like an afterthought.

Trembling with shock, he hoisted himself to his feet and veered toward the bathroom. He was halfway down the hall when he realized the intense pain above his eyes had vanished. A cautious hope took hold of him. He switched on the bathroom light. Hissed through clenched teeth at the sight of his blood-soaked hands. And careened toward the mirror, anxious for a glimpse of himself.

Twin rivers of blood trickled down each side of his nose. In the center of what had been his strange puffy bruise was a clean slit. His forehead was settling flat again. The wound was already fading to a rosy pink, healing even as he stood ogling it.

He ran hot water, grabbed a washcloth, and cleaned his face and hands. Gingerly (and not without holding his breath) he dabbed the skin of his forehead clean. He was vastly relieved when no hallucinations swallowed him.

It was healing. By god, it was healing! But how? Why?

His joy was so all-consuming it held these questions at bay, at least for the moment.

He felt tingly, as though a small electric current hummed through him. Different in a way he had no name for. Better. Stronger. The excruciating pain of the past few days had given birth to this blessed relief, and he was thankful for it.

A sudden weariness seized him, and it was all he could do to drag himself back to bed and flop upon the mattress.

Later, he told himself as he closed his eyes. I'll figure this all out tomorrow, when I have time.

But time, David was about to learn, had joined sides with the enemy.

3

Up onto the ledge. Poised like a diver, he jumped into the abyss. *I won't hit bottom,* he told himself with dreamy assurance. *If you hit bottom in dreams, you die—*

Head over heels he tumbled, outstretched arms ineffective wings slicing the inky black. Music clamored the air, a driving disco beat. From somewhere up above a voice shouted with malicious glee: "The healer awakes — now the fun begins!"

Dropping feet first, he suddenly plunged into icy water. Rank water surged into his throat. He sputtered to the surface, treading water. His hands knocked against an array of bobbing shapes. He grabbed onto one of the buoys in a desperate attempt to stay afloat and drew it to him.

It was Eddie.

His eyes, wrenched wide. Chalky face. Hair a tangle of seaweed. His mouth was a frozen exclamation point.

4

And David screamed awake, writhing naked on the floor of his bedroom.

5

Bessie Watson looked up with startled surprise as David fled the elevator. She scooted around the nurses' station and managed to grab a handful of denim jacket as he tried to pass. "Whoa, there. What's wrong?"

He spun toward her, both hands anchoring onto her fleshy shoulders. "Have you checked on Eddie this morning?"

She frowned. "I just now started my seven-to-three shift. Why don't we look in his chart and see what the night shift had to say. Hey, wait up!"

His tennis shoes squeaked purposefully across the highly waxed floor. He had no time for charts and pleasantries. Behind him, Bessie shouted in a stage whisper for him to stop.

He marched up to room 203. Knocking rapidly, David pushed it open without waiting for an invitation. And the smell hit him. Sour-sweet, like gone-over vegetables. He rounded the corner of the L-shaped room.

"Eddie—?"

A strangled cry lodged in his throat. His heart derailed off sure-footed tracks.

Long phlegmy ribbons of what looked like snot streaked the entire length of walls from floor to ceiling. Mossy green water pooled directly underneath the window. Droplets of water clung to the glass as though the window had been recently sprayed with a hose. A surge of hothouse air exhaled across his startled face, warm air rushing to greet the cooler air from the hallway.

He stared at the empty bed. A jellied substance oozed off the pillow and sheets, dribbling to the floor.

David bolted from the room. Bessie was just approaching the door, a sheen of sweat glistening on her dark face. "Where is he!" he screamed at her. "What happened in there!"

She recoiled from his verbal assault before her twenty years of nurse's training snapped into place. "Now calm down and talk sense."

"Eddie's gone."

"Gone? He can't be."

David waved her into the room.

A frown pursed her lips. She touched him on the shoulder, quietly commanding him to stay put as she ventured inside.

He almost counted the seconds to himself — one thousand one, one thousand two — before her startled scream cut the hospital silence like a fire alarm. Other nurses at the far end of the hall came galloping toward the room. He went back into the room.

Bessie threw him a mixed look of fright and shame, her arms extended for a hug. But he could not go to her. He blinked in astonishment.

The room was perfectly ordinary. Windows clean, letting in weak October morning. The ice-cream-colored stripes of wallpaper were unmarred by the mucusy web that had riddled its surface moments ago.

A perfectly ordinary hospital room. Except that where Eddie should have been was a human outline in blood, staining sheets and pillow.

"Where is he?" Bessie croaked.

David shut his eyes.

Promises in the light

"**H**ere we are. Fresh off the assembly line."[1]

David glanced up as Officer Alex Webster set a cinnamon roll and a styrofoam cup of coffee on the table in front of him. The policeman then proceeded to unload two cinnamon rolls, a large coffee, and a small container of orange juice from his tray. He sat across from David and smiled apologetically.

"Sleuthing always gives me an appetite," he sheepishly explained.

David, his face drawn, gave a small shrug at the breakfast laid before him. "I'm not hungry." He shook the image of Eddie's empty bed from his thoughts and forced himself to rejoin the world by glancing around. The hospital cafeteria buzzed with an early-morning crowd of staff and visitors. But he felt utterly alone and adrift, miles removed from the current of daily life around him.

"Now, partner, I know it was a bit of a shock," Alex Webster said with an easy drawl. He ripped open two packets of Sweet and Low and dumped them into his coffee. "You can't let every scrap of nasty business go right to the gut, if you catch my drift." Blue eyes twinkled at David. "Nothing wrong with developing a cast-iron disposition. It don't mean you cheat yourself out of feeling."

"He wasn't your friend," David said quietly.

"I know that."

"Then you can't imagine how I feel."

"Oh, I've got a pretty good idea," he said, cutting into the first cinnamon roll. He took a bite and grimaced. "You think it's a conspiracy that all hospital food tastes like cardboard?"

David smiled with wry amusement. This cop was too much, especially with that ridiculous southern drawl, like something lifted from a B-rated Civil War movie. Alex Webster wore his difference with an easy grace, a take-it-or-leave-it attitude that was charming and admirable. His professional composure had not broken at all when they'd led him into Eddie's empty room. Officer Webster had studied the wet sheets with a detective's fine scrutiny, then he'd talked privately with Bessie Watson while David waited by the nurses' station. After a quarter hour they returned, and the policeman had suggested the two of them grab some breakfast.

"Look, Officer—"

"Alex. Call me Alex."

"Okay. Alex." An awkward moment; he couldn't bring himself to meet the man's steady gaze. "I'm sorry." He rushed ahead. "I just don't understand any of it. If you could have *seen* Eddie yesterday..."

"How'd he look?"

"Terrific. Lots of energy."

"What did you talk about?"

David sipped his coffee. "He wanted to know what was happening around town. Hollywood gossip. Any men worth cruising in the Castro—" Feeling his cheeks flush, he retreated back to his story. "Eddie flexed his arm and said he couldn't wait to start pumping iron again. He acted like he was going to get out any day. He was still sick, of course. Dr. Allen had pretty much told me that he didn't expect him to recover enough to go home again."

Alex Webster wore a bemused expression. "He acted like he was getting out any day?"

"He was just ... excited. Happy to be feeling so good after feeling rotten. Like he'd just won the lottery and was waiting for the check to arrive in the mail." As soon as the words left his mouth he remembered just as clearly how artificial it had seemed, how much like a charade. Only Eddie had *believed* it, charade or no. Hook, line, and sinker.

Alex regarded him with a funny smile. "You didn't believe it?"

David was puzzled. "Believe what?"

"His good fortune. His health."

"I didn't think it'd last, if that's what you mean. I'd learned to take Eddie's health one day at a time. I mean, only a few days ago he was so weak he could barely talk. Do you know what it's like, watching a friend waste away like that? As if he'd just fade away into those white sheets—"

Suddenly tears threatened to flow. He didn't want to cry, not now, not here, in front of this police officer, but his last image of Eddie, alive and smiling at him, abruptly shifted to the slime-splattered room and the jelly crud smeared across the sheets. The image of all that strange destruction smacked him hard, taking his breath away. What he'd seen hadn't been real. It couldn't have been. If it had been real, the room would still be a slimy war zone for all to see. No. He must have been so worked up over his earlier nightmare that his imagination had carried it over into reality. That was possible, wasn't it? It explained everything. Except that Eddie was still gone. Vanished, without a trace.

He stared at the formica table, unable to bear the thought that this handsome policeman was watching him fall to pieces right here in the hospital cafeteria, of all places. He wiped away tears with the back of a hand and fought to control his sobs.

A hand reached out and touched David's hand. He flinched at the surprising touch of flesh upon flesh.

"That's right, buddy," Alex said soothingly. "Let it out, if you have to. Tears just show respect for your friend."

The officer didn't realize David was crying as much for himself as for Eddie. His hand felt warm and safe, covered by the policeman's palm. It impressed him, that this cop was unashamed to hold another man's hand in public. How old was this guy? Late thirties? Forty? Silver flecked his sandy hair at the temples, which only served to accentuate the blue of his eyes. And the black uniform, coupled with this show of affection, gave Alex an immensely appealing air.

Suddenly he realized what he was doing. David shook his head wearily and withdrew his hand. "It's so unfair," he sighed. "Where were all the goddamned nurses? Aren't they supposed to make rounds during the night?"

"You're right about that," Alex agreed. "Somebody should have heard — or seen — something. I've got Miss Watson calling every orderly and nurse on shift last night, but so far, nothing. All we've got is one hell of a disappearance and a bed that looks like Eddie may have been slashed by the creature from the Black Lagoon."

David jerked at that.

Alex looked at him, concerned. "What's wrong?"

"Nothing." But he was remembering his own attack last night, and the whirlwind that blew through his room. It seemed unreal, now. Another bad dream. He took a tentative bite of his cinnamon roll — which did indeed taste like sweet cardboard — and washed it down with coffee.

Alex polished off the first roll and attacked the second one. He chewed thoughtfully. "Eddie have many friends?"

David looked up, grateful for this change of direction in their conversation.

"Any that might want to help him out?"

"Help?" David's eyes narrowed. "What do you mean?" But once again he remembered Eddie's words: *The man in the steam, Davey.*

Alex slurped his coffee. "It's like you said. Hard to watch a friend slip away a day at a time, ain't it? Especially in a hospital room."

David bristled. "What are you implying? That I took him home so he could die outside of this hospital?"

Alex waved a hand. "Not you, no. But someone else. Another friend."

"He had no other friends," David shot back. "Only me." Which was true. Eddie had managed to cultivate only one friend during his busy schedule: David.

Except for the man in the steam. The MAN.

David shook his head. He saw Eddie's corpse in front of him, bobbing in water. "Eddie is dead."

"No. Missing. Big difference."

"I wish I believed that. His days were numbered anyway. That's why this makes no sense. Why kill a dying man?"

"Now nobody said a peep about killing—"

"Oh come on," David snapped. "You saw that bed. What the fuck happened in there? Something got him, and got him good. And I'm—" He cut himself off.

"You're what?"

"Nothing. It's nothing." He shifted in his seat.

Alex leveled him with a concerned stare.

"If you know something about all this, then please, speak up. It can't be any more bizarre than what's up there in room 203."

David glanced away from the heat of this policeman's stare. What could he tell him, really? That when he'd first walked into that room it'd looked like a scene from a disaster movie? Or how utterly shocked he'd been when he'd returned to find that nightmare vision gone, and blood in its place? While he was at it, maybe he should tell this cop about "shadows" swooping down out of the dark, shadows that growl and attack?

He began to stammer a response when a card was thrust into his hands. It bore Alex's name, and two phone numbers.

"I think you know more than you're telling me," Alex said, and immediately hushed the protest that sprang to David's lips with a wave of his hand. "You don't have to say anything more, not now. That top number gets me at the station. The other is my home phone. If you change your mind. If you make a connection, no matter how way out it sounds, or if you simply need to talk, give me a ring. Day or night." He waited until David met his eyes, and could see the truth written there. "Promise?"

"Why are you being such a nice guy?" David surprised himself by asking.

Alex shrugged. "The company I keep, I suppose." And this time it was his turn to shyly lower his eyes.

2

David crossed Church at Nineteenth Street and stood facing a bridge that gave onto Dolores Park. Directly in front of him, across the walkway bridge, sat a group of teenagers. They were sprawled across a picnic bench, listening to a radio. A handful of older men stood at the end of the bridge. These men were scruffed up, sullen faced but harmless-looking.

He plunged forward, walking down the steps to the bridge, and started across. His chest tightened with a familiar panic as his eyes surveyed every direction at once. He clutched his house keys into a makeshift weapon between his fingers and tried to steady his erratic heartbeat. Halfway across the bridge now. A J Church Muni car rumbled beneath him. So far, only three men had bothered to glance away from their card game and note his approach. One elbowed the other, saying something in Spanish. David felt his ears burn. He didn't have to know what was said. He knew. He knew.

He breezed past them unmolested and walked up the sidewalk to the crest of hill at Church and Twentieth. He took his hand from his pocket. His heartbeat steadied.

David sat down on the damp grass and drank in the sweeping view of downtown San Francisco, the Bay Bridge, and Berkeley and Oakland across the bay. A chill wind bit at his jacket. *Relax,* he commanded himself.

Officer Webster had driven him home from the hospital. David fancied he had felt an extra second or two of pressure as they shook hands good-bye, a private message of warmth directed only at him, but he was not sure. It all happened so fast.

Once home, he'd called Uncle Charlie's and asked for the day off, which they immediately gave him. Roger assured him that all his shifts could be covered until Saturday night. At first he had objected — he just needed a little time to sort out his feelings. But then he'd thought of his deadline and his unfinished short story that had to be mailed off, and all the confusing events of the past days. So many questions to sort out, examine, piece together. He *should* stay busy — but the thought of waiting tables with a shopkeeper's smile made him physically ill. So he accepted Roger's offer and took the days off.

He was home all of an hour before the silence of his apartment deafened him. He tried to sleep but couldn't. He flipped on a radio only to shut it off at once; the bright, bouncy music seemed a blasphemy. A picked-at lunch tasted of yet more cardboard. He paced in front of the sliding glass door and looked at the people trudging up and down Noe Street. Finally, in desperation, he smoked a joint down to a roach, the smoke harsh in his lungs so early in the day, and he walked the several blocks to Dolores Park.

Now he sat under a slate-gray sky, absorbing the view. This was a winter sky, premature even for a day in October. The skies had remained obstinately overcast ever since the freak thunderstorm.

A school bell jarred the afternoon silence. David watched as several of the younger kids bid their friends good-bye and walked downhill to the high school on Eighteenth Street. One of the teenagers caught him watching and flipped him the finger.

Now *this;* this was a fear he understood. The way his chest had tightened and his stomach clenched as he had walked past all of them. He hated himself for the fear, but at least he understood it. He had marched through their territory, determined to ignore the waves of hostility and contempt that rolled off them. He hadn't needed a boyfriend on his arm or to walk with a swish for them to peg him as gay. He was a single white male, and that was all the ammunition they needed. Their contempt was a given, a known quantity he could deal with and understand because he had battled it for so many of his thirty-one years.

What he did not comprehend was this new uneasiness that coiled about his belly like a live thing, squeezing.

The writer's side in him was a cause-and-effect man. He knew how seemingly unrelated incidents could all dump from various tributaries into one river, where the truth could be fished out with a little patience. As a reporter for his college newspaper, David had been dumbfounded to learn murders happened not because of great unrequited love or unbridled passions but because some jerk took the last parking space or wifey didn't do the dishes or the kids wouldn't shut up and watch "Sesame Street." Ridiculous arguments turn into murder. An insult to a nation escalates into war. Cause and effect.

So when had it first touched him, this sensation of danger?

The storm, of course. It had announced itself with comic-book ferociousness, as if to say, *Look at me. Deal with me.* From that day on, really, he had spiraled downward. His nightmares. His odd compulsions. The painful bump on his forehead. The visions.

David rubbed his hands over his face and sighed. *And one week after a freak storm I have hallucinations, am attacked by a murderous shadow that feels real, and now, Eddie is gone, his room a bloody battleground. Why? Is there a connection?*

It hit him. *It's me. I must be the connection.*

A strange excitement tingled through him. He would never have been able to describe this feeling to anyone, let alone articulate it for himself. It felt far away, belonging to another time and place, but meant for him. He faced it.

He was in danger. Something was circling, circling, drawing closer. Teasing.

He would find it. He would stop it. A promise, to Eddie.

He had never been more excited in his life.

10

Housecall

1

Alex Webster turned onto Natoma Street for a second time and prayed for a parking space. Natoma was choked with industrial vehicles this time of afternoon, all of them servicing the paper products and sheet metal shops, and a Chinese-owned sewing factory at the far end of the block.

This is what I get for not taking a police car, Alex thought. With a police car he could have parked out front, lights flashing, and to hell with this demoralizing search for a legal parking space.

But he was not coming to Natoma on official business. Not exactly, anyway. You follow strange hunches on your own time, and so Alex gritted his teeth as he maneuvered his red Toyota around the block before he found a space on Eighth Street. He parked and stepped out of the car, stretching.

A reporter from the *Chronicle* had tipped him. Back outside of room 203 he'd overheard a man say, "This one is even better than the disappearance of that bible freak."

Alex turned and looked at the man. The reporter was talking to an attractive woman who carried a small notebook and pen.

"You mean the guy south of Market?"

"Where you been Lucille, the Bermuda Triangle?" he razzed. "If you don't want to end up covering street fairs and lost puppy dogs, you'd better get on the ball. Some lunatic fairy papered his walls with pages from a bible before he was presumably murdered. Mr. Right for the night turned out to be Mr. Wrong, if you get my meaning. The landlord, an old lady who lives down below and watches the place like a hawk, she notices the guy doesn't go skipping off to work. Being the kind but nosey neighbor she is, she calls the apartment. No answer."

"So what happened?"

"Curiosity killed the cat. She finally took her passkeys and gave herself a peek — not to mention the fright of her life. The apartment was destroyed. Pages from a bible taped up everywhere. And the kid, gone."

The woman batted her eyes. "Any leads?"

The reporter shook his head. "Forget it, lady. All anyone knows is that Mr. Right decided to play too rough. Hell, who are we kidding here, right? Aren't they all into that sadomasochism stuff south of Market?"

2

It took several phone calls and a promise of a later favor, but by three that afternoon Alex had all the information he needed.

Jack Martin was the young man's name. Twenty-five. Word processor for Wells Fargo Bank, customer support. Originally from New Mexico. As white bread as a gay man could be living in San Francisco. No previous arrests. Not even a goddamned parking ticket.

Alex walked around the corner to Natoma. Once, years ago, this area had been part of his beat. And the Castro, as well. In the last two years he'd begun to work more special assignments concerning missing persons — like the early-morning phone call that had brought him rushing to Ralph K. Davies Medical Center. He preferred missing-persons work, and after ten years as a police officer, the higher-ups had started giving him his chance.

He dug into his shirt pocket for Jack Martin's address and walked midway down the block until he stood in front of the correct apartment building. He pressed the buzzer for what he assumed was the bottom apartment, and waited. A glass-paneled door looked into a dark hallway. An apartment door was on the immediate right, with a steep flight of stairs at the end of the hallway presumably leading to Jack's apartment.

The bottom door creaked open.

"Who is it?" croaked an old woman's voice.

"Police, ma'am." He searched for the landlady's name in his memory and found it. "This will only take a moment, Mrs. Kreitman."

The sliver of open door closed again, and for a moment he wondered if she was shutting him out. He saw this happen all the time; people who had experienced a recent loss often resented police intrusion. Locks and latches snapped back, and then Mrs. Kreitman stepped into the hallway.

"When are you going to pay for the damage?" she demanded.

"Ma'am?"

"The damage, the damage!" Her hands sawed the air impatiently. She was short and stout, seventy if she was a day, with steel-gray hair done up in curlers. Bifocals perched on a sausage nose. "I told them yesterday, how am I supposed to rent out that apartment with it shut up as evidence? What do I look, rich? Think I can afford to live off social security?" A stubby finger stabbed his chest in punctuation. "Why such a terrible tragedy should touch my life, I just do not know."

She had him practically pinned against the wall. Alex grinned to himself; Mrs. Kreitman had missed her calling as a police interrogator. Another five minutes of this and he'd be digging into his own pocket for cash.

"That's why I'm here, Mrs. Kreitman," he said with all the authority he could muster. "It's in our best interest to solve this case as quickly as possible. I'm here to take a few notes and inspect the premises."

"Where's your notebook?"

"Ma'am?"

"I have an itemized list of all the damage, if you care to see it." She turned to go back into her apartment, but Alex stayed her with his hand. He tapped the side of his head.

"I keep all my notes right here, if you catch my drift," he said with his best winning smile.

Mrs. Kreitman frowned.

"Perhaps on the way out?" he prompted.

That did the trick. Her iron expression softened. She dug into a pocket of her terry-cloth robe and produced a key.

"Very well, then. Follow me, Officer—?"

"Webster. Alex Webster."

They trudged up the flight of narrow steep stairs.

"Jack was a good boy," she said, puffing for air as they neared the top of the stairs. "He never played his music loud, even when he entertained his male friends. And he brought me the crossword puzzle every morning before he went to work." She halted on the final step to catch her breath.

"Did Jack have lots of friends?"

"Oh, a few, like everyone else," she answered. Her gaze narrowed into daggers. "But if you mean, did he often have overnight company, the answer is an emphatic no. Absolutely not." She touched his arm. "He wasn't interested in girls, you know," she confided, dropping her voice to a whisper. "As long as I didn't have to hear it in my own home, who was I to make judgments? Jack was very discreet."

"He had no particular friend, that you know of?"

"No. I think he was a bit lonely, actually."

"Did you hear anyone come home with Jack the night he disappeared?"

She fixed Alex with a stern look. He'd hit a nerve. "Are you here to inspect damage to Jack's apartment, or do I have to repeat myself to every officer who comes along and interrupts my privacy?"

"Mrs. Kreitman—"

"Look in your files, if you want my story," she snapped. "I'm sure if you'd done your homework, you would not be wasting my time."

She's not going to let me in, Alex thought suddenly. Mrs. Kreitman stood with her back and considerable bulk against Jack's front door, not budging. He was about to apologize and switch tactics when all at once something crumpled in the woman's expression, and fear rode the many lines of her face.

"You say Jack disappeared? Take a look at this and tell me he up and decided to take a hike."

She unlocked the door and slipped a hand inside for the light switch. Threw the door wide. She stepped aside for Alex to pass.

A damp scummy smell hit him at once. It was the smell of something trying to dry in an airless, closed-off apartment, and it had lost the battle.

Another battle had been waged in here, and lost, too.

The neutral carpet was polka-dotted with rusty splotches of blood. Most of it gathered near the bookcase, in a semi-circular pool. The TV was a gouged hole where the screen should have been. The bookcase had fallen over, with books flung in all directions. A pile of bibles lay near the center of the room. Alex went to them and picked one up by the corner. Most of the pages had been torn out, but those few that remained were stained with bloody fingerprints.

Which means he did this *after* he was wounded, not before, Alex concluded. What in god's name was Jack doing? More precisely, what was he trying to keep out?

The walls and windows were covered with the pages, with the heaviest concentration around the front door and the living room window. A few pages were haphazardly taped to the ceiling, but evidently the process had been either too difficult or deemed unnecessary. A quick check of the bedroom revealed bible pages in there, too, with most of them plastered to the window.

Alex walked back into the living room. He shook his head in the sheer wonder of it all. Mrs. Kreitman stood with a liver-spotted hand touching her throat as though to dislodge whatever words might be stuck there. They exchanged a glance.

"I know what you're going to say," Mrs. Kreitman blurted. "It's all the police asked me, over and over. Making me out as some kind of deaf fool." Her cheeks flushed with indignity. "I tell you I heard nothing. Nothing! No sounds of struggle! No cries for help! I slept like a baby while poor Jack fought off whatever did this!" She choked back furious tears and turned her face to the wall.

"Ma'am..." Alex stepped toward her, but she shooed him away.

"I swear I would have called the police, had I known what was happening," she said. "I'm only seventy-two, you know. I still have most of my hearing. Didn't I hear you knock at the front door? Didn't I answer right at once? Didn't I?" She looked away from the wall to meet his gaze. Alex nodded. Her face lit up. "See? I tried to explain that to the other officers, but I saw how they looked at me."

"Mrs. Kreitman, perhaps if you sat down..."

"Oh, I'm all right," she sighed.

They stood in silence as the old woman composed herself. Their eyes swept the room with a guilty fascination. Alex walked to the living room window and examined several of the bible pages taped there. They were dry to the touch, slightly brittle and crisp, the way paper dries after it has gotten wet. He checked the window latches. Locked.

"Was the front door locked when you came upstairs to check on Jack?" he asked.

"Oh, yes, absolutely. I knocked on his door for a good five minutes. I assumed he had overslept. But Jack was never tardy for work."

Alex stroked his chin. No blood on the staircase, so Jack hadn't left that way. The front door, locked. And the windows, locked from the inside. No smashed panes of glass. Absolutely nothing to indicate there had been a break-in — or a break-out. Only a missing person, and blood.

Just like Eddie Blake.

Mrs. Kreitman cleared her throat. "The entire apartment was wet, you know. When I came in to check on Jack."

"Wet?" He looked at her.

"Not as much as it must have been earlier, before I came in. But when I stepped inside, it was like walking into a greenhouse. Tropical, almost. Gave me such a fright, you have no idea."

He faced her. "Is there anything else you'd like to tell me? Anything else that happened that night? However trivial it may sound."

Mrs. Kreitman knit her brow. "No. Nothing."

"Anything at all. It's very important."

Her face clouded. "I've already given my report to the police. You promised we wouldn't go through this—"

Alex waved his hands to stop her. "Yes, yes; I know," he apologized. He gave the room a final glance. "I want to thank you for your time. You've been most helpful." He ushered her to the front door, and they entered the dim hallway. Mrs. Kreitman shut off the light in Jack's apartment and locked the door.

"There is one thing," she muttered, almost to herself. "It's silly. I'm sure you wouldn't want to know. Your kind of people want *facts,* not feelings."

"What is it?"

She motioned for him to follow, and together they trudged down the steep staircase. Alex steadied her as they walked, though he held no hopes of actually catching her if she stumbled and fell.

"I slept soundly that night," she said as she maneuvered each step with an added "Ooof!" She gripped Alex's arm. "Which at my age — ooof! — is pretty rare unless it's time to greet the Maker. I watch TV in my — ooof! — favorite chair, a great big Lay-Z-Boy recliner. I fall asleep in that chair all the time, and that night was no exception. I ate a bowl of tomato soup for dinner and conked out during the news. Out like the proverbial light I was! But sometime later, during the night — ooof! — I woke up."

To Alex's great relief, they reached the bottom step. The old woman squeezed his arm for them to stop. She met his gaze.

"Heart palpitations."

He looked at her blankly. "Ma'am?"

"That night, when I woke up. My chest was so tight. I couldn't breathe! I woke up, and such ... dread ... went through me. I couldn't move. I was afraid to move! I knew if I did, it'd see me."

"What? What would see you?"

"I don't know!" she wailed. "I don't know what it was! It was so *close* to me, something mean and horrible!" She fell into his arms, weeping. Alex was so startled by her outburst he remained stock-still, riding out her storm. "Maybe if I'd gotten out of my chair, called the police, Jack would still be alive—"

"Now hush that kind of talk," Alex ordered. "No one knows for sure if Jack is dead."

Her eyes blazed behind her bifocals. "You saw that apartment! That's Jack's blood all over that room. Don't tell me he disappeared. He was *butchered!*"

And Alex, who stood with his arms around Mrs. Kreitman, saying nothing, waiting for her to collect herself, heard David Walker's words echo in his head:

You saw that bed. What the fuck happened in there? Something got him, and got him good.

11

Hands in the mirror

D avid had his story. ¹

It came to him while he sat on the slopes of Dolores Park, a hand absently massaging his forehead. The wintery sky. The wind, whispering secrets as it pulled at his jacket. Mood and atmosphere perfectly matched for the tale. But did he have it in him, after all that had transpired in the past few days?

He rushed home, and by the time he sat down in front of his typewriter the first half of his new story danced provocatively in his head. He flipped on the machine and the story poured out of him, nearly intact. He was too afraid of taking breaks for fear of disrupting the flow of words, so he stuck with it until his neck and shoulders screamed with tension and his ass numbed in the wooden chair. After suffering through the stupefying pain of the bump on his head, he had the muscle to take quite a beating. When it was over, he groaned to his feet and paced the floor like an expectant father who had gotten his first look at his newborn child.

I did it. Hot damn, I finally wrote the sucker.

He padded into the kitchen and made himself a sandwich. He cringed when he saw the clock read eight p.m. How long had he been at it? Five hours? Six?

David retrieved the story from his desk and ate his sandwich while he read what he'd just written. Ah, it would be worth this pain, he was relieved to see. Not bad.

A little strange, no question about that, but enough cock and tease to satisfy the requirements of *Torso*'s editors. The events of the past week had inadvertently triggered his creative juices in a way that had never happened before.

He'd written a story about a man named Rick whose relationship with his lover, Bob, is jeopardized when, one night on his way home, he's seduced by the voice of a mysterious man who calls at a deserted phone booth. Creepy. Moody. Perfect for the magazine. Plenty of phone sex.

What a divine spark. He'd been given inspiration so suddenly and clearly, yet instead of thanking the heavens for this gift, he felt *spooked*.

Yes. As though he treaded on thin ice. As though somehow, just beneath the surface, these people might really be...

Naw. Impossible.

As his hand hovered above the pages, correcting spelling, checking the language, he found himself frowning at the name Rick one more time. He drew a line through the name and penciled above it: Mick.

There. That sounded better.

2

The grueling day had extracted its toll.

He had only slept a few hours the night before. Amazing he was even in one piece tonight. His muscles continued to ache from his nonstop writing session. What he needed was a long, hot soak in the bath. But first, a quick smoke to mellow out.

David hobbled into the living room (he was going to pay dearly for his writing marathon, he saw now) and retrieved his dope pan from underneath the sofa. He kept it there because of his affinity for smoking while watching the spectacular sunsets over Twin Peaks. He didn't get to watch that many sunsets any more, ever since he had started work at Uncle Charlie's last summer, but the dope pan remained in his favorite spot, if nothing else a reminder of those twilight evenings.

Chilly in this part of the flat. The drapes on the sliding glass door were open to the view. A cruel wind was tugging a blanket of fog across Twin Peaks. The glass doors rattled, emitting a mournful whistle. He watched the living fog with mounting disappointment. It was a depressing sight. September had been gorgeous, sunny and warm. October was supposed to be their Indian summer. Maybe it'd heat up again, once this weather pattern cleared.

He loaded the pipe with marijuana and took his first drag. The smoke stung his lungs — he never could adjust his inhaling to a pipe — and he coughed up most of it. The second drag was easier, and the third. A mellow wave rolled through him.

Pipe in hand, he returned down the length of hallway to the bathroom and started his bath. Sometimes he wondered if he should stop smoking grass. He'd given up everything else: the boozing, the late-night dancing, the quick toots offered by a friend. Gone, and good riddance. He didn't miss it.

Okay, okay — he knew he'd smoked more than his usual allowance for the week, but these were trying times. Besides, only marijuana took the edge off the phantom aches and pains of his mended bones. So what if it occasionally turned his brain into mush, or rendered him quite useless if he had to string more than two words together at a time in public — or on his typewriter.

David leaned against the hallway wall, reached down, and untied his sneakers. Enough of this debate about smoking; it was time for his bath. He shut off the hot water faucet and undressed. The overhead light in the bathroom was too bright, so he lit a candle that he kept by the sink for just such an occasion. A radio sat nearby. He flipped it on, but the rock music jarred him, and he shut it off. Better to have silence.

The bathtub employed a sliding glass door instead of a shower curtain. He rolled the door fully aside as he stepped into the water. Youch! It was too hot, almost scalding, but he knew how quickly water cooled, so he decided against adding a splash of cold water. He sank into the tub and leaned back, so that his head rested on the rim of the tub.

Ahh. Paradise.

Dr. Allen, Eddie's doctor, had taught him the therapeutic properties of a good soak. Over the summer, as Eddie's condition worsened, David's own stress began to take its toll. He'd had to dope himself into a stupor to fall asleep at night. Dr. Allen recommended hot baths at bedtime. Ready to try anything, he'd given it a chance — and happily discovered its benefits. Since the summer, he took soaks two or three times a week. With a puff or two from the pipe, and the calming effect of a flickering candle, he often found himself transported into another world.

And I can sure use that tonight, David mused dreamily. His sore, tight muscles began to ease as the hot water worked its magic. Steam drifted past his face. His cock rolled gently in the water.

His thoughts hopscotched in search of tranquility, and with a dreamy sort of wonder David found himself thinking of Alex Webster. Alex was the one good thing to come out of that morning's heartache. If he had been stuck talking to some stony-faced cop this morning, instead of Alex, god knew what kind of condition he'd be in tonight. In fact, the policeman had figured into his thoughts all day. How long had it been since that had happened?

His social life had ground to a halt years ago. Oh sure, men asked him for dates all the time at Uncle Charlie's, and every blue moon or so someone would catch his eye, and they'd have a date. But the rules for courtship had changed too much. As awkward as safe sex could be, David insisted on it. Most complied. A few walked away (but that had been early on, when safe sex seemed a matter of choice, not something absolutely necessary). It was easier to flirt, to window shop, to come home to a tape in the VCR, or to express his sexual needs in a short story. Dating became a quiet casualty in the war.

Alex Webster.

That uniform. That *accent*. And the blue eyes. He'd read of laughing blue eyes, but this cop was the first man he'd met who actually fit that description. Not to mention the wonderful sandy hair, silver at the temples, like some gallant knight.

His penis rolled to attention, poking out of the water. David slid a hand over it, his body shuddering with pleasure. His hand drifted lower and scooped up his balls, which he began to tug and pull. His other hand gently massaged his chest, pausing to tweak a nipple. There was no rush to his movements, no sense of urging this toward any conclusion. Just the delight in having his body come alive under his touch. With eyes closed, he imagined Alex performing a striptease for his benefit, the uniform peeled off layer by layer.

He drifted with this fantasy until he realized something had been added to it: music. The thump thump thump of heavy bass. Unmistakably disco music. Unmistakably Donna Summer, wanting to love you, baaaby...

David smiled. Walter. It must be Walter, his upstairs neighbor. He had a running joke with Eddie that Walter was stuck somewhere in the seventies; whenever Walter put a drink or two under his belt (which was often), out came the old disco records. Of course, he was a child of the seventies himself. He just didn't need it shaking the walls and his ceiling.

Only...

David opened his eyes.

Steam saturated the candle-lit room in impossibly thick clouds. The music floated in and out of his hearing, an echo, like music in a dream. Not real. And yet...

Images flickered through his mind as though he flipped through a catalog: Long, muscular arms. Massive square chests. A tangle of legs. Hands riding muscles. Gorgeous erect cocks. Bodies slick with sweat. Legs spread apart. But no faces; those parts of the bodies remained hidden.

Hands, suspended in the steam, beckoning, beckoning.

(Join us Davey)

(Join us...)

David scooted to a full sitting position, his heart in his throat. His erection still stood at full staff, encouraged by these erotic images. The music, rolling in and out on psychic waves. Distracting him.

So he would not hear.

But all at once, he did hear.

The sliding glass door in the living room rolled open. It had a distinctive catch, a clicking sound it made when opened.

He elbowed open the sliding door to the tub. Steam boiled around him, the air so cottony he could barely make out the bathroom door. *Lock it!* his mind shouted. *Lock the door!*

He could not move.

But something did move — inside the apartment. Careful, measured steps, quiet as a cat. Something soggy and impossibly wet was slushing down the hall toward him.

Squish. Squish. Squish.

With an involuntary cry, David wrenched himself up and out of the tub. He flew at the bathroom door and locked it, cursing the puny lock. Stepped back. Water ran into a puddle at his feet. Stone sober with fright, now. The images of naked men intensified in his head as though a movie projector had turned on that he could not stop.

He reached out to turn on the bathroom light, but the switch was beside the door. His feet refused to budge.

Squish. Squish. Squish.

In the light beneath the bathroom door, a shadow appeared.

"Go away," David whispered, his voice caught in his chest.

Suddenly, shockingly:

(Let me in)

"Go away!"

He spun in all directions. A weapon. He wanted a weapon. But what? He yanked open the drawer by the sink. No razor blades; he used the plastic disposable kind bought in packages of two. A tiny pair of tweezers. Fingernail clippers.

(Come play with us, Davey)

David felt his blood run cold. He knew that voice. Only one person called him Davey. But he choked on the name, afraid to speak it:

"Eddie?"

There came a terrible sound, like a huge cat scratching at the door to be let in. Fingernails scraped the wood.

(David. It's me! Help! Open the door! Let me in!)

The panic — and authority — of that voice was undeniable. *Could* that be Eddie? What's happened to him? He inched toward the bathroom door. His hand floated out to greet the marble doorknob.

And it leapt at the door, whatever stood on the other side, as if sensing victory. It pawed and scratched with maniacal fury.

David scrambled backward.

"Go away! I don't want you here! Go away!"

He glanced into the steamed-over mirror and whatever grasp he had on reality fled in that moment. Disembodied hands slapped against the glass from inside the mirror. Desperate hands that wanted to puncture through into his world.

He grabbed onto the open drawer for balance. The heat of the room was sickening; he swayed on the brink of fainting.

(Come and play with us, Davey. This is your only chance to come—)

"Shut up!" David screamed. In a fit of anger he slammed his fists against the bathroom door. "You aren't my friend! Go away!"

Maybe Walter will hear me, David suddenly thought.

His glance fell into the open drawer. Something silver caught his eyes. He scooped it into his hand. A whistle. Would he be heard, if he blew it?

The thing with Eddie's voice had turned angry.

(Let me in!)

"Go away! You aren't welcome here!"

In desperation, he put the whistle to his lips and blew. The shrill noise cut the air like a knife.

Whatever was outside the bathroom door suddenly howled as if doused with boiling water.

(Stop! Stop!)

Another blast. The whistle hurt his own ears in the small room. He glanced at the mirror in time to see hands retreat into the steam. He could hear the creatures cry in exquisite pain.

The Eddie-thing lashed out:

(I have failed! Failed!)

The voice rose to a high-pitched squeal of agony, and was gone. It flared inside his head, causing white-hot flashes of pain. David slumped against the counter, his legs no longer willing to support his weight. The searing pain inside his head shimmered like the afterglow of a fireworks display. The music ebbed into silence.

Is he gone? David wondered. *Is he really gone?*

A sureness in his gut told him it was true, but one hand still clasped the whistle in a death grip. He flipped on the overhead light. In the fogged-over mirror, marks swept down in foot-long slashes like the remains of some finger painting party. Trails of condensation dribbled miniature rivers on the steamy surface from the bottommost tip of the markings.

David hastily dried himself with a towel and slipped into his jeans. It took all of his courage to reach out and grasp the doorknob. He strained to hear any suspicious noise outside the door, but all was silent. Prepared for the worst, whistle inches from his lips, he opened the door.

Directly across the bathroom was the splattered imprint of a man. It was etched onto the wall in a mossy green outline. A trail of soggy footprints led down the hallway to the sliding glass doors, which stood open. Muddy, brackish water puddled in each footprint. A cold wind whistled through the apartment. David started down the hallway when a furious pounding at the front door stopped him.

"David? You okay? Hello!"

Walter stood at the front door.

"I heard shouts," he said. "And a whistle. Was that you?" He stood wrapped in a bathrobe, a bespectacled, chunky man in his midforties. He could tell David was fresh from a shower or soak, and he was suddenly embarrassed by his intrusion. "I hope I haven't interrupted anything..."

David shook his head. "I'm sorry, Walter. I ... fell asleep in the tub. Had a doozy of a nightmare. Thanks for checking on me, though."

"Well, sure. That's what neighbors are for, right?"

"Right."

Walter hopped foot to foot, as though he wanted to say more, but did not want to pry.

"Walter?"

"Yes?"

"Were you playing music a few minutes ago?"

"No. I'm watching the news. Why? Do you want to borrow some records?"

David shook his head. "I was just wondering. Thought I heard music." He leaned against the door. "Goodnight."

"'Night." Walter backed away from the door. "Oh — by the way. How's Eddie doing? Have you seen him recently?"

David bit his lip, and shook his head.

3

He slid the whistle onto an old gold chain he dug up from a dresser drawer. Laid it next to his bed.

Locked and bolted every door and window.

And slept fitfully, his dreams punctured by the image of clawing hands.

4

By morning, the footprints and the stain on the wall were gone.

12

Moonlight serenade

1

About the time that David was greeting his visitor outside the bathroom door, Mick stood beside the bedroom window of Bobby's flat, his eyes restlessly scanning the street.

Bobby watched from his position in the bedroom doorway, an uneasy frown on his face. Mick had picked at dinner. They'd watched a procession of television shows in silence. Is this how he wanted the night to end?

On impulse he slid up behind Mick and wrapped his arms around his lover's waist.

"Jesus!" Mick nearly jumped out of his skin. He whirled around, the fright in his eyes softening when he saw it was Bobby. "Don't *do* that."

"You're so nervous. You okay?"

Mick nodded.

Liar. "You're distracted."

"Yes. Sorry."

"You don't have to apologize." But Bobby thought, *Look at those circles under his eyes. What's the matter, can't he sleep?*

Mick rubbed his hands together. "Work's been a bitch. I — I guess I don't have much energy—"

"Shh. You're with me now. I'm here to take it all away."

That did it. Mick glowed. He folded Bobby against him and teased him with a kiss. This was better. They both felt it. But after a moment Mick gently disengaged himself.

"I'm going to hop into the shower," Bobby said. "Wash the day away. Care to join me?"

Something flickered in Mick's eyes. Then it was gone. He shook his head. "Not this time."

Bobby turned away, but not before Mick saw the obvious disappointment written on his lover's face. Bobby dutifully undressed.

Mick thought, *Why did I reject him?*

And Bobby thought, *Why is he so distant?*

Bobby walked into the bathroom and adjusted the faucets for the right water temperature.

Mick yanked off his own clothes and slid between the sheets. He picked up his book of crossword puzzles and flipped to an unfinished puzzle. He heard the splashing of a shower.

The phone rang.

"Answer that, would you?" Bobby called from the shower.

"Sure." The phone sat on Bobby's side of the bed. Mick scooped the receiver to his ear. "Hello?"

Silence.

"Hello?"

From the other end of the line: Drip. Drip.

Mick felt the blood run from his face. His mouth had gone dry. He worked saliva into his cardboard tongue and croaked, "Who is this?"

A man's voice purred, "Can't you guess?"

An icicle pierced his heart. That voice. That *accent*. He fumbled the phone. "I — I know who this is."

A laugh. "You sound surprised."

He glanced at the open bathroom door. A wave of guilt rolled through him, followed by a suffocating panic.

"How'd you get this number?" he hissed. *Please, god, don't let Bobby walk in on this.* But another voice inside his head screamed, *He found me how could he have found me?*

"I'm a man of many talents," the man with the Turkish accent said, amused.

"Listen," Mick said, his panic a spinning whirlpool, "If you bother me again, I'm, I'm, I'm going to call the police. Under no circumstances are you to call me here. Or anywhere else, for that matter. Understand?"

Drip. Drip. Water striking water. Where is that coming from? Somehow, that sound frightened him more than the bastard's voice.

"Oh, I understand all right," the man snapped. A blast of heat seemed to want to exhale right out of the phone. "Let me spell it out for you. You thought you were finished with me. You thought you could simply hang up and I'd disappear from your life. Now you know differently. I know where you live. I know where your buddy lives. Come back to the phone booth. Do not avoid me. Or I shall have to come and get you. While you sleep."

"Don't count on it." But his threat was empty, a paper sack filled with air.

"Remember: I picked you. Do not disappoint me. Perhaps I'll have to send a friend or two to convince you."

"What does that mean?"

"You'll see. Tomorrow night, then. Ciao."

The line went dead.

Mick slammed down the receiver. He stared at the phone. The only sound in the apartment was the running water of the shower. He let go a ragged sigh of relief.

The shower ended. The plastic curtain slid back.

"Mick?"

"Yeah?"

"Who was it?"

A lie sprang to his lips. "Wrong number. Somebody wanting Juanita."

A pause. "I heard you talking an awful long time."

"You ever try to talk to someone who understands two words of English? They insisted they had the right number." *Stop it,* Mick thought all at once. *Don't lie to him. What am I doing?*

Bobby asked no more questions. And when he slid between the sheets, warming himself next to Mick, neither said another word.

2

Sometime in the night Mick jerked awake.

Bobby lay beside him, sound asleep. Mick trailed a hand across his own chest and then lower, to discover a raging hard-on. He took himself into his hand, and the pleasure warmed him from head to toe.

Why am I awake?

A noise. He had heard a noise.

Something at the window.

He sat up and swung his feet to the floor. His erection jutted up and out between his thighs. The merest touch sent waves of pleasure rippling through him. He stood up.

Then heard it, clearly this time: moans of pleasure. Wet, happy sounds. Intimate whispers. Cajoling. Prodding.

Mick looked down at his feet. They were moving. *He* was moving, a step at a time, toward the window. A pale light streamed above and below the flimsy curtain. Each step closer was like plunging his erection into a warm, wet mouth. He didn't dare touch himself.

Voices, like a low-frequency radio:

(Join us)

(Join us)

(He wants you to join us)

Mick came to rest in front of the window. His dick bobbed with his heartbeat.

Whatever was outside now scratched and pawed at the pane of glass. Fingernails clicked against glass.

(Join us join us)

(Let us in!)

He pulled back the curtain. His eyes widened.

Two men floated outside the window. They were naked, their bodies translucent in the moonlight. One had his face buried between the other's legs. Mick could make out every detail of their handsome bodies, and yet he saw the alley below, as if through a soapy film.

The man who was getting head flashed his eyes eagerly on Mick's erection. He opened his mouth, where a dark tongue darted. He pawed at the plate of glass separating them.

(I'll take care of it for you — let me in)

And Mick, as if outside of his own body, watched as his hand reached for the latch on the window. His cock ached painfully, demanding release. He flipped the latch.

The man-ghost outside the window threw back its head, its lips curling into a victorious leer, and Mick saw the teeth, sharp as cut diamonds, teeth that could rip and shred flesh—

He latched the window.

Stumbled backward, arms thrust before him.

"Go away! Go away!"

3

"Go away!"

"Jesus Christ!" Bobby bolted upright in bed. "What the—?"

"Go away!"

"Mick? What's happened? What's wrong?" He reached over and touched Mick on the shoulder. Mick screamed, recoiling from his touch.

Bobby turned on the light beside the bed. Mick was petrified, his head swiveling in all directions, as though he could not understand why he found himself in the bed.

"Calm down, Mickey. Deep breaths now. Calm down."

Mick shot him a look of total horror. "Make them go away! They want in!"

Bobby pulled his boyfriend against him, enveloping him in his arms. He rocked him until Mick began to catch his breath. "A bad dream, honey. You had a bad dream."

Mick's glance darted to the curtained window. He shuddered. "You heard it too, didn't you?" His voice was a whisper.

"No. What?"

"Scratching at the window."

Bobby gave him a look.

"You don't believe me?"

Bobby patted Mick's arm. "Why don't I take a look," he suggested, swinging his legs over the side of the bed. Mick held him back.

"Stay."

"We're two stories up, Mickey." He gently removed Mick's death grip and stood up. Naked, he padded to the window.

Mick huddled into a ball. "Don't."

Bobby sighed. "Honey—"

He drew back the curtain. Glanced down into the alley, and overhead. "Nothing out here."

"Get away from there. *Please.*"

Bobby frowned at the unmistakable fear stamping his lover's face. The curtain dropped into place. He returned to bed and wrapped an arm around Mick, who could not stop shaking. "What'd you think was out there?"

Mick opened his mouth. Closed it.

"What's going on with you?" Bobby asked. A ribbon of irritation wound through his concern. "I know something's up. You're distant. Tense. You've hardly looked at me all night." He glanced into the open closet, where several pairs of Mick's suits hung on hangers. Mick had brought them over two evenings ago. "Or is it me, Mickey? Do you regret bringing over some of your clothes?"

Mick stared at him with complete incredulity, as if what he insinuated was the furthest thought from his mind.

"Honey, no. No. It's not you. It's these dreams."

"You've had more than one? Why didn't you tell me?"

"I can't remember the others. Just how they made me feel — cold. But this one—"

He shifted in bed. His mouth fell open with astonishment.

"What's wrong?" Bobby asked in alarm.

Mick lifted the covers and peered down at himself. "I ... I ... came all over myself!"

"You had a nightmare *and* a wet dream?"

"Don't make fun! This is scaring me!"

"Okay, okay. I'm sorry. Here." Bobby reached for the wadded hand towel he kept under the bed. None of this made any sense to him. But as he handed Mick the towel and watched as his lover cleaned himself off, an image flashed through his mind of the crucifix bursting into eerie light—

No, no, I just imagined that.

Bobby shook the memory away. He stared at Mick. "Now tell me about this dream."

"There were these ghosts ... men ... They wanted to get into that window." Mick's eyes were full of remembering. "To get *me.*"

"Honey, that's the oldest nightmare in the book, being chased by a monster when you can't move, or can't run, or whatever."

"You think so?"

Bobby nodded energetically. "It's all those 'Twilight Zone' episodes we're watching right before bed." He expected Mick to smile at that, but he only sat with his dazed expression on his face. "What else could it be?"

Mick shook his head.

"Well, you're with me now," Bobby said. "I won't let anything get you."

Mick smiled hopefully. "Promise?"

"Scout's honor."

They kissed. Bobby pulled Mick close, and they lay like that in comfortable silence, drawing strength from one another.

A fairy-tale wind shrilled around the apartment building, rattling the windows.

4

And in the morning, an unfamiliar silence.

He tossed and turned all night, Bobby thought, watching Mick from across the kitchen table. He sipped his coffee. *Look at those bags under his eyes.* He gave his lover a playful kick.

"A penny for your thoughts."

Mick glanced up from the paper. Sighed. "Sorry."

"Enough with the sorrys. How about the truth? You're a million miles away."

A shadow hooded Mick's blue eyes. "Oh, I was just remembering something."

"Tell me."

Mick cleared his throat. "It's nothing, really. A strange story. A friend told it to me. Uh — Larry. Have you ever met him? Tall? Mustache? I see him at the gym."

"No. So what happened?"

"Well, a couple of days ago he said he was — uh — waiting for a bus when the phone rang at his bus stop."

Bobby shook his head. "So?"

"Apparently some guy was watching Larry from a window. He'd called the pay phone. Larry had a feeling this guy could see him up close, as if he had binoculars."

"That's creepy. What'd the guy want?"

"What else? He wanted Larry to come to his place for sex."

Bobby sipped his coffee. "And did he?"

"No. He wanted to, but he was scared."

"He was *smart*. This city is full of nuts."

Mick toyed with a corner of the newspaper. "How do you know the guy didn't want to just get his rocks off and send Larry on his merry way?"

"That's not how those guys operate, Mick. First they lure you to their home. *Then* they go crazy."

Mick looked at him. "Crazy?"

"Torture. Rape. Kill, even. It happens all the time." He shook the newspaper in Mick's hands. "Don't you read the papers?"

"Sure. But this guy had a sexy voice."

Bobby cocked his head.

"That's what Larry said," Mick finished. He glanced at the newspaper.

Is he lying to me? It was an alien thought, totally removed from the mechanics of their relationship. So unnecessary. They had no need for secrets.

"Look," Bobby sighed, "I admit the whole situation sounds sexy in an offbeat sort of way. It's fine as a fantasy. But not for real life. I mean, what if the guy's not your type? What if the guy is a creep?" His eyes narrowed. "Or what if you find yourself buried in the cellar?"

"Oh, come on."

"Don't forget our friend with the bible pages. No one's found *him* yet. The world's a crazy place sometimes."

Mick nodded thoughtfully. "I guess so."

Bobby stared at him, and felt a tugging on his heart. He looked so lonely all at once. So scared. Bobby jerked the newspaper out of Mick's hands. He folded himself into Mick's lap.

"I'll be your fantasy man, if you want," Bobby whispered huskily. "Sure. I can talk in a gravelly voice."

Mick beamed. "Hummm — tell me more."

"Talk, my dear, is cheap."

And with that, they began to paw at each other, laughing.

5

"I need the mirror."

"Me too."

They jostled in front of the bathroom mirror, giggling.

"I have fifteen minutes to get to work," Mick laughed as he tightened his tie into place. He checked his suit for lint. "How do I look?"

"Like you just got laid. And me?"

Mick appraised Bobby's casual attire with a glance. "Gorgeous."

"Except for this bump." Bobby leaned over the bathroom sink and studied his reflection inches from the mirror.

"What's the matter?"

Bobby frowned at the unfairness of it all.

"Of all the bad luck," he sighed. He pointed to a reddish dime-sized lump on his forehead. "Looks like I'm getting a pimple."

13

Awakening

J
                           1
ust past noon David left his Noe Street apartment and trudged down
the steep hill into the Castro. Under one arm he carried an envelope
containing his short story. He'd added a note telling the editor to give
him a ring if there was a problem. He sincerely hoped there wouldn't
be one.

At this point, he was glad to be rid of the story. Gone, and good
riddance. Oh, he was proud of it, in his own way. Proud that he'd
been able to meet his deadline and come up with a story, odd as it
was. As he walked down the hill he harbored a superstitious belief
that all the disturbing events of the past week were somehow
connected to this work of his, and would magically evaporate once
the story was in the mail. He wanted to forget about the story, but he
knew he could never shake the nagging feeling that there was a lot
more to all of it — the story just another step closer — whatever that
meant.

As for now, he turned his thoughts to other things.

Like the weather. Which was clear, today. A low fog slouched over
Twin Peaks. Pushed by a damp westerly breeze, the fog would no
doubt tumble toward them in a couple of hours. Twin Peaks acted as
a shield for the Castro; it usually cut the fog into two directions: south
toward the airport, and north, through the Golden Gate and downtown. That's what was happening right now.

Actually, the biggest surprise was the return of the sun. Dark clouds
scudded across the hazy sky, but intermittent sunbeams poked
through the sludgy layer of rain-swollen clouds in a bizarre kind of
cosmic light show. For a city that had not seen proper sunshine in
many days, this was a welcomed sight. And as David rounded
Nineteenth Street onto Castro, he saw by the number of noontime
errand-runners that many appreciated the relief from the clouds and
the rain, however brief.

Men and women walked past him with animated smiles and excited chatter. A few men gave David the eye, surreptitiously glancing crotch to eye as they breezed past. It warmed him, this simple affirming glance. It helped put into perspective the events of the night before.

He knew he had to talk to someone about what had happened, but this desire was tempered with caution. He knew how improbable it all sounded. And in the light of this sunny afternoon, he hardly believed it himself.

David strolled past various shops and restaurants and arrived at Eighteenth and Castro — the Heartland, as Eddie had always called it. A black-haired man with a bleached blond mustache stood at the intersection cruising passersby. David stared at the man with amusement, and the man smiled back, misinterpreting his stare for interest. It had been a fad, some twelve years back, the bleaching of a mustache. Short-lived, with good reason. Yet here it was. The man's t-shirt read: "So Many Men, So Little Time."

The traffic signal switched to green. He crossed the intersection and hurried up Eighteenth Street. He broke his stride long enough to scoop up a *Bay Area Reporter* from outside one of the card shops on the street and scanned the headlines as he walked to the post office.

Ah, the *B.A.R.*, that local gladrag of gay news and entertainment. He always read the paper back to front, starting with the personals. The personals, where men bared their fetishes and desires for companions, were often an amusing source of story ideas. An unusual request or sexual fetish was often the springboard to a new porn story. After all, there were only so many ways of describing cock and ass.

So as he waited in line at the post office, David scanned the back pages first and then skipped around to various articles he intended to read when he returned home. He glanced approvingly at the latest muscle stud pictured in the leather column. Another picture caught his eye toward the bottom of the page: a handsome black man handing out AIDS-awareness leaflets. The caption below it read: "Anyone seen our pal Flint?" He searched the column for the accompanying story on Flint, and read:

> Worried friends Will Garter and Ralph Sutherland continue to cry foul over the suspicious disappearance of their pal and ours, Larry "Flint" Stone. Flint was the owner of that naughty hangout once reputed to have been the busiest bathhouse in SoMa — and full of fond memories for yours truly. It's been closed ever since a citywide ordinance shut down all remaining bathhouses. Rumor has it that Flint was unable to sell the property and that financial complications, saddled with his recent diagnosis of AIDS, perhaps triggered his disappearance. Ralph and Will insist Flint would never take his own life, and I'm inclined to agree. Flint always struck me as one tough customer. So if any of you out there know what's become of our buddy, give me a call and I'll pass on the information.

A strange feeling came over David.

It was like a gate in his head, opening.

He stared at the grainy picture. His right hand, suddenly cautious of this journey, reluctantly skimmed across the newsprint until his fingers rested on the image of Flint Stone. An electric shock buzzed through him with the contact. He jerked his fingers away.

Blood.

His fingertips painted with it, striping his fingers as it dribbled into his palm. Without thinking he shook his hand as though some creepy-crawly bug was attached to his fingers and would not let go.

"Next, please!"

David looked up. A female postal clerk crooked a finger in his direction.

He held up his right hand, bringing it close to his face for examination. Newsprint smudged his fingers.

"Are you coming, sir? Otherwise, please step aside."

Ink. Not blood. It hadn't been blood: of course not. David marched up to the counter amid a flutter of folding paper and announced he wanted to mail off his manuscript first class. He stared at his dirty fingers. Never had such a sight made him so happy. Blood. What nonsense.

To his chagrin he discovered his wallet to be bankrupt; he'd forgotten to go to his bank. Luckily, he carried his checkbook. Ignoring the scowl of condescension thrown at him by the pudgy female clerk, he scribbled a check for the amount. He peeled it off and slid it toward her, his glance resting on the folded *B.A.R.* on the counter. A dark wet stain was seeping out from the center of the paper. No ink was ever that color red.

"Sir? Sir? I can't accept this check."

"Huh? Why not?"

She thrust it toward him, her index finger stabbing the line where he'd written the date.

He had the October part right.

But for the year, he'd written 1976.

2

He stepped out into the weak sunshine and pressed himself against the steady weight of the post office wall.

He did not want to believe it. And this refusal was killing him, inch by inch. He saw that. The more he resisted the shaking earth, the closer he came to cracking open and falling apart.

He rubbed the flesh of his goose-bumping arms and thought, *Okay. Give in a little. What does it get me?*

Eddie. Gone. His gym buddy Jack Martin, also gone. And this stranger, this man with the cartoon name — something had happened to him, too.

Another thought. Those people in that so-vivid story of his — were they just his creations, or...

No; they're *not* real. They're characters. Made up.

But then David remembered suddenly, he and Jack on the exercise bike:

What's his name?

Mike. Mick. Begins with an M.

Okay, so he used the name. And maybe he borrowed the blond's good looks, too. He knew nothing of that man's real life.

But this sensation would not let go — the story *was* a link, somehow a link, and now this new intuition whispered clearly inside his head: *Mick's lover. He calls himself Bobby. They're real. And they're both in trouble—*

David pushed himself away from the wall and started back down Eighteenth Street. He'd meant to browse the shops and while the afternoon away, but his feet picked up momentum and soon he was running, brushing past men with bleached mustaches and men in t-shirts with cute sayings but that had to be his imagination too because everyone on the street couldn't suddenly look like they belonged in 1976 could they and all he wanted was a joint, he needed a joint to take him out of himself, take him away. He'd go home and pull out a few of his old records and pretend for just a few moments anyway that this dark future where overnight friends disappeared was not unfolding all around him.

His lungs burned from his frantic pace up the steep Noe hill. His hip felt stabbed by half a dozen knives. But he was home now. Safe, and alone, and home.

As David walked through his apartment first in relief and then with mounting panic, he began to question just how alone — or safe — he honestly was.

Scattered throughout the rooms — no, not scattered, he suddenly realized, but *placed* with exquisite care — in the bathroom, the kitchen, on top of the TV and VCR, by his desk—

Joints. Neatly rolled. Waiting to be smoked. A tiny puddle beside each one.

And in the typewriter, a new note:

MY COMPLIMENTS

it read. The black ink letters began to smoke as David stood watching. There was a cupped coughing sound and a tongue of yellow fire burst from the typewritten letters.

"Hey!" David cried. He yanked the paper from the typewriter and let go as it fluttered, burning, to the rug. He stamped it out.

He stared about his room as though it had become a witch's castle.

3

"What do you mean you can't tell me over the phone?"

David squirmed in his seat. "You have to come see for yourself."

He could hear Alex's exasperation, a long-winded exhale of air. David sat on the couch in his living room, one hand cupping the receiver. He heard a bustle of activity: A blaring intercom. The noisy jangle of a dozen phones. Shouts and catcalls.

All normal day stuff, David thought dejectedly. His world is the same. Nothing's changed.

Alex pressed his luck. "How about a hint to whet my appetite? What happened to you last night?"

Here goes, David thought. "I had an intruder."

"A burglar? Really?" There was a note of sharp alarm in Alex's voice. "For criminy's sake, why didn't you call the cops?"

"I am. You."

"Last *night*, David. Jeeze."

He was the only man David had ever heard say "Jeeze" and have it come out sounding perfectly natural. "Gee whiz" and "golly" were probably in his repertoire too — and the funny thing was, Alex could probably get away with saying it and not have anyone laugh.

Alex cleared his throat. "Did you get a good look at him?"

"No. But I know who it was."

"Who?"

"Not over the phone, Alex. I'd rather wait until you're here."

A puzzled sigh. "Boy, oh boy, I love a good mystery like anyone else, but this takes the cake. I thought this call was about Eddie Blake."

David said, "It is."

A stony silence.

Now I've done it, he thought.

"Hold on just a second," Alex stammered. "What are you telling me here? You saw Eddie last night?"

"Well — no. I didn't actually see him. But I think he was in my apartment."

"That's — that's great," Alex said in a voice full of doubt and sudden confusion. "Isn't it?"

David said in a low voice, "No. Not this time."

The confusion in Alex was giving way to a barely concealed irritation. "You're being very mysterious, David. I hope you know that. If this is your idea of pulling a fast one—"

"No, I swear." He rushed ahead before Alex could interrupt. "I know how this sounds. That's why I didn't want to discuss this over the phone. It's pretty unbelievable. But you said you'd help me, Alex, and that's what I need: help. Better I find out up front if you can — or want to—"

"Sure I want to help. But if you're withholding information I can't make any promises..."

"Don't worry. You'll get it all, tonight. When can you make it?"

"Six or seven too late for you?"

"No. That's fine."

They said their good-byes and hung up.

After a few minutes, David went to his desk and sat down. Put a fresh sheet of paper into the typewriter.

Speak, damn you, he thought. *Talk to me. Help me.*

The typewriter purred with electricity. Hypnotic, in its own way.

Before he even knew what was happening, his fingers began to move.

And he typed:

FIND THE WOMAN.

4

A red-haired woman steps out of her shop at the end of her workday. Breathes deeply the autumn-scented air of this twilight evening. She cranes her neck toward the west, glimpsing Twin Peaks and the winking lights of its three towers poking out of the fog. An indescribable ache in her bones. The ruthless march of fog across the gunmetal sky fills her with a confounding sense of doom. Briefly, she closes her eyes.

Words typed across a page. She's seen it off and on in her head for the past several days. Heard in waking dreams the smack of typewriter keys against paper and roller. Wondering what it all meant. She shakes the image from her head. *Go away,* she tells herself. *It won't touch me, whatever this is. I won't let it.* Trembling, she rushes back into her shop. Double-bolts the front door. And dreads the night's blanket flung across the city.

14

Deceptions, deceptions

W_{aiting.}

1

Waiting.

The hours tick by in agonizing slow motion.

Mick sits at the reception desk, answering the steady stream of phone calls to the law firm, typing letters and memos. To everyone's appraising glance he is a model employee. A tad young, perhaps, but resourceful, courteous. Quick to offer an important guest a cup of coffee, a magazine, and a dazzling smile able to soothe the most ruffled of feathers. His supervisors have discussed giving him a raise, which Mick will surely receive.

If he's around long enough.

Because all this insufferably long day, the image haunts him. Useless to fight against it, try though he does. It works in his blood like a drug, intoxicating him.

He shuts his eyes, and he sees it.

He opens his eyes, and he sees it.

It stands alone, shrouded in fog. The glass is cool, inviting, not damp in the least. The dark air of the booth whispers secrets, a tongue in his ear. The solid weight of the telephone in his hand is like cradling a giant cock, rock hard as his own.

He aches to pull himself out of his cotton briefs. He swells against the fabric of his pin-striped Bill Blass suit. Once, he had to stand up and fetch a guest executive a cup of coffee, his bulge clearly outlined in his pants, and the executive, a sixty-year-old married man with a male lover on the side, saw Mick's erection and sighed to himself, "Ah, the wonders of youth."

On his lunch hour, he can wait no more. Mick sneaks into a private bathroom and locks the door. He stands in front of the sink and mirror and scoops his hard-on out of his pants. His legs tremble. His freckled cheeks blush with excitement. The palm of his hand poises with ritualistic sacredness against the hot flesh of his cock. He surrenders.

He closes his eyes and he's at the phone booth, the voice urging him to taste, suck, fuck.

Breath upon his ear. A whisper:

(Not now)

Mick opens his eyes. His hand stops riding his dick.

(Not now, Mick. Save it. Save it for me, tonight)

And Mick, who has always been a good boy, does as he is told.

2

"Oh. I see."

"Don't be disappointed, Bobby."

"What else can I be? I thought I was making us dinner tonight."

They are on the phone, Mick at his reception desk, Bobby at the Quick Copy Shop. Bobby has to strain to hear Mick above the hot-air whine of the Xerox copy machines. He leans against the formica counter, his legs weak. The ground threatens to split open and swallow him in one convulsive gulp.

"I'm not feeling up to par today," Mick says. "Besides, tomorrow morning I have to take notes at an early conference meeting." A pause. "I'd rather lie low tonight."

"I could come to your place. Make you dinner there, for a change."

A too-quick response: "Oh, honey, that's not necessary."

Bobby bristles. *Necessary! These lies are what aren't necessary! Talk to me!*

But Bobby says none of this. Instead:

"Okay. If that's what you want."

"It's only for tonight. Don't be mad."

"Who said I was mad?" Bobby huffs irritably. He catches himself. Please: not an argument, not here, at work, over the phone. His co-workers eye him. He shifts away from their looks. "Mick," he says, "Is anything wrong?" He fingers the throbbing bump above the bridge of his nose. It's ached like hell all day long, and no amount of aspirin has gotten rid of the pain.

"N-No. Nothing."

"You can tell me, you know. Whatever it is."

Now Mick is the irritable one. "I'm *tired,* Bobby. I didn't sleep well last night. You know that."

Yes, he knows that. His thoughts fill with that strange story Mick told him this morning, about the "friend" and the phone booth. *He's in trouble.* Worry pulls at his heart. He chooses his next words with care. "Mick, if you ever fell into a jam — no matter what kind — you know I'd be there to help you out of it."

"W-What do you mean?"

Bobby chews his lip. "Whatever this trouble is that's pulling us apart—"

"Bobby—"

"No; I'm not going to pry it out of you. But for god's sake give me the truth here. You owe me that. I'm not blind. I see what's happening."

"Nothing's—"

"Whatever it is, Mick. You can tell me. I can't promise I won't be mad, but I do promise to at least hear you out. Let me be here for you. Okay?"

Silence. Bobby clenches the phone.

Then: a ragged sigh. "Okay."

Mick's voice is inches above a whisper, but Bobby doesn't care. Contact. Finally, he has made contact. His heart swells. "I love—"

But Mick has hung up.

3

The fog snatches away the sun on that Thursday afternoon. It sinks ignobly into the western sky, leeched of all color, as fog and wintery haze rob it of a fiery farewell. A fierce wind bears down upon the city, dragging a heavy curtain of fog behind it. Any respite from the day's intermittent sunshine forgotten. The city battens down for attack.

No one admits to an anxious fear. No one can understand why, on this night, the dark seems a villain.

In the Castro, many men postpone going home in favor of a drink or two in their favorite bar. With liquor their comfort and companion, they nervously eye the gray swirl of fog beating against the windows, which they will have to penetrate on their way home.

None can fathom the absurd excitement coiled in their bellies like an expectant child, nor their half-erect penises swelling against their pants. They begin to convince themselves that sex will cure this strange restlessness, although, oddly, they seek out no partners.

Gray gives way to blue, to black: true darkness.

As if on cue, the bars empty. Men scurry home without looking up from the sidewalk. Tonight, they have another date.

David will scribble notes at his desk and wait for Alex with mixed apprehension;

Bobby will pick up a pencil and doodle endlessly onto any scrap of paper within his reach — drawings of diamonds with light streaming out, and a stick figure hunched over what looks like a child's rendering of a toy typewriter. He will pop aspirin to get rid of his ever-increasing migraine, and pace, and in moments of utter despair hold onto his grandmother's crucifix as tears stream down his cheeks, and wonder if he has gone totally mad;

Mick will—

Well. Mick will keep his appointment.

Tonight, all will dream.

Tonight, some will believe.

And tonight, some will die.

15

Dear diary

1

Fifteen minutes before midnight. The appropriate witching hour, for this kind of tale. As I sit here and write this, I know whatever happened tonight — or may have happened — is over. Done. Maybe the man in the booth is dead. Or worse.

Sleep seems a long way off, tonight. I hope that writing in this notebook will help me sort everything out. My apartment is cold, even with the drapes drawn across the view. Truth is, I'm afraid to look outside. Afraid of the faces I might see pressed against the window. So I'm holed up in my bedroom pretending not to be frightened by the wind and rain gusting against the building. Stuck in the classic horror movie cliché: alone on a rainy night.

I miss Eddie. God, how I miss him. I'd be able to talk to him, instead of talking to myself in this notebook. He'd listen, and understand. He always did. But now, when I need his company and companionship more than ever, Eddie has not only vanished but somehow joined this ... this conspiracy to drive me crazy. So tonight, with no one else to turn to, I talked to that handsome policeman. Officer Webster. Alex. He keeps insisting I call him Alex, like we're buddy buddies, good ole boys from Texas or wherever the hell he's from with that accent of his. He means well, this Alex, but I didn't have to be psychic to read the expression on his face when he left tonight. Or for that matter, when he arrived at my door...

2

"Where is he?"

"Who?"

"Eddie."

"I haven't the slightest idea."

"I thought you saw Eddie here last night. Isn't he staying with you?"

...He had scowled, one eyebrow raised as though he was trying to decide if he'd been had. I paced by the sliding glass doors. I knew I had to proceed as if on eggshells. Instill trust in this man. And the reverse, too: Who was this Officer Webster, anyway? I had to tell somebody what was happening to me, that much was clear...

"I'm in trouble, Mr. Webster—"

"I told you to cut the Mr. Webster shit. Alex. Plain ole Alex. Now tell me what's wrong."

"Does anyone know you're here?"

"No. What are you so afraid of?"

"I think someone is after me, Alex. He's stealing my friends away and he taunts me with their deaths — well, not deaths, exactly; I don't know what to call it. This person wants to hurt me. Maybe even kill me. But he can't. Not yet, anyway."

...At the time I wanted to say *creature, monster,* but I held my tongue. I knew talking about it would make it real. There was no turning back...

"How does this tie in with Eddie Blake?"

"I think he was here, last night, but not as my friend."

"Wait a minute—"

"That's right. I think he came here to kill me."

...I had expected incredulity. What I got was anger. Alex moved toward me with surprising agility, a huge paw of a hand on each of my shoulders. He put his face right up against mine...

"Look. I'm the one doing you a favor here. I'm the one taking the time out to listen to what you have to say. So stop giving me this cock-and-bull story or I'll walk out that door fast as you please. You're in a jam, all right, boy howdy are you *ever.* And if you don't start giving me some straight answers, we'll never get to the bottom of this mess."

"In a minute. What's the official word on Eddie? What do your superiors think happened to him?"

"Let me tell you later."

"Tell me now."

"He's listed as missing. Nothing more."

"What about that ... that stain on his bed? The smell in his room?"

"Leaky pipes."

...His grip was like iron. I knew I'd caught him off guard. I had opened my mouth, but words died on the tip of my tongue. Leaky pipes my ass. Alex just shrugged. He still wouldn't look at me, the bastard...

"There's a vent on the ceiling. A faulty air conditioning system: That's what the report says. As for Eddie ... well ... they think someone helped him leave the hospital."

"Why would a dying man leave a hospital?"

"To die in peace. At home. Or wherever he was most comfortable."

"That's bullshit, Alex, and you know it!"

"Do I? What do I call the story you've been dishing out to me?"

"Eddie was *here* last night."

"That's exactly what my pals at the station believe. You brought home your buddy so he could finish out his days with you. It's perfectly understandable."

"He tried to attack me!"

"All one hundred and thirty pounds of him?"

"He wasn't alone!"

"Prove it."

...God, it sounded all so lame, even to me. Prove it. If I could've done that, there would have been no argument. But Alex just folded his arms across his chest, smug as a bug. I looked down at his feet. Last night, there had been footprints on that rug. The sliding glass door had been left wide open. There'd been little puddles of water in each bare footprint. Today, nothing but a little dried dirt. Nothing that a cop couldn't easily write off as imagination. But then I had an idea, and it caught fire in my imagination. Why hadn't I thought of it before? I made Alex follow me back down the hallway. He wanted evidence? I'd show him evidence. I entered the bathroom and flicked on a light. I crossed over to the bathtub, bent low, and turned on the hot water. It had gushed out of the pipe with a thundering roar. I could tell the cop's tolerance was wearing thin. That tight expression had returned to his face. It said, *This better be good.* We stood across from each other, Alex with his hands folded across his chest like the king of Siam, silent as smoky tendrils of steam began to drift toward the ceiling. Eddie hadn't been the only one here last night. He'd had company...

"Yesterday, in the hospital — you were such a help. I couldn't have gotten through all that without you. So I thought — hoped — you could help me again."

"I promised I'd help you. I wouldn't be here on my own time if that wasn't the case. All I demand in return, David, is the truth."

"I hope you won't change your mind."

"Why should I?"

"Because you may not like what you see."

"I'm a policeman with a job to do."

...When the steam had filled the room, I saw the claw marks in the mirror. The deep scratches on the inside of the glass. The steam had revealed them, as I'd hoped. I shut off the hot running water. But Alex just stood there. His face showed no shock or surprise. I thought at first he didn't see them. That he didn't recognize those foot-long slashes across the glass for what they were! I waited. *They had wanted to break through. They had wanted to break into my world, but I stopped them.*

Alex just leveled me with a look. There was such ... sadness ... in those blue eyes. No. More than that. Embarrassment. For me. And then I knew.

He thought I was crazy. He couldn't meet my eyes.

3

Maybe I am crazy. Hallucinating. Dreaming the whole thing up. Maybe I've got a tumor the size of a golf ball squeezing against my brain. In a funny way I could almost accept that. A tumor, scary as that is, is real.

I have an insatiable urge to smoke one of the joints that was left for me this afternoon. Smoke myself right into oblivion. The weird thing is, I know that if I smoke, it'll let down my defenses somehow. Believe me, I'm not becoming a prude or anything like that. But the pot will — I don't know — open a door. Create an invitation. Why else would they have been left all over the apartment, tempting me to smoke? So, as wired up as I am, it's sober tonight.

I told Alex everything. Well, I left out the part about joints all over the house (could he bust me on that?). But I did confess to a few tokes in a pipe before taking my bath.

You should have seen how his eyes lit up...

"You fell asleep. Makes perfect sense. You were exhausted. Your best friend had disappeared. You came home and wrote your little story, firing up your imagination. Smoked some weed. You were stoned. You were tired. You were in a hot bath. Perfectly natural you'd fall asleep."

"What are you implying: I dreamed everything up? What about those marks in the mirror?"

"I'm just an ordinary Joe, but it looked like plain ole water condensation to me. Nothing sinister about it."

"And Eddie?"

"You never *saw* anyone. You heard sounds. Music. What you thought were voices. Probably your upstairs neighbor."

"There was a stain on the wall. Wet footprints in the rug, up and down the hallway."

"But there's nothing here today, is there."

"I saw something in Eddie's hospital room, too."

"You were frantic from your bad dream and you *thought* you saw something wrong in his room. Think about it, David. Bessie Watson wasn't two minutes behind you into that room. Water don't evaporate that fast. That's just simple fact."

...That was true, damn him. But I knew that something had happened in there. That something had got him. I shouted this at Alex and his face took on this odd expression, as though my words rang true, but he wouldn't — couldn't — admit that to me right away...

"Put yourself in my shoes. I'm not calling you a lunatic. I'm not saying you should be hauled off to the funny farm. I *am* saying you've been under a lot of stress lately. The stress has given you these nightmares and hallucinations. Yes, hallucinations. I think you're suffering from a classic case of guilt. You obviously loved your friend very much. And I know you wanted to do all you could for him. But he was dying. Bessie Watson told me Eddie Blake didn't have more than a few weeks left to him, if he was lucky. And you — you're going about your life trying to keep it all normal but you can't, and that's an honest fact. Watchin' someone die piece by piece — it takes it out of you in funny ways. And I think in your depression and stress it was easier for you to accept some Bad Guy Boogieman coming and stealing Eddie away than recognizing it for what it was: this lousy awful disease."

...My shoulders started to shake then, and I couldn't stop. I wanted to curl up and make the world go away. Alex scooted down beside me on the couch and wrapped a big arm around my shoulders. As much as I didn't want to confess it then — or now — what Alex had said made a lot of sense. Not that it explained *every*thing, mind you. But enough for that part of me that craved rational answers to grab on to it gratefully. We sat quietly, side by side. After my earlier fantasies, it was rather nice to feel his warmth next to me, his steely strength...

"As for that bump on your head, that's serious stuff, David. You should have gone straight to a doctor. You can't fool around with your health, especially in this day and age. Now I'm not out to frighten you any more than you already are, but that bump could have been the precursor — or the cause of all your — hallucinations. The bad smells. The blackouts. Sounds like mild epileptic seizures."

"This isn't epilepsy, Alex."

"Maybe not. But if you look at it my way, it makes more sense than what you've suggested — that it's some kind of whatever you called it — psychic awakening. Don't you see there's no need to drag the supernatural into this?"

...Now that Alex Webster is gone and the house seems full of whispering footsteps, his words no longer reassure me. At that moment, though, I tried to see the logic in them. But I couldn't forget what I'd seen at the post office...

"You said it yourself. It wasn't blood on your hand at all. It was newsprint. Common everyday newsprint."

"Do the police *know* anything about that guy? Flint Stone? The article says he's not been seen in over a week."

"I'll check on it for you, if you'd like."

"Yes. I would like. And what about Jack Martin? There may be others. Some that the police have missed."

"What do you think this is, a conspiracy? Why do you refuse to let go of your ... boogieman?"

"Just — do me that favor, would you? Do that, and I promise I'll think about what you've told me tonight."

"Sure. I'll comb through some of the recent missing-persons reports. Look for any common thread that may have been missed."

...I had him. It was a perfect compromise. I knew if I was going to have to give up some of my way of thinking, so was he. I studied his face carefully, and I saw that it was clouded in an odd way. He already knew of a common thread, but he wasn't telling me. Not yet, anyway...

"What's so funny, David?"

"Psychic vibes."

"Oh? What: Are you reading something about me?"

"I don't know."

"Go ahead. What can you pick up on me, right this minute? I'll hold a thought in my head—"

"I'm not a mind reader, Alex. I just get flashes of ... of ... *knowing.*"

"Humor me, would you? I come from a long line of skeptics. I only know what I can see or feel when it's in front of me. If what you've been describing is more than a hunch or intuition, this is the time to prove it to me."

...I knew that. But did I have it in me? Was this feeling something I could harness and use to my advantage? Up until now it had revealed itself only as disturbing dreams, impressions. Quick, clear pictures, like flicking channels on a TV. So I took up Alex's challenge, to prove its existence not only to him, but to myself...

"Besides, isn't there anything about me you want to know?"

"Not really, Alex."

"Then why are you blushing?"

"Am I?"

"More than ever."

...I had wanted to ask him, *Are you gay?* Okay, okay. So the question bore no relevance to our discussion. I knew that. What could I say: Alex is an attractive man. Despite the fact that he's too damn rigid for his own good, I couldn't help but wonder if our friendship had a chance of going any further.

So I ... I reached out with my mind. I used the question as a sort of psychic shovel, trying to break the shell of his guarded thoughts. Nothing happened. No flash of insight. I just felt foolish...

"I told you it wouldn't work."

"What'd you want to know?"

"If you were gay."

"What does that have to do with anything?"

"I know it's none of my business. But don't you see? I'm gay. My friends are gay. Whatever seems to be happening is happening around me and my community—"

"—There are a dozen different reasons to explain what you *think* you're seeing—"

"I know! But maybe there's a connection. And since you're around me, I can't help but wonder if you've placed yourself in danger as well."

"Don't fret about me. The answer is no. I'm not gay ... You don't believe me?"

"Do *you* believe *me?*"

4

Here's the irony. I didn't believe myself. I wanted to believe Alex. His steady calm was like a flannel blanket I could pull around my shoulders to shake this chill in my bones. Let's face it: What was the alternative? A Freddy Kruger boogieman piercing my dreams? Eddie dead (undead?), come to drag me back to his new hell?

I could see it. In the past few days I had talked myself *into* believing. With Alex, I quite happily talked myself *out* of believing. Amazing, what a potent drug rationalization can be.

I was ready to ignore the gaping holes in this bag of answers Alex had handed to me. Ready to take it and smile and say "thank you."

5

"There's a difference, David, in believing the world has gone to hell. You'll find plenty of supporters for that. But a world given over to hocus-pocus? Hardly."

...At that moment, I'll never forget it: My eyes began to burn. Unmistakably chlorine. It stuffed my nose like a dirty rag, causing me to cough and sputter. Alex grew alarmed. He reached across with concern. It was happening again. My vision browned out. A curtain fell across my eyes, like one of those wire mesh screens covering a fireplace. Alex, the couch, the apartment sank into a bubbling gray soup. This wasn't a complete blacking out, as in the previous episodes. More like a ... displacement. I remained aware of myself even though my surroundings rearranged themselves. I could hear Alex shouting my name but his voice was far away, as if he stood on a street corner and shouted up to my apartment.

No; *I* stood on that street corner, and across from me was a phone booth and an old awning structure. A bus stop. A man stood in its shadows. He was bundled in a jacket and stamped his feet in the cold. I caught a flash of curly blond hair as he tilted back his head and took a swig from a small bottle.

Suddenly, the phone rang.

The blond swiveled in its direction. Swaying, he sauntered into the booth.

I saw it all up close, his hand reaching out from his jacket to grasp the receiver. And without knowing what I was doing I began to scream...

"Don't answer it! Don't!"

"Don't answer what? David, can you hear me?"

"Run! Run, while you still have a chance!"

...I found myself on the floor, squirming. Alex's voice had pulled me back and I didn't want to *be* back. I wanted to see what was going to happen. When I finally came out of it, Alex had been so concerned that I told him what I'd seen, but he couldn't seem to grasp it, the feeling of imminent danger for the man in the booth. He finally left, making me promise to rest. But I had seen too much: the phone booth, and its captive...

6

...Run. Maybe that's what *I* should do. Run, while I have a chance. Because now that Alex is back home where he can hold on to his sure and solid beliefs, I am deserted and afraid. It's long past midnight now, and I feel the dark gripping the apartment, taking my breath away. That queasy sensation of free-fall is back, but worse: I feel as though I'm about to touch ground deep inside some dark and alien landscape. I'd rather fall, fall and never hit bottom.

For the truth is — and that's all I can muster at this hour; the bullshit is too heavy to drag around any longer — I think I know who the man was, inside that booth. The booth I saw so clearly in my porno story. And if it's who I think it is, if what I saw is real — and happening — then it's too late. I'm inside that well. I've hit bottom. And there is no way out...

16

A waltz with the spider

1

It had become a dance of sorts.

Would Mick stay in his apartment or would he go to the phone booth, one-two-three, one-two-three. As twilight gave way to autumn darkness on that Thursday night, Mick fought the urge to return to that silent street, and the phone booth. Once, he was halfway out the door, his coat pulled around him, when he stopped, dazed, and realized what he was doing. He fled back into his apartment.

All day he had tantalized himself with visions of the phone booth. Shared drink with this dark desire. Yet, as the appointed hour drew near, he stalled. It was his old self rising, as if from slumber.

Don't go, this voice told him. *For once, stop listening to your cock. This guy, Victor. He can hypnotize. He wields a power ... an evil ... as if he were some kind of—*

But no; that word refused to be spoken. Even his thoughts skirted past it. To speak the word meant the overlapping of two worlds, old with new, a world of superstition melded to the world of electricity and skyscrapers and enlightenment.

He would not believe.

He refused to believe.

Because deep down, he was afraid he would keep his appointment no matter what his thoughts told him.

He tried to eat. He couldn't.

He watched TV without seeing it.

A dozen times he wanted to call Bobby, but stayed himself. This was *his* battle. That's what wound through his head like a reel-to-reel tape. He had to take care of this himself. Besides, to open up to Bobby now entailed spilling the whole truth. And what was that truth, exactly? That a whispered voice spoke to him? That it coursed through him like a fine liquor, erasing decency and good sense, urging him — demanding him — ever nearer? That this same voice brought visions that terrified and yet excited him beyond his wildest dreams?

Bobby would just love that, wouldn't he?

So the phone sat, unused.

Minutes ticked by.

His groin began to hurt. Something restless stirred down there, wanting to give birth. Sweat trickled down his chest and under his armpits. He threw open a window and drank in the cold like a man saved from drowning.

Fresh air. That's what he wanted. Fresh air. Maybe a walk around the block. And a pint of scotch to ease the shakes.

On went the jacket. Off went the lights. Door locked. He jogged to the corner store on Polk Street and bought a pint of Johnny Walker Red. He'd never bought it before, never even tasted this brand, but he bought a pint now. Stood on the street corner and downed a gulp. It burned going down, then fanned a mellow fire, easing the trembling in his knees. The beast in his belly was momentarily satiated.

With that first gulp flew the last of his resolve. His feet began to move beneath him.

But let it be said, to set the record straight: He went of his own volition.

2

It was a London night, fog muting sight and sound with a gauzy curtain. The air was damp and chilly, tasting of breezes off the Pacific, but Mick was warm. The half-empty pint of Johnny Walker bounced in his inside coat pocket. He was light-headed, dizzy. The distance between him and phone booth closed to just a few blocks. He was the only one walking Eighth Street at this time of night. He felt like a ghost haunting a deserted town. Even the homeless, the true wanderers of this neighborhood's streets and alleys, were nowhere to be seen.

When he'd first begun his walk, sipping from the bottle every dozen or so steps, he had chosen a plan of attack. He would tell Victor to leave him alone. Period. Sure, the man was a great fantasy. Scary, too — but that was half the excitement, wasn't it, this tango between them? What it lacked was a sense of completion. He wanted it to end, tonight.

As the liquor worked in him, however, his determination was wrestled to the mat by a greater anticipation.

What if we did play, just this once? he thought. *What if I make him promise that it goes no further than tonight?*

Mick trembled with desire. Ahh, for that first look at him! To put a face to that velvet voice, a body, a cock. To have this stranger feed on his youth and hardness.

Nothing wrong in doing this. If anything, he felt prudish in his lack of exotic experiences. If only he'd had a few more years before the epidemic came along and ruined everything. It was unfair. He was twenty-five, and this was the prime of his life. This should be his time to crow, to beat his chest, to test forbidden waters — and all the fun had been snatched away from him. He'd been too young to splash in that fantastic wave that had been gay pride in the late seventies, able only to watch it swell and crest from afar, in Denver. By the time he had moved to San Francisco at the age of twenty-two, the worst ills to befall a gay man could no longer be cured with a shot of penicillin.

Victor's invitation seemed to encourage a swelling of that long-ago wave. His message: We know how to take care of ourselves. So go ahead. Let's play.

These drunken thoughts bounced around in Mick's head. It did not matter that at odd moments it seemed as if someone else had placed these thoughts inside his head. It did not matter, that dream of ghostly men floating outside Bobby's window, and the man who drew back his lips to bare those incredible teeth.

And as Mick walked past Tehama Street, where Bobby lived, he discovered with a guilty shock that even his boyfriend somehow did not matter—

No.

He stopped dead in his tracks. Bobby *did* matter. He loved him. Sure, the guy got on his nerves every once in a while, and occasionally they'd fight, but Bobby was also his first serious relationship, and that mattered. It mattered a whole lot. This clear realization rippled through him. A joyous smile spread ear to ear.

He would tell this odd man to shove off. No more phone calls, no more games. Their dance was over.

A sudden thought: *Run. Run to Bobby's apartment, and tell him everything before it's too late. Don't trust Victor. He's too strong. He's—*

Mick looked down the street.

There it was, the phone booth, shrouded in mist.

3

"Look who's here."

Mick shuffled his feet. Since he had arrived, and answered the phone on the second ring, his mind fell blank. A lie sprang to his lips. "I'm on my way home."

"No. You kept our appointment, as I knew you would." Victor had that luring voice, like a spider to the fly, tonight. A silky purr, quiet and commanding.

Mick gathered himself.

"I want you to leave me alone. That's why I've come. I know what you're up to. So I'm telling you flat out: No more phone calls. No more games."

"No more sexy dreams?"

His blood turned to ice. *He knows about the dreams.*

Victor chuckled. "Don't be afraid, Vanilla."

"Don't call me that."

"Oh, I meant no harm. I'm glad you came. I knew you would."

"How?"

"I know all about men like you," Victor said. He sounded amused, enjoying himself. "You have sex the way you order food in a cafeteria. I'll have a little of this and a little of that. Perfect square portions. But inside, *oohh*. Admit it. You'd love your sex to be anything but perfect square portions, yes?"

Mick shrugged. "I guess so."

"You guess so. Come to me. I'll show you what you 'guess so.'"

"Victor, I can't. Not yet. I'm—"

"Too frightened?"

"I never said that," Mick snapped.

"You don't have to. Your whole attitude is one of fear. But you have nothing to be afraid of, my American friend. I want only what you want. Oh, admit it. Talking to me like this — wanting me — turns you on, yes?"

He sighed. "Yes. But—" *You're hiding something.*

"Mick, listen to me—"

Fireworks. A blinding flash.

"How do you know my name?" Mick demanded. His heart stalled.

"You told me," the spider-man said offhandedly.

"No I didn't! I'm sure I didn't!"

That patient — but patronizing — voice again.

"You have no reason to be afraid of me, Mick. You should feel flattered."

"Flattered? How do you know me!"

"Listen. You have come this far. You deserve the truth. Would you like that?"

"Y-Yes."

His voice dropped to a husky growl. "I'm special, Mick. So are you. I've been watching. Waiting. You're too good for your boyfriend. And I think we can help each other."

"Help?" Mick leaned into the phone. All the world was narrowing down to that voice on the other end of the line. He did not notice how the fog crept in through the doors and gathered silently around his ankles.

"You have yearnings you don't know how to satisfy. I have awakened something deep inside you. You have fantasies in the night, your hand wrapped around your cock, sheets kicked past ankles. I haunt your dreams. Yes?"

"Yes." His admission was very small, lost.

"And yet — there is an empty spot inside you. Your boyfriend can not satisfy this desire. Only *I* can satisfy you because *I* gave you this hunger. Do not be afraid of it, for we share the same appetite."

Mick swallowed hard. "What do you want from me?"

"I want you to prove your worthiness." The voice swelled, a proud father talking to a son. "I have waited too long for someone like you. With you, I could only plant seeds, and wait. I could not force. You had to come of your own free will. Otherwise, you would not deserve my gifts."

His mind reeled. Gifts? Seeds? He didn't comprehend any of this. Victor talked of free will, but the voice whispering to him since their first encounter had been impossible to ignore. Suddenly he flushed cold all over.

Impossible to ignore ... because in his heart of hearts, he *had* wanted it, after all. The undeniable lure of this man's dark power, whatever it was. To share in it, drink of it—

He felt himself giving in.

"You know you desire me, Mick. You know I am different from anyone you have known, just as your beauty separates you from others. Let me change your life."

A hoarse whisper. "How?"

"Simple. By enjoying yourself with me, now. By performing a test of obedience. I feel the heat of your desire." A pause. "I want you to show yourself to me."

Mick blinked. "W-What?"

A gentle laugh. "Such modesty, my friend, does not become you." The voice hardened. "Before we claim each other, I want you to work yourself right there. Pull yourself out of your pants. Isn't this what you've waited for, all day? The excitement? The release?" His voice was mocking, secure in its power. "So go ahead. *Do it.*"

Mick let go a ragged breath. A cool sweat beaded his skin. He opened the door to make the light turn off, and stepped back into the swirling shadows of the phone booth. As if watching himself from a distance, he saw his hand float down to grasp the upward arch of his hard-on. And yet. And yet...

Wasn't this why he was here?

But a nagging thought: *Why these feelings of something dark and unspoken, of gifts and power and dreams — all to have it reduced to this absurd show-off contest?*

A flame of rebellion flickered, but before he could protest, before he could open his mouth to question, something so astonishing happened, something so unexpected and deliriously erotic, all rebellion gave way with a tidal wave of glorious pleasure.

He looked down.

Tendrils of fog, swirling in invisible currents, swam around his calves and thighs. He was being kissed and fondled by its amazing touch. A recent memory came to him, of Bobby clamping down on his erection through his denim jeans, and that wonderful rush as he blew warm breath through the 501s and onto his dick. That's what the fog was doing to him, now.

Mick groaned. His back rested against the cool glass of the booth. He could drown in this. He slipped a cool hand beneath his tucked-in shirt to greet the warm, rippled muscles of his stomach. He reached higher and tweaked his nipples. Shuddered. The world began to fade away as desire stretched its wings.

Could Victor see him, through all this strange wonderful fog? Could he see the exposed angle of his neck as he moaned to the starless night? His heaving chest? Or his hand, hesitating before suddenly ripping open jeans to expose his thick erection jutting out at an angle?

Or — most unsettling of all — the smoky look to his eyes, blinking in surprise at the heat of his own excitement?

Apparently.

"That's a good boy," Victor said, low. He was panting, his moans timed with Mick's. "Show me. Show me!"

Now that he had taken this step, he was awash in the thrill of it all, of his own dick so hard in his hands. The breeze slipping through the open door of the booth seemed to blow all resistance out of him. He cradled the phone by squeezing shoulder to ear, leaving both hands free to tug and pull at his swollen cock. His knees trembled. All he cared about was the delirious rush splashing over him, the novelty, and, yes, he could admit it now, the danger.

"I'm your boyfriend now," the spider-man chuckled. There was a hint of smugness to his laugh, but a sense of comfort, too. How wonderful to simply let go, to obey, to follow. "You wish I was down there with you. Feel me now!"

All at once invisible hands pawed Mick's body. His pants were yanked to his knees. The feel of hands slithered across his chest and teased his nipples. A tongue seemed to dart from the telephone itself, licking his ear. And the final astonishment — an invisible mouth sank around his erection.

It seemed he stood in the middle of a steamhouse, the fog so hot on his face. He was spiraling higher and higher, his whole body locked in the power of eminent climax. Every nerve poised for the ecstasy of release. Phantom mouths and hands and tongues worked him over in every indescribable pleasure. He felt like a rocket shooting higher than he ever dreamed possible—

He gasped, tensing.

That voice in his ear, commanding:

"Now, Mick, I'm ready to take you! NOW!"

With a guttural moan he froze in exquisite agony and shot his load. Hot cum splattered the glass booth in steaming milky streaks. Spasms shook him so violently he dropped the phone. His knees buckled.

And suddenly: a humid shadow in the dark. Instinctively, Mick closed his eyes against it. A roar filled his ears, a subway-train sound, as something mauled the air around him. He felt himself embraced as if by a giant wet sponge, pressed into its suctioning folds. Air deserted his lungs. A panicked moment of suffocation, as though the whole force of his climax was food that could be gathered from the very air around him and consumed.

Stars winked in his head. He gulped for air, and found none. Dizzy, he leaned against the booth to keep from collapsing. And then it was over. The suctioning, the draining, let go of him slowly, as if with great reluctance. He could breathe again.

A gust of wind blew into the phone booth like a splash of cold water, and the fog disintegrated, scattering into a thousand silky threads. That sweet seductive touch of hands, lips, mouths against Mick's skin fled with this blast of cool air so that he might have imagined it all, if not for what he glimpsed as he opened his eyes and peered about him.

As if caught in a camera's flash, ghostly negatives of men, like sketches from an artist's inkwell, disappeared back into the misty night. Mick had not seen them before, had only felt their touch upon him, but in that instant, he saw their nakedness, their youth. The shadowy men were just shells of lines, nothing more. They threw themselves into the night, snatched and scattered by the wind, and were gone.

Mick still gripped himself in his hand, flushed with the intensity of his orgasm, knees shaking, all raw nerves.

The world spun back into focus. He glanced down at himself, at his pants pushed to his knees, his penis a soft toy in his hand. The cold night air abruptly raised gooseflesh. Exposed. Horribly, embarrassingly, exposed. He shook the last strands of cum free of his dick and stuffed himself back into his pants. A powerful urge to run surfaced in him, to leave the phone dangling and get the hell out.

As though reading his mind, he heard Victor quite clearly:

"Pick up the phone." This was no request. A command.

Hands shaking, he picked up the receiver and brought it to his ear.

"So," the spider whispered. "You have promise, after all."

Mick winced, squeezing shut his eyes. "Don't ... talk." That commanding voice, like puppet strings. Too much, after what had just happened. He was nauseated, as though he'd eaten something that didn't agree with him.

"You passed the first test. Do not be angry. Now I will show you other pleasures."

"Like what?" Mick snapped. "More jacking off in a phone booth? I feel stupid. Exposed and stupid."

A patient laugh. "This is kid's stuff. Next time will be different, yes?"

He shifted his weight. A silent alarm whirled in his head. "There won't be a next time."

"Of course there will. Next time, we meet in person." The voice dropped to a midnight whisper. "And when we are together, you and I, I shall give you a kiss."

Mick's throat went cotton-dry. His temples throbbed. He thought of the shadow that had fallen over him at the moment of climax. The weird draining. The other men (if he'd even seen them at all) scattering like so many broken branches in the wind.

With artificial calm, Mick said, "What's so special about a kiss?"

"You'll never want to leave me afterward," Victor cooed. "It will bring us together. A bond. I'll become your teacher. Lover. Friend. Wouldn't you like that?"

He gripped the phone with clenched fingers. He was sweating again. An answer to all this madness danced on the tip of his tongue. "I swear, when you talk like that, you make it sound as if you were some kind of ... you know ... a ... a..."

Victor let go an amused laugh. "Yes?"

"What happened just now?" Mick demanded. "Why am I so dizzy? And who were those men—"

"Questions! Such questions!" His tone became apologetic. "I took a little drink. Your equilibrium will return in no time. It was the only way I could be sure."

"Sure? Of what?"

"Of my suspicions. But do not concern yourself with this. Hearken to me when I say I need a companion. One with your extraordinary beauty, and talents. And in return..."

Mick had almost stopped breathing. The full impact of Victor's words reverberated though him, and yet he was helplessly lost to the wonder of it.

"Yes?" he gasped through cracked lips.

A surge of parental pride, the voice enormous in its galaxies of possibilities.

"Life. As you have never known it. Desire, as you have never known it. With me."

"How can I trust you?"

That gave Victor pause.

"I suppose you can't," he answered truthfully. "But understand that had I so desired, I could have taken you at any time."

Mick shook his head in a daze. He felt plopped into a nightmare, all sense of rhythm and linear movement lost. Scant hours ago he belonged to another lifetime. It seemed he was watching himself from a distance. He had never known such terror, or this strange calmness, in all his life.

Perhaps he had been lost from the first moment he saw this phone booth on that rainy night, waiting for him in the darkness. *Step into my lair, said the spider to the fly.* And off he had skipped.

He thought of Bobby, and his heart broke.

He felt guilty and unclean. Spoiled.

Thinking of Bobby tore at this darkness in his soul. Ideas clicked and whirled within him. Strategies. Plans.

But what it all came down to was Mick shaking his head.

"No. This is as far as we go. We played around. You got to watch me, and ... take from me. Now I'm standing here feeling so ... so..."

"I know how you feel," Victor said, his tone surprisingly gentle. "You have opened yourself to me. You are frightened — yes, frightened by the heat of your own excitement, and by what I propose. You've stepped onto a path which has no clear trail, and so you are confused. But I shall be your guide."

"What if I don't want you?" Mick blurted out. The boldness of his defiance surprised him.

"Oh, I believe you will choose life with me, after all, when you hear what I have to tell you."

Mick cocked his head. More? There is more to this madness?

"When I drank from you, just now, I saw into your heart." A pause. "You carry this new disease in you."

"W-What?" The world fell dangerously gray.

"Oh, it does not affect me," Victor continued nonchalantly. "But, so you see, even if I were to allow you life without me, you harbor this sickness within you. And it *will* take you, too, within a few of your years."

"Liar!" Mick practically spit. "You're trying to trick me. It's a lie!"

"Why should I lie? I tell you as a favor, to speed your decision."

Mick trembled uncontrollably. "Decision! I have no decision. You've taken care of that."

"Think upon my words. I am your salvation. We've no more need of this phone booth. Tomorrow, we meet in person. The confusion, the guilt will have left you by then. Replaced by the hunger."

Mick's eyes flared. Hunger?

"And together," Victor whispered, "we shall feed."

4

Darkness claims the city.

The evening tilts toward true midnight, that in-between time where day and night hang in precarious balance, each fighting for control.

From his steamy chambers He gazes out upon the sleeping city, and with an appeal to the dark heavens, sends out the dreams:

Throughout the city men toss and turn in their beds. They dream of steam, of disco music like a friend from another lifetime, and of water dripping from pipes. They see muscled flesh slick with sweat, bobbing cocks, a spread-eagled ass. They see whatever each wants to see, each to his own variation.

A playful orgy in a dimly lit room of hands cocks ass;

Men performing a striptease before an adoring naked audience;

Men in a circle, with the dreamer on his knees, taking them each into his mouth;

Others see the sort of visions that come only when inhibition sleeps, dreams of rope twisted about ankles and wrists, handcuffs, paddles. A room like a medieval dungeon, filled with exquisite toys for pleasure and pain, a shadowed Master bidding them welcome;

All of these men, these dreamers, wake with swollen cocks bursting, fountains of cum shooting across their stomachs, and in his palace He drinks it in, their ripeness, his strength.

Some chase after their dream, desiring it above all else, and to these men the shadows fly, scratching at their windows to be let in. These men are taken easily, even when they struggle and their eyes bulge with horror, scrambling backwards into their rooms. And with the new strength they leave no trace, save a knocked-over piece of furniture, or a puddle of rank water by the window.

In his palace, He is satisfied. With a rainy dawn breaking He calls the army home, and gathers them to his side. Time enough to take care of the rest.

5

One man stumbled through the night. Dazed. Weeping. He could not face home. He could not face his friend. When the fog gave way to a cold rain he let it run over him, cooling his fever. He stood for hours in an alley, peering up at a dark window. It took all his strength, all his humility, to go to the door and knock upon it. The alien voice commanded he leave, that this was pure folly, but the man bit down on his lip to draw blood so that all his attention could focus upon the bright burst of pain, and not that silky voice.

An eternity passed, waiting for the hallway light, the hesitant steps from within.

Bobby opened the door.

Mick stood there, blood a crimson slash upon his chin, his whole body soaked utterly by the rain. Impossibly pale. His eyes glowing furnaces. Hands limp at his side. His voice belonged to a wraith.

"Help me," he gasped. Tears streamed down his cheeks.

And Bobby, without saying a word, tears surprisingly hot and furious on his own cheeks, pulled Mick inside and double-locked the door.

17

Trespass

1

In bed, on the rim of sleep:
Alex thinks I'm crazy.
Maybe I am.
I've got to know more. Find out more.
I've got to be

2

Quiet.
Shh.
It's a secret, being here. Gonna take me a look.
The moist air was luxuriantly warm upon David's naked body. It caressed his torso, swirling past in almost visible eddies.

The hallway was lit with the flickering glow of torches hooked to cavern walls. Some distance away rainbow light swirled and spilled out of an opening in the wall. Watching it kindled a memory of walking into the I-Beam bar in the Haight: The disco lights saturating the dance floor would escape down the front staircase, urging him upward for his first glimpse of the dancing crowd. Oh, the promise in those kaleidoscopic lights! Would he dance all night with friends? Or would there be a face above the crowd, a man with a shy twinkle in his eyes, wanting to say hello?

The same promise, the same potential, was here in these lights. But the music issuing out the slash of doorway was absorbed by the rocky walls, robbing it of tenor and brass, reducing it all to bass. "Is There More to Life Than Dancing?" the current song.

David shook his head. Lights. Music. Caves.
Where am I?
The floor he stood upon was too smooth and cool to be the floor to a natural cave. He walked over to one of the rocky walls and stuck out his hand. Like a hard dry sponge, the wall had a slight give to it.

Curious, he padded a few feet farther and stopped to inspect one of the flickering torches. As he suspected — electric. A blue flame encased in a red glass frame.

He began to walk toward the disco lights, and the open door, when laughter cut him short. David whirled around, conscious of his nakedness, instinctively feeling that his presence here had to remain a secret.

Heartbeat pounding, he waited for the inevitable cry of alarm, of discovery.

But no; this laughter was intimate, hushed, not aimed at him at all. In the walls, he realized — there were doors, dark alcoves. He stood in front of one now and heard the "Ahhs" and "Ohhs" of men engaged in sexual contact. Their moans reached down inside his gut and awakened a ravenous hunger. The pleasant heat, the dim lights, his own nakedness, and the sounds of sex all combined to stimulate in him a lazy arousal. Like lying in bed in the morning, not quite awake but no longer asleep, a morning hard-on between his thighs. He wanted to give in to these urges suddenly, and indulge himself, but the very strangeness of his surroundings kept him alert.

David backed away from the lights and muted music, retreating to the shadows. He came upon the end of the tunnel, and a choice. A rock-slab staircase wound up, toward a whorish crimson light, and down, into a dark place where moisture hung in the air like mist from Niagara Falls.

Which way?

At the bottom of the staircase, a figure separated from the shadows. A black man, naked. With bones jutting prominently against his taut skin, he looked like a walking skeleton. The whites of his eyes were matched by dabs of paint on each cheek.

Oddly, he felt no fear of discovery from this man. And sure enough, the man raised a bony finger to his lips in that universal gesture: *Shhh*. He gestured for David to follow, turned in profile toward a whitish light, and walked through a doorway.

Who are you? David wanted to call out. His feet slapped against stone as he descended the staircase. The stones were warm, heated from below by the engine that ran this place. He could feel its vibration. His right hand brushed against the wall in search of a handrail. He grasped onto an object warm and sleek, jutting from the wall. Firm, but flexible in his hand. Several of them stuck out of the wall, spaced about a foot and a half apart, of various shapes and lengths.

Suddenly — his hand recognized what he touched. Fastened to the wall as macabre trophies, still pulsing with life: Cocks. Erections.

He jerked his hand away, recoiling, and lost his balance. His feet danced upon the steps, seeking a solid foothold and finding none.

Oh god—!

And in sickening slow motion he tumbled, hands thrust before him like a mad priest giving a benediction. He folded into a caterpillar ball and screened his face as he bounced and slammed against rock walls and floor.

He landed in a heap, air knocked from his lungs. Scraped and aching in a hundred different places. He groaned to one knee, then coaxed himself to stand. His hip hurt like bloody hell. He glanced about for the black man, his guide.

A white door sat in front of him. No, not white, glass: Clouds of steam beat against the door from the inside. A whistling rattle noise all around him, the artificial breathing of a life-support system. To his left were a row of showers, his right, a wide doorway that opened onto an impenetrable blackness.

Open the door, a whispering voice instructed. *What you seek waits inside.*

His flesh crawled. An unfocused dread squirted acid juice through his stomach. He understood, implicitly, that he had reached his destination, that this place was why he was here. Was this what the man, that walking wraith, wanted to show him?

He reached out for the wooden handle. It moved under his hand — like a snake shifting positions. He tried to ignore the blasts of panic that ran through him, warning him.

He opened the door. A billow of gauzy steam hissed out and up. David shielded his eyes with a cupped hand and stepped inside. Hot wet air rolled over him, clinging to every inch of his flesh with a pleasant stinging sensation.

He heard the voices first, a pagan chant:

(That's right baby)

(Show it off)

(Do your buddy)

(Take him)

David raised his eyes. A loosely knit group of men ringed two other men, who were performing for the crowd. The circle of bodies blocked a full view of the performing couple, but he saw two heads, one blond, the other with a short black crew cut. He edged closer for a better view.

Abruptly, he was struck by the beauty of the men. They seemed perfect ideals, not real at all. Shoulders exactly wide enough, arms ropy muscles that shook as they pumped their hard-ons. Broad backs, sloping into trim dancers' waists. No love handles on this bunch, even though some of the men in the group looked to be in their thirties and forties. Butts and thighs belonging to Olympic decathlon athletes.

Suddenly he realized: They were almost transparent, these men in the audience. As insubstantial as the steam floating up from the floor.

Not so, the two men in the center of the ring. As the crowd stepped back slightly to allow David passage, he got his first full look at the men garnering so much attention. Unlike the sculpted Adonises flanking them, these men were three-dimensional, real. He could see a smattering of freckles across the blond's shoulder blades. The rosy flush of high color as blood pumped below skin from the heat. Sweat dripping off slicked-down curls—

Wait a minute. The guy from the gym. The blond Jack had drooled over.

Mick.

Mick, the man he had inadvertently used as a model for his character in that story. Here. Why?

And his friend—?

He stared at the starched crew cut. Brown eyes. Thick mat of chest and leg hair. Solid wiry build. He had never met the man, never seen him, yet he had described him precisely as Mick's lover in his own story. This must be Bobby, the man he thought imagination alone had created.

His mind reeled. *Do I now exist in my own fiction? Or has my fiction come to life?*

"My god — are you real?"

Heads turned.

The man with the crew cut glanced away from his partner. His eyes locked with David's. A myriad of expressions — wonder, caution, interest — exploded with rapid-fire swiftness across a face too lean and angular. Was that a flash of recognition on that slightly turned face?

And David again spoke:

"Are you ... Bobby?"

The man jerked as though he'd been shot. His hand slapped against his forehead with the comic timing of a vaudeville routine. Something dark squirted out between his fingers.

That gesture, more than all that had preceded it, made David go cold with recognition. *He has a bump between his eyes—!*

He saw the man go wild with fright, staring behind David in terror.

And then—

Something leapt onto David's back and drove him to the floor. No time to even finish the thought, to digest how a man he had thought only an imaginary character seemed to be flesh and blood, and to also share his affliction of an awakening psychic eye. A rain of blows showered upon his head and shoulders. He threw up his hands for protection and snatched at whatever was squirming against him. He nabbed a tiny wrist, a clawing hand — and howled with pain as teeth sank into the fleshy pad of his own hand. He heard a chattering squawk, and then the creature sprang away.

Immediately, he rolled onto his back and sat up. His left hand screamed where he'd been bitten, an ugly row of teeth marks below his thumb.

The men were gone. A steamy fog roiled about him, obscuring the floor he sat upon. He was no longer in the steamroom but somewhere else, dark and impenetrable.

(Do not move)

growled a voice inside his head.

(Let me gaze upon my foolish trespasser)

If an animal could talk — a snake or spider, perhaps — it would own such a voice. Each hissing syllable sent chills tingling down David's spine. He was afraid to look up, to face the owner of that voice. A weight lay upon his head and shoulders — fear, wrapping him in heavy chains. *Caught. I've been caught.*

He saw calves and thighs, skin the color of polished coal. Was it a man? Yes — and no, the proportions too exaggerated, like a balloon stretched beyond normal capacity. Each thigh the size of iron posts for a building's foundation, knee joint the size of a basketball. Descending calf and foot lost in the bed of swirling white air.

Looking up, he saw nothing above the broad solid waist that served as anchor for the enormous penis dangling between the iron-post thighs. A skein of white drifted above the waist, feeding the illusion of a black giant, an Olympian with head and shoulders above the clouds.

Something nestled by the giant's foot. It squatted on its haunches, one hand wrapped adoringly about his master's calf. A tangled mass of black hair writhed above a sooty face whose only set of features seemed to be a pair of eyes and red swollen mouth. A wicked grin twitched on the full lips, as if the creature had forgotten how to smile but was producing the best facsimile it could muster. A puppy dog's tongue popped and lolled out of the mouth, licking its chops with anticipation.

It was a boy.

A Spanish boy of no more than ten or twelve.

Revulsion overpowered David's senses. A child! Here!

A hand the size of a cast-iron skillet dropped from the obscuring mist and pawed at the boy's head. Each finger seemed a foot long, raking the hair like a crab skittering along through seaweed.

The animal voice again, obscenely close, a rape:

(What's the matter? Don't you approve of my pet?)

And with each pat of hand upon head, the boy began to change. Humanness softened, like heated wax, and dripped away. Skin bubbled and cracked, blackening. Something grotesque appeared in the boy's place, an apparition foreign to rhyme or reason. Part chimpanzee. Part bat. Mulish snout and ears. He transformed into something vaguely resembling one of the wicked witch's flying monkeys.

"Stop it!" David shouted. He had been unable to speak for himself, could not voice his own terror at his fate, but he found he could at least speak up for one so innocent, changed so horribly into this abomination.

"Stop it! Stop it!" mimicked the monkey boy. He licked between the fingers the hand that had transformed him so.

Crushed by confusion, horror: "Why are you doing this!" David gasped.

A bully's reply:

(Because I can)

"Who are you?"

"Who are you? Who are you?" squealed the impish boy. He bounced and bobbed.

And the reply, like a cobra's lunge of venomous fangs:

(Your *future,* healer. I am your future!)

Nothing educated in that voice. Disaster. Rage. An implacable steamroller. A voice as black as a pit in the earth. David flattened against its fury, his head tucked, quaking.

(See?)

gloated the giant.

(You have no power here)

The boy, gibbering with insane delight, pointing: "See how he shakes! How he trembles! Victor—"

But that was as far as the boy got before the hooked fingernail slit his chest with a scalpel's precision. The huge hand knocked the wretched boy from his post and sent him sprawling. The chest zippered open with a wet explosion; tiny fists scrambled to halt the flood of innards. Peals of terror and pain.

And from the giant, a violent rage so terrible steam spontaneously erupted from all directions at once. The heat was stifling.

(Silence, pup—!)

But too late. Damage done.

David burned with knowledge. He cloaked himself with it as a shield against this dragon's fire. Pointed at the giant in triumph:

"He has revealed you — *Victor!*"

The impish boy, on his feet now, the geometry of his chest rearranged and somehow sewn together: "Didn't tell! I won't tell! Forgive! Forgive!"

A roar filled David's ears. A wind with a banshee wail slammed into him—

3

—and he catapulted awake upon his own bed, sheets drenched from his sweat, the dragon's frustrated howl blasting inside his head. David rolled onto his belly, head poking over the rim of mattress, and promptly threw up, retching the awful dream place out of himself.

4

A gray dawn.

Wind-whipped rain tattooing the window.

He'd stopped shaking, finally. Comforted by the fragile dawn breaking outside.

Every muscle in his body ached, their dull pain a testament to the reality of his dream journey.

A victory, with the morning light. Somehow he'd trespassed, actually been in that dampness, gotten too close, punctured an enemy's world. And learned two secrets.

Mick. The man from the gym. He was definitely caught up in this, a player of some kind in this deadly game. So, it *had* been Mick he'd seen at the bus stop. Acting out the scenario he'd written in his story.

Which brought him to Bobby. *If* the man with the crew cut was Bobby. If the characters from his story were real ... That swollen bump on the man's forehead had certainly seemed real enough. Were he and this Bobby somehow ... connected? Could that explain why he'd written their story so easily, so effortlessly — because they shared this strange affliction?

David frowned. These men — if they were, in fact, real — were strangers to him. He knew nothing of their personal lives. Was there some kind of psychic bridge being forged between them?

Questions. So many questions.

One answered, though. The Grand Prize.

The enemy had a name, and his name was Victor.

Worth the terror of the dream, to own that knowledge. For it seemed to anger the thing to have its name revealed.

With a groan, he hobbled into the kitchen and made a pot of coffee. His hip complained. He studied his left hand where the boy had bitten him, and he could see a faint outline of the boy's teeth. With a shudder, he recalled the giant's exact words:

Your future, healer. I am your future.

You have no power here.

He dragged out his journal notebook and returned to bed. With blankets wrapped comfortably around him, his back propped with pillows against the headboard, and a cup of coffee in one hand, he flipped the pages to his entry of just a few hours earlier. It could have been written in another century. He picked up a pen.

...Last night, all that mattered was getting Alex Webster onto my side. I wanted to convert him over to my beliefs as a way of wrestling my own doubts, and quieting them. I'd needed him to say, "I believe you. You aren't crazy."

But he didn't say that. If anything, this is exactly what he believes. And to my great relief and astonishment this morning, I've discovered it no longer matters.

For you see, I've seen inside the monster's home, and I believe. I went there, somehow, in a dream. His name is Victor. His arrival — it's like it created an echo inside me and awakened this ... this ... ability inside me. Self-preservation, perhaps. Is this any different from a mother suddenly possessed of superhuman strength who lifts a car off her injured child? In the face of danger, the impossible is oftentimes born. And if I can grasp one truth out of all this, it is this: I am in danger.

I have to trust this power implicitly. Allow it to guide me.

For I think there are others. Others who are in danger, and fighting. Mick. Bobby.

And the woman. She may be real as well.

I have to find them, all of them.

Before dark, before the creature can attack me once again.

18

Walls of Jericho

1

The first phone call was easy.

"He's come down with the flu," Bobby said. "A temperature of 101 degrees. I'm taking him to Kaiser later this morning."

That last bit about a hospital was a lie — but what did the secretary need to know? Bobby sat wrapped in his robe at the kitchen table, a steaming cup of coffee in one hand. Every few minutes he angled his head toward the bedroom, where Mick slept.

"Well," grumbled the secretary with an Ernestine whine, "This is terribly short notice. We have a board meeting in half an hour." She let go a long-suffering sigh. "I suppose we still have time to call in a temp. Mick did seem under the weather yesterday."

Bobby's ear's pricked up. "He did? In what way?"

"I'm not sure I can say," she said, becoming irritatingly vague as she held his full attention. "He wasn't sneezing or coughing. No real signs of a flu, if you know what I mean. But he had no attention span. Talked to you like you weren't actually there. Maybe he'd taken a couple of decongestants," she added, trying to be helpful. A buzz from another line. "Anything else?"

"No, no; that's okay. Just wanted to let you know Mick wasn't coming in today. Thanks for your help."

He hung up. Whistled a sigh. One down. One to go.

His boss was not so accommodating.

"We need you today," Mr. Chesley barked when given the news. "I have to have fifty copies of the Concord report collated, boxed, and shipped out by one p.m. I need *you*. And you say you can't come in because you're playing nursemaid to a sick boyfriend? What kind of horseshit is this?"

Bobby shut his eyes. For $5.50 an hour he should have such grief.

"Truth is, I'm not feeling so great myself." His fingers skimmed the tender spot between his eyes. "Look. I know it's a busy Friday, but this is an emergency. When's the last time I missed a day of work, huh?"

Back and forth they went. Finally, a compromise. He would come in and work from ten until one, making sure the Concord reports made it out the door. He wasn't thrilled with the arrangement, but it was the best he could wrangle under such short notice.

He hung up the phone and listened to the silence of his apartment. Rain droned against the skylight above the kitchen. A gray dawn. Gray morning. Gray day. The kind of day where he wanted to crawl back under the covers and sleep it away. Or watch game shows and soaps until they blended one into another, all boundaries gone.

Boundaries. A good word.

Boundaries meant a beginning and an end. Borders. Definitions. Do not cross this line for fear of losing all marbles. Trespass this border, face the consequences. The world mapped itself with territories and zones. Good thing, most times.

What happens when that boundary is stretched to the limit? What happens when the preposterous smacks up against reality?

Moans from the bedroom.

Bobby lurched away from the kitchen table, splashing coffee in the process. Cursing his clumsiness, he darted to the bedroom doorway and took a look.

Mick stirred beneath the blankets. His head tossed side to side, eyes rolling beneath tightly shut lids. Asleep. A dream, Bobby thought, watching. He's having a

nightmare.

An involuntary shudder went through him. For the umpteenth time, his own nightmare from last night reared across his vision. No good to push it down, not when he stood scrutinizing Mick asleep, knowing that Mick's condition and his own strange dream were tangled, somehow.

It had dominated his thoughts since waking, and once again it spun its familiar tale:

He and Mick stood in the center of what seemed to be some sort of steamroom. The warm air around them was wildly erotic. Words from an old Diana Ross song echoed overhead with a dreamy sluggishness:

If there's a cure for this, I don't want it, don't want it...

Steam rose from the floor, cocooning them with its feather-light touch. Mick's nimble fingers danced across his nakedness. Bobby glanced away from his lover and was surprised to discover they were surrounded by men, the kind of astonishingly beautiful men who filled the glossy pages of *Advocate Men* and *Torso* and *Inches*. All tantalizingly real, just a few feet away. They stroked themselves unhurriedly, enjoying this show with Mick and Bobby in the center ring. Their murmurs of approval excited Bobby, but it was Mick who had never appeared more desirable. Sweat dripped freely from his crown of blond curls. A broad smile stretched his face, and when Mick laughed, it sent a shower of water bullets thrown from his hair. With a pang for what once was, he remembered: This was how Mick had looked the night they met, dancing across from him at the I-Beam.

"Don't be shy," Mick said to him. He clasped Bobby's hands into his own and brought them to rest at each plum-colored nipple on Mick's smooth chest. He urged Bobby's fingers to explore and awaken.

Whispered voices around them:

(Do your buddy)

(Show it off)

(That's right baby)

Bobby needed no encouragement. He ran his fingers over the gym-toned muscles of his lover's chest. Felt the satisfying fullness of his erection growing long and heavy. A hand feather-brushed the curve of his ass and swam down his thighs, his calves. The men were closing in, moving with the synchronized grace of an underwater ballet as they jerked themselves off and encouraged the lovers with their touch.

Somewhere, a door opened.

Bobby didn't bother to look. If someone else wanted to join them, fine. And he wouldn't have looked, not ever, except for the voice that cut through the steam with its icicle shock: "My god — are you real?"

He had never seen the tall, dark-haired man who stared at him and Mick as though they were a cartoon that had come to life. The sleek face, full jaw, green eyes (yes, even in this dream he saw them, two emeralds in a sea of gray) were unknown to him. And yet. Familiar ... He stared across the void at the man.

And heard him ask:

"Are you ... Bobby?"

Suddenly — a staggering pain in his forehead. A spear driven between his eyes. He yelped with agony and slapped a hand to his head as though it could stem this sudden tide of pain. Between his fingers — oh god, no! — blood!

What happened next was a blur.

Something jumped onto the stranger's back and drove him to the floor. Bobby caught a swift shape — it looked like a midget, small and wild and brown. It pounced onto the man with a warrior's fiendish cry, tiny fists pummeling, then both vanished with a billow of steam and exclamations.

The men shrieked and scattered, like monkeys fighting for territory.

Mick pulled away. Bobby tilted his head in puzzlement, then glanced back to where the man with the green eyes had just been standing. A new figure had appeared there. It seemed to just rear up from the floor, as if the steam had rushed to fill an invisible container of dark and polluted water. The sight of this giant struck terror into his heart. Suddenly hands pinned him from behind, and chains were thrown about his wrists.

"Hey!" he cried. "What's going on?"

A jet blast of steam squirted him full in the face. He gagged and shut his eyes against the searing of his flesh. Blind terror now. "Mick! Help me!"

A terrible laugh, icy in all this steam.

He squinted open his eyes. Mick was walking toward the dark man as though swimming through mercury. An odd bewitching smile sat upon his lips. The giant raised one arm and his lover slipped into the shadow below it, enfolded in a voluminous cape. He dropped the arm. Mick was gone.

Now the real nightmare began as the figure moved to greet him. Bobby shrank against his chains and tried to pull away. Was it human, this man drawing near? With each step toward him the features melted and blurred, like tallow wax exposed to flame. Black skin bubbled and oozed, cracking open to rearrange its very geometry. The harder he tried to make sense of its features, the more alien it became. It settled into something leathery and vaguely reptilian, a gargoyle statue come to life. Red eyes blazed at him. A slit of mouth creaked open, pink tongue darting, before splitting into a grin. Bobby went cold with recognition.

"No," he gasped, remembering the night of the storm, the figure out in the alley, staring up at his window in challenge. Here was the Cheshire Cat grin, once again.

And suddenly a torrent of hate, words spit at him like a ghastly stream of vomit:

(Mick is mine. You can't have him and now I'm going to have you!)

"Get away from me!"

A strange current thrummed through his bowels. Bobby, aghast, felt his limp penis spring to attention. He was sick with excitement. The creature sank in front of him, drawing back livery lips to bare fangs like something out of a comic book. A gnarled paw snaked forward, grabbing his balls with the strength to rip them clean off, and twisted cruelly.

(Worship me)

he snarled.

Bobby shook his head. The steam had found his tender nasal cavities. Star-blinding pain with each inhalation.

Defiantly: "Never."

(Then Mick is mine)

the giant bellowed

(And you're no boyfriend *at all!*)

Claws hooked into his testicles. Tears of pain exploded out of Bobby's eyes. Before he knew what was happening, his genitals were ripped free with a gush of blood—

—Only it wasn't blood, after all, but his own swollen cock erupting across his stomach.

He had shot awake in bed, sheathed in sour perspiration, as nausea claimed him. He'd had to grip the side of the mattress and will himself not to be sick. In those seconds before his eyes adjusted to the darkness of his room, he'd thought he was still trapped in the bowels of that terrifying place, the warm liquid ribboning his stomach blood from his own castration.

Only then had he noticed the stickiness dripping into his eyes.

Blood. *Real* blood, from the painful pimple that had swelled and ached like a motherfucker the night before.

He'd gone to the bathroom, shocked by his haggard appearance in the mirror, and cleaned himself up. Allowed the real world to filter into his consciousness bit by bit as he pushed the dream away.

As he pushed it away now.

Bobby shook his head. Scary, the hold that nightmare had on him. Even now his intestines froze at the thought of it.

He stared at the prone figure of his lover, head buried beneath the pillow as though even in his sleep Mick sought to keep out unfriendly whispers. They would have to talk soon, before he left for work. Mick shouldn't wake up alone to an empty apartment. No telling what he might do.

Besides, he had questions. Lots of them.

Mick had been impossible the night before. Delirious with fever. Muttering about some kind of monster who was tricking him. He had wanted to laugh, but you don't laugh when your lover comes pounding on your door half-crazed at three a.m.

No wonder he had such a nightmare last night, what with all these unresolved questions swirling in his head. Mick's evasive behavior. The excuses. The lies. That story about the phone booth, and a "friend." All laced together with patchwork images of glowing crosses and a lightning-lit alley. And that *headache* from this pimple or bump or whatever the hell it was; the more he worried about Mick, the worse the pain had become. At least this morning his forehead had settled back to normal, even though the spot still ached dully. Perhaps the headache bore as much responsibility for his nightmare as his un-spoken worries. But to have a wet dream on top of a nightmare? Why, it was just like

the dream Mick had had!

Bobby thought all at once, the dream where men tried to get in through the window.

Blood pulsed in his ears.

The walls of the apartment leaned toward him.

"Dear god," Bobby muttered. "Dear god in heaven."

His legs wobbled, seeking refuge from their task. Careful not to disturb Mick, he slid into bed and leaned against the headboard. Listened to the rain.

What's it mean?

What could it possibly all mean?

A sound like lightning and thunder in his head. No: It was the boundaries of reality, as they cracked and crumbled.

19

Crazy animals

1

"**Y**ou're not going to believe this," his friend Harry wheezed, plopping down two styrofoam cups of coffee onto the desk.

Alex doctored his coffee until it was candy sweet and leaned back in his chair. "So tell me," he said, forcing his voice to stay calm. "What made last night so special?"

Harry held up a finger for patience and clicked on the computer terminal directly in front of them. He was a huge burly man, shiny as a newly minted penny on the top of his head, with bushy Albert Einstein eyebrows and a thick walrus mustache that completely camouflaged his upper lip. His bulk overflowed the tiny computer chair he occupied, devouring it like some sort of circus clown balanced on a unicycle. Harry had ten years' seniority on Alex, and while he might appear buffoonish, when it came to tracking down missing persons he was one of the best.

He was also a buddy of Alex's, and owed him a favor.

"First, let me ask you a question," Harry began. He gulped his coffee and pointed to the terminal. "Every day I'm fed information about missing persons. Ninety percent of the names that pop up on that screen are runaways. Teenagers. Kids from Fresno who hightail it to the Big City. You know the types. But every blue moon, the statistics change."

"Did they change last night?"

Harry shrugged. "Too early to tell. You know as well as I do that a person isn't classified as missing until after forty-eight hours."

Alex leaned forward. He was beginning to sweat. "Something happened?"

Harry frowned. "I'll know for sure tomorrow, when we go official. But let me ask you." And here his voice dropped in pitch, as though embarrassed by what he had to confess. "Have you heard any rumors — or seen anything odd — when you've been out on patrols in some of the neighborhoods?"

A cool chill whispered across the back of Alex's neck. He had to ask. "What do you mean, Harry? Which neighborhoods?"

Harry blushed. Two hundred and forty pounds, and the man blushed. "You know. In the Castro. Or Polk Street. The gay neighborhoods."

Despite the beginnings of dread working within him, Alex smiled inwardly. Harry had lived in San Francisco twenty-four years, but getting him to say the word "gay" required a pair of pliers.

Harry was waiting for an answer. Alex nodded. "I've heard a few rumors, if you want the truth. I'm working on a couple of cases. And keeping my ear to the ground to hear of any more."

Harry downed the last of his coffee and grimaced — perhaps from the coffee, perhaps from what he had to say. "You don't have to put your ear to the ground." He patted his chest and managed a sour smile. "You can hear it straight from the horse's mouth."

"What are you saying?"

Harry crooked a finger. He dropped his voice to a whisper. "Between you and me?"

Alex nodded.

"None of it's official until tomorrow, understand. Maybe one or two will show up by then. But I've received some pretty weird phone calls this morning. Distraught roommates. Boyfriends."

"What's happened?" Though he knew. Of course he knew. The sweat on his brow told him.

Harry snapped his fingers, the set of his round face grim. "Eight men. Gone. All — you know — homosexuals. Vanished without a thank-you or a good-bye."

2

Back at his own desk, Alex stared at the pile of manila folders in front of him. He was sweating heavily now, his blue cotton shirt a wet rag.

Belief.

It poked him in his ribs. Dared him to reach down and grasp its truth.

Where he came from, in West Texas, belief was what you saw with your own eyes, wrestled with your own hands. Not this slippery fish of an answer that demanded he check his disbelief in favor of what stared him in the face.

David, at his front door, had warned him more men might be in trouble.

Had that prophesy come true? And if he let himself believe that much, if he allowed that inkling of truth to seep in — then what of his dream?

Alex fanned out the folders like a game of solitaire across his desk. They contained every man, woman, and child who had disappeared in the last two weeks — and god in heaven, there were too many of them. So far, at least, he could rule out the missing women, and all of the kids appeared to be runaways except for that Spanish kid, Miguel Garza. And there was the fact that he lived south of Market.

Like Jack Martin.

A warning bell inside Alex's head: *Leave it alone. Last night was a dream. Period.*

But he couldn't leave it alone. He was after the truth, wasn't he?

He picked up Jack Martin's folder. Opened it to the photograph of the average face, the inviting smile on lips too full for cheeks so angular. He held the photograph between fingers that shook ever so noticeably. Stiff brown hair rounded out a face stubbornly bland and innocuous, a face determined to blend into any crowd, void of any special features.

Yet it was Jack Martin's very ordinariness that burned into him. Because he ... Because he...

Dreams could be senseless things.

The subconscious tapped into everything, mixing real life with fancy and emotion, all poured into the grist mill of dream logic. No telling what would spit out...

3

Tapping at the window. That's what spit out for Alex in the flat dead darkness of early morning before dawn. He'd awakened. Sat up on one arm and peered toward his shuttered bedroom window. And heard the most delicious moanings, the cooing of some fantastic plumed bird.

Ah, what had smiled at him as he peered through the wooden slats of his shutters! Unembarrassed by his nakedness, he boldly drew them back for a look.

You don't greet an angel with a roaring hard-on, but since Alex had never met an angel before he hoped she'd excuse any lapse of good manners. It helped that she was naked as well, shoulder-length hair silver, voluptuous skin the finest mother-of-pearl color he'd ever laid eyes on. Her eyes flashed blue sparks, ruby lips a Marilyn Monroe pout. One slender hand caressed her breasts with intimate knowledge. The air behind her all but glowed, haloing her, and he decided it was her hummingbird wings, fanning the night air — after all, they were four stories up. Something held her aloft.

And her voice, chiding at his astonishment which held him rooted to the spot, yet layered with urgent desire:

(Open the window, my lover. Let me in)

A moment of hesitation. Self-consciousness at last: his bobbing erection, mushroom cap swollen pink.

Her eyes fastened upon this prize, and she responded to his downcast bashfulness by gliding a hand through the silver forest sprouting between her creamy thighs. Wet with anticipation.

(I, too, my lover — I too)

The window thrown open. She blew in as though a curtain gusted by a wind, settling like a delicate scarf upon his bed. Her amusement rich, bubbling from some secret core. One hand roamed her exquisite features, teasing him with her display, her ripeness.

And Alex himself seemed to fly as he swooped toward this angel and sank into her flesh. Oh god! Wonder of wonders! An explosion of lust and desire so all-consuming that any reality — which should have warned him he was awake, *awake* — splintered into a thousand shards.

She bucked against him. Met his urgent thrusts with little gasps of pleasure. Her cool fingers combed the sprinkle of hair across his shoulder blades and the thick patch above his ass. Clutching him with the desperation of her own need.

Her hair — a sea of silver across the pillow.

Her eyes — fantastic jewels, reflecting back his own heat and desire.

They fell into perfect rhythm, a harmony rarely achieved yet fiercely sought after, Alex groaning in syncopation with her hot breath upon his ear. A fine sweat oiled their lovemaking.

(Darling—)

"Oh god—"

The crest reached much too quickly, carrying him up onto a swell of indescribable pleasure. Her fingers dug into his flesh. He lifted his head so that he might see their imminent climax reflected in her eyes—

He felt her clamp down hard on his spurting cock, so that he couldn't pull out and away.

And with a sickening crack, her head split open.

She cracked as though her shell of skin was no more substantial than a fortune cookie. It steamed off of her with a liquid gush, like some kind of trick photography in a B-grade movie.

Horrified and repulsed, Alex choked on his scream.

Another face reared up out of that pulpy mass that was her face, shoving itself against him, wet tongue stuffed into his mouth to stifle his cry of revulsion with a kiss.

He whipped his head to the side, disengaging the foul tongue from his mouth, gagging. He stared into the face that had been his angel — his eyes popping open like window shades snapped wide. *No! It can't be!*

Jack Martin.

Jack Martin, with a face slimy with god-awful goo, but still him, unmistakably him, his body pressed against Alex like a wet glove, an asshole now clamped tight around his erection. A schoolboy's giggle at the prank, this trap executed without a hitch.

A leer, Jimmy Cagney style:

(You wanted to find me, copper — here I am!)

Alex pitched violently onto his side. Heard a wet plop as he freed his penis from that hot canal. The force of his roll hurled him over the side of his bed. He landed on his hipbone and elbow with a painful crunch, then rolled onto his back, stars exploding in his eyes.

(Next time, copper! Next time!)

Even with the taunt, he stayed where he was, unable to move. Hyperventilating. He felt drained and sick. Sweat streamed out of every pore on his body.

An infinity passed before he dared himself to look. The silence of the bedroom mocked him as he hoisted himself to a sitting position and peered over the edge of mattress—

—and saw only the familiar: Pillows. Sheets. Bedspread kicked back.

Eyes snapped to the window.

Shutters: sensibly drawn shut.

He dragged himself to the bathroom, dizzy and reeking with perspiration. Determined to wash himself clean. He flipped on the shower and stepped under the massaging spray of water.

By the time he'd stepped out of the shower, he'd washed the dream away too.

Crazy animals, dreams were. What else could it be?

4

And Alex, at his desk, answered himself:

What else could it be — except some living nightmare from David Walker's delusions come to attack me, me!

He sighed wearily and pushed the stack of folders to the side of his desk.

Maybe it was worth a phone call. Patch up any hard feelings about his abrupt departure from David's flat last night — although David had been too dazed and disoriented over his vision (or whatever the hell it had been) to be upset about his taking leave. He took out a scrap of paper from his wallet, read David's phone number, and dialed.

On the third ring, the answering machine.

"Just wanted to touch bases again," Alex said airily after David's message. "Give me a call when you get in, okay?"

An hour later, and still no David.

"Look," Alex said, "I'm sorry I wasn't responsive to what you said last night. Can we give it another try? There's a few things I want to tell you. So give me a call at the station, would you? I'm ready to talk. Ready to listen. So if you don't call me back within the hour, I swear to god I'm gonna come find *you.*"

5

The hour came. And went.

Where the fuck can he be, on such a rainy afternoon?

Alex began to have his own visions: a torn-up apartment, walls and furniture soaked, and no trace of David, not a single trace...

Oh, it was crazy, all of it.

He yanked on his jacket, dug for his car keys, and ignored the startled expressions of his fellow officers as he hurried through the lobby to his car.

20

Tricks, no treat

B

1

obby tells him, "I'll finish up at the shop just as fast as I can. You'll be fine. I'll call every hour—"

Mick's hand shoots out from underneath the bed covers. For someone so weak, a fierce grip. "Don't leave me alone. Please. Can't you get out of work?"

Bobby shakes his head, but adds as consolation: "I'll call—"

"No!" Terror dances behind the feverish eyes. "No more phone calls. I wouldn't know ... I mean ... if it was you or..." Mick recoils into the pillow, as if willing himself to disappear.

A deal is struck. Bobby will let the phone ring once, hang up, and dial again. Mick is to stay in bed, doors locked, windows latched.

The hour grows late. Another ten minutes, and a definite chewing out from the boss. Still, Bobby hesitates as he sits beside Mick on the bed. So many questions between them, saturating their silence. He cradles Mick's hand and sighs. *This* gesture says what needs to be said; the questions, the doubts, can wait.

Mick is looking at him. "I'm so sorry," he whispers. "I never meant—"

"Hush. Get some sleep."

A squeeze of the hand. "Bobby?"

"Yes?"

"Don't let him get me."

Bobby tenses. Him, again. The one who did this to Mick, frightened him so. This man with the name like a conqueror: Victor. Anger percolates below his surface calm. He holds it in check, where it simmers, waiting. Not now. Later. Later.

"I promise, Mick. I swear."

But how hollow his words, as he prepares to leave. He lingers at the bedroom door, watching Mick toss and turn with fitful sleep. His beautiful, beautiful lover, desired by so many with his perfect gym-muscled body, handsome strong face — Mick, reduced to a cowering child, hiding under the sheets. Turning away from him, bolting the front door: These actions require more strength than ever he imagined.

One insidious fear flashes neon-bright:

That he might never see Mick again.

2

He is companion to the King.

Men kneel before him. He is paid tribute, respected. He has his choice of any in their domain; the Master is not a jealous creature. Here, in this kingdom, he is revered, for he is the only one who can move about in daylight as well as darkness. He has been infused with the Gift. His strength is of ten men. When they are finished with this place, when the Master has had his fill and destroyed their enemies, only the two of them will move on together. The rest shall finish out their purgatory in the palace.

They will travel to other cities, and wait, until all proper conditions are met. As with this city, they will not have to wait long. There is always a weakness, an opening. It signals the Master much like the scent of quarry, running with the currents of the sky. No one can be claimed who does not wish it so.

Mick knows this, for he has been shown. Images of where the Master has been flicker like home movies across a screen in his mind:

On a water-starved caravan crossing a vast desert.

In an Egyptian kingdom in flames from a conquering tribe.

In the bowels of a slave ship, somewhere on the Atlantic.

In London, amid the stench of unburied bodies.

Too much, these images, these histories: too much. Mick tosses in his sleep. The scenes evaporate, replaced by a whisper:

(Come to me if you want to live)

One voice. Urging.

A phone booth. Ringing.

It's—

3

Ringing.

Mick bolted upright. He was sheathed in sweat, heartbeat a wild drum in his chest. Something vile in his dreams. He snatched at it, willing himself to remember, knowing he had glimpsed a terrible truth, but the ringing scattered the images, blew them apart.

Ringing.

It was the phone beside the bed.

He stared at it with tribulation. Had it rung once, while he was asleep? Was this Bobby? Tentatively, he lifted the receiver to his ear.

A frantic voice from the other end: "Mick? Is that you?"

Relief! Mick sank against the pillows. "Bobby. Thank god it's you."

"What's happened? What's wrong?"

"N-Nothing. I was asleep. I didn't know if I'd missed our code, or..." He closed his eyes. "Please come home."

"Soon. I promise. I'm working my ass off to finish. You just stay put. Understand?"

"I'm not going anywhere."

"I love you, Mick."

"I love you too."

But as Mick hung up the phone, a whisper, the only remnant of his dream:

(Come to me if you want to live)

He listened to the steady drum of rain outside his window, letting it lull him. He tried to fall back to sleep, but couldn't get comfortable. His body ached. His feet ached. Mick reached below the sheets and grasped his right foot, intending to give it a quick massage.

And was swallowed by a wave of horror so powerful he numbed with disbelief.

He had to see for himself what his fingers telegraphed, but it required all the courage he could muster to draw back the sheets, and take a look.

Ah, the reason for his aches:

Between his toes, his elongated, flattened-out toes: webbing.

Skin had grown like soft putty, as though he was in the process of transformation, feet flattening into something part animal, part man.

And on that rainy late morning, alone in the locked apartment, no one answered Mick's anguished cries, drowned out by the falling rain.

4

But David heard them.

Mick's shocked cries blasted through him like a radio station switched on inside his head, raw and purple, the color of absolute panic — and then just as quickly faded away with the glitter of dim stars.

"Hey — are you sick?"

David glanced at the muscle boy behind the counter and wearily shook his head.

"I don't need anyone going sick on me, know what I mean? So if you're gonna throw up or—"

"No." David held up a hand and offered a plastic smile. "I'm fine. Just — look in your computer, would you?"

"Last name?"

"Uh — I don't remember it. I'm trying to find out if you've seen him the past couple of days."

A smirk. "You realize how many men come to our gym?"

"You'd remember Mick. Real handsome. About my height, five-ten, eleven. Curly blond hair. Wide forehead and high cheekbones."

Another smirk. "Those aren't the kind of cheekbones *I* notice."

David bit back the urge to tell this silly queen to go fuck herself.

From the doorway: "I remember him."

David lit up. "Mick? You a friend of his?"

The tall, red-haired instructor shook his head. "Naw. But occasionally we spot each other on the bench press."

"Have you seen him around here? I think he's in a bit of trouble." *Like right at this moment,* David thought. "And I can help."

The instructor stroked his chin. "Come to think of it: No. Haven't seen him in a week, almost. He usually shows up on his lunch hour and then finishes his workout after six, when he's off work."

"Would you do me a favor and look up Mick's last name in your computer?"

A furrowed frown. "You said you were a friend."

David dipped his head in mock modesty. "He's got a boyfriend, see, and well — Mick didn't give me a last name or a telephone number."

It was the wrong tactic. The redhead shrugged apologetically. "I wouldn't get tangled up in family affairs, if I were you. And as for our computer, we can't look anyone up with just a first name. Even if we could, I wouldn't give it to you. You're just going to have to wait until you bump into him here. But as I said — I haven't seen him all week."

"Okay." Shit. "Thanks anyway."

David turned to leave.

The twinkie behind the counter began to punch buttons on the stereo. "What the fuck?"

The redhead chimed in: "Is this song on the tape? Where'd it come from?"

Too engrossed with his mission, David hadn't paid attention to the steady drone of music played for the benefit of the men on the workout floor. As he zippered his jacket and readied his umbrella to face the misty leaden afternoon, he recognized the old disco tune:

> Burn, baby, burn
> It's a disco inferno

The twinkie said: "What a stupid-ass song."

The redhead pushed him aside. "Leave it alone. I remember this one. I used to dance to it at the Troc."

> Burn, baby, burn
> Burning down the house y'all

"But it's not on the tape!" protested the twinkie.

"It has to be, you idiot!"

Not any more it doesn't, David thought — and he was out the door, leaving them to their confusion.

5

The car slammed on its brakes, horn blaring.

Bobby leapt back onto the curb.

Shit! Pay attention! Do you want to get killed?

The driver of the Pontiac shot him the finger and sped down Mission Street with a wet squeal of tires. *Smart. Really smart. Keep this up Bobby boy, and they'll be peeling your body off the cement. That would really help Mick, now wouldn't it?*

Mick.

His senses cleared. Home. He wanted to get home. Fast.

Because something very strange was afoot, and not just with Mick.

At work, the oddest thing...

He'd loaded all three hundred and twenty-two pages of the Concord report into the high-speed copier. Plopped himself down at his nearby desk to keep an eye out for any trouble as the machine went to work. He'd grabbed a yellow note pad and pen, intending to jot down a follow-up list for the reports. Instead, his worries had interfered. His hand had moved across the paper sketching pictures — an old habit from his school days, a method of keeping himself busy while he nursed worries and fears.

He drew a flaming torch hooked to a cavern wall.

A pyramid, with light rays streaking out in all directions.

A grass hut sitting under a canopy of stars.

A box with lettered keys on it. A man who sat beside it.

And underneath the figure, he'd scribbled the initials: D.W.

A weird tremor, as Bobby stared at the figure he'd drawn.

Then he saw him again, the man with the green eyes from his dream: *Are you Bobby?*

Suddenly the copy machine jammed, crumpling several pages in the process. Bobby tossed aside his note pad and settled into the painstaking process of running handfuls of pages at a time. Pulled all twenty-four finished copies from the racks and repeated the whole process all over again — he needed fifty copies. Then: Three-hole punching the paper for binding. Double-checking pagination and graphics.

The minutes ticking away, ticking.

No time for lunch.

Finally, the reports all packed up, shipped UPS.

When the reports went out the door at two-fifty, so did he.

The driving rain of that morning had slackened to a heavy mist. Gusting winds wrenched at his umbrella, threatening to turn it inside out. He hugged it against his body and walked as fast as the wind allowed. His thoughts matched the wild wind. His phone call to Mick had done nothing to alleviate his mounting fears. What they needed was an honest heart-to-heart, all cards laid on the table. Find out who had scared Mick so badly, and decide on a course of action.

And as Bobby crept home he couldn't help but notice how much like twilight the afternoon had become under the rainy gloom. How in a few scant hours true darkness would reign.

He hugged the umbrella close, his feet rhythmically slapping wet pavement. Lost to the daydreamy quality of his thoughts. And when he absently glanced up from the sidewalk, his stomach pitched forward in a high-dive somersault.

One block away stood the dilapidated bus stop awning and old-fashioned phone booth. It's presence was so commonplace as to render it almost invisible. Yet this is where it had started for Mick, blocks from the safety of Bobby's apartment.

I was waiting for the 19 Polk. Minding my own business. I looked down the street. And it called to me, somehow.

As it now called to Bobby.

He had walked past his own street — right past Tehama, lost in reverie. The phone booth sat in mute defiance, daring him to come closer.

A fucking phone booth can't *dare* — or so he told himself — but there was no shaking off this undeniable curiosity. The wheels of thought began to turn as a scheme entered his head. Five minutes. A quick look around, that's all. Maybe he'd find evidence, something tangible he could give to the police to help track this guy down. Something tangible so *he* could believe. Accusations and fears were one thing. Proof, concrete proof: What a difference that would make.

His feet began to move.

I was afraid to tell you, Bobby. Embarrassed. I'm sorry I lied to you, and said it happened to a friend. I thought I could control this guy. Have some harmless fun, and forget about him. But the moment that phone rang, I was lost...

No one stood at the bus stop. No one waited for the 19 Polk. Of course, this particular area south of Market was not close to any of the hotbeds of activity; most of the nightclubs were several blocks away, as were local businesses. This was a quiet, rather sad residential stretch of sagging Victorians and hollowed-out buildings long abandoned.

A queer chill rippled through him as he approached the booth. It stood patient as a Venus's-flytrap, waiting. *Step inside. Step inside...*

Up close, it was certainly commonplace enough. Ignoring the green awning and bench of the bus stop, Bobby walked directly up to the booth. He touched the glass. It was cool to his touch, streaked with muddy grime from traffic.

Perfectly ordinary.

Yet his heart jackhammered in his chest. Blood sang through his veins with an almost audible hiss. His nerves sparked with anxiety — and he hadn't even stepped inside the booth.

He closed his umbrella, pushed open the folding door, and stepped inside. A stale urine smell assaulted his nostrils. He spun around in a clockwise turn, taking in the claustrophobic confines of the booth with a cursory glance. All maddeningly ordinary. Nothing to suggest anything unusual, except for the tingle of his nerve endings shouting: danger. What had he expected?

The phone to ring?

That was his answer, when he cut to the bone of his suspicions: He wanted the phone to ring. He wanted to hear the voice that had worked such a dark spell on Mick. Challenge it. Laugh at it. He wanted to outwit. Outsmart. Conquer.

He looked at the phone.

Nothing.

Of course nothing — this guy only comes out at night, right?

Bobby sighed with resignation. His heartbeat returned to normal. This was silly. *Silly.* He'd promised Mick he'd return home early, and look at him, wasting valuable time in this most unlikely of places. Mick was waiting for him. He was afraid. He was

alone.

Suddenly the phone booth door snapped shut. Bobby eyed it in stunned fascination.

What the—?

He reached for the metal door handle — and jerked back with a yelp of pain. He stared at the fingers of his right hand. Three blisters were already rising from his scorched flesh. Grasping that door handle had been like sticking his hand over an open flame.

Stars. Fireworks. Wild panic.

He jabbed at the door handle with his left hand, but without even touching it he could feel the heat radiating from it. The abrupt heat was fogging up all the glass of the booth. He watched, slack jawed, as the world outside the phone booth dissolved into a wall of white.

In that instant, Bobby believed.

Any last scrap of doubt vanished as absolute terror gripped him. He'd been tricked. Lured. Something wanted him away from Mick. It was somehow keeping him here, trapped, buying time to make sure Mick stayed alone — and that thought terrified him more than any concern for his own safety.

Steamy mist swirled about him, sucking at his clothes. Sweat trickled down his shoulder blades and under his armpits from the sudden humid air. Seconds ticked away like gongs from a grandfather clock. He made another stab at the door handle, felt its blistering heat, and retreated with a whimper. He had to get out. But how?

He lifted his eyes — and the black pay phone challenged him. Abruptly, he scooped the receiver into his hand. The line buzzed a dial tone, waiting for its quarter. Bobby sucked in his breath.

"Hello? I know you're there! I know you can hear me." In his desperation he let his fear be taken over by a healthy dose of anger. "Come on, you bastard. Talk to me! You can't keep me here forever."

The dial tone clicked off. He waited. His knees were shaking so badly he had to balance himself against the glass of the booth. Dead silence on the line. Then: What was that?

Drip. Drip.

Water hitting water. Like in the bottom of a deep well, a cave: a place never warmed by sunlight.

The hairs at the nape of his neck stood on end: Someone was on the other end of the line. They made no sound, but Bobby knew, he *knew*. He had a sensation of ice, as if frigid air could miraculously travel out through the phone and blow into his ear.

Ice. Steam. Heat. Crazy, all crazy.

He found his voice. "Leave Mick alone. You can't have him."

Silence spun out.

"I know you can hear me," he challenged. His voice echoed down into that deep well, unnerving him. *What's going on? Why doesn't this guy answer?*

From the fathomless bottom of that well: a sound. Bobby strained to hear it, his face a map of concentration. The flesh on his arms crawled into goose bumps.

Because what he heard made no sense.

> *Take it, take it*
> *Take it like a man*
> *I'll love you, love you*
> *The only way I can*

An old disco song, like an echoing memory. But below that song, taking precedence, he heard a wet, intimate slurping, the sound of flesh slick and ready. The rhythmic slurping of someone getting his dick sucked. From somewhere, the movement of bodies shifting position, followed by a gasp and the moan of penetration.

Ecstatic grunts of approval.

> *Let me love you, love you*
> *The only way I can...*

A momentum built, flesh slapping flesh, thrusting, harder and harder.

As it dawned on Bobby what he was listening to, he heard the moans of pleasure become sharp intakes of breath, mewlings of pain, as if all pleasure in the act was left far behind. He could almost see hands trying to still that insistent plunging that had crossed the line into violence.

The slap of skin against skin grew fierce, devouring. Moans turned into protest, pain — and a sudden high-pitched wail:

"Stop, that hurts, that hurts, somebody help meeee!"

Tears of outrage. A knife jabbed into Bobby's guts could not have hurt more.

For the voice belonged to Mick.

"You bastard!" Bobby roared. "Leave him alone!"

154 ✦

The music, the fucking, climaxed with a frenzy of grunts and shouts, exquisite pain married to pleasure. Underneath a savage sigh he heard a terrible whimpering, like a broken animal whose body had been shoved aside. Bobby butted against the confines of the phone booth, helpless, trapped — and wounded as the accusation floated out of that darkness, through the phone — a plaintive voice:

"You promised me, Bobby. You said you'd protect me but you lied. You lied!"

His heart broke, just snapped in two. "Mick!"

Suddenly a demonic laugh roared up through the phone, like the snorting of a dragon. And with it, plunging into Bobby's skull, raping his thoughts: the vision of the face of that gargoyle, the creature from his nightmare, grinning through teeth streaked with blood.

With a strangled cry he threw the phone back onto the receiver. He whirled within the confines of his prison, his hand grasping the sturdy hook of his umbrella handle. He raised it to smash through the glass itself, if necessary.

It wasn't. The door popped open, smooth as silk, cold rainy air rushing in to greet the steam of the booth. Fun and games over now. This was an invitation to leave.

Bobby sprang out of the booth and ran. He ran as fast as his legs could carry him, tears spilling down his cheeks.

Branded by Mick's accusation:

You said you'd protect me but you lied. You lied.

6

Preoccupied with his umbrella, fumbling for keys to unlock the gate, David tensed up like a coiled wire as the shadow stepped out from the murky gray of the adjacent open-door garage.

"David?"

"Alex! What are you doing here?"

He said nothing, but in his eyes was the glimmer of reconciliation, of kinship, of some new awareness.

"What — what's happened?" It was all he could manage.

Alex's eyes became wild and distraught: "Last night — I had a dream, David."

A dream. He nodded with abrupt understanding, and not a small touch of dismay. For if Alex had been touched by these dreams, what did that imply about this evil's growing strength and influence?

"It's getting dark," David said uneasily. He handed Alex his umbrella, freeing one hand to unlock the gate. "Let's go inside."

21

Twilight confessions

A *dream—*
1
Me too.
Tell me.
With cups of coffee, stories told.

2

"And when I sat up beside the bed and looked at the window, she — he — it — was gone," Alex finished with a shaky laugh. He broke into a bemused grin and shook his head.

"What's so funny?" He feared they were opposites, once again. David serious with every word of Alex's story, while the policeman's amusement increased as he related his dream.

"Aww, come on buddy; listen to it." Alex cupped both palms in an open gesture as if to say, just kidding. "A beautiful woman outside my window. *Float*ing, mind you, several stories up. Suddenly we're doin' the wild thang, all over each other like horny teenagers, and right as I shoot my wad, out pops this Jack Martin." He shook his head again. "I was more inclined to believe it when I kept this to myself. Telling you now — hearing my own words — it sounds just like the goddamned crazy dream it was. Period."

David glanced out at the leaden sky through his sliding glass doors. He summoned conviction into his voice. "It wasn't just a dream, Alex. Jack Martin came to you last night."

"Oh, I don't know—"

"Then why are you here? You left half a dozen messages on my machine and then staked out my apartment until I returned."

Alex gave him a flustered look. "I was worried."

"About what?"

"About — you."

"Why? What'd you think was going to happen to me?"

"Whoa, partner. Put down the club. Why are you so mad at me?"

"Because I want the truth. I don't have time for this bullshit dance, Alex. So tell me: Why are you here?"

"Look, I wanted to talk with you, okay? I found it rather peculiar that after all your talk of premonitions and dreams, I'd suddenly have one of my own."

"Only it didn't feel like a dream, did it?" He pinned Alex with a piercing glare and wouldn't let him glance away. "You had a real orgasm. You picked yourself off the floor. You showered. There was no moment when you woke up and knew you had been asleep. From the moment you heard someone outside your window, you were awake."

"Okay," Alex conceded. "Uncle. What's your point?"

"Jack Martin came to you last night. They're starting after you because you're a threat, because you're helping me. I really feel this. There's a deadly purpose to it all."

Alex held up a hand in protest. "I still don't believe it—"

"No one says you have to. But while we sit around moaning that this can't be happening, something's picking us off one by one."

"What makes you so almighty sure all at once? Last night you bounced back and forth like a ping pong ball, not sure what to believe."

David hesitated. He wasn't aware of it, but his face turned gray with the remembering. "I was there, last night. Face-to-face in a waking dream so vivid, so real, I can still see the creature. It's burned into my brain."

"Creature?"

"Yes. Creature. Monster. It's definitely not a man, whatever it is. And you can wipe that silly grin off your face, Alex. This thing calls itself 'Victor,' but what I saw was something counterfeit, something impersonating a human. I barely got out of that place alive. And there were others there: a man I used to see at my gym named Mick. And the man I think is his lover, named Bobby. Last night when I blacked out, I saw this Mick going into a phone booth. I could sense that he was being lured, tricked. I don't know why, or for what purpose, but we're all connected somehow. I can't ignore these constant visions of them. I can't deny they are real any longer. There was also a ... boy."

A ripple of alarm. "A boy?"

"Yes. About ten or eleven years old. Dark complexion, like he's either Filipino or Spanish." He caught the light bulb going off behind Alex's eyes. "I've just described someone who's disappeared, haven't I?"

Alex nodded. "Miguel Garza. Miggy. Disappeared while playing catch football with a friend named Kevin."

"So how do you explain that, Sherlock?"

"I can't."

"Well, then give me an inch, would you? How else could I have known about this boy if I hadn't seen him with my own two eyes?"

Alex chewed on that for a moment. "So where is this ... this place you went to last night?"

He frowned. "I have no idea. It wasn't a house, actually. It seemed much larger. There were hallways. A staircase. Strange rocklike walls — steam — lots of steam — and there was a man, thin and starved-looking, who beckoned me, guided me."

"Who is he?"

David shrugged.

The policeman scratched his chin. "How'd you get there?"

"In some kind of dream that was no dream." David stared at Alex as if defying him to disbelieve.

"Great. Just great. Okay. Let's lay all our cards on the table. Leave out the hocus-pocus and see what's bare-bone fact."

"All right." *Finally,* David thought. *We're getting somewhere.*

"A series of curiously similar events: A young boy named Miguel disappears south of Market as he's kicking around a football with another neighborhood kid. Later that night, in the same general neighborhood, your gym buddy Jack Martin vanishes, and the apartment is left a total wreck—"

David held up a hand. "Wait a minute. How do you know all this?"

"I heard about it the same morning I met you at Davies. I managed to get a look into Jack's apartment with a little help from Mrs. Kreitman, the landlady."

David leaned forward in expectation. "What'd you find?"

"As you may have read in the papers — it garnered about two paragraphs on page six — he'd plastered bible pages all over his apartment walls and windows. The place was damp, like it'd gotten wet and was still trying to dry. Nothing was left but blood. And no one saw or heard a thing."

"Why didn't you tell me this before?" David scolded. "I knew you were hiding something from me last night. Eddie's disappearance was just like that! And as to what I saw in his hospital room — the stains and water may have disappeared, but you couldn't get rid of that moldy wet smell."

Alex nodded, then indicated he wanted to get back to basics. "So suddenly we have this little flurry of disappearances — Miggy, Jack, Eddie. In two of the cases, all that's left is a splotch of blood and the smell of stagnant water. This same night, you claim Eddie — or something you thought was Eddie — broke into your apartment and tried to attack you while you were taking a bath. Last night you had some kind of seizure and—"

"It wasn't a seizure, Alex. How many times do I have to tell you that? Something is inside me ... something beyond my control. It's some kind of intuition, for lack of a better word ... and it's growing more pronounced with every disappearance. And you know what it's telling me right now? That you're afraid to admit how much that dream frightened you last night. Deep down you're afraid that even a little bit of what I've been saying is true. I mean look, even if we do trim away all this supernatural stuff, we're still left with several men and one boy who are missing. You can't pin that on my supposed guilt over Eddie. And except for that boy, two of the missing are my friends. I may not be at the center of what's happening, but I'm certainly no bit player. *I can see things.* I think you realize that, and left all those messages on my machine because you realize the danger involves not only me, but *you*. And the danger is something none of us have ever been up against."

They glared at each other, frightened, a glassy look in their eyes. David thought, *We approach this from different angles, but bottom line is, we're both scared to death. Maybe this fear will pull us together, after all.*

For the truth was, with the soupy gray of twilight quickly fading to black, the fear was coiling around him again, snatching away his breath. Earlier, in the daylight, he'd been prepared to chop through this dark forest alone. Now a superstitious dread clamped onto his feet with the weight of chain shackles. He'd come no closer to finding Mick or Bobby today. Or the woman, whoever she was, the most unreal of all — just a single typed message on a page. He didn't know if today had been his last chance. Perhaps tonight was the night his luck would run out.

The phone rang. It jarred their solemn silence, causing each of them to jump. David reluctantly excused himself into the kitchen and took the call. Alex stood up from the couch and went to stand at the sliding glass doors to allow him a bit of privacy.

Scattered lights sprinkled the hillside slopes of Twin Peaks and Diamond Heights. Below the rain-swollen sky, a carpet of fog advanced down the slopes.

David hung up the phone and cursed.

"I don't believe this. I have to work tonight."

Alex swung away from the view. "What?"

"Two of the waiters didn't show up. Tom called in sick, and no one's heard a peep from James. Roger needs me ASAP."

"Why don't I give you a lift?"

"Thanks." But David's expression clouded again. "You still don't believe any of this, do you?"

"No," Alex admitted. "But I'm listening to you tonight. I'd say that's a start."

That struck home. He met Alex's gaze and nodded with appreciation.

The policeman cleared his throat. "You are right about one thing," he said.

David looked at him expectantly.

"When it's all said and done, we're still left with one unalterable fact: Men have disappeared under pretty suspicious circumstances. And maybe, somehow, you have this gift to see things connected with the cases. It *has* been known to happen. So what does that psychic whammy of yours tell you?"

David bit his lip. "That this is only the beginning."

Alex frowned as though he'd tasted something bad. "While you're at work, I'm going to pore through those files again. See if I've missed anything. I'll give you a call when your shift is over."

And in front of Uncle Charlie's, as David stepped out of Alex's Toyota, he said, "I'll try to come pick you up after your shift."

David looked at him with genuine surprise. "You don't have to do that."

A flash of teeth. "I know I don't. But now that it's dark, I can see fear has turned you three shades lighter in the last ten minutes. Seems like a good idea we stay in touch, know what I mean?"

The weight on David's shoulders lessened a little. "Yes. I do. And — thanks."

As Alex sped off down the rain-slicked street, David offered up a prayer to the drizzly sky: *Let us all get through the night. Please.*

For a feeling began to nag at him, a feeling that could explain Alex's concern for his safety.

He thinks I'm next. That's why he was so worried when he showed up at my apartment today. He thinks I may be the next to disappear.

And underneath that, his own fear added reinforcement: *It* could *be me next. Locked forever in that dark, steamy place.*

He sighed with resignation. Rubbed his forehead.

Rope. Wrists. Bedpost.

"David?"

"Huh?" He shook out of himself to see Roger, manager of Uncle Charlie's, waving him inside, out of the drizzle. "Coming," he said, and Roger, pacified, stepped back through the door. The bizarre image shimmered in afterglow inside his head. Baffling. Hands and feet, wrapped and bound with

Rope?

No. Clothesline. Clothesline?

Suddenly he was afraid. The wet night pushed against his shoulders.

Underneath the damp chilly air, he thought he smelled it: gunpowder.

A pistol taking aim, soon.

3

Relief.

It sighed through Bobby like a June wind. He sagged in his bedroom doorway, knees buckling, lungs bursting from his run.

Mick was curled up in bed, asleep.

He had been so sure of that whimpering voice on the other end of the phone. So sure Mick had somehow been snatched. Bobby closed his eyes and heard that dragon's laugh again. He shuddered. *All a trick to frighten me.*

Bobby staggered toward the bed, a sober man with a drunkard's walk, and sank thankfully onto the mattress. Gently, not wishing to alarm him, he nudged Mick's shoulder. Mick woke up instantly, eyes cartoonish in their terror, nostrils flaring. He took his lover's hand.

"It's time we talked," Bobby said.

4

Mick spilled everything. Almost.

He again confessed his first conversation with Victor. He told of the phone call into Bobby's apartment the night he'd dreamed of men scratching at the window. How this man's voice had wormed inside him and begun to grow like a crazy kind of cancer, eager to control him.

"When Victor talks, I lose myself somehow. I've never even seen him—"

"—But?"

Mick lowered his gaze. "I want to. *He* wants me to. I don't think I'm strong enough to say no."

"You have to fight him, Mick."

Mick wrapped his arms around his knees and began to rock back and forth. "He's gotten inside me. I'm afraid of what he'll make me do. You see, I — I went to the phone booth last night, like I told you. And ... something happened."

Bobby's breath stalled in his chest.

Mick's knuckles were white shards of bone. He plunged to the heart of his confession. "I had sex with him." He saw Bobby's incredulous look and quickly amended: "In the phone booth. I've never seen him, ever. But he's seen me."

Anguished: "Why? Why would you do that?"

And Mick, his voice taking on a flat, foreign tone: "He wanted to drink from me."

"...Drink?" Bobby's thoughts raced. He wanted so much to understand. The door to that understanding felt so near, despite the shroud of dread that he knew full knowledge would bring.

Mick rolled his eyes, a wild flame sputtering in the blue. "You still don't get it, do you? It turned him on. Nourished him, somehow. It was as if he could drink my energy. Feed on my sex—"

In his mind, Bobby grabbed the handle and flung the door wide to face it all. He saw once again the dark creature of his dream, kneeling before him in that godforsaken dungeon, felt how against his will his cum had squirted into that hideous mouth as blood spurted from his genitals.

Mick shivered uncontrollably.

"You've got to help me, Bobby! Because ever since last night, I keep getting hit with these waves of ... Like a craving ... A — A — *command*—"

"Now stop it! Right now!" Bobby gave him a rough shake. "Nobody can control someone else like that, nobody!"

Mick laughed — a jagged wound. "You've never heard him talk, or you'd know. He's coming to get me, I know he is!"

"Not if I have any say in it." Bobby, too agitated to sit, paced the bedroom. "We have to think. Protect ourselves."

The phone rang.

The effect was like being splashed by ice water. A palpable fear leapt between their terrified glance.

"Don't answer it!" Mick wailed.

"I won't."

"I don't want you talking to him. He'll trick you."

"He already has," Bobby said.

Mick stared at him in wonder.

The ringing phone was an insistent jangle, fraying their nerves.

Bobby couldn't stand it any longer. He swooped upon the instrument, meaning to crush it with his bare hands, smash it against the wall. Sanity stalled his raised hands, however, as a better solution came to him: He plucked the plastic connection to the phone from its home, killing that siren call in midring. He threw the disconnected wire to the floor. "Now let the bastard talk to us!" Bobby roared, flushed with his success.

Mick's gaze never wavered. "What do you mean Victor already tricked you?"

He set down the phone. "I went to that booth this afternoon."

He gave Mick the nuts and bolts, finishing with: "I was so frightened. I just knew he'd somehow broken in here and gotten you."

Mick grasped Bobby's hand. They sat close together on the bed, his lover's need for motion having been replaced by the need for comfort and warmth. He thought of the trick played upon him that day: the weird disfiguration of his feet. God, how he had screamed! But when he'd screwed up the courage for another look, the strange webbing around his toes had vanished. He thought of telling this to Bobby, but in his misery he asked, "What are we going to do?"

Bobby rubbed his eyes with his free hand. "I don't know, honey. I just don't know." The tension momentarily eased, his eyes searched for answers within the confines of the room, eventually resting upon an object beside the bed. Leaning across his lover, he scooped the gaudy crucifix into his hand. "I wish we had a dozen more of these."

Shadows under Mick's eyes. "Why?"

Bobby couldn't bring himself to tell his troubled lover of the glowing cross of the other night ... It was all too fantastic to contemplate. Mick made this "Victor" sound like some modern vampire. Crosses? Vampires? No!

But he held the crucifix with a sudden appreciation. Perhaps it could recognize evil — hadn't it proved that by flaring into life that night he held it in his hands? Perhaps it could conquer evil as well. It was a hope worth nourishing.

Better to say nothing. Better to have this moment between them, air cleared after a week of lies and confusion, doubts and fears. Bobby sought out a clock, and shrank at the time. What an interminable night this was going to be! Still, his spirits were buoyed by this highway of sharing running between them, swept clean of deceit. Enjoying this eye of the hurricane even as the winds seemed to be gathering its army. The air was charged, full of electricity.

Before morning, a showdown?

5

Mick, who sat looking at his hands like a lost child in a department store, felt buffeted by those electric currents in the air. An invisible line was being drawn in the apartment: Bobby on one side, "Victor" on the other. He was relieved to have spit out the story of this man who had choked him into silence and had twisted truth into lies. He was relieved that Bobby believed him.

There was just one problem.

In his confession, he had forgotten to mention the real cancer buried inside him, working its evil. It scratched at his throat, demanding to be let out, to be talked about, but he held it inside. He knew it would be the final capper to this whole nightmare, somehow more terrible than all that had preceded it. But in the dark tunnel of his narrowing thoughts, Victor's voice, whispering:

You have the new disease in you.

Another trick? A scare tactic to win him over? What if it *was* true? If he believed that Victor had already gotten inside of him, wasn't it also possible Victor could tell if he was sick?

His hopscotching mind ticked off a list of maladies.

He *had* felt tired lately. Out of breath when he climbed stairs. His workouts at the gym not so great, even when he pushed himself. No night sweats, though. No telltale purple spots. Then again, when was the last time he'd thoroughly checked himself?

Was he balanced on the edge, about to tumble? Colds that never go away, congested lungs, a lingering cough—

If it was true ... If it was true...

Then Victor offered a way out.

Life, as you have never known it. Desire, as you have never known it. With me.

Yes, the ground currents were swelling, the storm brewing on twilight's horizon, lines drawn—

"Mick?"

A liquid glance at Bobby.

"A-Are you okay?"

Mick sought his voice, and found it. "I'm fine." He seemed to speak from the end of a long tunnel. And Bobby, so small; like looking at him through the wrong end of a camera lens. Bobby's lips were moving, a fish in an aquarium.

"You don't look so good," Bobby said.

What Mick heard was:

You have the new disease in you.

22

Wrestling

1

The day retreated early, tail tucked between its legs, as night bullied over the landscape.

So began a wrestling match, desire pitted against fright.

All across the city men sat in darkened apartments. They slid on t-shirts they hadn't worn in years, shirts with funny sayings like "You can't be first, but you can be next" and "Daddy's Toy" and "So many men, so little time." They yanked on the tightest pair of 501 blue jeans they owned. Dug around in the bottoms of dresser drawers for forgotten gold chains to slide over their heads.

And waited.

They told themselves they were going out later, and would let impulse direct them when the time came. So to pass the hours they dragged out scratchy albums with faded covers and homemade cassette tapes and listened to the sounds of the old days flow through their apartment like fine aged wine. That part of their mind that should have reasoned, Why am I doing this? What's happening to me? remained strangely silent on this restless night.

Only the bright bubbly music mattered, so loud in their ears. It made them think of hope-filled times. And then, in the silent intermission as they flipped records or changed tapes, a memory would sneak upon them, and they'd remember waking up from last night's erotic vision, sick with longing and sick with dread, pinned against their mattress as something monstrous fed upon their ecstasy.

Easy to forget, if they cranked up the music and washed away the memory with booze and pills and dope. All the recent priorities of maintaining health, of popping vitamins instead of black beauties, Quaaludes, acid — all priorities stalled as the minutes ticked toward midnight.

Other men sat in silent dark apartments, eyes closed, swaying as if in the grip of a mystical experience. Sugar-plum visions of cocks and ass and steam swirled through their thoughts. In this darkness they pulled their dicks from their pants and stroked themselves with lazy anticipation, while in their other hands they clutched what they had mysteriously found beside their beds that morning: tickets, and on them the words Admit One.

There were men who suspected a wrongness in the air, men who recognized that a monumental trick was being played upon them. A vague, childlike fear settled over these men. Afraid of the dark. Afraid of the shadows under the bed, the inky blackness of bedroom closets. Jumping as wind-blown tree branches rapped against their windows.

But most of all, afraid of the ghosts that whispered at the backs of their necks: *Go to sleep, and you shall have paradise.*

And so all across the city, alone with their worries, alone in the dark, men wrestled with equal parts desire and dread, as the shadow creatures perched, awaiting their siren call.

2

"Slow night."

David turned to Roger, manager of Uncle Charlie's, and nodded.

"Sorry to have asked you in for nothing."

"S'okay."

Roger, a handsome man in his midforties, was pinch faced and troubled. He couldn't stand still. Nothing satisfied his eye. His lean face looked appallingly birdlike, two beady eyes set between a hawkish nose. Perspiration gleamed on his ashen forehead.

David put a hand on Roger's shoulder. "Take it easy," he said lightly — but Roger jerked under his fingers, startled at contact.

"Don't!" Roger snapped.

"Relax, would you? You want to chase away our only customers?"

That caught his attention. Roger glanced at the two occupied tables by the window, where a total of six men sat in subdued conversation. He hooked a thumb in their direction. "If business stays this bad, it's curtains, buddy boy. May as well file Chapter Eleven and put an end to this misery."

"This will pass," David said, but even Roger caught the halfhearted enthusiasm.

Roger sighed. "Every day I see fewer and fewer people out on the street. I'd like to blame this shitty weather, but Christ, where is everyone? Holing up, waiting for it to pass? What if it *doesn't* pass?" He shook his head. "We've got a long winter ahead."

David glanced at the two tables of customers. How many others have had dreams? Are they keeping it to themselves, this secret of the steam, afraid to tell someone else about it?

One of the customers signaled Roger for the check. As Roger went to help him, David took the opportunity to sneak into the back office, fish through his wallet, and dial Alex's home phone number.

The phone rang and rang, a dozen times.

Each ring was like a knife insinuating itself into his ear.

Where are you, Alex? What's happened? You said you'd be home.

He returned to his boss, who stood fidgeting at the salad bar.

"I don't know about you," Roger said, "but I can't wait for this shift to be over. I'm so wound up I'm ready to go through the roof."

David nodded in commiseration. His thoughts were black fluttering shapes dive-bombing through his head.

"When I go home," Roger said dreamily, "I'm going to take a long hot shower and steam this horniness right out of me."

3

Alex raked a hand across his face. God, he was tired.

The pool of lamplight shining onto his desk seemed to spear him directly between his eyes, no matter how he adjusted the lamp. He wanted to shut off the light and rest, but no: miles to go before he slept. A pile of police files lay open on his desktop, demanding his scrutiny. He'd managed only a couple of pages before the lines began to blur and his eyes ache.

He downed the last of his scotch and soda and debated another one — his third. Ordinarily he wasn't much of a drinker, but this was a drinker's night, what with the howling wind and rain. Very Edgar Alan Poe. He smiled at his own imagery.

But no; no more drinks. David's phone call wouldn't come until after eleven. He had to stay awake and finish his research, despite his bone-tired drowsiness. Must be the result of last night's unfinished sleep.

He shook his head to clear his vision and flipped through the files.

Miggy Garza. Vanished not more than one block from his own house, on Roberts Alley. Interviews with the distraught parents had turned up zilch. Likewise, a talk with the boy Miggy had been playing with, a Kevin Bates.

Larry Frank Stone. Flint Stone. What a downhill ride *this* guy had been on. An Officer Pena had interviewed two of his buddies, Ralph Sutherland and Will Garter. Quite the sad tale they told about their friend. Flint's business shut down. A string of lawyers in a futile attempt to get the city to let him reopen. What was it he owned? Alex frowned. A *bathhouse*. Great. One big AIDS factory in the making. And this joker was pissed because the former mayor had shut him down?

He shook his head. He knew this wasn't a popular opinion — David Walker would probably lay into him if he'd heard such an opinion — but, hell, a man has a right to believe what he wants to believe.

Officer Pena's scratchy handwriting blurred and doubled in front of his eyes. He tried to read the next paragraph, something about this Flint character getting sick and probably offing himself, but, oh, to rest his eyes. He dug a fist into each eye socket. Swirling images swam in that darkness behind each eyelid.

Alex yawned and stretched. He forced himself to read the next several lines of Officer Pena's report. Despite pleas to the contrary from Ralph and Will, the evidence pointed to suicide. Flint Stone had a stack of legal and medical bills a mile high. He'd been pushed into a corner, needing a way out. But no body had been found.

He suddenly thought of David's words.

I touched his photograph, and there was blood on my fingertips. Blood.

Flint Stone. Owner of the Caverns bathhouse.

Rocklike walls ... It wasn't like a house. It seemed much larger ... There was steam everywhere...

Despite his weariness, a little spark went off inside Alex's brain. He flipped back through the report on Miggy Garza, and near the bottom found a statement from Miggy's friend Kevin: *We were playing near that haunted house — you know, where all those men used to go...*

Images were swirling behind his eyes again, distracting him from what should have been a profound excitement.

All these scattered cases, reported by different officers with seemingly no connection to each other. Yet here it was. Miggy and Jack, both living within blocks of this place called the Caverns. The place was shut down, condemned — but had anyone actually searched the building? Had anyone stopped to think this Flint Stone may have faked his own disappearance, and was now hiding out in the bathhouse? The guy knew he was sick and dying. Maybe, in some twisted way of thinking, he'd decided to take as many people along with him as possible. Striking back at the very community that had contributed to his downfall.

Alex leaned back, immensely satisfied with himself. Now *here* was a thread of logic that made sense. It even tied in with David Walker's suspicion that the gay community was being targeted. Perhaps Miggy Garza had stumbled too close, and spotted Flint in the building. Flint had had to nab him to keep him silent.

Wait until I tell David about this.

He shut his eyes.

How heavy, his eyelids. What a relief to close them. In the darkness behind his eyes he saw hands reach out for him, a beautiful woman's fingers coming close to caress him with a massage. And, boy, didn't he deserve a massage right about now. Wouldn't it feel great to lay back and allow himself to be worked over...

He sighed with pleasure and imagined the smooth touch of those cool fingers. Only a faint spark of awareness was left as he slumped onto his desk, brushing aside the pile of manila folders. Dimly, he thought he heard the phone ring.

And too late, recognized the source of this false drowsiness. It swooped upon him like a sack thrown over his head. He tried to hook his fingers under the edge of it, willing himself into wakefulness

Hey wait a minute—!

but the hands were upon him, massaging him into deep sleep.

And on this night, while others dreamed of steam and men, Alex slept in a web of forgetfulness, caught in its silky threads.

23

Siege

Bobby drew back the curtain.[1]

The street below was alive, though no one walked upon it. Scraps of paper and cardboard skittered across the pavement, blown by fairy-tale winds. It was hard to make out anything through the rain-pelted glass of his bedroom window, but he could see a drunk sitting on the loading dock across the street merrily drinking himself into a stupor. Shadows jigged and danced to the music of wind and rain. What was that, crouched in a doorway? A figure? And there: a flash of yellow, like demon's eyes. No: just a cat darting through the rain, the ruined corpse of a mouse in its jaws.

For all the tricks of his exhaustion, the street remained barren of human traffic. However, that couldn't keep Bobby's fevered imagination from conjuring up the man with no face, even if deep down he knew their game had progressed way beyond such transparencies as looking at each other through a pane of glass.

The lines had been drawn. The first shots fired. Now the smoking barrel was aimed at his head. He may not see the gun, but he recognized the whiff of sulfur and metal that no wind could blow apart, the smell of worlds about to collide. The enemy was near.

Another reason, closer to his heart, kept him in his role as sentinel: It gave him an excuse not to look at the bed, and what he had done. He was afraid to turn. Afraid to give in to the pleading eyes, the don't-do-this-to-me expression. Safer to stay like this, his back to the room, and watch the storm-swept street.

But the hand, aching from its task, turned traitor. The curtain fell back into place.

Immediately, from behind and on the bed, the whimpering. The cajoling. The gag, securely tied, couldn't muffle all the sound.

Bobby clapped his hands over his ears. "Stop it! For the love of god, stop it!"

A muted shout. Legs thrashed against the mattress.

I can't take this, Bobby thought. It gutted his insides. He was a fish trapped in the hunter's steady hand. Each muffled cry like the bite of a knife, slowly disemboweling him.

A cold certainty chilled him suddenly: *What if he feels Victor taking over? What if he's trying to warn me?*

He could drown in this sea of what-ifs, just sink like a stone, and no matter how hard he splashed to stay afloat...

Concern beat out intellect. Bobby turned and looked.

Mick was nodding his head, an undisguised eagerness in the whites of his eyes. A fever burned both in front of and behind those orbs, so that he appeared to be bathed in the coppery reflection of a huge fire. Sweat cascaded from his rosy cheeks. His blond hair was matted and dirtied from perspiration. He pushed against his restraints and worked his mouth to speak.

Bobby nibbled his lower lip, hesitating. "You made me promise..."

Mick's eyes blazed: *Hurry! Do it!*

"Is — is it him? Is he coming?"

A vigorous nod.

They hadn't taken that consideration into their plans. How could Mick warn him, in his present condition? What had they been thinking, in their rashness?

Bobby bent forward.

And sprang back as Mick lunged at him, hands twisted into claws. The rope held, but he bucked and kicked, his back arched like some sort of crazed gymnast's. His feet were bound together and secured to a knob under the bed to keep him from packing a mean kick, but he still had ample leeway to thrash and struggle. He howled at Bobby through the gag in his mouth, the sound a cross between a wounded wolf and a hungry jackal.

"Stop it!" Bobby shouted. *It isn't him, I know it isn't!* he thought feverishly.

He spun away from the bed, from the pleading eyes, and staggered into the den. Oh, how the fisherman's knife worked on him now, dissecting his very sanity. He was going to go nuts, absolutely one hundred percent looney tunes if this night didn't end soon. Which it would not, considering that the clock on the wall read just past eleven o'clock. He had to hold on to his sanity — for the both of them.

Because Mick had gone — well — a little crazy.

It began with the descent of darkness, hours earlier. Mick had folded into himself, not answering questions, not responding to Bobby's gentle proddings. At first he was not overly alarmed. Mick was content to stay in bed, sometimes dozing, sometimes working on a crossword puzzle. Certainly easy enough to watch.

Bobby fixed them dinner. Mick wouldn't touch a bite, claiming no appetite. Okay, fine: He could live with that. He rolled in the portable TV to help pass the time, but the Friday night lineup of sitcoms was even more dreadful than usual, so off it went after half an hour.

The rain began, a soft pattering against the window.

He glanced up from his murder mystery, cringing at the sight of Mick with his head cocked to one side, as though he listened for secret messages in the patter of the rain.

He went into the kitchen to make himself a cup of coffee. While grinding beans he heard a rustle from the bedroom, and returned to find Mick slipping into jeans and a t-shirt.

"What are you doing?" Bobby asked.

Mick walked the floor. Muttered to himself. First he was too hot, and wanted a window open for fresh air. Bobby cracked the window. Then he was too cold. Bobby shut the window. Then he whined for fresh air again.

"Mick, what's the matter with you?"

"I'm not sick!"

Bobby was taken aback. "I never said you were."

Mick paced. "I'm too young to be sick. It isn't fair. It isn't right. I'm not sick!"

He went to him. "Tell me what's—"

Mick shoved him, hard. Completely unprepared for the blow, Bobby stumbled backward into a wooden dresser. "Get away from me! I can't breathe! I need fresh air." Slippery as an eel, Mick dove toward the bedroom door.

Bobby was faster, cutting him off. Mick grabbed hold of Bobby's shirt to yank him aside, and suddenly they were spinning in all directions at once. They dug into each other like hometown rivals on opposing football teams.

"Get out of my way," Mick snarled. He yanked himself free.

Bobby immediately blocked the doorway, and shook his head.

"I mean it! Get out of my way!"

He stood his ground, chest heaving. In that split second he saw the fire burning behind his lover's eyes, the glow that wanted to consume him.

Mick charged. Bobby scooted to the side as though, in terror, he had decided to allow Mick passage — and then grabbed and locked him in a power grip as he tried to dive past. With an arm hooked around Mick's chest, Bobby propelled him back into the room. They tumbled onto the bed.

"It's him you have to fight, not me! Fight it Mickey!"

Mick wrenched free, scrambling for the edge of the bed. He teetered to his feet, but Bobby was upon him in an instant. He clipped Mick in the knees. Toppling, they both crashed to the hardwood floor. Smack! Mick's forehead took the brunt of the fall.

Fear rushed through Bobby. "You okay, Mick?"

His boyfriend lay still, the fight all out of him.

Bobby rolled him onto his back and winced at the half-inch gash on Mick's right temple. A puddle of blood gathered there; he wiped it away with his thumb. Quite a lump by morning, no doubt. He gave Mick a gentle nudge. "Honey?"

Great. I've given him a concussion. Now what?

No. Mick was conscious. But he was shaking as if in the grip of an earthquake. He blinked rapidly, his eyes swimming in and out of focus, the fire momentarily subdued. He seemed to be summoning himself up from a bottomless well. He started to sit up.

"Lie still," Bobby ordered, though his command was a whisper. Aghast at the violence that had brought them to this. "You'll be okay, I swear it."

Mick fumbled for Bobby's hand. Found it. Bobby tensed: another fight in the air? Was he about to be thrown to the floor? No. His lover's touch was reconciliatory.

"Thank you," Mick gasped.

2

"You *have* to."

Bobby shook his head.

"You saw what happened to me."

"Mick—"

But truer words had never been spoken. Bobby felt it in his bones. This lucidity was only temporary, a lull in a night promising hurricane winds. Even so... "I just don't think I can do it."

Mick walked into the kitchen. Bobby trailed behind him, wary and watchful. Mick went to a cupboard and dug through the junk drawers: masking tape, nails, string, scissors; all scooped up, examined, tossed aside. "It's the only way, Bobby. Otherwise I'll go to him. I don't have any other choice." Finished with one drawer, he knelt to look through a box under the sink. His hands were rotary blades whipping through the rubble.

"Maybe we should get help," Bobby offered.

A derisive snort. "Who do you suggest?"

"I don't know. The police."

"Should we flip a coin to see who tells them the good news?" Mick's tone was bitter.

"I — I don't understand."

"Here it is!" He triumphantly pulled out a thick bundle of clothesline. He saw the puzzled expression on Bobby's face and sighed. "How can we possibly explain Victor to San Francisco's finest? They'll hang up on us in two minutes."

"Not if we aren't the only ones."

Mick stood up. The clothesline dangled at his side. "What do you mean?"

Bobby hesitated; this was delicate going. "What if we aren't the only ones he's after? Several gay men have disappeared, don't forget. Maybe someone is keeping track of it all. As for this guy — well — maybe you and I are just two more people for him to get out of the way."

"N-No." Mick faltered. Impossible. He knew he was special to Victor; all this craziness hinged upon that indisputable fact. Victor wanted *him*. Desired him, above all others. Was calling to him. Calling—

He shuddered. He blinked at Bobby.

"We have to hurry," he said.

3

In the end, what other choice did they have?

Bobby cut the clothesline into workable three-foot lengths and bound Mick's feet together. The hands presented a problem: Should they be wrapped together, or tied separately above the head? He opted for the hands together on the chest. He tied Mick's hands at about chest level and then secured the other end on the headboard.

Mick tested the play in the rope. He shook his head. "It's too loose."

Bobby frowned. "What is this, *Son of the Exorcist?* I just want you to remain on the bed, not be uncomfortable."

"We don't know what's going to happen," Mick answered, giving voice to the unspoken dread between them. "Just do it."

It felt strange, wrong, an overreaction — that is, until he watched as Mick began to change again.

He had dropped back into that sulky well of silence. Bobby hoped that he'd drifted off to sleep, but when he checked, Mick's eyes were wide open, focused on the ceiling. Listening, again. After ten minutes or so, Mick became restless. Couldn't get comfortable. He started muttering to himself.

"It doesn't mean I'm sick," Mick said. "Just because I get out of breath now and then. I feel okay. Tired, but okay. It's a lie."

And then:

"This was a stupid idea, Bobby. You were right. Why don't you let me up? Let me stretch my legs. We could take a walk, you and me. We'll be okay."

And then:

That shudder, like throwing something off of himself. An anguished moan. The red-rimmed eyes searched frantically about the room.

"It's happening again," Mick said in a faraway voice.

"What!" Bobby jumped as if he'd been struck by lightning.

"Listen to me," his lover gasped, his breathing asthmatic. "Quick. I want you to cover my mouth."

Bobby was aghast. "That's crazy, Mick. You don't need a gag."

"I don't trust myself any more. I'm afraid."

"Of what?"

"That I'll trick you."

"No, you won't."

"Just do it!" The voice booming out of Mick was alien, huge. It startled Bobby into motion. He went to one of the dresser drawers, rummaged briefly, and pulled out a San Francisco State t-shirt.

Trembling, he approached the bed, and the prone figure that was his lover.

"You'll know when it's safe to take it off," Mick assured him. There was a steel to his voice, despite a tone of resignation.

I love this man, Bobby thought, an incantation to appease the gods for this trespass. *I've never cared for anyone so much in my entire life.*

He stuffed the gag into Mick's mouth.

4

Now:

The interminable muffled shouts. The blazing eyes. Hands that attacked like lobster claws.

The night, a yawning cavern.

5

Go to sleep, and you shall have paradise.
Go to

6

Sleep.

Bobby snapped awake. He was slumped in the armchair in the living room, his shirt and pants wet against his damp skin.

What the—?

He'd dozed off, apparently. His sleep-thickened mind struggled to remember his last waking moment. He'd been reading a mystery. The sound that awoke him was the book striking the floor, where it had slid off his lap. Had he shut off the light, to rest his eyes? He didn't think so. Yet the only light source was the 25-watt bulb above the kitchen sink. A seed of panic stirred within him.

He was drenched with his own perspiration. The apartment, oven hot. Maybe Mick had gotten cold and cranked up the heat.

Except that Mick was—

The last vestiges of sleep dropped away. Memory, and his purpose as sentinel, flooded him. *Damn it! I'm supposed to stay awake!*

He reached for the reading lamp beside the chair, groping for the switch in the murky half-light. Something wet splashed his forehead.

Huh?

His fingers instinctively leapt to his forehead to prevent the liquid from running into his eyes. He sniffed his fingers and jerked at the brackish stink, like sewer water. *What is it?* he thought wildly. *It feels like*—

Plop! Another direct hit, this one on top of his head. Trembling, he ran his fingers through his hair and withdrew gooey fingers, as if he'd stuck his hand into a jar of Smuckers jelly. Bobby groped for the reading light, located the switch, and turned it on.

The scream flew out of him.

His apartment was alive with motion.

Water oozed out of pores in the walls. The ceiling seethed and boiled, droplets of grimy water rushing out from the center to embrace all corners of the room. The light fixture in the ceiling overflowed with startling swiftness, sending a machine-gun spray to tattoo the hard-wood floor.

He stumbled to his feet. The impossibility of what he was seeing stunned him.

The water cut a riotous path, gushing down the length of the walls in muddy strips. An acrid, coppery smell assaulted his nostrils. The reading lamp was knocked from its perch and exploded with a wet flash, extinguishing its light. He hopped away, careful not to step in the electrified puddle.

The destruction of the room was swift and absolute. No piece of furniture escaped the water's ruinous touch. Pictures crashed to the floor with a spray of tinkling glass. Soggy books plummeted off shelves. A pile of old newspapers on the kitchen floor let loose a river of ink. Bluish green globs, like the muck of a river bottom, splattered the sofa and chairs with its fouling excrement.

His arms windmilling as if to ward off the ooze, Bobby wrenched himself away from the living room and spun toward the bedroom. His foot caught a slimy puddle, sending him skating into the door frame. He hit his head, and for a moment stars danced in front of his eyes. My god, he had to warn Mick, they had to get out—

He stared at the bed in shock.

Mick lay across the covers, head thrown back, eyes rolling in ecstasy. His bonds still held him prisoner, but his hands had loosened the rope.

Instantly he understood who had set this battle in motion. Despite the rope, the gag, his watch — despite everything — Victor had found Mick.

Mick's erection poked up from his pants. Both hands rode his hard dick, milking it. Glazed eyes swept Bobby's features, showed no recognition, and looked away.

Feeling betrayed, Bobby stared in wild-eyed helplessness, his breath coming in hitches and gasps.

Something thumped behind him.

He turned.

The pregnant mixture of heat and water was quickly turning the apartment into a steamroom. Plumes of it hissed into the air. It sizzled off the moisture streaming down the walls. Pools of water on the floor jerked and danced. In the dim light he watched as steam shot out of one of these writhing pools and then sank back, a grotesque genie taking form. A network of bones and tissue took shape, red and steaming, arteries and veins twitching with life. Heart and lungs beat as though suspended in a sea of red, glistening as the form congealed. Out of the vapor, a pair of eyes fastened upon him.

Bobby shrieked. He smacked up against the bedroom door frame, his bladder emptying in shock. He sucked in his breath and held it, as though by not breathing he could make this insanity go away.

A creature from his nightmares leapt onto the floor, as vaporous as the steam that had given it birth. It hunkered down, long arms swinging, skin mottled and cheesy, as it surveyed its surroundings.

He struggled to make sense of what stood in front of him. A stone creature, like those that guard old castles, with the simian features and batlike ears — gargoyles — but with a shock he realized that the creature was a man, horribly transformed. It alternated between man and beast, like those holographic pictures, a metamorphosis yet to be completed. He was naked, an erection poking out obscenely from between his legs. His eyes, squashed to red slits, gleamed with a hellish light. A serpentine hiss escaped his throat as it focused on him. Liver-colored lips parted to reveal fangs of yellow ivory.

Two other men-things leapt out of the steam as if a door to their world had opened. They hung back, naked and slick, waiting. They were equally grotesque, though more recognizably human than their leader, as though the metamorphosis corrupting them had only recently begun its handiwork. One of the men pointed at the telltale stain darkening Bobby's groin and shrieked laughter.

He bolted.

He threw himself into the bedroom and stood at the foot of the bed, staring down at Mick. His bound lover, as if understanding what was happening, had stopped jacking himself off. Hands lay patiently folded atop his chest. His blue eyes were dark and flat; impenetrable. Despite the gag in his mouth, Bobby could see his lips curled into a hint of smile.

Bobby was stunned. *They want him, and he'll go, if he's set free. He's lost to the spell.*

Movement in the living room.

They were coming.

One hope remained. Offering up a quick prayer, Bobby scrambled to the side of the bed and snatched up his grandmother's crucifix. Instantly the cross burst into radiant blue light, as it had before. Power hummed up his hands and forearms, tingling with an electrical charge.

He took strength. All the old stories, the late-night movie monster lore revolved around one unalterable fact: the power of the cross. What greater demonstration of its power than this blue rainbow energy coursing through it? Even Mick seemed to shrink from its light.

He spun around, marching toward the doorway. He held the cross like a shield, arms outstretched. His hands were numb. Blood pounded in his ears, his heart a runaway train.

In all their wretchedness, they appeared.

"Get back!" Bobby shouted.

White cartoon faces twisted into unreadable grimaces. Was it terror in their eyes?

The leader jumped forward.

"No! Stop!" Bobby swung the cross.

The creature fell upon him. A clawed hand shot forward and clamped onto his wrist. Fingernails dug into the pliant flesh there, making him cry out through clenched teeth.

"No!"

He made to push the crucifix into the flesh of the creature's face — surely it would burn its holy imprint into the skull, just like in the movies — but the grip on his wrist was absolute. Bobby lost his purchase on the cross as the man-creature in front of him wrenched it from his grip.

The cross flared into a mini supernova, sputtering miserably in the hands of the creature before it died. The leader threw back his head with a howl, his cry taken up by the two men behind him. He clamped down upon the cross. It shattered with a dry cough, pieces of plaster jettisoning in all directions.

Bobby let loose a defeated cry.

They stared into each other, the living and the dead.

Fingernails bit into his wrist. Suddenly he was flung around, spun like an unwilling dance partner. Pinned against the cheesy flesh of the creature as its stinking breath rushed into his ear. Bobby moaned and kicked but could not free himself.

From the bed, Mick watched with his liquid gaze.

One of the other men-creatures came round. He tore at Bobby's soiled jeans, ruthlessly yanking the pants down. He dropped to his knees, fangs bared.

(Do not resist)

whispered the man, his voice inside Bobby's head. A razor-sharp fingernail perched beneath his Adam's apple. But having his neck slashed to ribbons was the least of his worries; he stood stock-still as a clammy hand pawed at his testicles.

(Resist, and I take this as my souvenir)

said the man on his knees, and to Bobby's utter horror and disgust he felt his limp penis drawn into the creature's maw. Pinpricks of teeth nibbled at the base of his cock, a teasing threat.

The world swam gray, wanting to brown out. *Don't faint,* he commanded himself. *Please god, don't let me faint.*

The third creature loped to the bed. Bobby watched nimble hands untie the ropes binding Mick. Flush with freedom, Mick sat up in bed and immediately removed the t-shirt gag from his mouth.

"Run!" Bobby shouted. "Run!"

Mick scooted off the bed, stretching his limbs. He buttoned his jeans. Slipped on a pair of shoes. Totally indifferent to Bobby's plight. A funny angle to his head, cocked as though he heard the sweetest music. The man who had untied his bonds ran his fingers lovingly over Mick's torso.

What does he see? Bobby wondered, repulsed by the display. *What illusion cloaks their hideousness?*

Finally, Mick faced him. Button eyes swirled twin galaxies of madness.

"Fight it," Bobby yelled.

A fingernail dug into the ripe flesh beneath his Adam's apple. Pain shot upward, burning into his brain. He felt something warm and sticky trickle down the concave corridor of his chest.

"I'm sorry," Mick intoned. "You don't understand."

Bobby whimpered in his confusion. He was sweating in the steamy heat, but his insides had frozen into one great chunk of ice. His thoughts raced: *I'll never see him again. This is it. He'll become one of these things, a pale shadow, a puppet—*

"I'm sick," Mick said.

Bobby flinched. *What?*

The creatures fidgeted, impatient with this talk.

Mick blinked rapidly, as if desiring to roll back the spell just long enough to unburden his confession.

"He saw it in me," he said. "He could tell. He's promised me life."

"It's a trick!"

Bobby winced as the teeth about his cock drew blood. Excruciating pain blotted his vision.

"I'm sorry, Bobby. Good-bye."

As if he saw nothing — as if this nightmare could not touch him — Mick turned and walked out, a path through the muck opening before him.

Bobby struggled against his captor. Lost. He had lost. If he hadn't been pinned, he would have collapsed to the floor. Grief choked him.

He heard the front door open and close. What seemed like interminable minutes passed as the creatures continued to hold him. They were laughing — that riotous sound like souls burning in hell.

Rage gathered fire in him. If Mick was going to be taken, then they'd have to take *him,* too. As far as he was concerned, his life had walked out that front door. He went lax, playing possum, as he summoned his strength for one more attack.

But something was happening.

The air around him shimmered with heat. The steel grip holding him grew putty-soft.

A growl upon his ear:

(We'll be back for you later)

The creature on its knees spat out Bobby's penis.

Immediately he jerked his full body weight to the right. He came loose easily, almost too easily, as his momentum threw him angling toward the bed. He gained his balance, yanked up his pants, and spun around, hands up, to do or die.

Instead, he only watched.

Steam flew up from the floor. The three men stood in a semicircle, a contemptuous expression in their eyes. They grabbed their hard-ons and wagged them in a lecherous farewell.

And then their skin flew apart.

A crimson line bisected the bridge of nose and angle of chin, zippering down the length of chest. Steam blown, their flesh peeled off in a wash of blood and guts, innards revoltingly displayed. Liquefying, they turned transparent.

Bobby lunged at the two that had held him, arms swinging. But nothing three-dimensional remained of these beings: As his fists punched the steam their image evaporated, obliterated by his kamikaze swing.

"Come back!" he screeched. "Come back you shits so I can fight you!" Tears of frustration and rage rolled down his cheeks. He wanted to strike out, smash.

The phone rang.

Bobby jerked, the red haze of his anger cut to the quick.

I disconnected it. How can it ring?

He spun in a circle, trying to remember where he'd last put the phone. He spotted it on the lower shelf of the nightstand. Sure enough, no cord dangled from the phone.

He put the receiver to his ear.

Pregnant silence, each listening. At long last, the voice, a velvet growl:

"He's *my* boyfriend now."

"You son of a bitch," Bobby spat. "I'm going to kill you."

Victor laughed. "That's the spirit!"

"If you hurt Mick in any way..."

"What will you do, hmmm? Slap my hand, perhaps? Wave a cross in my face? That was some display, my friend. Such heroics. You've been quite an annoyance for one so young."

"I'm going to put you in a grave!"

That laugh again, cold, cold.

"I would be disappointed if you did not try," Victor chuckled. The laugh fell back into his throat and transformed into a dragon's growl.

The receiver in Bobby's hand grew warm. "Which is why I have prepared a special room for you, Bobby. Your flesh will be our pleasure. You'll beg to join my ranks. Yes, my friend, come to me now, you and your companions! Be a hero! I'm waiting!"

The phone blazed with heat.

Bobby, yelping, hurled it against the far wall. The phone struck the wall with a satisfying explosion of plaster, tumbling to the floor with a jangled crash.

His chest heaved. He gasped for breath. He could still hear Victor, laughing.

But underneath that, suddenly, a grasped straw of hope:

Companions? Does that mean there are others *fighting this thing?*

He slumped forward, and the world swam into black.

7

Mick studied the dark silent building in front of him and uttered a hollow laugh. Of course. Of course. *This* was Victor's home.

The Caverns bathhouse.

Behind him, a cartoon cutout of Bobby's front door sat squarely in the middle of the street. It squatted on this dark street as though it were a parked car at ease in a comfortable parking space. He had simply walked through it. One moment he stood in the apartment; the next, here, in front of this place — Victor's home. What greater proof of power.

Its purpose terminated, the apartment door bubbled like celluloid caught under the hot glare of a faulty projector, collapsing into itself. With a steaming whoosh! it splattered across the wet concrete and soiled puddles with its muck.

Mick turned his back on the oily puddle. Even had the door remained open, escape was closed to him. Not that it mattered. He had no intention of going back.

Because he had never felt such an excitement.

His erection strained against the cotton fabric of his pants. It was alive with anticipation, responding even to the rub of denim against his cock-head.

The bathhouse towered above him, eager.

Mick threw this thought against its brick and concrete walls:

You promised me life. You promised!

Silence.

He waited. A wet wind gusted around him, the break in the rain threatening to dissolve.

Faint at first, like an echo of an echo: music. The thump thump thump of disco, all bass and driving beat.

The black double doors seemed to shudder. Inside, a latch was thrown back. The door swung out on protesting hinges. Flashing neon lights — red, white, blue, dizzying — spilled through the slash of door.

Warm air steamed out, the heat of many bodies. The music boomed louder, woven with the surprising bark of men's laughter. Mick recognized an old disco tune:

> *Let's party hearty*
> *Till the break of dawn*
> *Start all over again*
> *Till our fun's been done*

A joyous wonder consumed him. *It's like 1978 in there,* he thought. *Before all the trouble began.*

The hypnotic lights reached out for him.

Songs folded one over the other, no longer just the one tune but all songs somehow, a retrospective that echoed magically inside his head.

A dim part of him knew it spelled his damnation to fly up those steps and go inside. He no longer cared. Victor called from the center of this palace, waiting. Victor, who had chosen him above all others.

He glanced up and beyond the Caverns building to the tormented fog that rode the night sky. A sliver of moon poked through runners of clouds. No: He would not blaspheme himself with a final prayer. He took in the sky, the sickle moon, the fog with a convulsive gulp, consigning it to memory, and lowered his gaze to the open door in front of him.

Inside lay his new allegiance.

Swiftly Mick crossed the threshold, embraced by music and lights.

The door shut with an echoing clang, its secret nightmare locked inside.

2

Don't leave me this way

Now can't you see it's burnin', out of control...
—Thelma Houston

24

Seashell whispers

1

The night is a jealous lover, holding its secrets pressed against its breast. But, as any proud parent, it yearns to boast of its deeds.

They will never know, David and Alex and Bobby — they will never learn of all the workings of the night. The vast city, the thousands of men, the many hands of darkness.

Come closer.

It seashell whispers, with tales to tell.

Listen:

2

Sixteen years had passed since Margaret Kreitman's husband William had held her in his arms, yet here he was, beside her, slipping beneath liliac-scented sheets. She knew it was William because of the soft steady patter of kisses he rained on her body with such gentle, intimate knowledge. Swimming up from an unusually heavy sleep, she yawned and stretched her flabby limbs, grateful for his touch. But it was a sound that had disturbed her, a slushy thump from Jack Martin's empty apartment up above.

Her room was dead-dark, buried behind thick green-and-gold draperies that allowed only the faintest mockery of light to creep around its fabric edges.

"William?"

(Yes, my love?)

"Is it really you?"

He answered with a kiss upon her sagging breast, teeth gently tugging back her flimsy nightgown to expose the brown pear of nipple. His tongue lit a fire upon her. She gasped as the heat consumed her utterly.

"Ohhhh…"

Memory skirted her thoughts: arriving home one late-November afternoon from a grocery expedition to find William sprawled across the Lay-Z-Boy recliner, "ABC World of Sports" on the unwatched television, bag of potato chips and half a bottle of Coors on the coffee table — William, dead of a heart attack at sixty-seven.

Dead — yet here he was, awakening a passion cooled to glowing embers by sixteen lonely years. He licked her breast and slipped a hand beneath her cotton nightgown and it felt too wonderful to protest, this warmth that rocked her like waves lapping over the forgotten foreign land that was her own passion. He began to push the nightgown up and up, exposing her to his roaming hand.

"Wait—"

(Yes)

"It's been so long—"

(I know)

He climbed above her, gentle but insistent, and to be so desired, so *wanted* after the barren wasteland that characterized the past sixteen years — it broke the ice of her resolve, hushing any further protest. He slipped into her, bigger than she remembered, impossibly huge, and the gasp that escaped her lips was equal parts pain and pleasure.

"Oh, William..."

(Dear heart)

He pinned her to the mattress. She writhed under him, head whipping side to side. William had been a hefty man, solid and wide as a door in life, but this William did not crush her with his weight.

He impaled her.

And when she began to murmur protests, when he thrust at her with a cruelty her husband had never possessed, she clawed at the shape above her, gagging with shock and revulsion as chunks of flesh came off in her hands like soft putty, screaming to no avail when a cold hand clamped down over her mouth, and a voice whispered into her ear:

(Pretty good fuck for an old lady)

It was Jack.

Jack, who loved her to death, in the empty black of a cold bedroom.

3

The kid had skin the color of Esther Williams's backside, an underwater green from too many laps around the pool. A jet-black pair of sunshades perched on a liquid nose. Hank wasn't so hip on the glasses, which hid too much of the boy's face, but the boy himself was A-okay in his book, yes indeedy. So what if the kid looked green around the edges? No Mediterranean glow on himself either, Mr. Desk Clerk Manager of the San Francisco Suites.

It was 12:05, the dawn side of midnight.

Hank had been waiting fifteen minutes for the J Church bus, here in the Powell Street Station. An ill-fitting suit bit the crack of his ass and hooked under his pudgy arms. He was a man in his midforties, hair salted with gray, gym-toned muscles of yesteryear going to fat. Hank wore blinders when it came to his ever-widening girth, still able (when he squinted) to see the man he had once been. He ached to adjust himself under his clothes, anxious to be free of his suit, but he couldn't stick his hand into his jockeys with so many people milling about.

Even at this time of night, with the underground buses winding down for the day, the station buzzed with activity. A Chinese family stood gathered in a circle, yammering with animated gestures. Two teenagers with spiked hair leaned into each other against the wall, a bored expression on the girl's face as she let her boyfriend's fingers roam. Two men about Hank's age gave minireviews of a play they had just seen, fresh from the Golden Gate Theater or ACT. Hank frowned. Not even one decent man to cruise to help pass the time.

Behind him, the rolling escalators ka-thumped ka-thumped ka-thumped, a conveyer belt in a coal mine. An oddly unsettling sound. Then again, maybe it poked at his already frayed nerves because he hadn't slept well the past two nights. Twice last night he had slammed awake, heart pounding, hands trembling. No reason, except perhaps his neighbor's tree scratching at his window. Fitful sleep until dawn.

Tonight, he intended to pamper himself, and soothe those jangled nerves. Pop on a porno tape when he got home of cute young boys with dancing eyes and eager mouths and dicks like the stick shift of an imported sports car. Afterward, blissful sleep.

He had drowsed in this thought, killing time, and then there he was, this kid with the pale skin and sunshades. He walked past Hank with mild indifference, all casual-like, but Hank saw the swelled crotch, deliberately thrust against baggy pants. No underwear.

The young man walked away from the crowd to stand alone beside the platform. He seemed to be fingering himself under the folds of his pants. He half turned to Hank, the glasses hiding his eyes, but he fancied he saw a glimmer of a smile on red lips. *Come and get me,* he seemed to be saying.

And Hank, who could not believe his good fortune, ached for the boy, his blood on fire.

He heard cables clanking and great metallic moans from the subway tunnel, and a bus roared toward the station. Stale warm air puffed ahead of it, tousling his hair. The J Church, his bus. A ribbon of hope wrapped around him: Perhaps this was the boy's bus as well, their secret cruising about to be extended.

The underground bus squealed to a stop. Doors popped open.

The boy did not move.

With a longing parting glance, Hank sighed at the inequities of age and stepped onto the bus. Row upon row of empty seats greeted him: He plopped down by a window.

A shadow moved to his right, and as he looked up from his disappointment there was the kid, sliding into the aisle seat directly across from him. Hank slapped on a poker face, but inside he danced a jig at his full house. Hot damn!

A buzzer rang and the doors clanged shut. They shot down the tunnel.

Civic Center and Van Ness stations next. Afterwards, the J Church would climb above ground and veer left, clanking up Church Street.

As they pulled out of the Van Ness station he and the boy teased each other with quick sideways glances. The boy adjusted himself exaggeratedly in his seat, and when he looked over, the boy's hand had casually dropped to his lap, outlining the significant bulge cradled there.

He had seen this once, in one of his porno movies. Two men on a subway in New York. Staged. Fake. This was better, the natural subtlety of their tease, the way each pretended they were not locked together. Raising the stakes for when they might come together.

The train emerged from the tunnel, chugging past the Safeway. The boy stroked and massaged himself. He stared fixedly out the window as the night pressed against the glass.

Hank shifted in his seat. He was hard, too. His hand drifted to his erection. He rubbed the outline of his hard-on for the boy to catch in the window's reflection.

They stopped at Market Street, where half the passengers disembarked. One or two people boarded, but miraculously, no one wandered into their section of the streetcar, spoiling the game. The train whined forward on electrical skates.

Hank stared at the boy, all pretense pushed aside. This time the boy did not shy away from the glance. Fire leapt and danced between them. They showed off their hard-ons through the fabric of their pants and pawed at them with their hands. A delirious joy swept through Hank. God! To bed this young man, tonight. To flip him over and spank that pale ass for being such a naughty boy, showing off on public transit. What would it feel like to slide into him from behind, a fistful of neck hair in his hand?

Hank's breath, all short gasps and pants.

Then the unbelievable happened.

The boy reached into his pants and pulled out his erection. Pale and lean, bowed slightly. He waved it at him.

Hank devoured it with his eyes.

He wanted to pull himself out of his pants too but trembled at the audacity of it all, the raw spunk and nerve. But he could scoot over onto the seat beside the boy, oh yes, and wrap his hand around that lean hard shaft. Whisper promises of an adventure. Hell, he'd even pay him money, if that's what the kid wanted. Hank had never bought anyone before but there was a first time for everything. He made to scoot across the aisle.

But the boy zipped himself back into his pants, one two, and sprang to the train doors. They were at Twentieth and Church, the top of Dolores Park — the place where David had come to sit that gloomy afternoon of Eddie's disappearance from Davies Hospital. The boy cocked his head for Hank to follow.

The train squealed to a halt, doors flung wide. The boy threw him a parting glance and stepped outside, waiting. Hank shot out of his seat, all thunder and sweaty palms, stumbling after.

He was hit by fog and moisture-laden wind. Hank lowered his eyes and waited for the J Church to sail by. When it passed, he raised his head with a foolish grin on his lips, ready to say hello.

Only no sound came out. His jaw dropped.

The boy stood ahead of him about ten yards away.

But Twentieth and Church: gone. Dolores Park, the view of downtown: gone.

Instead, he stood in the center of some back-alley street. The fog was so heavy it churned the air three-dimensional, clouds spinning off like newly formed galaxies. The only light streamed from the building looming in front of him, where the boy stood framed in a doorway. The boy had taken himself out of his pants again, wagging his hard-on. He leaned against an open black door.

(Come to me)

he said, all invitation.

Hank's feet scraped across pavement.

Red lips stretched into a smile. A flash of teeth. The boy was reaching for his sunglasses.

Hank shuddered: *Wait a minute! I know this place!*

And then he began to scream.

4

Seashell whispers.
The hum of telephone wire.
Listen:

5

What's your name?
Joey. And you?
Whatever you want it to be.
What does that mean?
I'm but a shadow. A voice in the night. Here, for your pleasure.
How'd you get my number?

Oh, I've been watching you. You use the phone like a hard dick in your hand. Call strange men and whisper to them. You stroke yourself while you talk, am I right? Aren't you in bed right now, touching yourself?

Maybe I am.

I am. I'm tugging on my balls right now, wishing it was your hand grabbing me. How about joining in?

...Sure. What do you look like?

I am blond, like you. Blue eyes. Five foot ten. Brown hair all over my chest, a line of it running down to my dick. Thighs and legs furry with it.

Jesus! We could be twins.

That's why I've watched you. I know you have a secret fantasy of playing with men who mirror you.

Wait a minute. Nobody knows about that. Nobody.

I am your twin, Joey. We're so handsome together, don't you think? Let's pull our dicks. Run our tongues over each other's nipples. Finger each other's sweet asshole.

Ahh...

Ohhh...

Talk to me, whoever you are.

I know of a palace, Joey. I want to take you there. I'd lead you into a mirrored room, where you'd strip out of your clothes. You'll show off for me, won't you?

Sure. You bet.

And when you are completely naked, you will kneel and wait for me. Hand upon your manhood. Waiting for my command.

God, I wish you were here!

You do?

I want to see you. Touch you.

Let me hear you work yourself, Joey. Let me hear you.

Ahhh ... Uhhh...

Faster.

Ohh ... Ohh!

You really want to see me?

Yes!

Look out your window.

And Joey, a likable guy with years of living ahead of him, a man surrounded by loving friends and supportive family, a man who watches his health like a hawk and who planned to live to a ripe old age, glances away from his erection and out his bedroom window and screams at the grinning devil face pressed against the glass. The creature holds a telephone receiver to his ear, the wire cord a dangling, chewed-off end. Joey hears it chuckle through his phone receiver, a sound as cold and jagged as Arctic moonlight.

An explosion of glass and fury.

As the creature falls upon him, and takes its communion meal.

6

Kevin sat up in bed.

The voice was calling to him through the wall.

Louder, tonight. Usually it remained a faint whisper, riding the patter of rain against his window, a ghostly, hair-raising sound. He'd heard it — or thought he'd heard it — almost every night, right after his worried parents would tear themselves from his bedroom with shaking heads. It was as if the voice knew to wait, to not reveal itself until Kevin lay on the edge of slumber, lulled into false security.

Yes, it would wait until he was all alone, and then buzz buzz buzz in his ear, an insect voice that somehow knew his name: *Keeevinnn.*

Mom worried a lot these days, her once-beautiful eyes clouded with concern. Dad worried too, only he tried not to show it. Sometimes he'd be sitting on the bed, talking low, coaxing Kevin into sleep, and Kevin would shut his eyes and open his small mouth as though it had popped open all by itself, wanting to be asleep but not asleep, and see Dad with his head in his hands, a terrible dry sound coming from him that was worse than the voice that waited for Dad to leave the room. He'd dig the palms of his hands into his eyes, and then catch himself, lest Kevin wake back up.

Most times, though, Dad would just hold Kevin in his arms and say how proud he was of him. Many of the other neighborhood kids had been sent to live with relatives in other parts of the city, but their family had no one close by, and so he stayed.

Kevin didn't mind.

For many days and nights parents had scoured the neighborhood for Miggy Garza, and turned up nothing. He tried to tell them — deep in his heart he knew where Miggy was, he just knew it — but everyone, his parents, Miggy's parents, his neighbors, even the two policemen who had sat him down on the couch — everyone talked *at* him and not *to* him, a frightened, glazed look in their eyes, not really listening at all. He told them Miggy had gone after his football next to *that place* — but instead of searching the building they talked and talked of men who lived in the streets, men who wanted Miggy for reasons that made his mother gasp as though she'd been punched. And so they had searched, and found nothing, and every night the voice in his bedroom got a little louder, a little closer, and the ticking of his bedroom clock sounded like the mournful gongs of the neighborhood church bells.

For he understood with a knowledge far ahead of his years that his life was narrowing down somehow, narrowing not just in years or months but days, hours, minutes. He knew, because the voice in the wall told him it was so. He waited out his days like a prisoner on death row, sleeping with a night light on and his closet door firmly shut, trying to ignore the sly whisperings that his parents said was only the wind.

When the water began to trickle down the Snoopy wallpaper in his bedroom on this Friday night, Kevin watched with an expression Miggy would have well recognized. He opened his mouth to call his parents back into the room, but dumb wonder held his tongue.

A fountain of brown water gurgled down the length of wall. Instead of spewing across the floor, it sank into the floorboards, somehow vanishing. A ripe toilet smell issued out; Kevin wrinkled his nose in disgust. The water began to thicken suddenly. In the dim penguin glow of his Opus night light it looked for all the world like pancake syrup oozed down his wall.

He hugged himself into a ball, gathering the sheets and blankets about him. "Mom," he gasped. "Dad." His tongue was a chunk of dry wood in his mouth. He thought he'd never be able to speak again — and then a choked rattle escaped his lips.

A football popped out of the wall. It arched high in the air, in miniature rainbow trail, before thumping to the carpet with a sludgy plop. Kevin scooted across the bed, flattening himself onto his stomach, to peer at it.

In the glow of Opus's light, he saw the signature: *Joe Montana*.

He sucked in his cheeks. Terror sparked across his vision like fireflies, winking points of light like Tinkerbell on that Disney show. His head swiveled, taking it all in: The football. The fountain. The football. The fountain.

And out of that waterfall, a voice — *the* voice — gargling through a mouth full of water:

(Toss me the ball, Keeevinnn)

Kevin bunched his hands into fists. The scream was stuck in his throat, lodged there like a Thanksgiving turkey wishbone, not going up, not going down. He scrambled up onto his knees, giving himself room for the wild heavings of his stomach, his chest. He managed two words: "Go away!"

But it didn't go away. In fact, something swelled out of the middle of the waterfall. A bubble shape twisted and unscrewed loose of the syrupy concoction that cascaded in seemingly slow motion around its sides. It shook itself, sending a spray in all directions. Lifted. White insect eyes blinked open below a tangled mass of hair. A raw slash of mouth ruptured open into a grin.

Miggy's head hung suspended in the middle of that dreadful waterfall like a mounted trophy. His eyes fastened upon him.

(Come and play with me, Kevin. Grown-up games. Come and play!)

The wishbone rose in his throat, pushed higher, to grant him his last request. He worked saliva into his tongue. Filled his lungs with air. And let go a wail of such black terror it shrieked through every corner of their house.

From down the hall, shouts answered his cries: "Kevin Ashley!"

And when Kevin's dad bounded into the bedroom, the missus right behind him in a whirl of white nightgown, all they found was an empty bed, and a football sitting on the floor in a puddle of water.

7

Maybe it will chase the blues away, Ralph thought as he positioned the twelve-inch disco single onto the turntable. He punched buttons and watched the mechanical arm purr into place.

And whatever rides the night sky, tonight.

Ralph backed away from the stereo as "Let's All Chant" tripped through his apartment. Sipping his screwdriver (he was one-third of the way through a bottle of Absolut and going fast), he felt a goofy grin spread across his wide face. For a few minutes, anyway, it was going to be 1977 again.

Not that he wanted the Old Days back, exactly — the smoky discos, the endless nights staggering back home strung out on the latest designer drugs — but, god, wouldn't it be wonderful to go just one day without It? To not have disease crash through every single day, week after week, year after year.

He'd lost track of the number of friends who'd gone under; it took too much out of him, to mourn every loss. He wasn't a callous son of a bitch (as Flint had often accused him of being). Ralph had simply discovered the days passed easier when he numbed himself. It was like having a sharpened triangle in his chest. With every death, the triangle turned, digging into his heart. Hurt like hell. But after a while, with every twist, the triangle's cruel edges dulled. The more it spun, the less it hurt. Shoot, these days he could pick up the *B.A.R.,* browse through the obits, and feel only the faintest remorse whenever familiar faces stared up at him from their final resting place.

Yeah, he'd been doing just fine, thank you very much — until Flint Stone disappeared. Vanished, without so much as a thank-you or good-bye. Something rotten about that, sure as shit, cause Flint was many things in his life but coward wasn't one of them. It smelled of trouble.

He and Will figured it out real fast: bad news from the clinic. Last Saturday night, right before they got dumped on by a huge fucking rainstorm, he and Will had hurried over to Flint's apartment, pounding on the door, demanding to be let inside. Flint was hiding inside, Ralph was sure of it. Flint was a kid when it came to bad news: He had to pout and sulk for a couple of days until it washed out of his system. That's what Flint had been doing, pouting, as they pounded on the door and demanded entrance. Flint wouldn't let them inside, and that was okay, in the long run, 'cause everybody deserves a little time to wallow when the axe hangs overhead, taking aim.

But the next day, when they cajoled the landlord into checking the apartment, Flint was gone. Ralph had expected to find Flint passed out on the bed, or moping in front of the TV, or simply sitting on the couch, staring into space — anything but *gone*. Gone was like dead, only worse somehow.

From that day forward, for Ralph, Flint's disappearance spelled the beginning of the end. He slid into a downward spiral that knew no end. The stormy weather and gray fog depressed him during the days, while at night his sleep was interrupted by the strangest visions. He awoke to find pools of sweat dripping off him, as if he'd spent half an hour in a sauna, and it didn't take a Jeane Dixon to figure out what night sweats meant, no sir. He was no fool when it came to guessing his odds.

Getting sick put the fear of god into his heart, sure it did, but it didn't spook him nearly so much as the *dreams*. And at forty-two, a black man from the rolling hills of Virginia, he hadn't been spooked in many a long year.

The other night he thought he saw Flint in his dream. It looked like Flint, only it wasn't him. They stood in the basement corridors of the Caverns, and Flint had motioned for him to enter a room. There were men in chains down there. It should have been sexy and right, but it was wrong. And he went anyway: That's what made him wet with fear. He had followed Flint into the dungeon, and the love was pain and dark and unutterably soiled. Ralph had careened awake with his own cum squirting out of him, the suffocating weight of that place upon him.

And beside the bed, on the nightstand, a ticket. Ralph recognized it even before he picked it up: a ticket to the Caverns, Admit One. His image was drawn upon the ticket, a ghastly vision, with his eyeballs gouged out and his black skin sewn with stitches, like Frankenstein's monster. He'd had to clamp a hand over his mouth to keep from screaming hysterically.

That had happened two days ago, and all that mattered now was locking every door and staying inside and dreaming of a time when the world was sweet.

As Ralph drank tonight, he began to see it all clear. That wasn't supposed to happen when you put a couple under your belt, but, hey, he was here to say horseshit. He saw clean through to it all.

Something had snatched hold of Flint and made him spoil, just as the city was spoiling. Something had snuck into town while they all had their backs turned, and it was mean, with sharp teeth. A couple of nights ago he and Will had swapped stories while they downed a few drinks at the Eagle. Seemed most everyone in the bar knew of someone who had "disappeared." Even Will, who drove a cab primarily in the gay neighborhoods, had had a few customers spin tales of vanished roommates or disappearing neighbors.

Thinking about that conversation greased the wheels of thought. Something rotten was happening, you betcha, and traditionally enough ole Flint squatted smack dab in the thick of it. Flint always did enjoy the limelight. How he was involved Ralph didn't know, but an inner radar told him he was on the right track.

He sipped his orange juice and vodka and shivered suddenly when he thought of that creepy downstairs dungeon inside the Caverns.

I'll help you, Flint, if I can. Whatever's gotten hold of you. I promise.

The bouncy refrain of "Let's All Chant" came to an end. Ralph flipped through his records and replaced it with Donna Summer and Barbra Streisand, "No More Tears (Enough Is Enough)." Vodka splashed onto the record jacket. Tonight, the shakes a wild beast. This music was supposed to remind him of happier times, but dread hooked its fingers into him even tighter.

Finishing his drink, he checked the double-bolted locks on his front door and secured the locks on his windows. He lived on the third floor of his apartment building, and while he doubted anyone could force themselves in through his windows, better safe than sorry was his motto. He was beyond caring what anybody thought, should they see him being such a 'fraidy cat (although that was how he saw himself: a 'fraidy cat).

Satisfied that every door and entryway was locked tight, Ralph meandered into the bedroom. He wanted to call Will and spill the beans about his theories. They had already talked to the police, and even to a couple of reporters (who wanted to dredge up their pet theory of gay devil-worshiping cults — why, right here in River City!). All to no avail. Will was a practical man who didn't take kindly to half-baked notions of satanic cults and secret kidnappers. Even though Will agreed that something fishy was going on, he had not yet come around to Ralph's assumptions that Flint and his bathhouse might be a part of it. He'd surely scoff at haunted bathhouses and ole Flint rattling chains from the Great Beyond.

He had to ease Will into it. This required kid gloves and a clear noggin. He couldn't talk to Will now, no siree, not with his thoughts all swimming in liquor.

Ralph stared into the bathroom, and an idea seized him. He'd take a shower. Shake this coiled restlessness with a quick hand job under the water. Slip into a robe. And call Will, the late hour be damned. With thoughts fresh and uncluttered, he'd ladle out his theories in bite-sized portions, and win his buddy over.

Jeans and shirt slid to the floor. Off came his socks with a funny jig. Vodka splashed onto the carpet. He drank a final gulp for the road and set down his glass.

Donna and Barbra became dreamy voices heard through intermittent splashes of water as he stepped into the hot spray. He let it play over his tension-wound muscles. Dipped his head under the shower nozzle and how good that felt, a massage of watery fingers on his scalp and neck and shoulders. The stinging slap of hot water was like the love blows of a lover's raised palm.

Time melted into the steamy mist.

Yeah, baby. Donna and Barbra on the speakers. The massaging spray. Steam rising in billows, up and across the ceiling, coating everything. How familiar it all was. How much like—

Before his mind even completed the name, he felt the hand cup his ass.

Ralph whirled around.

His ass stung where it had been touched.

Now a hand snaked up his inner thigh.

"Hey!" He hopped foot to foot, hands madly brushing his legs as though they swarmed with spiders. Too startled to even suspect what was happening, Ralph simply knew he was being groped and that he saw no one.

He waited — but it stopped as suddenly as it had begun.

He stood under the spray, eyes huge with fright, hiccupping for control. Briefly, with a lover's tease, he felt a lick of tongue upon his uncircumcised cock.

Ralph jumped back, hands sawing the air, and this time, with the steam-heavy cotton clouds, he glimpsed a shadow leap back into the steam's embrace. Something frog- and apelike, if such a thing was possible. The shower wall shimmered, throwing off its three-dimensional geometry.

He buried his upturned face underneath the full brunt of the shower, determined to rinse these illusions right out of his head. His legs wobbled, threatening mutiny. *Hurry!* his mind shouted. *Get out of here, quick, before it comes back!*

He squinted through the cascading water to double-check the solidity of the tiled wall, but before he had an opportunity to look, the world splashed a rusty mud color.

What's this? Ralph wondered. He dug his fists into his eyes, withdrew. And shrieked with childhood terror.

Blood.

Head-to-toe covered in it.

It poured out of the shower nozzle in a ghastly effluence.

Ralph pinwheeled backward, gagging. His hands flew to the shower curtain and tore it aside as he stumbled out onto white tile. Mutiny! came the rallying cry of his legs, and too sick with disgust to help himself, he sagged onto the floor. Tears blurred his vision. His stomach heaved.

Something dive-bombed and plopped against the wet floor. Ralph, sick and disoriented, gasping with dry heaves, opened his eyes and looked. The blood — if it had ever splashed over him at all — was gone.

But directly in front of him on the floor, something even worse: Admit One tickets to the Caverns. A dozen of them. The red ink was running, blurring the images upon the tickets, but he easily recognized his face on all of them, distorted by a thousand horrors.

He raised himself to one knee and spied his surroundings. His bathroom, his apartment, gone. He knelt by the entrance to an enormous steamroom.

He had imagined himself in the Caverns, and here he was.

From loudspeakers overhead, warped and dreamy: Donna and Barbra.

The steamroom door swung open with a hiss of hot wet air. Every muscle in Ralph's body tensed. *Slow down!* his mind shouted. *I don't understand what's happened! Let me think!*

He stared at the open mouth of the steamroom and a penny-dreadful premonition gripped him of monsters with glowing red eyes, creatures with claws and fangs come to feast—

A blond man emerged from the steam. Sweat-slicked. Naked. Tousled hair dripping into his eyes. A swimmer's lean build. Full lips pulled back in a shy greeting. Another man coughed out of the steam, this one older with brown hair that lay as a fur upon his body. This was a man who worshiped at a gym, every muscle perfectly defined, without an ounce of extra fat upon him. He stepped up to the blond and draped an arm about his shoulder. The combination of the two men, one older, muscular, the other boyish and slim, inflamed Ralph with an unexpected — yet somehow calculated — lust.

Who are you? What are you doing here? he wanted to ask, but they began to glide toward him in all their delicious nakedness, eyes twinkling and lips parted. They circled him in a sort of dance, fondling him with smoldering eyes.

And Ralph, despite himself, reached out his hand.

Touched the blond boy with the eager smile.

And watched as his fingers sank into the boy's chest cavity, a pus-and-blood mixture squirting out with shocking suddenness, speckling his own face and chest. It was like sticking his hand into a bowl of gone-over cottage cheese. He tried to withdraw it, but some inner working held it captive among the blood and guts, the stew of the boy's insides making a meal out of his hand. The blond was grinning.

Ralph's shocked cries echoed in this steamy chamber, bouncing back to haunt his own ears.

The boy grabbed Ralph's forearm and withdrew the hand from his chest with a slushy wet plop. It was almost unrecognizable, smeared red with a syrup too ghastly to look at. The gaping hole of the boy's chest rearranged itself, correcting this affront to its anatomy.

Both men held him down, mildew-slick hands greasing each armpit. They were forcing him to kneel down. The tile floor bit into his kneecaps.

Riding a wave of eucalyptus-scented steam, a voice:

(You've been a bad boy, Ralph)

Ralph jerked his head. "Flint?"

(I can't have you poking your nose where it doesn't belong, now can I?)

It had Flint's voice but the inflection was all wrong, something European where it should have been Georgian smooth. And the *malice*. Oh dear god, the malice oozing from those words.

"Flint!" Ralph wailed. "I'm — I'm — I'm your friend! Your buddy! Don't let them hurt me!"

(Hurt? Why, I'm giving you your dreams, Ralph. All your secret desires!)

The steamroom door swung shut, white clouds beating against the glass.

And Ralph, who had come close to understanding what had happened but never would know for sure, was dragged, protesting, through tunnels he did not know existed, down into the earth, as the men at each side took on the true shape of their corruption. He was dragged through inky darkness into an earthen chamber and chained to a wall, and all the terrible rites and desires he had performed in his dream nights earlier were now performed on him. In that soulless dark they howled at his screams and rent his flesh with teeth grown long and hideous until madness became his blessed refuge, and he embraced its muddied waters.

Ralph knew nothingness, and nothingness was good.

Until he flew awake some time later, arms and legs in chains, and the feeding began all over again.

8

Victor, in his palace, drank.

He grew fat upon the slaughter, semen sluicing down his chin like the blood of a ghost, consumed by an unquenchable thirst. He wallowed in the offerings of his shadows. Scooped bowls of man sweat and ripe jism into his cupped hands and poured it over his mouth, his face, Adam's apple bobbing as he drank, reveling in the strength and power that infused him.

And he began to change.

His kinetic being sought new geometries, punching through and beyond the masquerade of a body he had assumed. He drilled into the raw ore of human emotion that infused these walls, melding its energies with his. Lust had splattered these walls, its imprint steeped into the woodwork, and Victor was heady with it. Let them all come to him: men, women, children. Let them all feel his breath upon their faces. To perish by their own desires, and fuel his life in return: not a bad bargain.

Victor's eyes gleamed.

He flexed his new muscle, and felt the outer walls of the building ripple with his thought.

Ahh. Let it begin.

25

From beyond

D avid felt it — like a door slammed shut upon his soul. Like the inescapable clang of a jail cell.

Roger swung by him with a bus tub of dirty dishes. "You okay?"

He waved him away.

"You look like someone just walked on your grave."

"Thanks, pal," David retorted. "I could say the same about you."

"But you're too nice a guy," Roger quipped. He carried the bus tub into the back kitchen where Sam, the only cook to report in that night, was studiously scrubbing down the double set of oven burners. "Thank *god* this night is over!" he trilled out from the kitchen.

David steadied the erratic thumping of his heart. He kept seeing and sensing it, a black door clanging shut. The image was disconnected, frightening in its very simplicity, its ordinariness. Yet it stood for a decision that had no back door, no emergency exit. He knew that whatever happened on this night bore the same finality as death.

He tended to his chores with a precision born of familiarity. He'd had only a handful of customers, so setting up the tables for the following evening took a fraction of the usual time. He reset tables, checked salt and pepper levels, restocked sugar packets and sweetener. Since they were shorthanded, David helped Sam and Roger clean up the kitchen.

Besides, keeping busy held more dangerous questions at bay. Why wasn't Alex answering his phone? What had happened?

And since no ride would appear at the end of his shift, that meant he was walking home. He could handle the trudge up the Noe hill. But these nagging images of doors slammed shut...

Roger whirled past. "Why don't you pack it in for the night? Sam and I can finish up here by ourselves."

"You're the one who wanted to leave."

"And I will. Soon enough."

Sam, a short burly man with a ribbon of auburn hair wrapped around his bald head, waved David on with a pudgy hand. "Go on. Scoot. I'm outta here in ten minutes." He glided across the floor balancing two saran-wrapped bowls into the giant walk-in freezer. He moved with a dancer's grace, his upper body bulk rendered invisible by his satin-smooth footwork. "I'm hitting the cha-cha palace tonight," he boasted, fingers snapping. "These feet are in a dancing mood." He caught David's sharp glance in his direction, and saw the temptation to comment on his desire to go out dancing — but then David walked away, silence chosen. Sam nudged Roger. "What's eating him?"

Roger shrugged. "It goes double for me, whatever it is."

David emerged from the back office, where he'd gone to fetch his jean jacket. Glum faced. "Good night, guys."

"Still no word from your friend?" Roger asked, intercepting. And an odd thought: *This boy looks like he's about to face a firing squad.*

David shook his head.

"Let me call you a cab."

"That's okay."

Roger pressed the issue. "No sense walking home in this shitty weather, even it if is only a couple of blocks."

"Don't bother. Really. See you guys later."

When he stepped out of Uncle Charlie's, his resolve faltered. Castro Street was a morgue. Oh, a few hardy souls braved the street, clustered in tight knots. One lone man meandered by in jeans so tight they could have been painted on, wearing a t-shirt that said, "No one looks bad after 2 a.m." A tan sport coat — polyester-leisure-suit style — topped off his odd appearance. The suit was much too big for him, the sleeves hanging down past his wrists, and the shoulders looked as though they had been draped. One of the huge lapel collars stuck out at an angle into the air.

David stared — and the man acknowledged him with a nod and a goofy smile. He continued down Castro Street toward Eighteenth, whistling a bouncy refrain that sounded vaguely familiar.

David hurried up the street. He'd expected a sharp wind to howl down the street — from inside Uncle Charlie's, it certainly looked freezing outside — but the air was surprisingly humid. He didn't even bother to button his jacket.

His anxiety increased as he neared the corner of Nineteenth and Castro. He was leaving behind the lighted storefronts and streetlamps, heading into huge gulfs of predatory darkness that lined the long blocks to Noe Street. He paused at the corner and glanced up to Twin Peaks, where the three towers glowed like lights from an alien spaceship in the fog. He shivered at his own nervousness. And thought: *Just get the hell home.* He started across Nineteenth Street.

And jumped out of his skin when the phone in the public telephone booth across the street began to ring.

Jesus. David stepped onto the curve in front of the closed-up Mandarin restaurant on the corner. There were two phones placed back to back in one of the new-style open phone booths. The phone closest to him was ringing. He turned to leave.

The second phone began to ring.

He stared at it. The flesh on his arms crawled. He stood, rooted to the spot.

Don't answer it.

He remembered his short story, and Mick, and the feelings of danger. *Don't pick up the phone.*

He retreated, heart hammering. He walked briskly up Nineteenth Street toward Noe. His right hip began to hurt from his pace, but he ignored it. The ringing of both phones pierced the night muffled by drizzly fog, as though there were no other sound in the world but that jarring cry, demanding that he listen, and answer. His head whipped side to side, scanning the dark stairwells, the tiny alleyways between houses. He began to whistle, a childhood defense to ward off evil spirits as he walked, but then stopped almost immediately when he realized he was whistling "On and On and On," an old Abba tune. The man in the polyester leisure suit had been whistling it.

As he neared the corner of Nineteenth and Noe, David sucked in a breath. Only a month ago the market had installed a pay phone outside its doors. Amber light from the overhead street lamp reflected off shiny metal. He slowed to a halt and regarded the phone with curiosity.

Back down the two long blocks he had walked, he heard it: the two phones axed in midring, like birds felled by a hunter—

—And then the phone in front of him burst into a ring.

David jumped and glanced quickly around him, ready for anything that might swoop out of the dark. No: He was alone, alone with these pay phones, each daring him to pick up its receiver. Each brittle ring bit into his indecision.

I'm out in the open. Alone. This is meant to scare me, and it's working. Leave the fucking thing alone.

Keeping his eyes fixed on the telephone — as if any moment its structure would melt and shift and mold into some horrible breathing creature — he stepped beyond the phone and chanced a couple of backward steps up the hill.

The ringing was insistent. Daring him. Answer. Answer.

David took the bait.

He marched up to the phone and drew the receiver to his ear. He couldn't be afraid forever; he had to face up to it, see what this was all about.

"Hello?"

He expected a man's voice, but what he got was Grace Jones.

Watch out, punk
You haven't a clue
Coming to get you
Get you

David jerked the phone away, the disco song a dynamite blast in his ear. He made to slam down the phone when a voice rose above the song like a long sigh: "Daaavid..."

An icicle stabbed his heart. His scalp crawled. That *voice*. Could it really be?

"Heeelllp meee..."

Full of trepidation, he brought the phone to his ear. Grace strutted her stuff, the old tune ingratiatingly coy.

From high, from low
Better watch your backside, boy
Coming to get you...

"Eddie?" He didn't dare believe it, but oh, how he ached with hope against hope. "Is it really you?"

"I'm not supposed to be here," rasped the voice. "I've come to warn you."

It sounded like Eddie, but the words were spit out, gargled, like speaking through a mouthful of water.

Was his friend — somehow — still alive?

"What's happened to you? Where are you?"

A sobbing cry. "It hurts, David."

He shut his eyes, not wanting to hear.

"I have a message..."

He held his breath.

"Bring Him the stone."

"The what?"

"Bring it to Him," Eddie said. "Or—"

"Or?"

"Or we will feast upon you."

Something wet seeped into his ear. He pulled the phone away and cringed with disgust. Syrupy ropes of sludge bubbled up out of the phone, like a toilet overflowing. The Eddie-thing was laughing, a sound like the gurgle of a drowning man.

David dropped the receiver. It banged against the storefront and dangled in midair, oozing entrails to the ground. Now Grace needed a man, perhaps a man like you.

He fled. The horrible gunk muddied his left ear, where he had pressed the phone to it. He half ran up the Noe hill, gasping for breath, desperate to be home, his face burning with this joke played upon him.

Relief as he slipped his key into the gate and he stepped inside. Home.

2

He had to take the risk.

Last night he had posed the question, and somehow seen inside the monster's domain. Since he had succeeded without even knowing how he did it, perhaps tonight, with conscious effort and willpower, he could do it again.

But David was afraid. He sat white-knuckled on his bed, listening to a wind that had picked up, howling around his apartment. Fear: the barrier behind which lay all knowledge. He didn't have to move the huge boulder out of the way, not completely — and he doubted he owned enough courage for the task — but if he could move this rock of fear aside just enough to slide on by, then perhaps its crushing weight would lighten into its true shape: a mirage, created by his own mind.

He shook his head.

God, he wanted a joint.

He wanted Alex. Why hadn't Alex answered his phone? Had something happened to him?

Most of all, he wanted to wake from this nightmare.

Smoking was out of the question. Yes, the marijuana would relax him, and take away the ache in his hip from his panicked run up the hill to his flat. But he could not chance the muddled thoughts, the misdirected intentions. He had to be of one purpose, one mind. There was nothing moralistic about this decision: He simply could not chance getting high.

So he filled his lungs with deep regular breaths and imagined a blank screen in his mind. This technique was nothing new: He used it often when creating images for his stories, for once a picture in his head had the rightness and texture of a memory, he could describe on paper what he was seeing.

He adjusted the pillow that he'd stuffed behind the small of his back and leaned against the headboard of his bed. His legs were folded into loose pretzels above the covers. His limbs tingled with sleepy pinpricks as body and awareness numbed to automatic pilot. His chin drooped to his chest. His forehead pulsed with phantom energy.

On that clear blackboard in his mind, he wrote:

Show me how to defeat this thing.

The tingling in his hands and feet trickled up the rest of his body to join forces around his heart. A curious sensation rocked him, as though he sat in a canoe that tilted side to side. A roar in his ears was the sound of his own blood pulsing through his veins. The waves underneath him gained strength. His entire body was caught in the grip of powerful vibrations.

Show me.

He lost all notion of where his body ended or began; the vibrations, like some kind of electromagnetic energy, were an embryonic soup that encased him completely. No pain: just this warm pulsing current.

Show me.

The back of his head bumped against the headboard, and David — who knew his chin had rested against his chest — opened his eyes in surprise.

And got an even greater surprise.

He was bouncing against his bedroom ceiling, legs uncurled, stretched out flat.

Below, immobile on the bed like a mannequin posed for a store window display, lay his body.

What happened? Am I dead?

His panic brought on a sudden bobbing and wild fluctuations as he bounced against the ceiling. He felt a tugging on his back, and a sinking sensation that seemed to encourage a return to his body — but almost at once he calmed himself. Frightened? Unquestionably. Yet this was fantastic. So this is how he'd traveled into Victor's lair!

Victor.

Show me how to defeat—

And the spirit, wish granted upon command, took him into

3

a roaring tunnel
shooting stars

4

to a place totally unfamiliar.

He hovered in the air, an unseen witness to a clustered group of men, women, and children, huddled outside a squarish thatched hut. Their black skin garishly outlined bones in their too-thin bodies. Crying babies nursed against mothers who had no milk. Tiny children, their bellies distended with disease, sat in the sun-baked grass and dirt.

A man squatted in front of the largest of these huts, guarding the entrance. He was lean-limbed and thin, a short man reduced to angles and bones. His eyes were closed, making his head appear too big for the meager neck and shoulders supporting it. A piece of tree bark sat before him on the ground; some kind of design had been drawn on its smooth underside. The man's lips moved with religious fervor. All of the adults surrounding the hut were bowed in prayer, their softly uttered words the buzzing of a hundred bees.

It was early evening in this world, the heat of a scorching day only now retreating with the setting of the sun behind the distant jungle. The multitudinous chirp of nesting birds competed with the slice-the-air cries of locusts.

What dream place is this? Who are these people?

That last question glowed brightest of all in his consciousness, and generated movement. He felt himself lowering toward the hut, powered by decision. He drifted, invisible, toward the hut's entrance — but the guard seemed to sense his presence. The man jerked his head, concern and wonder a deeply etched expression upon his hunger-thin face. He groped for his drawing upon the ground as if for reassurance. Then the oddest thing: An almost completely toothless smile stretched ear to ear. He shut his eyes and resumed a singsong prayer.

David entered the dim interior of the hut. It was lit by a few spurting candles on the dirt floor. A stifling heat flowed through him. A paper-thin string of smoke twirled up into the air from a wooden bowl: incense, hickory, wildflowers. Smoke wafted past his face, the aroma sharp in his nostrils, and it was this smell, so undeniably textured and authentic, that convinced him this fantastic experience was no mere dream.

A man with jet-black skin, dark as a winter's night, lay on a straw mattress. He appeared to be thirty-five, forty years old, with a close crop of grizzled hair going gray. A wide nose, full lips. His cheeks were dabbed with paint, and his forehead glistened with a reddish, crudely drawn circle. Emaciation painted his face with harsh strokes. Was this ceremony a deathwatch? His legs were gnarled, his arms stringy ropes of muscle. A simple loincloth covered his genitals. Both hands lay upon his stomach, upturned in supplication. An object the size of a baseball was being held, and David felt himself inexplicably drawn to it.

It was a gemstone of some kind, the bottom half a rounded crusty shell of rock. It rose out of this shell into a central jagged point. The crystal-clear peak snatched the flickering candlelight and broke it into a dozen fractured rainbows. The stone's center was a majestic royal purple.

The black man popped open his eyes.

David recoiled in shock.

The man raised the stone in offering and whispered one word: "Kahmaal."

Does he see me? David wondered. No; the eyes swept about the entire room, not resting upon him at all. So why did he feel the offering was unmistakably for him? And the word: "Kahmaal." An incantation? A name?

The man hugged the stone to his chest, touched it lightly above his heart, and then raised it into the air, toward him. "Kahmaal," he whispered.

David stared at the sparkling stone. A sudden darkness thudded down around everything but the stone, and the pair of hands holding it. A windstorm roar filled his head. Syncopated flashes burst through his mind with a dizzying velocity. He saw a succession of hands holding the stone: black white brown white white black white. And the stone itself being chipped at, polished, losing its outer earthen crust, diminishing in size but hewn into extraordinary beauty. He was pulled along at this hair-raising pace, a witness to the stone's journey through many owners, young and old, wealthy and poor.

The dark curtain lifted a little. The whirlwind roar subsided. David saw a kitchen table, upon which sat the crystal. It had been shaped into a pyramid, its triangular point rising out of a milky base, with the tongue of purple buried within its center. It sat upon a white bed of silk.

He lifted his gaze from the gemstone. Cupped hands surrounded the stone. The hands belonged to a woman with long, flowing rusty hair — red hair that had dulled with age, streaked silver. She had a plump pumpkin face with a wide, wrinkled forehead. A trace of freckles sprinkled her nose and both cheeks. A fluffy blue robe folded across her ample figure.

She looked exhausted, worn out. The only part of her that seemed vibrantly alive was her hazel eyes, which stared with transfixed intensity at the gemstone before her.

Hope shot through the soil of his consciousness like a magnificent flowering plant: Was *this* the woman who could help him? He wanted to talk to her, reach out to her.

Suddenly she tensed, like a cat sniffing out an enemy. Her bowed head snapped to attention, blue-green eyes startled as they bore into him. Her jaw dropped.

"Get out," she hissed through clenched teeth.

And David, confidence in his invisibility shattered, reared back. He felt a powerful tugging from his back, as though he were attached to a rope that had now drawn tight into a tug-of-war, urging him backward.

The woman was beside herself, trembling with indignation and naked terror. "Get out!"

From across the room a young man's voice rang out: "Mom? What's wrong?"

The tugging on his back was undeniable.

No! I have to talk with her! Let me stay! — but it was too late; he was lassoed backward out of the small kitchen, into a dark room crowded high with bookshelves stuffed to overflowing, drawn through the wall somehow so that he glimpsed a storefront with its big glass window, rows of brick and solid oak door. There were words painted onto the glass window, the store's name written in a half-arc, but David couldn't catch it, saw letters but had no time to grasp the full name, and he felt himself flipped upside down as though on a carnival ride—

5

And plopped back inside his own body.

David startled awake, limbs tingling in shock, a gasped breath drawn like an infant's first taste of life. A sharp pain flared in his hip as he unwrenched his stiff legs and stretched them across the bed. His heart banged against his chest. His physical body felt heavy, cumbersome.

And he heard it once again, whispering up from the lips of a man long dead, the mysterious word:

Kahmaal.

26

Oblivion,
and back again

1

Now it was Bobby's turn to hide.

He needed it. Needed the black well he'd parachuted down into — deep corridors where the walls were soft cotton and draped him like a comfortable, well-worn robe. This was his haven, a place within himself that no Halloween monsters could raid. And so he rested.

2

After being left alone, he had crawled to his bed and passed out, numbed by shock and exhaustion. At one point he awoke with his fists pummeling his pillow, *betrayed betrayed* branded into his brain by red-hot pokers: angry at his desertion, at being left this way.

And then he'd discovered, as he sank back into a feverish sleep, that the mind has secret corridors in which he could roam, corridors of fleecy cotton that stroked and soothed with a mother's gentle touch.

It's not so bad down here — so he stayed.

3

He might very well have remained inside this padded wonderland except for a sudden discovery: He was not alone.

A black man glided toward him, head bowed in shy greeting. He was about Bobby's height, and excruciatingly thin. Shoulder blades stuck out like curtain rods in an attempt to hold up the weight of his body. Every cruel detail of the black man's starvation was humiliatingly visible; he wore only an animal hide wrapped around his genitals. Row upon row of rib cage framed his stomach.

His nose was flat and broad, with black button eyes on either side almost obscured by a thick bush of wiry eyebrow. He smiled at Bobby obsequiously and bowed as if to apologize for interrupting the solitude of his master. He motioned for Bobby to follow, his hands like anxious blackbirds.

Bobby — who had lost all sense of time, down here in this cotton world — followed. The man's identity did not matter; he was simply another dream-prop in this comforting gray maze where he had come to rest. So he followed the man down a flight of stairs, each step creating itself as they walked, down to a secret place. Out of the cloudy landscape appeared a table hewn from a large slab of tree trunks, thick paper spread upon its surface, with charcoal and chalk at its side.

The black man gestured toward the table, guiding him toward it.

Bobby furrowed his brow. "What do you want?"

In the ancient one's hands a sheet of yellow note paper appeared, and with a jolt of recognition, he saw his doodles scrawled across its face. He could see the torch, the pyramid, the hut, the man with the typewriter. The man then pointed to himself, indicated the blank paper and chalk, and gestured to Bobby, drawing him toward these accessories. Compelled by this dark man so like those tribesmen pictured in *National Geographic* magazines, he approached.

The African repeated his gestures, seeming to say, "I draw, you draw."

"Okay." Bobby stepped up to the table and took a piece of charcoal into his hand.

The African bobbed with enthusiasm, contact at last. He grinned a gap-toothed smile of half a dozen crooked teeth.

"What should I draw?"

The hands encouraged: anything, anything.

He shook his head and sighed. The charcoal took on sudden life as it touched paper. His hand flew across the parchment. He drew a triangle. Shaded it in, and added rainbow light emanating out of it by drawing squiggly lines.

The African nodded his head, pleased. He took a piece of charcoal into his own hand and Bobby stepped back to give the man elbow room. The hand worked at a frantic pace without jerky stops and starts. With confident strokes he drew the face of a man very much like himself: broad nose, wide cheeks and forehead dabbed with ceremonial paint, solemn piercing eyes, and full, almost feminine lips. When he was finished, he withdrew to give Bobby a good look.

"Who is it?" Bobby asked.

The African pointed to the man's face and then rested a thin finger on the triangle shape Bobby had drawn.

And softly intoned, "Kahmaal."

"What?"

"Kahmaal." He repeated his gesture, face to triangle, face to triangle. Cocked his head to stare into Bobby's eyes, and the intimate contact of that powerful look shocked him with its naked pleading, its insistence that was an energy all its own.

Bobby struggled to understand.

Danger signals were going off inside his head, flares with red-ribbon trails. He felt chosen, his escape threatened. Visions of Mick. Like shards of glass—

The gray landscape quivered: *No. This is why I'm here, don't think about it — about Him—*

The African was drawing again. He took the side of the charcoal and swirled an S shape, like a tornado whirlwind, and drew a circle around it. The shape contained the unspeakable violence of wind and storm. The black man's eyes were grave when they lifted away from his drawing.

Bobby could sense the incredible power of evil emanating from that shape, and he knew. Dark shadows tore at him. He remembered, and dared himself to whisper that name. "Victor."

The African nodded. The eyes, black liquid pools, sparked with alarm. Once again he pointed to the drawing of the pyramid shape and the man. "Kahmaal."

Slowly Bobby began to feel it. This "Kahmaal" was somehow connected to the nightmare that had been his life in the last few days. And if there were others, then there was the possibility of salvation. This place was no padded cell of refuge, but instead one of clarity, and knowing.

Another nod. And more encouragement for him to use the charcoal in his hand.

Acquiescing, he began to doodle across the paper, drawing shapes and figures as they popped into his head. He glanced away from his drawing of a man with books, looked up through the well of gray, and saw a hole up above. The ceiling contained a trapdoor to the heavens.

Bobby knew what lay beyond that trapdoor: his apartment, his life, his reality. Scribbling onto this paper would take him back, if that's what he wanted. "Knowing" would take him back. But to wreckage, and hopelessness?

He stared at the African, who met his gaze with sad, doomed eyes.

"I have to go?" He knew the answer but required the nod, the confirmation, that the man gave him. Oh, but there were so many delicate corridors to explore down here, so many chambers. Hadn't the African appeared through one of those very doors himself? Who else waited to greet him with enigmatic games to play?

The African pointed to the whirlwind symbol, and a glittering, frightened look came into his expression. Charcoal skimmed the paper. Bobby watched as lines and shapes came together to form Mick's face. Shocking, to see his lover's image appear under this stranger's hand.

"Do you know where he is?" Bobby coughed out. His throat was sawdust.

The hand responded by drawing the tornado design over Mick's face: Victor and Mick, intertwined.

Bobby's lower lip began to tremble. "No," he said, breathless at the thought of it, the horror. "No; I won't let it happen, I won't—"

He gazed up at the trapdoor from his position at the bottom of the well. A frantic wind tore at the cotton clouds, hurled paper off the table, charcoal and chalk flying.

I won't let it—

And he awoke to a midmorning, watery light pooling across his bed sheets.

4

He began to draw.

Which meant he was more than a little crazy. Off the deep end. Nuts, big time.

What did it matter? Who was here besides himself, to see the wreckage of his apartment? No law said he had to clean it up. He tiptoed around shattered glass strewn across the hardwood floor to make himself a pot of coffee. Rummaged through drawers for a spiral notebook, and a couple of number-two lead pencils. Returned to his bedroom, coffee, notebook, pencils in tow, and settled in for the next couple of hours.

Fragments of his encounter with the African hurled disjointedly through his mind, but instinctively he understood that details of this dream were not the important issue. This overpowering urge to sketch and draw — that's what was significant. There were answers in the shapes he'd been doodling over the past several days; Bobby knew this without understanding how he knew, or why it was important. Ever since stirring awake he'd been seized with the idea that if he began to put pictures onto paper, he'd find his route to Mick, and a way to combat this Victor.

His first drawings were frustratingly aimless: faces with no definition or identity, amorphous buildings whose only characteristic were big black doors at the end of a short flight of steps. Quite by accident, he discovered that when he lay the fingers of his left hand against his forehead and sat in contemplation with eyes shut, images began to flood over him. His right hand couldn't keep up with the flow. He sketched hurriedly, boldly, allowing the drawings to take shape underneath his hand.

He drew a dozen variations of a triangular-based pyramid. Bobby liked these pictures the best, because a certain warmth, a certain strength emanated from the pyramid-shaped object, which he found to be enormously comforting. In the last of these he added two figures above the pyramid: a woman with long flowing hair and a thin man beside her, taller but younger by many years. No other features were clear.

Then he began to draw pictures that greatly disturbed him: infants cradling empty stomachs; two feet bound together with rope; a net falling out of the sky. They chilled him, these horrible images, and puzzled him. What did crying babies have to do with Mick?

Morning gave way to afternoon. Bobby flipped to a clean page. He wanted something concrete, an image that would give him clear direction. He closed his eyes, touched his fingers to the area of his forehead that had once throbbed like a bad tooth, and asked himself: *Who can help me?*

The pencil responded.

He drew almond-shaped eyes set in a strong face and topped with wavy black hair. No, wait; not so much hair. The man has a receding hairline. A high forehead. He shaded in the pupils of the almond eyes, suddenly knowing their color should be green.

Heard the voice ask: *Are you ... Bobby?*

The pencil tapped the page. A smile, hesitant at first, spread across his lips. *This man. I saw him in my dream with Mick. And I drew him yesterday afternoon at the copy shop; I drew him hunched over a typewriter. Is he the one? Can he help me?*

How can I find him?

He flipped to a clean blank page in the spiral notebook.

I ought to get dressed.

I can't waste the daylight.

His hand moved, and wrote:

Find him.

27

Out of mind

1

Davdid woke up tasting tea in the back of his throat. He could almost smell it too, an aroma of herbs and cinnamon and lemon drifting through his chilly apartment. He downed cups of black coffee in an effort to squelch the taste, but it coated everything like heavy cough syrup. Occasionally he caught a whiff of something unpleasant. A musty smell. Woodsy.

He thought about what had happened to him last night.

He thought about what *may* have happened to Alex Webster. For here it was ten in the morning, and still no answer when he called. Each unanswered ring only took him deeper and deeper into despair.

In his lowest moments he knew Alex could be dead. Alex, who would refuse to believe even as he opened a window to allow one of those creatures inside.

And when he glanced out his own window, no definition separated land and sky: All was a metallic gray, silent and unmoving. Not a soul trudged down Noe Street toward the Castro. There had been casualties during the night. The smoke from last night's battle clouded the morning air, mixing with this cloying aroma of tea.

The more he thought about what had happened to him — where he had gone, what he had seen — the more he knew the woman was a key to solving this complex puzzle. If not the woman herself, then what he saw she possessed: that magnificent stone. Even that impostor with Eddie's voice had said:

Bring Him the stone.

What powers did it possess? How did it tie in to the African? Most important of all, could he use it against this evil?

David stared out his sliding glass doors as if wanting its depressing view to seep into him. Ten in the morning, and yet the day seemed defeated, already dropping over the edge into eternal twilight.

Well, I'm not defeated. Not yet anyway. I've got to use this daylight, such as it is, before it slips away from me. Face facts. Alex Webster is of no help. This Mick and Bobby, even if I am somehow seeing their lives, are on their own. I can't find them. I've tried.

But I can look for the woman.

If I can trust my visions, what I saw last night was some sort of shop — a bookstore? The store's name was written in a half circle on its glass window. I'd recognize it when I saw it again. And I'll recognize her, too. She had felt me, and I had undoubtedly scared her last night. If I could just talk to her, I could allay whatever fears she might have, and let her know I'm on her side...

Half an hour later he was showered, dressed, and out the door. The keys to Eddie's Audi were tightly clenched in his hands. Eddie had always made it clear that he was free to use the car whenever he needed it. Even with such permission, he felt funny about it. This was Eddie's car; it represented that last foothold into a normal life outside of hospitals. He'd respected that, kept his distance with an ungrounded hope that one day Eddie would be able to drive it again. Deep in his heart he'd known it would never come to pass, but the hope had remained, a tiny flame burning inside him.

Sorry, pal. Hope you understand.

David unlocked the driver's side and slipped into the cold interior. No time for sadness now; he had to be strong. He gave the engine a few minutes to warm up.

Now where?

He steadied himself with several deep breaths and mentally opened the door inside his head. *Show me where you are.*

The tea taste tickled the back of his throat. He thought of what he'd glimpsed last night, a shop crowded high with books and curios. An old storefront sandwiched between other shops. It was hard to reconcile his visions with what his mind now remembered as reality.

He backed the car out of the open garage and headed down Noe. What the hell. A full tank of gas. There was a bit of time before he would lose this precious daylight. He came to a halt at the stop sign on Eighteenth Street and nibbled his lower lip in contemplation. His intuition seemed to whisper turn right, which would take him into the mostly Spanish Mission district. Then he thought of the Haight Ashbury. With its weathered Victorians and tempered charms, the storefront he held in his head like a photograph fit in perfectly with the funky nature of the neighborhood.

He could almost hear a voice inside his head: *Go to the Haight.*

Okay, okay.

He turned left.

2

Where the Castro had been nearly deserted, the streets of the Haight Ashbury were filled with a curious mix of aging hippies, vagabond homeless, university students, and transplanted yuppies.

David prowled the neighborhood, his head rotating side to side, searching. He crept past used clothing stores, used bookstores, funky new wave coffee art shops. He tried side streets like Parnassus and Cole. In his head, two words: *Show me.*

But his quest rapidly degenerated into the frustration of aimlessness. The brick-and-glass storefronts were hopelessly blending together. Who was he trying to kid? He was no psychic with gifted powers of intuition. This was searching for a needle in the proverbial haystack.

Anticipation sank into irritability with each stop sign and dead-end turn. A drizzly fog began to slick the windshield. He flipped on his headlights and windshield wipers with a muttered curse.

He faced facts.

Nothing was coming. He couldn't concentrate. The only thing he seemed to be aware of was the ticking of the clock. Lately, nighttime lasted forever; daytime, the blink of an eye. The tide was running against him and he could do nothing to stop it.

He slapped a fist against the dashboard. "Fucking hell!" he cursed to the empty car.

A wild-goose chase. This Victor — or whatever the hell it was — must be getting quite the laugh over this. He was no sleuth. He was certainly no psychic. He couldn't find the shop. The woman. Or Mick. Bobby.

Another voice nagged at him.

You can't find them because they don't exist.

That would be the capper, wouldn't it? Chasing after phantoms. Maybe his first assumption had been right, when his forehead developed that strange bruise: All these years since his fall were false, counterfeit. He should have died from his fall. Now time had caught up with him and was reeling him back, back toward death—

Stop it!

These doubts swarmed inside him, egged on by the sad drizzly day. Resigned to defeat, David drove back home with a desire to rush into his bedroom and pull blankets over his head. If he couldn't make it all go away he could deny it, if only for a short time. It'd help if he got good and stoned.

When he pulled into his garage he heard the phone ringing in his apartment. Had he put on his answering machine? Was it Alex calling, at long last?

He bolted up the steps to his apartment.

Damn. The machine wasn't on. And when he fished out Alex Webster's phone number from his wallet and called, he got an answering machine. He left a brief message for Alex to call, and his phone number.

Only as he sat stuffing a little marijuana into his pipe did the significance of the machine occur to him with a white-hot flash.

Wait a minute! Last night and earlier this morning there was *no answering machine. Now it's on. Which means Alex is alive.*

Good. At least nothing had happened to him during the night. Now if he'd only get off his duff and call...

He finished loading the pipe. Oh, the hell with the consequences. He wanted to jump off this merry-go-round, if only for a short time.

But instead of smelling the pungent odor of marijuana as he brought the pipe to his lips, he smelled it once again: cinnamon and lemon. Herbal tea. He took a drag from the pipe and coughed up most of the smoke. Another toke, and then he put it aside.

The silent apartment settled around him. Above, he heard bouncy music coming from Walter's flat. It pricked at his ears, unnerving him.

Opposites warred in him, flip-flopping desires that agitated and annoyed. Sit. Stand. Sober. Stoned. What in the world was going on? Depressed, and yet so wound up. As if he were of two

minds.

David wagged his head. Yeah. Sure. The boogieman's creeping into my brain, muddling it all up.

He pulled on his blue-jean jacket again and grabbed an umbrella. He couldn't stay, now that he had come home. Perhaps a walk to throw off this restlessness, an activity to rid him of his sense of helplessness.

A surprisingly warm mist sprinkled his face before he popped open the umbrella. The wet weather was aggravating his hip, but perhaps it wouldn't complain so much once he walked on even ground. At Nineteenth Street he glared at the public phone next to the corner store.

Bring Him the stone.

That's what the Eddie-imposter had told him last night. But there could be no stone without the woman, and so far there *was* no woman, only this maddeningly cloy aroma that tickled his nose and throat.

He meant to walk into the Castro for a while and just browse some shops in an effort to clear his head. But his feet, if not his head, held to an alternative plan. He began to walk Nineteenth toward Dolores Park. Well, that was fitting, wasn't it: this place he commonly sought out for comfort, when depressed. The uninterrupted view of San Francisco often recharged his batteries.

When he arrived, the sight only further compounded his sadness. San Francisco's skyline was lost to a heavy gauze of gray clouds and fog. The city seemed ... caught, somehow; trapped and squeezed into the ground. Like a bully had pushed the city's face into the mud and wouldn't let go.

His glance shifted to South of Market. A particularly black sky dominated this region. Storm clouds boiled the sky and seemed to spew out across the city.

As he stood watching, a bit of his old self crept back in. Imagination or no, it hurt to stare at this beautiful city with its nose ground into the mud. Time to throw off the bully.

His thoughts turned to Eddie.

I promised I'd help you, but I'm no closer to solving this riddle. Help me. Please. Anyone. I swear I'll find out who took you away from me, Eddie. I'll stop whoever's doing this.

Of course, he had a name for the monster, didn't he: Victor. A name belonging to someone triumphant in battle. Well, not this time. Not if he could help it.

He shut his eyes, and saw a flash of diamond.

The restlessness tugged hold of him again, and he began to walk down the wet grassy slope of Dolores Park. If he could have held a mirror to his face at that moment, David would have been surprised to see how unplugged his expression looked. Disconnected, as though something had been shut off to make room for another switch to be thrown. He moved across the hillside without question or rational thought, moving because it seemed the right thing to do, just as leaving his apartment had been the right course of action.

He crossed Dolores at Eighteenth and began walking toward the Mission. This was the direction he'd thought of going earlier, in Eddie's car. He sniffed the air and his nostrils flared at the now-familiar aroma. A sharp, almost vinegary smell of glue binding mingled with oak and pine and dust. It tickled his throat and made his eyes water. His thoughts tumbled all over themselves.

Don't question this. Walk. Follow this instinct. You asked for help and by god—

Another hundred yards, and he stopped dead in his tracks. Anyone watching would have mistaken him for a clown who had mimed running into a brick wall. A tingling flush traced a path down his scalp and across his spine. He folded up the umbrella and used it as a crutch to help support his weight.

The dream sat in front of him.

Sandwiched between an antique shop and a closed bakery sat a brick building with a wide plate-glass window. In a rainbow arc across the glass:

DÉJÀ VU

Books — Curios — Fortunes

3

The dark days were over.

He knew it, in that instant.

At long last, here was proof that his dreams were not just dreams. And since this place was real, was the rest of it real, as well? Mick. Bobby. Victor. Finally, he had stepped out of the realm of his mind and into the physical.

How much did she really know, this woman? Would she be able to tell him anything about the stone? About the evil attacking them?

A tinkling bell announced his arrival as he stepped into the shop.

28

Drawn in

I
1

t was almost obscene, this sexual heat that fanned his skin like the glow from a huge fire. Bobby was feverish with anticipation. Disjointed images overlapped and fell upon one another with the chaotic intensity of foreplay, smothering him with photographic kisses.

He was unaware of any gate inside his head that opened and closed upon command, though intuitively he knew that he had opened himself full throttle. He tumbled toward the answer, toward the destination, and the anticipation was greater than any longing he had previously experienced, greater than all the Christmas mornings of his childhood, greater even than that giddy moment when John, a high school crush, had slyly suggested they shower together, the rest of the gymnastics team having departed.

So: Here he was curled upon his bed, little gasps escaping clenched teeth, hand pumping across the notebook paper with masturbatory frenzy, drawing closer to that final crest of hill where the answer would shine as bright as a newly risen sun upon his face. And with the answer, Mick. He was sure of it.

Whatever image came to his mind, he immediately transcribed onto paper. If he stopped to consider what he was doing, doubt crept in, and that was no good, a mistake. Drawing pictures to find out what had become of Mick? Crazy.

And then the face of the black man from his dream would float before his eyes, that wide, gap-toothed smile encouraging him to continue.

Who says the world makes sense? — and he'd return to his notebook and pencil.

He was still no artist, despite this burst of creative outpouring. His figures were amateurish, frustratingly childlike. Yet an energy infused them. An ... earnestness. Like this man he kept sketching, with the high forehead and almond eyes. He drew him in a bathtub, while above him hands seemed to float out of a wall. He drew this same man at a desk.

The man with the green eyes. *Are you ... Bobby?*

Was he a friend of Mick's? Was he also a victim of this creature's web?

Victor's parting words came back to him:

Yes, my friend, come to me now, you and your companions! Be a hero! I'm waiting!

He had no companions to help him. Not yet. But somewhere, this man with the green eyes was also fighting. Why else would he continue to draw him? Why else would he have seen him, in his dream? And of course, the man knew his name. Perhaps he would lead him to Mick.

Bobby flipped to a clean page. *Keep going. I'm close. I can feel it.*

He began to draw a series of pictures of black double doors. Shadowy figures whisked up steps to the doors, desperate to be allowed inside. In one of the drawings the door was pushed open, and beams of multicolored light streamed out. A figure wore something on his chest. A shield? No. A badge. Over this man, he superimposed a pirate's skull and crossbones. A rash of goose bumps fanned across Bobby's arms as he stared at what he had drawn. He was afraid to guess who this was, this man with a badge.

It felt like death lay behind those double doors.

Victor lay behind those double doors.

This was part of the answer. Everything has to have a place to call home, and these doors were of that place — where this Victor had hidden himself. He knew Mick could not be far behind.

Where? Bobby demanded of this current vibrating through him. *Where is he hiding?*

His hand began to move across the paper. He sketched a rectangular block. Added windows, then boarded them up. These windows no longer looked out on the outside world; they preferred darkness. Below the windows he drew in the black double doors. Beside this warehouse-looking shape he added a fenced-in parking lot where (as though the drawing needed an extra touch) he penciled in a boy holding a football.

When he'd finished, he lay aside the pencil and studied what he'd drawn. His skin felt clammy and raw. His stomach gurgled with nausea. Any moment now he was afraid he would have to bolt for the bathroom.

It was familiar, this place.

The steps leading up to those double doors.

The parking lot. Full of cars.

An image came to him of standing in the cool dark, music echoing the night as men in leather jackets swept purposefully up the stairs. Over a decade had passed, dulling the edges of this memory, but time could not rob him of the name of the place.

Bobby's eyes popped open.

He remembered.

He *knew*.

He stared at his rendering of the building. It was almost unrecognizable, but his memory easily sketched in the three-dimensional details lost by his amateurish stab at a drawing. Except for the double doors. They—

An exhale caught in his throat.

As he watched, one of the black double doors popped open. A tinny sound issued out, like music from a child's radio. Music, high-pitched and squeaky. Something began to trickle down the steps. A stain quickly spread across the paper. It changed from the color of his lead pencil into an ugly maroon.

Blood.

Blood, seeping across the page, obliterating the drawing.

And inside his head, a taunting sneer:

(Come and get your boyfriend, then. I'm WAITIIINNNGGG—!)

Bobby slammed the notebook shut and threw it across the room.

2

He allowed himself to breathe again. After a few minutes he stood up. Ideas and strategies clinked in his head with the clatter of loose change.

Twenty minutes later, showered, dressed, and an eight-inch steak knife concealed within the folds of his jacket, Bobby locked the door to his apartment and hurried down the steps to the street below.

29

Double-crossed

U_{nplugged.} ¹

Alex Webster drew the cord into his hand and stared at its pronged end. *Speak, damn you. Give me some answers.* But there were no easy answers, not this morning.

His face closed down into a scowl. Had he unplugged the telephone last night? No. Of course not. He was waiting for David Walker's call, and...

And ... what?

His head ached with a colossal hangover that far outweighed his consumption of alcohol. Never mind that he'd had only two, three scotch and sodas at the most. He'd conked out at his desk, but when he woke up—

He shook the thought. Where he woke up was another story. Right now he had business. He checked his wristwatch. Five minutes to noon. *Noon,* for christsake. He'd lost the morning. And if David had tried to call — of which there was no doubt — he'd probably given up in frustration.

Alex bent down on one knee to plug the phone cord back into the wall. Something cool seeped through the fabric of his cotton sweatpants when his knee sank into the carpet. He stood up and saw a dark wet circle outlining his kneecap. An alarm whispered across the back of his neck. He squatted onto his haunches and patted the carpet with his hand. Lifted damp fingers to his nostrils, and sniffed. A ripe, sour smell.

He could almost hear David's voice inside his head: *Explain that one, Sherlock.*

He couldn't. Yet. But talking to David would be a start.

He wiped his palm onto his sweats, flipped through Ma Bell's white pages, and dialed David's phone number. One ring. Two. He gave up after the tenth ring and reluctantly returned the phone to its cradle.

Okay. He's out and he forgot to turn on his answering machine. Now what?

The Caverns. Flint Stone. The possibility of a man hiding out, a man who had given up on life and who would now take life with him, whenever and wherever he could. Alex flushed with anticipation as he relived that moment from the night before when the jigsaw pieces had snapped into position. Good-bye to David's ghosts and goblins, to creatures from the Black Lagoon, to dreams that didn't feel like dreams.

Only...

The memory bobbed beneath conscious thought. Alex neatly thumbed it down with his excitement. None of it mattered any more, this extraneous gobbledygook that gummed up his thinking. Purpose, direction, action: These attributes were his.

He strode into his bedroom and began to dress. No uniform today; until he could show actual proof, this little investigation was on his own time. Besides, he didn't want to alert whoever might be hiding out in the bathhouse to the knowledge that police were sniffing out his trail. He changed out of his sweatpants (the wet spot around his knee looked like a bloodstain) into a pair of comfortable old jeans that buttoned down the front. His belly pushed against the front, threatening to hang over, but the jeans felt good against his skin. He dug around for a flannel shirt to go with it, wasn't happy with any of them, and settled on a splashy, yet slightly faded shirt of palm trees and sunny beaches. He'd worn this one out to clubs, years ago. The collar was way too big, but what the hell. Being fashion conscious had never been one of his top priorities.

As he began to walk out of the room, his glance fell to the chair by the foot of the bed. This chair usually collected several days' worth of discarded shirts and pants, with rumpled pinecones of dirty socks and underwear littering the floor just underneath.

The slacks he had worn last night lay crisply folded over the back of the chair. His shirt was on a hanger, hooked to a corner of the chair. His pile of assorted dirty clothes were laid out underneath the chair neat as you please.

Alex grinned bemusedly. *God, was I drunk last night. Turned into my own maid. Either that, or Donna Reed tucked me into bed...*

Another jagged shard of memory poked through, a face with a hand raking across her mouth.

Alex stepped up to the chair and studied the folded slacks. If Donna Reed *had* tucked him in last night, she was one lousy maid.

Near the cuff of the pants were the dried remains of a muddy handprint.

2

"Harry? Alex Webster."

"Where the hell are you?" Harry asked through what sounded like a mouthful of sandwich. The phone connection buzzed with static.

"Hey — Saturdays are supposed to be a day off," he joked with false jocularity. "Listen. I have a favor to ask."

"Shoot."

"If it's okay with you, I want to hold onto those files I borrowed through the weekend."

"Getting close to something?"

"I think so. I'm checking out a hot lead right now."

Harry slurped a drink. "Just remember your buddy when it comes time to pin on a few medals."

"Don't you worry, Harry. If I can pull this off, we'll crack this story together."

Harry grew serious. "I gotta level with you, Alex. I'm worried about all this secrecy. If these cases have a common thread, I want you to spit it out. I won't have fingers pointed at me, I'm telling you up front. I've got Katie to watch out for."

"Don't you worry about that pretty wife of yours," Alex said. "No one's going to get into any trouble. I'm real close to some answers, but I'm out on a limb. With a little more time I can crack this."

Silence spun out. Then: "You owe me. Remember that."

Alex broke into a grin. "I'll pay you back for this, I promise. Thanks."

And he would, too — in a way neither one of them could have imagined.

3

Alex stamped his feet with impatience and rang David's doorbell for a third time.

Where the hell is he?

He backed away from the gate and stared up at the fire escape balcony and sliding glass door. The opened drapes looked into a dark apartment.

What was this, another rotten example of Murphy's Law? Two answering machines between them, and yet they couldn't manage to connect today. Maybe David was still annoyed with him for not swallowing all of his story about ghouls and goblins. Maybe this was his little way of getting even. It sure seemed as if something was determined to keep them separated.

He walked over to the passenger side of his car, opened the door, and reached into the glove compartment for a note pad and pen he kept stashed away.

We seem to be crossing paths today, he scribbled. *Are you mad because I didn't call last night? I'm checking out a hot lead. I'll be home about three. Call me. Alex.*

He tore off the page, folded it into thirds, and stuffed one end into David's mailbox.

It was time to root out the bad guys.

4

He turned left off Eighteenth Street and swung down Mission. Now *that* was a mistake, he saw at once. Even on this gloomy Saturday, the streets were jammed with a curious mix of Latinos and blacks, the homeless and the hopeless, with a few gay men and lesbians peppered in like so much exotic spice. If a city had a pulse, the Mission was where it thumped beneath the city streets. But Mission was not a street you wanted to maneuver if you had to be somewhere in a hurry.

And he had a destination, oh yes.

At Sixteenth and Mission he hooked right and dropped down several blocks to Folsom Street. This would give him clear passage into South of Market.

Answers. He wanted answers.

Like, what happened to me last night?

Ah, yes, that was the question, now wasn't it?

That black curtain of forgetfulness, swooping down upon him as he sat at his desk...

Drive, he commanded himself. *Don't think about it. It's not important any more.* This *is important, what's in front of me.*

He was reminded of a cartoon where a line of people wait at a bus stop, and poor Joe Schmoe, last in line, stands with a small rain cloud over his head. No one else is even wet, but this poor guy stands drenched head-to-toe under his personal thunderstorm. Alex remembered chuckling at the cartoon, thinking: It's true; some guys go through life with clouds over their heads, like prophets of doom.

South of Market had a rain cloud over its head.

The demarcation line between day and night had whittled away. The city's overall gloomy weather was magnified a hundredfold down here. Brooding clouds and joyless light cast a slushy pall over everything. The fog hung so thick and dense Alex had to switch on his windshield wipers and headlights. It was like driving under the vortex of a fast-building storm.

He drove down Folsom Street. Unlike the Mission, this section of town was deserted. Not surprising, given the nasty weather. Alex glanced at the houses on this block. Curtains were tightly drawn. No lights in any of the homes, despite this wintery gloom. Maybe they were all sleeping.

Maybe they were all dreaming.

His mind returned to it, like a tongue probing the empty hole where a tooth had been pulled, drawn by phantom sensation. Memory finally jabbed through.

He'd had a dream, before awakening. No: not a dream, exactly; more a sensation, one long sensual foreplay of hands upon his body. He'd given himself over to the dance of hands, not even bothering to open his eyes as he luxuriated in their touch. Feeling a heaviness in his crotch as his cock swelled into an erection. Heaven, this dream sensation. Especially when a mouth swallowed his hard-on with liquid grace, and he had exploded in fantastic fury—

Drive, Alex commanded himself. His hands bit into the steering wheel.

For what sickened him now was the ease of the deception. He'd startled awake in his own bed, gobs of semen pooled around his belly button, aching like a son of a bitch from the raw teeth marks nibbled around the base of his cock. He'd looked up and there was Mrs. Kreitman, stark naked, fish-liver white and sagging raw-dough breasts, raking the back of her hand across her mouth and snickering at her prank. She'd tossed back her head with laughter and disintegrated before his own eyes, blown apart like a cartoon explosion on a kiddie show.

Hard to remember much after that. He'd meant to jump out of bed, but a dizzy exhaustion claimed him, and threw him back onto the sheets. When his eyes eventually fluttered open, it was almost noon. He'd swung out of bed, his hangover dull screwdrivers twisting into his brain, when he'd looked about his room.

Saw his clothes laid out just so.

Realized he could not remember leaving his desk.

And heard that broken-glass cackle of Margaret Kreitman echo inside his head.

No, Alex thought as he drove Folsom Street, he most definitely was not the same man of less than a week ago.

Because *this* Alex Webster was suddenly, unquestionably afraid.

5

I'll just drive by and take myself a good long look.

He slowed the Toyota and peered through the windshield for Roberts Alley, which he knew should be coming up within the block. Drizzly mist, combined with the low fog, made visibility difficult. The metronomic drone of the windshield wipers — thump-*thump,* thump-*thump* — was loud in the quiet car. Alex suddenly realized he was holding his breath. He exhaled noisily.

Relax, he told himself. *Don't be spooked.*

But it was hard not to be spooked, with the car wrapped in fog and tenement buildings whispering by in the gauzy maroon undertones of a bad dream.

There — Roberts Alley. He skidded on the slick pavement, the rear tires sliding to the right as the car jerked to a stop. He cursed over his mistake and finished the left-hand turn at a gentle crawl. He was wound tight with tension. A headache pulsed at his temples; the last vestiges of his hangover. The Caverns stood at the end of this block.

His head whipped left to right, left to right. Fog swirled around the car. It was like driving through a rain cloud.

Where is it? Where's the goddamned building?

All at once Alex slammed on the brakes. The car squealed to a halt. Seconds ticked away in confusion. Absorbed in his preoccupation, he'd somehow blown it, made a mistake.

He faced the end of the block. Roberts Alley emptied into another street. A one-way street sign informed him to turn left.

He had passed the bathhouse. Missed it in the fog.

How could he have missed it? *As if the Caverns were gone, vanished, hidden so no nosy cop can come snooping for monsters—*

He clamped down hard on that, banishing those thoughts. His hands shook with the jitters; he grabbed the steering wheel to steady them. He sat there contemplating what to do next, windshield wipers thump-*thump*ing in the silence, when his glance strayed to the immediate left of the intersection. There was a parking space on the corner.

...Convenient.

Yet there it was. Alex crept the car forward, turned left, and glided into the parking space. He forced his thoughts to shift away from his anxiety. He would follow his original plan of attack and go take a look.

He shut off the car engine. Silence thundered around him. And try as he might to suppress it, to stay cool, the vast army of nerves that plugged into his system hummed with unmistakable knowledge: *I'm afraid I'm afraid I'm afraid.*

Lady Luck, don't leave me now.

He zippered his windbreaker and stepped out of the car.

6

He had taken all of three steps when he smelled it: an unmistakable whiff of spoilage. The air was poisonous with it, as if the fog misting his face was an accumulation of tears and sweat and rot.

Alex walked slowly, a blind man in this pea-soup fog, eyes focused on the sidewalk. Concrete slabs of tenement stairs and red brick floated past as though disconnected, objects in a void. With each step, his resolve crumbled. What his logical mind marginally believed, his body began to recognize and accept unconditionally, with no modern hesitation. His heart jackhammered painfully in his chest, his fight-or-flight switch flipped to overdrive. His stomach rumbled with queasiness.

For as much as he prided himself on being a levelheaded good old boy, not given over to flights of fancy, it was simply impossible, up this close, not to be afraid.

Of course he knew fear. In his line of work as a police officer, he'd been a part of dozens of shootings, drug busts, close calls. He'd been screamed at by angry mobs, dodged bullets during shoot-outs. Had stones hurled at his face. Suffered the blistering heat of an apartment on fire as he carried a terrified little girl to safety. Yes, he knew fear.

Yet none of that fear could compare, none of it could come close to this inescapable superstitious dread which snaked through him now as the fog rolled back enough to reveal the three-story building in front of him.

The Caverns.

A moan escaped Alex's tightly clenched lips.

Earlier, it may have hidden itself, but now the building welcomed him. He looked at the row upon row of crumbling brick, the shuttered windows of the second and third floor, the black polished doorway of its entry, and he knew that it could hide any manner of evil.

This was a haunted house straight out of childhood nightmares, a place that could conceal anguish and bitter tears and secrets, dirty little secrets. A perfect home for a madman. Was this Flint hiding somewhere within its walls?

Warm fog, like the smoke of a forest fire, boiled around him, its fingers like the arms of an octopus, drawing him up the steps.

All his resistance to superstition, all his doubt, let go with a rush of fear.

He thought, *No one knows where I am. I'm alone. And unarmed. Oh, David—*

He stood frozen like that until, through the drumroll of his terror, he heard movement behind him, and — too late — was forcibly spun around by hands upon his shoulders.

30

Red and black

David breathed in the now-familiar aroma that had assailed his
senses not five minutes earlier: paper, dust, wood, herbal tea. The
ghostly scent of binding glue.

The cramped shop was overloaded with shelf after shelf of used
books on the metaphysical, each stack divided into specific areas of
interest. Edgar Cayce. The Tarot. Ghosts and hauntings. Reincarnation.
Holistic healing. With a quick glance, he noticed the store's inventory
was not limited strictly to the supernatural. The back walls, lined with
dark oak bookcases, were a hodgepodge collection of mystery and
science fiction books. Obviously, the store's bread and butter depended upon clients in search of metaphysical concerns — an irony
he found wryly amusing, considering his present condition — but it
also serviced those in search of a good used book at an affordable
price.

For a bookstore, the Déjà Vu was not particularly well lit; or had it
just taken on the gloom of the day, saturating its walls with a gray pall?
Yes, the shop was scruffy, in need of a good cleaning, but down to
earth, too. Sturdy. It comforted him with its familiar informality.

"Can I help you?"

David turned to the voice — which, judging by the tone of it,
sincerely hoped he did *not* require any help. A young man stood
partially hidden behind a wide desk and antique cash register. Tall,
with shaggy carrot-orange hair that fell over pink ears and a pale
forehead. A closely trimmed beard the color of rusty pipes rounded
out a lean, hard face. A spray of freckles peppered both cheeks like
a second skin. His eyes were ice blue, calculating David's presence
with a thinly veiled contempt. A shopkeeper's smile was frozen upon
his lips. He looked boyish, a recent graduate into his twenties.

"Just browsing," David answered, rattled by the hard stare. He
turned away from the man's gaze and spotted a white cardboard sign

✦

beside a curtained doorway. "Rachael Black — Fortunes told — $25," it read. An idea fell into his lap. "Actually," he admitted, head bowed like a schoolkid addressing the principal, "I'm here to see Rachael. Is she free?"

The redhead made a face as though he was answering the stupidest man alive. "She's twenty-five bucks," he said with a can't-you-read? sneer. He made a hitchhiker gesture toward the curtained partition. "Mom's with another client. Do you have an appointment?"

"No." He fastened on a please-help-me expression. "It's an emergency," he added by way of explanation. Inside, his thoughts buzzed with this new information. *Mom? He's her* son? *Oh, great.*

The boy softened; perhaps he smelled money. The shopkeeper's smile reasserted itself. "Give her a few minutes. I'm sure she'll see you."

"Thanks." David browsed the shelves for a few minutes, drifting toward the section on ghosts and hauntings. He was the only customer in the store, and for once he wished others were around him. Images from last night were flooding over him, now that he had the reality of the shop around him. He wanted to scout around, explore. But the young man behind the counter watched him suspiciously, making him self-conscious. There was something disquieting about the man that went beyond the cool plastic reception he'd given David. Something contained behind the veneer of shopkeeper. He glanced at the man and was startled when their eyes met.

"Do I know you?" asked the redhead.

"No," David answered.

"Funny." His freckled face was a map of puzzled concentration, as though a name danced upon the tip of his tongue. He scratched his rusty beard and then pointed at him. "But you've been in before, right?" He seemed to demand this confirmation.

David repressed a grin. *You could say so, in a manner of speaking.* "Once or twice," he said, to be polite. He crossed the hardwood floor and extended a hand. "My name's David."

The man behind the desk stared at his hand as though it contained a booby prize, then awkwardly thrust out his own hand to shake. "Red."

"Nice to meet you, Red." They perfunctorily shook hands. David thought, *I'll never get near this guy's mother if I don't win his trust.* "You know, your mother comes highly recommended. That's why I wanted to see her."

That seemed to butter him up. Red smiled and boasted, "Yes, Mom's one of the best. There are plenty of fakes around; you have to be careful who you see."

"I agree. How long have you been in business?"

"Over seven years."

David nodded, impressed. "Business must be good."

"Getting better and better," Red proudly answered. "Lots of guys like you coming in."

Guys like you? What did *that* mean? The kid appeared a little too pleased that men "like him" were coming in desperate and distraught, anxious for kind words and fast remedies.

Voices escaped the partition, male and female, wishing each other good day. A frail man elbowed through the curtain. The poor guy; he resembled a bag of sticks bundled into a long raincoat. A harrowed, haggard face scrutinized David first with startled surprise, then with an expression reflecting kinship. He breezed past him.

"See you next time, Red," the man said, and stooped beside the front door to retrieve a long black umbrella from a cylinder. With dramatic flourish he looped a giant scarf about his neck, but not before David recorded a cluster of purplish lesions uncomfortably swelled beside the Adam's apple.

"Okay, Chuck," Red called after him.

The man favored David with a parting glance. Then he was out the door, a shadowy silhouette against the fogged-over glass.

It gave him the queerest chill. One moment a man; the next, a passing shadow, an indistinct blur upon the glass. First the quick smile, the open friendliness of an exchanged glance — then the vanishing into the mist, a soldier joining his troops, perhaps never to be seen again. David shuddered.

Red circled around the desk. "Wait here," he instructed, and disappeared behind the curtain.

Now anxiety found its home in David's belly. He paced the narrow runway between the desk and a mahogany table piled high with books by Louise Hay. He dropped his umbrella into the bin. If only Alex were here to share this moment with him. He reached out with his mind, searching for Alex as though the policeman were a radio station he could tune in by adjusting dials inside his head. Something was brewing. Something...

Red brushed through the partition. "Mom will see you now," he announced.

2

David walked though the curtain. He found himself in a small cozy kitchen, a round formica table in front of him with the kitchen necessities — stove, sink, refrigerator, and multiple wooden cabinets — shoved against the left wall. Rachael Black had her back to him; she busily filled a tea kettle with hot water.

"How about a nice cup of tea to get things started, shall we?" she said gaily, not even bothering to look away from her task. She bent to check the pilot light on the stove, popped a match, and lit the gas burner. She was humming to herself.

"Mrs. Black?"

"Oh please — call me Rachael—"

She spun around, Rita Hayworth style. Sparkling hazel eyes, broad friendly smile. Fifty if she was a day, but her red hair, threaded with silver, was parted down the middle and worn like a woman half her age. It seemed weightless, the hair: like the spun glass of an angel-hair Christmas ornament. It floated around her oval face and cascaded onto her shoulders.

She had enough time for that, for the routine politeness, before she laid eyes on him. Those words that had been uttered so nonchalantly tens of dozens of times to clients, in the tone an invitation to relax, settle in, we're pals — died suddenly on her lips.

Yes, in spinning around to face him, she had just enough time to launch into her routine before the friendly smile trembled beneath her freckled cheeks and bent south in wordless horror. Her throat muscles bunched into knots, Adam's apple bobbing. Her pale skin mottled with crimson fury. The glitter in her eyes no longer spoke of friendliness but resembled more the hard glint of sunlight bouncing off newly fallen snow.

She whistled harshly between her teeth, an involuntary gasp.

Even David recoiled, shocked by her response to seeing him. "Mrs. Black?"

"Get out." Quiet, deliberate: Her tone allowed no room for discussion.

"I must talk with you."

Rachael shook her head. "You aren't welcome here. I'm sorry. You must go."

He stepped toward her. "You know who I am?"

"Yes!" she spit at him, a cat backed into a corner. "You and your ... your pornography!"

David was taken aback. "My what?"

She folded her arms across her chest. "You heard me." Her equilibrium was returning, now that the surprise of his presence in her kitchen no longer paralyzed her.

"I don't know what you're talking about."

"Makes no difference to me what people do in the privacy of their own homes," she said airily. "I've counseled many gay men in my time." She stabbed a finger in his direction. "But I don't have to see what goes on behind closed doors. I don't have to witness it, night after night. And I won't!"

David shrugged with exasperation, palms open toward her. "Please — what are you talking about?"

Despite the urgency of their exchange, both of them had automatically adopted a whisper. He knew why, without having to be told. The answer was in the front room, sitting behind the desk and cash register.

"You're the writer," Rachael accused. "It's all your fault. That perverted place. It's all your fault I see it!" Her lips twisted in a grimace, disgust and loathing plain on her face.

He chanced another step toward her. Rachael shrank against the kitchen sink as though he were a vampire after her blood.

"You know what's happening," he challenged. "I don't know why, but you're seeing it all through me. How long were you just going to sit back and ignore it?"

"I'll have no part in this. How can you write about such an awful place! Such perversity! I have nightmares every night."

"What place?"

"That *bath*house. Or whatever you call it. For pity's sake stop writing about it! Break this connection with me and leave me alone!"

Cold water flooded David's veins. This woman had unwillingly seen his own visions of that hell, had assumed he'd written it, had given it a name. A bathhouse.

It had been waiting there all along, this connection. Waiting to be named, to act as a magnet to draw all the pieces home: The steam. The rock walls. A bathhouse.

The *Caverns!*

Eddie used to go there, years ago.

Yes. The steamroom. The hallways. Music.

Victor.

He gasped as though struck full on the face. Rachael Black stopped jabbing the air with her finger and stared at him with eyes round with fright.

"Mrs. Black, listen to me. It's real, what's happening. People are dying. You've got to help me. You're my only hope."

"Don't be so melodramatic," she snapped.

"It's *him* you need to be frightened of, not me. It's this Victor who's giving us nightmares."

Naked terror shone through her eyes. "I'm warning you. Get out. Don't force me to call my son. He won't like it, not one bit."

"You have a stone. A crystal of some kind. It guided me to you—"

That did it. The mention of the gemstone brought absolute panic. "Randall!" she screamed.

From the other room: "Mom?" The scrape of chair against the floor.

"Shhh!" David pleaded, but too late, the denouement set in motion.

Red burst through the curtain, puffed with rage and concern. David turned to him, apologetic, open mouthed. Red descended upon him like a locomotive. He grabbed a fistful of blue-jean jacket in each hand, spun him around, and rammed him up against the wall. "What are you doing to her?" he snarled into David's face. "Huh?" He smacked him against the wall.

"Let me go—" David protested.

"Randall—"

Red closed in, powerful with a son's protective fury. David was stunned into submission, unable to loosen himself from the boy's grip. "You listen to me, wimp," Red sneered. "Get out of here and don't come back. I so much as see you outside the shop, I'll beat you into a bloody pulp. We understand each other?" They were eyeball to eyeball.

"Yeah," David muttered. He was hot with embarrassment, confused by this violent turn of events. He glanced at Rachael, who was wringing both hands in front of her ample waist.

"Let him go, Red."

"He tried to hurt you, Mom."

"No," Rachael said. "He's mistaken me for someone else."

Red glared at David, determined to have the last word. "Don't mess with me again."

David nodded. "Okay, tough man," he said — and rammed his knee into Red's groin.

Red's eyes rolled heavenward as the excruciating pain doubled him into a ball. He howled in agony and cupped his hands over his genitals.

David pushed the boy away from him; he'd only meant to free himself. He beseeched Rachael, who had gone stone-white, to forgive him. She folded Red into her arms and seared David with a scorching glare.

He held up his hands in truce. "I'm sorry," he apologized, taking a backward step through the heavy curtain. He fixed Rachael with an accusatory stare of his own. "You can't ignore us while we all die. You've got to help us."

"You brought this upon yourself," she shot back. "You'll get no sympathy from me."

"I'll be back."

"Like hell," Red grimaced through gritted teeth.

She waved a hand dismissively. "Get out, before I call the police."

David burst into laughter.

Rachael and Red looked at each other, confused. They didn't know he laughed because he'd used up all his tears; that he laughed to hold back sorrow and frustration as he lurched out of the shop and emptied onto the street, a defeated man.

3

He ran away from the shop, down Eighteenth Street. It was drizzling, and he'd left his umbrella back in the bookstore. Too late now. Desperate highs and disparaging lows hit him from all sides. He cast about in search of an anchor and found it: a pay phone.

He ran over to it, glad for the overhang of roof that protected him from the rain, and dropped in two dimes. He dialed Alex Webster's number from memory.

Please oh please answer—

After the second ring, the automatic machine clicked on.

Another wave of despondency rolled over him.

Now what? Alex not home. Rachael Black and her son unwilling to help. What's left?

The Caverns.

No! Did he dare? Alone?

She'd given him the name, unwittingly. A name — and now, perhaps a destination as well. He had at least two hours of daylight left. What if he took a look? If he could approach Alex with hard evidence, then the policeman would have no alternative but to help him.

He mumbled a message for Alex to call him when he returned home and hung up. The drizzle turned into a steady rain. His hip began to ache in anticipation of running back home through the rain.

Should he go home first, and take Eddie's car? Or go back to the Déjà Vu and demand another entrance?

Out of the gloom a yellow cab appeared. It moved slowly, trawling for customers. On the spur of the moment David rushed to the street corner and flagged it down. The cab obediently halted in front of him. He jumped inside.

"What a lifesaver!" he exclaimed, and folded himself into the backseat. "Noe and Twentieth, okay?"

The driver nodded. "I gotta make a quick detour — do ya mind? I won't charge ya, okay?"

David waved his assent and settled back against the seat. His eyelids drooped shut. Yes. He'd return to his apartment. Change into dry clothes and put on a raincoat. And if he couldn't hook up with Alex, then he'd check out the Caverns alone. Despite the outcome at the bookstore, just seeing the shop had bolstered his confidence. Checking out the Caverns would give him that same feeling, for it would keep this whole situation embedded in reality, and out of the realm of his mind. It would give him a sense of progress, to know for certain that this monster existed, and called the Caverns home.

He retreated into himself, eyes shut, and let his thoughts replay the whole frustrating scene with Red and Rachael. How could she turn her back on him? Didn't she realize what was at stake?

Under this cloud of disappointment he gradually became aware of a smell in the taxicab. He crinkled his nose. Wet dogs: something wild and unpleasant.

The driver began to whistle.

David glanced up from his reverie.

He saw the back of his head. Sweat streamed down the man's neck. A little black leather cap perched jauntily atop the driver's head. His brown hair was soggy with perspiration.

He shot a glance at the cabbie's identification papers. Underneath a small picture of an ordinary-looking man — short-cropped brown hair, brown eyes, wide self-conscious smile — a name: Will Garter.

Will Garter?

He dug around in his memory. Found it.

The leather column in the *B.A.R.*

Worried friends Will Garter and Ralph Sutherland continue to cry foul over the suspicious disappearance of their pal and ours, Larry "Flint" Stone...

He glanced into the rearview mirror. Will Garter was watching him. His eyes were polished glass.

David's mouth went utterly dry. For the first time, he noticed the direction in which the cab was taking him. *Oh god no.* "Stop the car," he demanded. It came out a squeak.

The driver pulled doughy lips into an amused leer.

"I said stop the car!"

Will Garter whistled. He reached for the radio, and his whistling tune was in sync with the sprightly disco that gushed out:

> *Come dance at Club Valentine's*
> *Make your dreams true*
> *There's men and women waiting*
> *To get their hands on you...*

The cab zigzagged Folsom Street like a shark prowling familiar waters.

31

On the doorstep

1

The knife was an uncomfortable wedge sticking out of the inside coat pocket of his jacket, but Bobby rather liked the feel of it all the same. To keep from jabbing himself as he walked, he'd wrapped the blade with a hand towel from his kitchen. He counted the cement blocks of the sidewalk. Brightly colored litter stuck to the wet sidewalks like the forgotten confetti of an abandoned parade. It made Bobby unaccountably sad.

He tried to keep his mind blank as he walked — especially as he approached the phone booth where it had all started for Mick. He crossed to the opposite side of the street. In this pewter landscape of grays and purples and mist the phone booth stood silent, truly a Venus's-flytrap in a spoiled garden of wood and steel and concrete. It seemed to watch him hurry past — or so Bobby believed, neck hairs rising.

His unease intensified as he turned the corner and aimed for Roberts Alley. Except for the handful of cars slinking by, he might have been the last man alive in a dead city. That's how he felt, as though he'd been deposited inside someone's science fiction novel — *The Last Man on Earth*. Ordinarily he would have laughed at such a notion, but he'd left ordinary times far, far behind. His life, before this had happened, seemed eons in the past.

When at last he spied the street sign to Roberts Alley — almost literally bumping into it, hidden as it was by yellow fog — his hand dropped to the handle of his knife to reassure himself it was still there. Seeing the sign brought it all back.

Roberts Alley. Not quite as notorious as Ringold Alley, that infamous stomping ground where men prowled shadowy nooks and crannies for quick sex, but during its heyday this street had certainly rivaled it. All because of that bathhouse. The Caverns.

Bobby shuddered, thinking of his drawings.

He had never played within the Caverns walls. Mind you, he was no prude. In the candy-store atmosphere of the late seventies and early eighties he had worn his youth and dark Italian looks as a badge, secretly pleased at the entry it provided him. In the late seventies, too young to be allowed entrance into the bathhouses, he had stood in hopeful anticipation outside its doors as men flowed in and out.

It saddened him suddenly to think of this — to remember all the light and music and laughter. If freedom had been roughly played, if they had all stepped over the line at times, at least it had been mindlessly enjoyed with the high-spiritedness of adolescence. Their party may have gotten out of hand, but no one had any right to criticize its beginnings.

And now it's come down to this, Bobby thought, depressed. His feet made tiny lost slaps as he walked the sidewalk. *Victor. He makes us remember. He makes us desire. And then we are lost. Lost.*

Like Mick.

His hand fell to the knife handle.

God, no. Please don't let it be too late. I'll cut Victor out of you, if I must.

Would they bleed, these creatures?

He hoped so.

Anger was good. He stoked it, allowing its heat to thaw the chill in his bones. The poisoned atmosphere of this place was enveloping him, warning him of danger. A hothouse-warm drizzle fell upon his face, the odor of chlorine and chemicals in the air.

And here he was: the Caverns.

On his immediate left stood the burned-out foundation of a Victorian. A set of stairs led to empty air and charred debris. The bathhouse towered above the debris on this side, its upper roof lost to the fog. Bobby's heart hammered against his chest with just the sight of it. There: the twin black doors of its entrance, just like in his drawings. And there: the chain-link fence surrounding an empty parking lot.

Behind him, suddenly: the skim of tires zippering along wet pavement.

He whipped the knife out of his coat in reflex and bolted up the stairs of the Victorian. He crouched behind a charred pillar. No one was going to catch *him* by surprise, not if he could help it. He squinted against the drizzle and waited.

Twin headlights carved paths into the mist. A red compact glided into view. He glimpsed an older man hunched behind the wheel. A rolling wall of fog descended upon the car, and Bobby, who squatted not twenty feet away, lost all sight of it. Not even the taillights were visible as it passed.

Spooky. The fog, as if alive, swallowed the car. Surely whoever was behind that wheel must feel the ... the wrongness of this place.

He'd driven slowly, as though *looking* for something, not running away.

Bobby wrenched out of his squatting position and stretched his legs. His thoughts swirled with confusion. Should he go after it?

No. Better not to advertise his presence.

In this underwater world of muffled sounds he heard a car engine shut off, and a few minutes after that, the slamming of a car door. His spirits buoyed with hope — for he knew, then, how awfully afraid he was, how alone, beside this terrible, haunted building. It would be folly to underestimate his enemy's influence, up this close.

So he waited, and watched.

Out of the gloom, a man appeared. He moved cautiously. The man's wariness proved it: It *was* impossible, up this close, not to feel the Caverns' corrupting influence. He half expected it to be the man with green eyes, but no, this one was older, perhaps in his forties, with silvery blond hair. Who was he — and what did *he* want here?

Bobby tiptoed down the cement staircase.

The man had stopped directly in front of the Caverns, mouth agape as he stared at its black doors.

He didn't want to startle this man and have him cry out — and thus give themselves away, if they hadn't already — so he moved quickly on sneakered feet.

The man must have heard him. He began to turn toward the sound.

Bobby touched the stranger's shoulder and held a hand to his lips with a shushing gesture.

2

They stared at each other, both of them white-faced with fright.

"Who are you?" Bobby demanded. "What are you doing here?"

The other man's eyes narrowed, taking in the knife with a trained glance. Before Bobby knew what was happening, the man grabbed his wrist and pried the steak knife from his fingers. Bobby tried to wrench away, but the man's grip was like iron. He propelled them away from the Caverns' front doors and back toward the burned-out stoop. Bobby wriggled in his grip like a fish caught on a hook. The man raised the knife, its point in Bobby's face.

"You. Hold. Still."

He obediently stopped jerking. His eyes blazed. "Who are you — some kind of watchdog? You keep an eye on this place while that thing sleeps?"

One of the man's eyebrows popped up. "What did you say?"

"Is that accent for real?" Bobby sneered.

The man yanked cruelly on his arm. Bobby felt his bravado falter. "Keep your voice down and answer me straight. Who are you? Why are you here?"

"To kill that son-of-a-bitch pal of yours hiding inside," Bobby snapped.

"Who?"

"Don't jerk me around, okay? You know who I mean. *Victor.*"

Another eyebrow popped up in astonishment. "How do you know that name?"

"Let me go. You're hurting me."

"How do you know it!"

"Because he took my lover last night," Bobby spat at him. "And you'd better stay out of my way—"

It was absurdly easy, this age-old trick. Bobby stuck one of his legs behind the man and pushed. The man's eyes went wide with surprise as he toppled backward and landed on his tailbone. The knife flew out of his hand. Bobby lunged after it, scooping it from the sidewalk. He whirled to face his assailant.

"Stay where you are!" he said. His heart pounded in his chest. Adrenaline jumped through his veins. "You get off that concrete and I swear I'll stick this knife right through you. We understand each other?"

The older man brushed himself off. "Yeah, I get your drift."

"What are you doing here?"

"I'm looking for someone called Flint."

Bobby wrinkled his brow. "Who's that? Is he in cahoots with Victor?"

"Why don't you let me stand up, and I'll tell you."

"No chance." Bobby gestured toward the bathhouse with the knife. "Is Mick inside? Just answer me that."

The man's square jaw dropped. It was almost comical.

"*Mick?*"

"Don't play games with me. I'm getting him out of there, whether you like it or not."

"Is your ... is your name Bobby?"

Stunned. He could summon no answer to his tongue.

"It is. Your name is Bobby. Well I'll be goddamned."

Blood rushed to Bobby's face. "How did you know my name?"

"We've been looking for you," the man said softly, wryly. "Well. Not me. David."

"David?"

"David Walker."

"Describe him."

"Tall. Lanky. Dark hair. Green eyes. What's the matter? You gonna be sick?"

The knife drooped in Bobby's hand. Images spun behind his eyes. His drawings. "You're a friend of his?"

"Yes."

"Then you're — you're not with Victor?"

The man shook his head. "You know, the only other person I've heard call him that is David. I think you two have a lot to talk about."

Bobby remained wary, not quite ready to throw down his weapon. "How do you know so much about me?"

"It's David, not me." He ran a hand through his silver-tinged hair. "He's told me about you. And your friend. Mick. David ... see ... he sometimes gets pictures inside his head. Does that make sense to you?"

Bobby nodded with wry understanding. "More than you know."

A gust of wind swooped around them. An unearthly moan raised a chill.

"What the fuck was that?" Bobby whispered. He clearly did not want to know.

"Do you mind...?" The man raised himself to his feet and briefly massaged his tailbone. He stuck out a hand. "Officer Webster. Alex."

"You're a *police*man?"

"That's right."

"Sorry about ... this. Bobby Volanti." He took the man's hand into his own, glad for the sudden safe harbor. "I thought you were ... you know..."

The policeman nodded. He glanced away from him and peered into the purple shadows, where building dissolved into swirling chaos. "I came here to scout around. Between the two of us, I'm afraid we've lost the advantage of surprise. If anyone's inside this building, they must have heard our little scuffle."

"That's okay. It's still daylight."

"What has that got to do with anything?"

Bobby's cheeks colored. "I think Victor is ... you know ... like a..." His voice trailed off. Giving the monster a name suddenly felt too weird: Movie-monster clichés could not be spoken with a straight face. Yet it lived, this cliché. They could be standing upon the monster's doorstep.

"If anyone's in there at all, it's a man named Flint Stone," Alex asserted. "He used to own this place before he disappeared about a week and a half ago. That's who I think this Victor is that you and David keep talking about."

Bobby shook his head. "It's not a *man*. A man can't do what this thing does."

"Have you seen him?"

"No. But a couple of his 'buddies' broke into my apartment last night. They kidnapped Mick, tricked him into following. So that's why I'm here." He brandished the knife. "They can't have him. Victor can't have him, not without a fight."

The officer shook his head. "Listen to me. There's to be no fighting, understand? I want you to stay right here. I'm going to take a quick look around this place and then you and I are hightailing it straight over to David's apartment." His expression was bemused. "He's gonna flip when he gets a gander at you. I hardly believe it myself, and I'm standing here talking to you."

That haunted moan sighed through the air again, then was torn and shredded by the fog. A palpable fear leapt between them. Their eyes were shiny with it.

"Let's just get the hell out of here," Bobby said. "Take me to this David. Can't you feel it?"

"Feel what?"

His eyes were child wide. "It's like we're being watched."

Alex frowned. "Listen," he countered. "I'm a cop. Let me do my job and we're outta here." It was said not so much as an answer, but as an oath he'd sworn to himself, and meant to keep.

Another low moan of wind, like the baying of a hound. With an exchanged glance both arrived at the same shivery conclusion. The sound was emanating from inside the building.

Bobby held out the knife. "If you must go, take this."

Alex shook his head. "You keep it. David will skin me alive if any harm comes to you, now that we've met."

"What about you?"

"This old dog can take care of himself." But his blue eyes darkened.

Oh, this was crazy, just crazy. "I'll wait up there," Bobby sighed, and indicated his perch up on the charred stoop. "But if you aren't back in five minutes, I'm coming after you."

An affirmative nod. Alex stepped away.

Bobby took a couple of backward steps toward the stoop, reluctant to allow this new ally out of his sight. He watched as Officer Webster crept toward the building, one hand outstretched as though to guide his way. Less than ten feet away, the fog waited like a curtain of wet smoke. As the policeman moved toward that misty curtain, an odd doubling came upon Bobby. He saw a figure from one of his drawings and Alex blend together, like a flashing neon sign with two messages, each illuminated independently, yet intertwined.

He saw the badge, a policeman's badge superimposed over Alex's back, watched it snuff out, and in its place — shockingly — a skull and crossbones appeared. That universal symbol for death.

A cold chill with the impact of wet rags slapped against his face. His mouth dropped open but no words tumbled out. This premonition shook him to his core.

"Alex," he croaked.

But Officer Webster was consumed by the smoke-fog, gone as if he had never been there at all.

3

The mist swirled around Alex, hugging like a glove. It stung his eyes when he looked up, so he shielded his eyes and pressed ahead. Sour perspiration soaked his shirt. His skin crawled and itched. His right hand kept dropping for his holster and gun, a reflexive gesture even while he reminded himself he was unarmed.

Sweat popped from his forehead like oil on a hot griddle. *Keep moving,* he commanded himself.

This was silly. He'd made such a big show about having himself a close look, and now that he neared the building his internal watchdog barked *danger! danger!* and would not shut up. The atmosphere around the bathhouse kept hitting him in waves, as though his body, with its network of nerves and sensory switches, recognized evil and could not be silenced.

He was moving toward the soot-grimed brick wall when out of the corner of his eye he caught movement. He glanced up the three steps to the black double doors.

One of them had popped open. A teasing slab of darkness loomed behind the open door, which jutted out about six inches.

Alex halted. *Well. What do you think of that?* He glanced behind him for Bobby. The smoky fog was an ominous shroud cloaking the distance between them. He could no longer see him, hidden on the stoop no more than fifteen feet away. *Bobby. Christ in heaven! Wait until I bring him to David!*

He held a quick debate with himself. Was this a trap? Maybe. Then again, his whole purpose in being here was to get a look inside.

He whisked up the stairs. Reached for the door. Its metal surface was oily under his fingers, cool, like congealed grease. Suppressing a grunt of revulsion, he pulled open the door. It yielded further on screaming hinges. The dishwater light of the afternoon pried weakly into the darkness, cutting a watery path a few feet inside. Alex saw gray carpet.

He slipped through the door. An overwhelming silence plugged his ears. The loudest sound was the gonging of his heart. But this entryway hosted a silence which felt full of ghosts, their voices and shapes swarming this darkness, pressing against his ears in an attempt to be heard. His bowels ached painfully in sudden spasm.

He forced another few steps, and squinted.

To the right of center, a glassed-in booth. To the left, a turnstile which emptied onto more darkness.

Suddenly, he stiffened.

I'm not alone—

A giggle, to his right.

He began to turn toward the sound when pain exploded with a sickening bolt directly behind his right ear. A loud ringing erupted through his head. A bright burst of savage pain as his body accordioned into a folded jack-in-the-box. He collapsed heavily onto the carpet, which was splattered with something purple and dark, so much like his own blood.

The giggle again. Victorious.

Blearily, he raised his head despite the pain. A young man stood over him. A two-by-four swung from the boy's hand, one end of the wood horribly smeared. He raised the makeshift club.

Alex tottered at the rim of a bottomless well. His last conscious thought:

Who is th—

Then he fell into it.

The young blond man stepped back and took a satisfied appraisal of his handiwork.

"Gotcha," he whispered.

4

Bobby jumped off the stoop, his heart a wild drumbeat in his chest. He held the steak knife clenched in one sweaty paw, its steely point a warning to anyone — or any*thing* — that came near.

Every fiber of his being screamed, *Don't let the policeman go there alone.*

He moved forward stealthily, his upper body stooped and prepared for attack from all sides. The knife sliced the fog, which whipped against his face like sticky tears. No sign of Officer Webster. Had he gone around the back of the bathhouse?

An echoing giggle cut the silence.

Bobby jerked toward the sound. His eyes alighted on the open double doors. A cold wave of unimaginable fear. Seeing that open door, daring him to enter, seemed the accumulation of every childhood fear rolled into one. No swatch of darkness in the closet, no bottomless pit of black beneath the bed was any match for that six inches of darkness waiting for him behind that double door.

But Officer Webster had gone inside, he was sure.

Mick. He might be inside, too. Prisoner to that accursed creature.

He steeled himself and sprinted up the steps. With his free hand he pried open the door and slipped inside.

"Alex?" he whispered into the darkness. His voice sank without echo. He squinted, forcing his eyes to adjust to the nonlight. His gaze fell upon a dark stain soiling the carpet at his feet. He squatted. The stain was tacky to his touch.

Fresh blood. He knew to whom it belonged.

He sprang to his feet. His legs shook so badly they were rubber bands. The darkness sucked against him, tugging at his clothes, his knife. Urging him away from the door.

"Alex!" he whispered as loudly as he dared.

Somewhere in this ocean of black, a grunt of exertion. A sliding, raspy sound.

Bobby held the knife before him. "W-Who's there?"

A chuckle answered him, off to the left. Childish and unreal. Something dragged across the carpet.

"Who's there!"

That labored, draggy sound answered him again, like a body being hauled into the very depths of this place.

All instinct told him to get the hell out. Retreat, while he still had time. There were forces in the dark. Changes, as though something asleep was now awakening. Blinking stars twinkled the black void. The air trembled with change.

He hugged the knife to his chest. Backed toward the door.

He said, louder now, "Alex? I'll come back for you. I—"

A hyena laugh.

The familiar voice came out of nowhere:

"That's what you promised me, too."

He blanched. *No. It can't be.* A sob broke out of him.

"M-Mick?"

Again, floating across the dark, plaintive:

"Join me, Bobby."

The dark writhed with shapes. A ripe-smelling wind blew across Bobby's face. He sensed something rushing toward him. Something with the impact of a train, churning up the dark, eating a path toward him.

"Mick! Come with me. Get out of here, now—"

A rank explosion of wind. And out of the dark reared a shape unlike anything Bobby had ever seen. A huge face like a carnival devil, a hellish monstrosity of fire and steam. It roared down a hallway toward him.

He bolted, unaware of his own screams as he turned and fled. Bobby slammed against the metal door release and threw himself out into daylight. Heat blazed against his back. A trickster's mocking laugh rang in his ears.

He tripped over his own feet on the concrete steps. With a startled cry, he collapsed into a tangled pile at its bottom. The knife skidded across the pavement and came to rest not ten feet from where a yellow cab screeched sideways to a halt.

32

Face-to-face

1

Will Garter whistled with the disco song pouring out of the radio. His fare was being an annoying pest, shouting and demanding to be let out, like he was the king of England or something. Or in this case, perhaps *queen* was the correct noun. His chapped lips tugged into a smile.

This was working out great. The promises whispered into his dreams were all going to come true, once he brought this man inside.

I give you anyone, anyone at all.

No death, here.

Do my bidding, and I reward.

He hadn't wanted to listen to those whispers, at first. He was a changed man, content with the new directions of his life. Then, at night, he'd started having ghastly visions of himself wasting away into the sheets, of endless days and intolerable nights alone, always alone. Oh, how this future had frightened him. His past had begun to look better and better.

"Okay," he'd called out into the dark just a few nights ago. "Show me what I have to do."

This blending of past and future could be his, for a price. Fine. That's how the world operated. No free lunches, as the saying went. His visions at night became infinitely sweeter as the plan was laid out before him.

Since that night, he'd haunted the streets with his cab, waiting for the signal. In his head multicolored lights bounced off mirrored walls, as though he stood dead center on a dance floor, head tilted heavenward. Was this one of his rewards? Yes, dangled like a carrot before him.

He didn't sleep for two days. Vague recollections of downing coffee in doughnut shops and 7-Elevens. Empty bags of chips and ice cream wrappers piled around his feet.

Finally, word from the Top Gun.

Sure enough, his mark flagged him down on Eighteenth Street, just as the Big Guy said he would.

Now his immortality shone before him like the promised land of a children's fable. If only the guy in the backseat would shut the fuck up. Will twisted the volume dial on his radio to drown out his fare's indignant protests.

He pulled a hard left onto Roberts Alley. Sure enough, his passenger bounced forward and to the right, banging his head against the metal door frame. The guy slumped in his seat.

"Now stay there!" he chuckled, wildly amused at his own inventiveness. Will Garter began to slow the cab for the first time, but not too slow, no sirreee: He didn't want his fare to get any ideas about jumping ship. He slammed on the breaks at the last minute, his cab executing a sideways skid.

Immortality, next stop.

2

A shambling caricature of a man stepped out from behind the driver's seat. Bobby froze, paralyzed by this new vision. But the man seemed completely unaware of his presence there on the Caverns' steps. He jerked and wobbled like a marionette, a slim, muscled man wearing a t-shirt that stuck to his wet torso like glue. A leather cap poked out at an angle from his head. He hoisted himself out of the cab and turned his face toward the bathhouse, an expression of mystical awe and revulsion warring on that wan, twitching face.

"See!" the marionette-man shouted. "I brought him to you, as I promised!"

He ran a tongue over fever-dried lips, bowed self-consciously, and spun like a driven thing, hands clawing at the door to the backseat of the cab, which he threw open. He crouched at its entrance and began to jerk and sway as though he grasped a slippery fish between both hands.

From inside the cab:

"Hey — stop!—"

3

Will Garter lunged at David, an insane strength infusing his scrawny limbs. His words were hurled razor blades:

"Come with me, bastard! Get out of this fucking cab!"

David kicked at the driver's hands, but the man had managed to grab onto his ankles and would not be shaken loose. His own hands scrabbled for something to grab onto, but his fingers raked uselessly against vinyl. No use: He was being drawn out of the cab.

"Help!" David screeched. "Somebody help me!"

"Too late," Will Garter snickered. "Too late for—"

He stiffened. His eyes bugged out like window shades snapped fully open. A gargling rasp of pain and surprise issued out of his mouth.

To David's astonishment, the man let go of him. He immediately retracted his legs and curled into a ball. Will's hands slapped about the back of his head and shoulders as though trying to dislodge some foreign object. His leather cap fell to the ground. The muscles in his neck bulged with an effort to speak, and all at once a sickly fountain of blood spurted from his mouth.

David cringed.

"He promised," Will Garter said through a mouthful of blood. "Promised..."

Red-rimmed eyes rolled backward into his head. He collapsed with a messy sprawl across the backseat. He twitched and shuddered, then lay still.

David tasted vomit at the back of his throat.

A knife handle stuck out of the cab driver's back, where it had been thrust between the shoulder blades. David's gaze lifted away from the corpse and into the shocked countenance of a man with a crew cut. The man was trembling uncontrollably at the violence wrought with his own hands.

It was Bobby — his vision made flesh — here at the Caverns!

Suddenly, their eyes locked.

Bobby saw the man of his drawings come to life. He stood, frozen.

And then David was scrambling out of the cab, tears welling in his eyes as he grabbed Bobby and they fell into each other's arms like long-lost friends.

4

With a lover's touch, David brushed tears that had fallen from Bobby's cheeks. "Don't cry," he whispered. "It'll all be okay, now."

Bobby shook his head: how to explain this relief in seeing the dream made real? And then he glanced directly behind David to the nameless man sprawled half in, half out of the taxicab, and he felt a pain as though he were the one stabbed. He blanched and twisted out of David's arms. "I think I'm going to be sick—"

"It's okay," David said, stepping out of the way. "You were right to do it. You saved my life."

Bobby doubled over with dry heaves. He indicated with a wave of his hand to just give him a minute, and true enough, the retching soon passed. After a moment he straightened and stared at this man with the piercing green eyes. He had sketched them quite accurately, in his drawings. How about that?

"You're Bobby," David said.

He nodded.

"What a sight for sore eyes," David grinned. "We have lots to talk about, but first I want to take you to a friend — a policeman — Alex Webster."

A look of absolute horror from Bobby.

"What is it?"

"Inside," he stammered.

David grabbed him by both shoulders. "What?"

"Your friend's inside!"

"What!" Thunderstruck. "Alex is *here?*"

"Yes. I saw blood. And ... and ... *It.*"

Fright lay as a white sheet upon Bobby's features. He pointed weakly at the double doors. "He went inside. I followed him. He wouldn't take the knife. I told him to, but he wouldn't! I heard... I *saw...*" His face contorted with horror, his eyes flashing with dark memory. "Mick is in there! My lover! Please help me—!"

"Shh," David whispered, and pulled this man against him. He shook in David's arms. "Of course I'll help you." But he lifted his gaze toward the building and stared at it with foreboding. The very air around them grew menacing as it snatched at their jackets and stung their faces with its drizzly stingers.

"It almost got me," the man was mumbling. "I was so afraid. I had to run."

"Listen to me," David ordered. "Don't go soft on me. We've hooked up. And that's important. I know it. Now let's go get our friends." He stared at Bobby, whose eyes widened with understanding. He turned and glanced upon the broken body of Will Garter.

Pushing down a surge of revulsion that tasted of bitter herbs in the back of his throat, he grabbed a leg with each hand and dragged the body out of the cab. The upper torso flopped to the pavement with a gut-sickening crunch. Will Garter's face struck the asphalt, splitting his right cheek. A red pool seeped out and mixed with the puddles of greasy water.

"Jesus." Bobby had spun away again, nauseated.

I have to do this, David commanded himself. He placed his foot in the small of the man's back, bent over, and grasped the wooden handle of the steak knife. Some inner working held it captive; bone and muscle and tissue refused to release the foreign object, as though it had welcomed its violation.

He grunted, "It won't come out."

"Oh, great," Bobby muttered thickly.

He threw his weight into it, straightening as he pulled. Like slicing through a thick steak, the knife gradually slid free. His legs felt wobbly. A dizzy light-headedness rolled over him. But it was done: He had the knife, the weapon to protect themselves while they searched for Alex and Mick.

"I've got it," David dutifully announced — but there was little triumph in so macabre a trophy.

"What now?"

"We get our friends."

David stepped away from the cab driver's body and he felt it, the earth trembling beneath his feet. He and Bobby exchanged a frightened glance. A low rumble shook the ground, followed by metallic moans.

"An earthquake?" Bobby, incredulous.

No. Something worse.

5

They heard the cough and sputter of a generator. The metallic grinding of gears flipped into appropriate slots. A disco tune bubbled out of the building, the pulse of this song slow, warped, like a record played on the wrong speed. It started up in midsong.

> *Born in the shadows*
> *Born in the dark*
> *This resurrected life we crave*
> *Ain't no lark*

Beams of light shimmered through the slats of two-by-fours covering the upper-story windows.

David blinked in confusion. "It can't be," he sputtered. "It's still day..."

True enough; but the sickly fog hovering about the Caverns had created its own night out of day — dark enough, just dark enough at last for the building and all its occupants to waken.

Bobby whispered, "What should we do?"

There would be no time for decisions; that gift was robbed from them. For as they stood upon the threshold, both watched a sudden darkening upon the brick facade, a shimmering like a heat mirage upon hot asphalt. Something resembling oil bubbled up between mortar and brick.

Bobby took a halting backward step.

David stared incredulously at the building, which was no longer the stubborn brick front to an empty bathhouse. The Caverns wall was rearranging itself, its structure remaining intact even as it changed shape. The slatted upper-story windows became huge lantern eyes, hypnotic pools of swirling red lights. The black double doors began to bulge out and liquefy, forming the snout and jawline of some feral animal, disappearing finally to become a gigantic, gaping mouth. They could see the inside wall of the Caverns at the back of its throat, untouched. A welcome mat became a lolling tongue. Music issued ever more brightly out of this mouth, yet remained low and stirring, like dreamy background music:

Gonna live the life of the boogie
From here on out, yeah yeah

It was a face three stories high, a devil mask belonging to a float in a Mardi Gras parade. The face seethed across the brick restlessly before eyes the size of beach balls fixed on them, and the face settled into itself. A growl — a mad dog sound, amplified a dozen times — rumbled through the flesh-and-brick structure to shake the very ground they stood upon.

David wanted to be brave; oh, how he wanted to be brave. But the monster, three stories high, burned its image into his brain like hot icicles. His mouth felt stuffed with sawdust.

The gargoyle face on the building drew brick-and-mortar lips into a leering grin.

(WELCOME)

David flinched as the baritone voice raped the inside of his head. Beside him, Bobby made dry rattling noises: He, too, was terrified into speechlessness.

(NOW THAT YOU BOTH ARE HERE, LET'S PUT ASIDE OUR GRIEVANCES, SHALL WE? PUT DOWN THAT RIDICULOUS STICK TOY AND COME INSIDE. YOUR FRIENDS WAIT FOR YOU. CAN YOU HEAR? WE'RE HAVING A GRAAANNDD PARTY!)

Tremulously, David shook his head.

Bobby stepped forward, terror making him foolhardy.

"What have you done with Mick?" he shouted.

(FULFILLED HIS WISHES, AS I CAN FULFILL YOURS)

"Fuck you," Bobby spat.

The wolverine face upon the brick rippled sibilantly, ripening with anger.

(EVEN NOW YOUR CIRCLE GROWS SMALLER WHILE MY NUMBERS MULTIPLY. THE POLICEMAN WILL MAKE A *FIIINE* ADDITION. YOU'VE SAVED ME THE TROUBLE OF BRINGING HIM HERE MYSELF)

Oh, that news about Alex: like a one-two punch to the stomach. Something hardened in David at that moment. He turned to Bobby and saw the boy trembling uncontrollably. "Give me your hand!" he cried. His voice was as sharp as the knife he carried in the other hand.

Bobby turned, confused, his face burning with an eerie light. He reached out and grasped David's hand.

And quite unexpectedly they both felt it, a tingly energy that ballooned with their touch, like two electrical cords plugged into the same socket. The power seemed to start with David and rush through Bobby. Here it was, in its utter simplicity: a connection completed, the psychic energy which had brought them together, channeled. And strong.

Briefly, an image rose before both their eyes, momentarily obscuring the dreadful sight before them: the black man with the ceremonial paint, raising the stone as he whispered, "Kahmaal."

The awful face twitched like a spider clinging to a swaying web.

(WHAT GOOD IS POWER WHEN YOU DON'T KNOW HOW TO USE IT?)

"Wanna bet?" David retorted, and he took a bold step forward, Bobby at his side.

Their show of strength was a gamble that paid off; the charcoal face retreated just a little, like a crab scrabbling back to dark waters. Doubt swept its features. The building host began to appear beneath it, as the face faded in and out on waves.

Their triumph infuriated the creature.

(YOU DARE MOCK ME!)

From inside the bathhouse terrible, ear-splitting screams of agony rose up and reached a pitch beyond human hearing. Steam gushed out of the fanged mouth-door in great boiling clouds. It rolled past them with a furnace blast.

Instinctively they ducked, faces turned away, as the stinging heat boiled over them. They broke apart, each protecting themselves, and whatever concentration of power that had armed them was snapped.

(YOU WILL NOT WIN! I HAVE ROOMS IN HERE FOR YOU! YOU'LL BEG FOR DEATH, A THOUSAND TIMES OVER, BEFORE I'M FINISHED!)

Scalding air shot past them.

Above the disco beat came the screams of men and women trapped inside. Their cries rose to an unbearable shriek and blended with the cyclone roar of wind.

Sensing the worst of the blast was over, David slapped Bobby's upper arm and shouted, "Run!"

They turned away from the Caverns, away from the Halloween face—

—and there stood Will Garter. He faced them like a zombie out of some bizarre horror movie. He swayed unsteadily on his feet, arms raised in a boxer's stance. His right cheek was a mottled open wound where his face had struck asphalt. Bits of gravel were wedged into the open flap of skin. The eyes were soulless black dots punched into a doughy face. He growled at them.

Bobby leapt back in stunned surprise.

Will Garter stabbed a finger in his direction.

(You. You did this to me)

All color leeched from Bobby's face. The guilt he carried for his deed — despite the unavoidable rightness of his violent act — contorted his slim face. He glanced to David for support.

Behind them, Victor laughed. The earth rumbled.

The zombie charged.

But David threw himself in the way. With a warrior's cry he thrust the knife into the thing's stomach and sprang away.

Will looked down in shock; he grabbed hold of the hasp and tried to tear it from his guts.

David backed away, keeping his distance.

"Quick!" Bobby shouted. He stood by the passenger's side of the cab, having run to it during the fight. "The keys are inside!"

David needed no encouragement. He bolted for the cab, threw open the front door, and slid inside. Bobby was right behind him, his expression pallid, moonstruck. Keys dangled from the ignition. David locked the door and gunned the engine.

Will Garter threw himself onto the hood with a soggy thud.

They screamed — high, girlish cries.

Steam was rising off of him. He turned his ruined face toward them and slapped a bloody paw against the windshield.

"What's happening to him?" David gasped.

Will flailed his arms as a steamy fire began to consume him. He rolled onto his back, the knife handle a stump poking from his belly as he jerked and twitched. His mouth stretched impossibly wide, surely snapping bones and cartilage with the effort to vocalize this star-blinding pain.

And then he looked seized by a gigantic hand. His back snapped backward as he was hauled away from the cab. The crisp lines of three-dimensionality muted suddenly; his features softened, turned transparent.

"Go!" Bobby implored. "Let's go!"

But David was transfixed by this disintegration. He watched as steam liquefied Will Garter, his features blown apart. For one instant the knife bobbed in the air as though held by invisible strings, and then gravity yanked it to the wet concrete.

"David! Come on!"

He shook out of his spell and floored the gas pedal. Tires spun without purchase on the wet asphalt. He eased up on the gas as his driving reflexes took over. The taxi veered out of its start-up spin and roared forward.

Neither of them wanted to see if the face still clung to the Caverns' facade, but the monster's warning abruptly blasted through their heads:

(NOWHERE TO RUN, MY PUPS! MY HOUR HAS COME! JUST *SEE* WHAT SURPRISES AWAIT YOU!)

Fresh tears of fright and dismay coursed down their faces. Bobby sobbed with naked relief, but David managed to hold back his tears until he recognized Alex's parked Toyota as they shot past. He felt a knife insinuate itself into his heart; that's how keen was the pain.

Oh, Alex. I'm so sorry—

6

They could not comfort each other on that terrible drive to David's apartment. Yet it was a comfort, in its own way, to be together, to share the horror and tears. Bobby never asked where they were headed. He seemed to know without having to be told.

But neither one was prepared for the sight that greeted them as David pulled into his own driveway.

"Oh no," he moaned. "Not my *house.*"

Bobby sat stone-rigid in his seat.

No lights shone through the sliding glass doors of David's apartment, but they could see them there, cavorting on the fire escape balcony. He recognized the little boy, Miggy, who had mistakenly given the creature a name. Another young boy bobbed and bounced beside him. They looked like a pair of chimpanzees.

An even greater shock was the naked old woman who stood with her legs defiantly spread open, her sex obscenely displayed. She pawed at her breasts with whorish delight and cackled at their scarlet expressions. Behind her, a man slipped his arms about her bloated waist and grinned down at them.

David flinched as though he'd been struck.

"Do you know him?" asked Bobby.

He nodded. "Jack Martin. We worked out at the gym together. I don't know the others."

"What should we do now? We can't go inside."

David picked at his lower lip.

"We're trapped," Bobby whispered with shivery horror. "Just like Victor said..."

David frowned. "Not yet, we aren't." He shifted into reverse.

"Where are we going?"

"Trust me," he answered, and drove the taxi back down Noe Street toward the Castro.

33

Requiem

1

The pounding of his own heart woke him. Every beat was pure agony to his head; each pulse, a gong of brutal pain.

Awareness seeped in and out on a flowing gray tide. Sometimes the pain at the back of his head would lift him onto a cresting wave and toss him through the surf. He'd swim back into consciousness as though he moved through thick syrup.

How long it took before Alex reached consciousness, he did not know. Perhaps minutes. Perhaps a lifetime. Real clock time belonged outside of himself, divorced from where he now lay. His thoughts darted around a giant hole, afraid to fall in, afraid to remember. Remembering would be worse. So he floated.

He thought at first that he must be in a hospital. After all, he was in pain. He'd been hurt. He lay on a bed. As the tidal pain rolled back a bit, he grew aware of other sounds besides the labor of his own breathing. That's when reality reached up and tapped him on the shoulder with the message: *This ain't no hospital.* Hospitals smelled of cleaning fluids and starched white sheets. Hospitals have intercoms where buzzers buzz and voices sound like men and women holding their noses as they talk.

The overriding sound in *this* place was breathing — but not his own. Huge, rhythmic, like the pain rolling in and out; it ought to have lulled him. Except it was wrong. Period. Huge intakes of breath, like the rumble of a stoked furnace. A wheezy, growling exhale. What *was* that? And why did it steal all the heat from him?

He dared himself to open his eyes. His eyelids felt weighted by bricks, ridiculously heavy. Alex summoned what little reserve of strength he had and pulled them open. A harsh light blinded him, sending in a roaring tidal wave of agony. He gritted his teeth and rode it out. After a few moments his eyes adjusted to what was a low-wattage bulb hanging from a gray ceiling.

He lay on a narrow mattress built into the wall like a shelf. Otherwise the room was bare, walls stark and high.

A prison? Alex thought wearily. *I'm in a prison?*

He wondered if the door to this cubicle was locked. If he had owned the strength, he would have tried it.

He lay very still and listened. Echoes of shifting metal pounded the walls, screeching and banging, like a ship cutting through deep waters.

In midsong, a disco tune revved into life. It piped though loudspeakers outside his room.

> *Gonna live the life of the boogie*
> *From here on out, yeah yeah*

He remembered.

The man with the club. Being dragged through darkness.

A fresh sheen of sweat popped out on his forehead. He glanced about his room with new understanding. A prison? Yes, though that had not been the original purpose of this room. Once upon a time this cubicle had operated as a playground between men, a private nook for men who walked the halls with white towels wrapped about their middles.

Screams and shouts cut the air around him; frenzied, sobbing cries. Alex's skin crawled at the sound. *What in the world?*

The voices were male and female. With their shouts, a dawning horror set in. The sprightly music pounding through the hallways may have once been dance music, but he recognized an undercurrent, as if it were being played at a strange speed: the sadness of a funeral march.

A woman's scream rent the air.

And a man, gibbering: "Not again! Not again!"

The pounding of many fists upon walls.

Alex tapped his reserves of strength and pushed himself into a sitting position. Pain roared through his head like a crackling brushfire. He blacked out.

He came to a moment or so later. But at least he was sitting, head against the wall, feet on the floor. An unmerciful thirst parched his throat. Moisture poured profusely from his head — perhaps it was blood, his wound open again from his movement.

Was he dying? The pain told him yes. And if he lived much longer, if he clung to life in hope of salvation, what fate awaited him? Another bashing with a club? Some other, far worse end?

He could not, would not, allow that to happen.

He sucked in a tortured breath and made to stand up from his bed, but again he was swept up in a dizzy tidal wave. He made one frantic attempt to stay conscious before the undertow dragged him into darkness.

2

He awoke to music, and sounds of commotion.

Footsteps outside his doorway.

Groggily, Alex lifted his head.

A voice slithered into his brain:

(Your friends have misbehaved, Alex. I'm afraid you'll have to take their punishment)

Alex prayed with sudden horror, *Dear god, let me die—*

A latch was thrown back.

The door banged open.

34

The woman: Inevitabilities

1

Inevitable.

Inevitable, that she should enter this particular line of work, considering her remarkable childhood.

Inevitable, that her marriage should crumble around her feet after eight ill-spent years, leaving her stranded but wiser, little Randall only six years old.

Inevitable, that the blessing of the crystal should disintegrate into such baffling and disturbing questions.

"Stop thinking about him," Red admonished. "He won't be back."

Oh, but he would. She knew. Two plus two did equal four. He'd arrived, despite her attempts to hide her whereabouts by conjuring faulty images and wrong directions. He'd found his way to her doorstep, and damn him to all hell, he would come back.

"He's a creep," Red told her. He raised a fist. "And a stupid creep, if he shows his ugly face here again."

Rachael Black smiled indulgently. Red was a good boy, loyal to the end. Hotheaded, but in his own way, it was part of his peculiar charm. She'd escaped many of the usual traumas of single parenting relatively unscathed. She had never had to lay down a curfew, never had to have a heart-to-heart about drugs or alcohol (sure, he occasionally drank far too many beers — what boy didn't?) He had his girlfriends, and always treated them courteously, even though the lot of them were whiny little things with no interest except themselves.

Yes, they'd sailed through his stormy adolescence with hardly a squall between them. Now Red was twenty-three, and if he still wanted to live with his old mom, if he preferred her company to some of the scrappy young girls who giggled too much, that was fine by her. She was never the recipient of Red's temper; that he reserved for anyone who got in their way. And he was such a help running the bookstore.

"You sit here," her son had instructed after that man stormed out. "Have yourself a cup of tea. I'll close up shop."

"But it's too early," she had protested. "It's not six o'clock."

Red waved that away. "Have you looked outside lately? Nobody's gonna come in, not in this weather."

Closing early ran counter to her principles, but today, she'd acquiesced. Her legs had no strength anyway, so shaken was she by that ... that pornographer's appearance. What was his name again? David? David something. Thank god she hadn't left the crystal out on the kitchen table, in plain sight. What if he'd tried to take it? Oh, the horrors that thought set into motion!

Rachael pushed herself away from the kitchen table. The desire to gaze upon it burned within her — to know the stone remained safely within her possession. Silly, of course: That young man with the haunted face hadn't been near it. Still, she could not quell the fire, could not rest easy, until this need had passed. She hoisted herself off the chair and ducked into her bedroom. Through the partition she could hear Red at the cash register, counting the bank. She approached the antique jewelry box upon her dresser with the anticipation of a starving woman about to gaze upon a feast. Her heart pounded unmercifully against her bosom.

She was unused to this feeling of dread that had hold of her. *Calm yourself.*

She opened the box. Folded back the white silk handkerchief.

There it glittered. Just looking at the crystal soothed her frayed nerves, took away the rough edges of her panic. It never ceased to astonish her, its intricate prisms and points within points, that blue tongue buried within its center. The bedroom where she stood was dimly lit, yet the stone caught all the available light, magnifying it, casting rainbow shadows onto its surrounding bed of white silk.

A jewel without price. Truly.

And if anyone deserved to benefit from its charms, Rachael Black knew she was just that person.

2

Life — well, life just hadn't lived up to all her expectations. Mind you, she expected no miracles and understood perfectly well that certificates guaranteeing the best of everything were not doled out at birth. Forge whatever path you can, her mom used to say. Don't be afraid to blaze a trail.

Well, she'd been doing that for as long as she could remember, ever since the day when ten years of an uneventful childhood had been interrupted by a near-fatal accident.

She used to revel in the telling of it; myth made real. Her son would sit across from her, moony-eyed with a child's familiar litany: "Tell me again! Tell me again!"

And Rachael, who denied her child nothing, would clear her throat and begin:

3

"When I was ten years old, I fell off a swing set and landed in a pile of scrap wood. A rusty nail punctured my right foot. We lived in a tiny dot of a town a hundred miles outside Tucson, and Daddy, a devoutly religious Christian Scientist, did not believe in penicillin, or tetanus shots, or any kind of doctoring, for that matter. My foot swelled to the size of a football. I ran a temperature of 105 degrees for several days. They told me I was delirious. All I can remember is Mom and Dad praying over me. I knew I was getting worse. On the fourth or fifth day I distinctly heard my father command my brother to go round up wood. I was frightened, because I believed it meant only one thing: a coffin. They were going to make my coffin.

"Some time that night, I was startled awake. The whole bedroom was bathed in a sort of lilac-colored light. At the foot of the bed stood a radiant woman in a flowing robe. She was indescribably beautiful, her whole being an expression of love and kindness. I wasn't the least bit afraid.

"'Are you the Virgin Mary?' I asked.

"She shook her head patiently. 'I have come to help you,' she said. She drifted to the side of the bed and offered me her hands. 'Come with me.'

"When I took hold of her hands, the terrible pain that had racked me all that week evaporated. For that relief alone, I would have followed her anywhere. Holding one of my hands, she began to lead me out of the room. On impulse, I glanced at my bed. And there I was, still half-covered in sheets, my head resting on the pillow. Eyes closed. Mouth open.

"In that instant I knew I was dead."

Dead? little Randall would cry, squirming in delicious terror at the thought of Mommy gone, Mommy taken away. He knew the outcome, yet had to ask: *What happened next?*

"Yes," Rachael would somberly intone, "Dead; yet feeling so alive, with this woman. One moment we were in my bedroom, and in the next we stood in an empty chamber.

"Immediately, the woman set me upon a wide examination table. Anxiety welled in me, and sensing my fear, she calmed me with soothing strokes of her hands.

"'Where am I?' I asked her.

"'Hush,' she replied. 'Do not be afraid. I am going to heal you, but you must be very still and close your eyes.'

"I did as I was told. My eyes fluttered shut. Her hands rested on my swollen right foot. They were hot, like an iron. She massaged and manipulated my foot, hurting me at first, until the warmth sank in. She sent me reassuring thoughts, telling me what a good girl I was, how brave and strong.

"Her manipulations continued for several minutes. Suddenly, I heard a strange ringing in my ears. Without warning, the table dissolved beneath me. I was flying through a dark place, a tornado sound all around me. I wasn't scared; that was the funny part. I was saddened because I no longer felt or saw the Lady around me.

"At that very moment, whispering into my ear, the Lady said, 'You have much work to accomplish for us. Go, and prosper, and share in all your gifts.'

"The next thing I remember is coming awake in predawn light back in my own bed. I felt weighted down, heavy, as though my body was made of bricks. I threw back the covers and looked at my foot. All the purple discoloration, the swelling, had disappeared. Even the puncture wound had healed. My first thought was to get down and pray to thank the Lady.

"And then I became very still, and listened to the sounds of the house around me, and I felt — oh, how to explain this — like a new muscle was being flexed in my head. I thought of my brother, and knew he was asleep. I thought of my parents. Mom was awake, her hands curled about the covers of her bed. I could sense waves of distress flowing through her. Confusion. Fear. Guilt at not being able to make me well.

"I was so upset with this image of my mother that I jumped out of bed and rushed into their bedroom. 'Mommy! Mommy!' I shouted. 'Don't feel bad. I've been cured!'

"I told them excitedly about the Lady, and how she had helped me. They were skeptical, of course, but patient the way only parents can be, until it suddenly dawned on them that I should be half-dead in my bedroom. They quickly examined my foot, and finding it healed, Mother burst into fresh tears and proclaimed it a miracle.

"It wasn't until days or even weeks later that I began to appreciate some of the changes that had occurred in me. I was so happy to be free of pain, to be alive, that I wanted to experience *every*thing. Gradually, I became aware that if I concentrated very hard, I seemed to sometimes hear what people were thinking — or at the very least get a sense of their thoughts and mood. Also, if I lay very still at night or in the morning, I had lovely dreams of leaving my body and flying about the room. I enjoyed the freedom of it, because it reminded me of how it felt with the Lady. Sometimes I traveled great distances, but always, at the end of these flights, I felt a tugging, and a need to return.

"One day Mother sat out on the back porch, resting in the noonday heat. I could tell she was thirsty, so I brought her a tall glass of iced tea. Her eyes shone with the oddest light. She patted the seat next to her. I joined her.

"'How do you know these things?' she asked.

"'What things?' I saw the confusion and worry in her thoughts.

"'You bring me tea before I ask for it. In the kitchen, you are always one step ahead of me, bringing me just the pot or pan I need. Sometimes, I swear you can see right through me. Just this moment, I deliberately thought of iced tea, and minutes later here you are, with a glass.' She took my hand. 'Rachael, honey, tell the truth: How do you know these things?'

"I shrugged. The color of her thoughts told me she wasn't angry, or upset: She just wanted answers, and deserved them. 'Sometimes I hear people in my head. Like a radio station that I can tune in. Everybody has their own ... channel, and some come in clearer than others. Like you, for instance. You're easy.'

"She fixed me with a stern look. 'How long have you been able to do this?'

"'Ever since I was so terrible sick. After the Lady made me well.'

"An image of Mother Mary flickered across her mind. It was like one of the stained-glass windows in our church. Not at all the Lady who had helped me, but this image soothed her fears. After all, a miracle *had* happened. She should have lost her little girl, yet here I was, talking of this strange gift.

"'Listen to me,' she said. 'You've been given something special. Only the Lord knows why. But I don't want you broadcasting this — you hear me? You'll have time enough for that later, when you're older. Right now it's to remain our secret. Anytime you want to talk about it, or have any questions, you come to me. Not a word of this to your brother or father. Daddy wouldn't ... understand.'

"I didn't need to look into her thoughts to know how Dad would react. Daddy, for all his goodness and well intentions, was a superstitious man, and in many ways fearfully ignorant.

"Years passed. Mom and I would take trips into Tucson, where we'd go to the public library. I read every book on the paranormal I could lay my hands on — which, unfortunately, were hard to come by. Most of all, I learned that I was not the only one with these gifts, and that comforted me very much."

Here Randall's face would light up, the unburnished curiosity of a child. "What about me?" he'd ask. "Will it happen to me, too?"

She would shrug; and throw open her arms for Red to come to her for a hug, and tell him, "It might. It just might, when you get older."

"What happened next?" he'd ask.

"Well," she would answer very seriously, "I went to college. Met your father. And we lived happily ever after."

And Randall would giggle and laugh, absurdly happy, for *he* was the product of what came happily ever after. The child of a maiden straight out of a magical tale.

In the reflected glow of her young son's face Rachael would persuade herself that it was true, this "ever after" — and then she would glance up and away from Randall and stare into the unwavering disgusted frown of Steven Black, her husband.

4

She married Steven Bishop Black just about the time she'd resigned herself to the solitary life of an old maid. College had brought her to Los Angeles, a degree in philosophy (which amounted to a hill of beans, that's how much good it did her), and a clerk's position at a bookstore servicing UCLA students. It was 1965. The plaster cast of 1950s morality began to reveal the first cracks.

Ruddy faced, blond haired, Steven Black swept her off her feet with his good looks and forceful personality. He was one year her senior, finishing up his last year of law school. His dreams of powerful courtroom oratories, which he spun on their frequent dates, intoxicated Rachael; here was a man intent to change the world, to make it a better place. And since her own drowsy life lacked direction, since she was still attempting to sort out which road to travel, it was ridiculously easy to be his cheerleader, and let her own dreams sleep on undisturbed.

In so many little ways she began to help out: cooking dinners, giving the spartan apartment where he lived a good thorough cleaning, typing his papers for class. They dated all through early spring and summer, and by Thanksgiving they were married. Steve had wanted her to move in with him, and delay marriage until after his degree; Rachael was nothing if not old-fashioned, and she drew the line: marriage or nothing. Marriage it was.

She never came out directly and announced her specialness; she kept it for herself. Besides, somehow the topic never came up in casual conversation. Steve was impressed with her ability to stay one step ahead of him, to read his moods, but he never thought to question it. So they lived, that first year, in mutual ignorance. If he sometimes wondered how on earth she had known it was him on the phone before he spoke a word, or puzzled over the packed dinner she had already prepared before he told her he was studying late at the library, he never said a word.

Their marriage remained steady and uneventful — that is, until her husband came home with his head swirling from the afternoon tryst he'd spent with another woman. He'd walked in the door, kissed Rachael on the cheek with a mumbled excuse to go soak in the tub — and she'd turned on him, screaming.

He could not lie to her, he found. He may as well have come through that front door and tossed her photographs depicting every sexual position he'd tried. Yes, she was furious. So was he: How could she know these things? How long had this been her little secret? Served her right, to go peeking into someone's thoughts without their permission.

Like taffy, the marriage pulled apart, but did not break. Days of sullen silence gave way to a truce. Outwardly, each forgave the other. Inwardly, each stored the resentment for a later date, should such ammunition prove useful.

Meanwhile, she worked part-time to support them while Steven finished school. Indulging her love for kids, she found a job at a nursery school in the mornings, and worked at the bookstore in the afternoons. Her husband buried himself in his studies, but allowed himself no outside dalliances. Rachael was grateful for that, and in appreciation, without quite being aware of what she was doing, she began to clamp down on her talents. No more would she poke around where she didn't belong. The gifts, she discovered, were like plants in a garden; without nourishment, they began to wither.

Steven finished law school, and out of their celebration they conceived a child. With the birth of her son, Rachael at last found a purpose for her life. Steven worked grueling weeks as the freshman aboard a big law firm, paying his dues, while she now stayed home with Randall. The years went by. Theirs was not the best marriage, perhaps, but an arrangement of convenient compromises. Every once in a while Rachael would feel the need to revitalize her gifts, to put them to good use, but Steven still frowned upon it all. His reasoning was clear: He made more than enough to support them. She should just stay home and take care of Red. She could read her books on all that psychic junk if she wanted, but leave it at that.

Funny how she allowed so intrinsic a part of herself to sleep all those married years. If not for Randall, she might have rebelled earlier. Inevitable, that a time would come in her life when she knew she had to act before all was lost — just as it was inevitable that she should discover once again that her husband had been having quickie affairs behind her back.

She could not forget, or forgive, this time. And his resentment was a hard stone that could not be dislodged. He'd had it up to his eyeballs with her talk of ESP and precognition. He wanted out. So did she. They parted on amicable but cool terms, he to another apartment in Los Angeles, and she to San Francisco, Randall at her side.

She secured a flat in the Haight Ashbury district. Rents were cheaper there, the streets of her neighborhood filled with a curious mix of leftover hippies, itinerant vagabonds, and a recent influx of homosexuals. She found work at a bookstore called Uncommon Ground in the Mission. Its proprietor, a Mr. Dotson, dabbled in the occult and psychic phenomenon. He welcomed Rachael, and encouraged her to exercise her unique powers.

She then uncovered a sad fact: What she'd taken for granted, her one uniqueness, her gift, had ebbed away to nothing. Her garden was a wasteland, and she doubted if she could summon it back to life. The seeds to this garden had been planted long ago; nothing waited in reserve. She would have to make do.

At Mr. Dotson's suggestion — and considerable encouragement — she began to read palms for people who came into the bookstore. At first she was terrified, and consented to this masochistic exercise only with her steady, familiar customers. But how easily led they were, these lambs who needed — demanded! — answers. It required no special talent to dig around and tell these people what they wanted to hear. How repetitious, their questions and wants: Would they love, and be loved; would they meet a man, would they meet a woman; should they take this job...

And she: Of *course* take the job — if that is what you desire. Of *course* some day true love will knock upon your door. Be free of guilt, move on from the past, enjoy the present. Oh, how they swallowed it all, these desperate people! Each one went away convinced Rachael had spoken directly to them, having peered in upon their very soul.

Rachael the Impostor — that's what she called herself now, in her darkest moments. Here she was doing her life's work at last, helping others, but the power was almost gone, a mere shadow of its former strength. Fitfully, it would appear only when confronted with raw emotion. Once, for example, a Vietnam vet had come to her, his mind black with crimes committed in rage and confusion, under cloak of night. It had required days to rid the shop of his stink.

Mostly, there were only faint glimmers, stray thoughts or colored emotions to be picked up and interpreted when she could. So she cultivated her talents for reading body language, of intuiting what her desperate customers needed to hear, and, impostor or not, she was a success in her own modest way.

Mr. Dotson died of a heart attack in 1984, and after much legal finagling and months of paperwork, the bookstore was hers. She and Red moved out of their Haight Ashbury apartment and into the small but cozy rear of the store, renamed the Déjà Vu.

It was tougher than she'd expected. Times were lean. Red tried a semester of college at UCSF and promptly dropped out. He preferred working with his hands, and searched out jobs at construction sites. But he got into frequent fights with his co-workers and bosses. In between these jobs, he worked with his mom in the store.

Just when Rachael feared possible bankruptcy, she began to notice a distinct shift in her clientele. She could not keep her shelves stocked with enough books on holistic healing. Interest in New Age thinking had dawned, and ever the shrewd businesswoman, Rachael rode these currents. Pyramids, crystals, healing stones; holistic health strategies, reincarnation, life after death — whatever they wanted, she provided. And if she didn't believe in half of it, well, it was up to her customers to buy or not buy. Her job was to provide the merchandise.

Then it happened, the miraculous: Red's present.

All that long, dry spring Red worked at a shipping warehouse out at Hunters Point. Its location in a rundown section south of San Francisco wasn't the greatest, nor did he enjoy having to wear a safety mask to screen out dust that was possibly laden with deadly germs from exotic locales. The pay was good. Red enjoyed the work, the shuttling of crates to and fro, and the lack of supervisors hanging around. He was left alone, and he liked that just fine. All sorts of merchandise passed through his hands: umbrellas from Taiwan, pottery from Bombay, multicolored fabrics and dresses straight from the Philippines. He would come home with stories to tell, and Rachael's eyes would shine with excitement as the places rolled off his tongue: Taiwan. Tokyo. Hong Kong. China.

Then, on the summer solstice, he brought home a gift-wrapped present.

"What in the world?" A delicious thrill as she ripped into the package with a child's delight.

"A crystal," he told her as she held it up to the light, her lips pursed in awe and wonder.

Beautiful. It was absolutely beautiful. "This must have cost you a fortune," she said to him, but he shook his head and looked away, embarrassed. She studied him a moment and stole the thought from him without meaning to. So *that's* how he could afford the gemstone; a five-finger discount from the shipping warehouse. She was about to reprimand him when it came to her that this was the first time in months she'd picked up such a clear thought so effortlessly. How had she accomplished such a feat? And she looked at the gleaming crystal, which began to feel hot in her hand.

Okay. He stole the crystal. Big deal. Who was going to miss it? It had been done out of a son's love; no crime of drugs or illegal gains. A present, aimed to please her. Sweet, in its own way.

Imagine her astonishment, then, as the crystal began to reveal its true self in the coming days and weeks, as though normal perception was a gray thing obscured in layer after layer of onion skin. The stone peeled all that back, heightening her awareness to a level equal and above the powers she had cherished as a teenager. With the crystal in her hands, her clients truly became open books, their wants and desires nakedly displayed.

Word of mouth carried her deeds all over town. Soon she had a steady stream of customers. Rachael tried to keep a low profile, but at night she positively danced, Red at her side, laughing. The sweetness of this victory!

Inevitable. She deserved success, after all the difficult years.

Golden summer chilled into autumn.

And with autumn came the visions.

She wasn't sure what they were at first. Old memories of past owners of the stone? Random, intuitive flashes? Daydreams?

She began to fear the twilight. Such an odd, groundless fear, but there it was. True dark, true day; neither one bothered her. It was only as the sun sank behind Twin Peaks, slanted afternoon light yielding to the gloom, that dread twisted knots into her stomach. In twilight, the day lost all definition. Comforting, solid shapes grew hazy and indistinct. Something stirred in the air, blowing upon her face; something carried on the wind, moving inexorably closer. The smudge of gray fog upon the land was like a creature dredged from the sea, hugging the hillsides with its tentacles.

She would sit in her kitchen, the stone in her hand, and see a man — a writer. She knew he was a writer because she saw his words as well, and they disgusted her. Stories of rumps and penises, men having intercourse with other men. He wrote pornography, this writer, and try as she might, she could not shake the visions of him. She was a helpless Peeping Tom to his intimacies, his written fantasies of exaggerated sexual acts.

With the crystal's help, she saw it all. Even while giving a reading for a client, certain aberrant images flickered, intruding, unwanted: a man in a phone booth, pants pushed down to his knees, penis in hand; men floating in multicolored lights, or sitting in darkened rooms, all of them squeezed into clothes obviously dug from the bottoms of dresser drawers; hospital rooms smelling of sickness and death. And through it all, the writer squirming with terrible agonies.

The realization was slow to build, but once up, Rachael caught its full implications: These images did not all stem from this writer and his filthy stories. All across town a deadly web seemed to have been thrown, and these men she saw twitched in its threads.

Yes. Her feelings were undeniable. Something blown in with the ocean fog, something with no shape — and yet was all shapes. A fire demanding fuel, and these homosexual men were the first to feed it. Yes, a fire: That described it exactly. An invisible fire that ravaged in silence. And the fire lived within that abandoned building she had seen.

She had never encountered anything so malevolent, so virulent in all her life. It numbed her, flattened her with its force, so that relief came only when she shut herself off from it. No problem; hadn't she mastered the art of denial during her eight years of marriage? Easy to put on the blinders, to go about her business.

And then her hands would cradle the stone, and she knew the writer sought it, sought *her*. Forget it: The crystal was hers. He couldn't have it. This was *his* fight, whatever was happening. Besides, wasn't that what the baritone voice whispered into her ear each night before she tossed and turned with dreams of underground caves and hands clawing the steam: *Stay out of it.*

She agreed. She obeyed.

She shut herself down, tried to block the emanations that might give her away.

What a shock, then, to look up from the crystal only last night and see the writer's ghostly image before her. She'd scared him away, and hoped — prayed — she'd seen the end of him.

Until that very afternoon, when he faced her in the flesh.

He'd be back, all right. Two plus two equaled four.

This isn't your fight. Stay out of it.

She did not need the voice outside, yet inside her head, to warn her off. It was nothing personal against these people; she just wanted to be left alone. And if this writer was foolhardy enough to think he could waltz into her store and take the crystal from her, he had a nasty surprise coming.

He wanted a fight?

She'd give him the fight of his life.

35

Borrowed time

Roger and Sam huddled in conference by the salad bar.

1

Roger and Sam huddled in conference by the salad bar.

"What are they doing now?" asked Roger.

"Talking," Sam answered, rubbing his jaw in thought. "It sounds like some kind of fuckin' shorthand. David starts to ask a question, and his friend — Bob, is that his name? — answers before he even finishes the question. Damndest thing I ever saw."

Roger scowled. He knew the damndest thing *he'd* ever seen: David and that kid stumbling through the archway door of Uncle Charlie's, both of them bloodied and white as ghosts. His few customers had sat at their tables in horrified silence.

Furious? God damn he'd been furious! He'd hustled them into his back office, away from his patron's prying eyes, and, good waiter or no, intended to fire David on the spot.

But how pitiful they looked, the two of them. David dutifully introduced his friend Bobby, who was tight-lipped and drawn, deferring completely to him. And David: Christ, the front of his shirt was greased and spotted with blood. Red stuff was splattered over his hands. They smelled, the both of them: sour and coppery.

"We've been in a fight" was all David would say.

This wasn't enough to explain their condition. "You were supposed to be at work hours ago!" Roger reminded him, flushed with indignation.

And the *look* David had given him then — so sad, so hurt, was full of the unspeakable.

"Okay," Roger had sighed, wilting under that penetrating gaze. He waved his right hand toward the dining room. "Hell, you see we have no business tonight. Between Sam and me, I guess we've got the shift covered."

"Thanks, Roger." David had glanced protectively at Bobby, and for the first time Roger sensed this strong bond between the two.

Interesting: He had never known David to be at a loss for words, yet here he was hours late for work, blood all over him, monosyllabic in his answers. Yet in a single glance to his quiet friend he said a thousand words.

They had excused themselves, and used the bathroom off the office to clean up and change into some of the fresh shirts David kept in a locker.

Now David and his buddy sat together in the lounge office, voices low but excited, close to each other like old friends eager to catch up.

Roger and Sam were going crazy with curiosity.

"What the hell happened to them!" Roger sputtered. "Why do they look like they stepped out of *The Texas Chainsaw Massacre?*"

"I'll get closer," Sam said with a wink. "And here's how." He dished up two platters of lasagna and marched over to the office door.

"Alex wanted to help," David was saying. "But he just refused to believe what was happening—"

"Din-din," Sam cheerily called out. He pushed open the door, ignored their surprised faces, and set the plates of food before them.

Bobby glanced at David. "I'm not hungry."

"Eat," Sam commanded, "or you'll make this Jewish mom one unhappy lady. It ain't a pretty sight. Ask David if you think I'm lying."

David smiled gratefully. "Thanks, Sam." He handed Bobby a fork. "Go on."

"I can't. I keep seeing—" He bit himself off and glanced self-consciously at Sam.

"Don't mind me," the cherubic cook said airily. "Talk about whatever you want. I won't tell a soul."

Sam didn't budge; he rocked up and down on his heels.

This kind gesture dictated he provide some sort of explanation; David cleared his throat. "I ... know we must have looked..."

"— ghastly—"

"Yes — when we walked in. But trust me, Sam: You don't want to be involved in this." He finished with a no-hard-feelings smile. "Nothing personal."

"One day you'll explain?"

David nodded. "The whole enchilada. I promise."

That mollified him. Sam shrugged and left, closing the door behind him.

Roger handed Sam an order slip. "Table five. A cannelloni and a fettucine Alfredo." He motioned toward the back office. "So what's the dirt?"

Sam made a zipper motion across his lips.

"Oh come on. Give."

Sam couldn't help himself; he leaned in conspiratorially and stage-whispered, "Well. If they haven't killed anyone, they damn sure act as if they're *planning* to before the night's out."

So would Sam. And much sooner than ever he would have imagined.

2

With his first forkful, Bobby's appetite was unleashed. An English muffin munched with his morning coffee had served as his only meal for the day. Even so, he thought he'd never eat again, not after the gruesome events of the past several hours. But when that chubby cook Sam waltzed out of the office, and when the pungent odors of tomato and garlic and Parmesan cheese hit his nostrils, he rediscovered an old secret as he dug into the lasagna: Even amidst horrors, life goes on.

"Hey," David chided him. "You'll make yourself sick. Slow down."

"Sorry," he mumbled through a mouthful.

"Don't be sorry. It's good you have an appetite."

"Knock knock!" Sam called out. He waddled into the office with a basket of garlic bread and two glasses of red wine.

"Sam—"

"Bon appetite," he answered with a wave of his hand, and was gone.

"Not bad service," Bobby grinned, "considering *you're* supposed to be the waiter in this joint."

David pointed his fork toward the office door. "I know what's going on. They're only being so nice to us because they're dying of curiosity."

"Wouldn't you?"

David nodded. "I'm just thankful they let us in. I don't know where else we could have gone."

A needling worry rose in both of them, unspoken: that their hiatus here was only buying a couple of hours.

David's red flannel shirt was a little too long in the sleeves for Bobby, but otherwise fit him fine. David wore one of his work shirts, all white. Their other, splattered shirts lay in a rolled-up pile on a chair; David intended to toss them into the garbage out back.

"Do you think they'll call the police on us?" Bobby asked uneasily.

"Naw. They're my friends. And even though it looks like we—"

"We did," Bobby interjected darkly.

"No." He shook his head emphatically. He leaned in. "We did *not* murder him," he whispered. "We just finished what Victor started. And incidentally, you saved my life." He sipped his wine. "Now tell me what happened last night when Mick was taken."

It poured out of Bobby in white-hot bursts. Whenever he stumbled with the story, his face distorted with pain and horror, David reached out with his mind and he, too, saw. It occurred between them spontaneously, and felt as natural as breathing.

"The truth is," Bobby said, and pushed his plate away, "I don't really give a shit what's going on. If we were meant to meet, then you've got to help me. All I know is, this son of a bitch has taken the only man I love."

"It's not just you, Bobby. It's the whole city."

Bobby's eyes ballooned at that.

David continued. "My best friend Eddie Blake was one of the first to disappear. And that man we saw on my fire escape. Jack Martin. We used to work out together at the gym. Shoot, he's the one who pointed Mick out to me. He knew his name. And because of that, I wondered if the Mick of my story — and you — were real people."

Bobby brightened. "It *is* amazing, isn't it, that I drew you on paper."

"Yes. It is. And now, here we are. Together. It was meant to happen."

They looked at each other a moment in grateful silence.

Then Bobby shook his head. "What I don't get is this: What you've been telling me. The lure this thing uses: a couple of dusty disco tunes and goopy nostalgia. What is that? I mean — hey — I listen to everything from Patsy Cline to New Wave punk, and I'm soft for a few tunes myself. But that doesn't mean I'd let myself get killed over some desire to have it all *back*. See what I mean?"

David sipped his wine. "That music has special meaning for me. And a lot of other gay men and women my age."

Bobby nodded. "I know that. But I still don't get it."

David hesitated for a moment. Suddenly the answer came to him. "It reminds us of Before. That's it, in a nutshell. Now you; you're probably right on the cusp of things when they first changed in the eighties. Most people seem to think disco popped out of nowhere with *Saturday Night Fever,* but hell, disco started in the gay clubs *years* before that movie came out. Gloria Gaynor. Barry White. Donna Summer — shit, we *made* her career! Now I'm the first to admit that in retrospect, most disco music was pretty awful. But at that time, for me and many others in the mid-to-late seventies, disco was like having our own national anthem. So much seemed within our reach. It was the music of our new freedom."

Bobby nodded, smiling at his own bright memories. Then his expression clouded. "And then — the party was over."

David grimaced. "I hate it when people say that, but, yes: The party was over. In its own way that's all right, too. It was time to grow up, move on. But all those freewheeling desires — at least with me, anyway — had to be locked up. Pushed into a private drawer. And every once in a while it rears its head and shouts, *I want to come back!* Do you know what I mean? The desire to ... enjoy life again without having to worry about the consequences."

Bobby shook his head with solemn understanding. He'd begun to feel a little like that himself, every time he opened a newspaper and read the latest grim statistics. He cleared his throat. "So this Victor — whoever or whatever he is — has some key to that drawer?"

David's eyes lit up. "Yes. Exactly. From what I've seen in the neighborhood, he's been flaunting our old desires right in our faces. He tempts us by saying the party *isn't* over — not if you come to him. Pretty irresistible offer. And if we gay men have one fatal flaw, it's that: We are easily tempted."

Bobby chewed on that for a moment.

"Look," he hastily went on. "I'm not claiming to know everything, because I don't. I wish I could say differently. All I know is, I've been aware of you and Mick from almost the very beginning. We're parts of the same solution. In a way, I admire you."

"Why?"

"You responded against this threat right away. It didn't matter how preposterous it all seemed. You charged in without thinking about the consequences."

"That's because I wanted to save Mick," Bobby said. A pang of remorse hit him with his words.

"Maybe we still can," David said, as though catching the color of Bobby's thoughts. "And Eddie. Alex. Jack. We just have to be brave and try our best. I'm just relieved — and a little in awe — that my ... my premonitions have proved correct. That's why I admire you. While you were fighting for Mick, I kept wondering if I was totally crazy. No one believed me. Not even Alex. And now—" His face darkened. "Now we'll have to wait and see if it's not too late."

Bobby drained the last of his wine. "Where do we go from here? We can't return to your place. I suppose we could go to my apartment — though I should warn you it's quite a mess."

David shook his head. "No. They could be waiting there, too, in ambush. But I met a woman today, and her son. Rachael and Red. She owns a stone, a crystal — and I'm convinced it has a power we need and Victor wants for himself."

"I've drawn it!" Bobby exclaimed in wonder. "And maybe her and her son, too. Does she have long hair? And he's tall, right?"

David rubbed his head in amazement. A crooked grin. "I wish I'd met up with you sooner. Yes. That's them, all right. I don't understand what the power of this stone is, exactly, but I'll bet it's a key to stopping Victor. I think the crystal can be used as a weapon."

Bobby's face was alive. "You suppose that's why I drew it, and you? Because it ... it called to us?"

"Yes."

He considered his own words a moment, then scowled. "Don't you think it's a little coincidental that Victor and this stone appeared in the same town?"

David leaned back in his chair. He shook his head. "Maybe it explains *why* this has happened. Hell, I don't have a monopoly on the answers. But coincidence? No. I don't believe in coincidence any more. There are no acciden—"

A muffled thump-thump on the roof, directly above their heads. A winged sound.

"What was that?" Bobby whispered.

David stood up from the table. He'd gone a little pale around the edges. "I'll go check—"

The lights went out.

3

The office became a black hole, stupefyingly opaque.

"David—!" A plaintive cry, little brother to big brother.

"Give me your hand."

They groped for each other in the dark.

"Come on," David said. He stumbled toward where he assumed the office door to be, tugging Bobby along with him. His stomach was doing flip-flops as he grasped the door frame and pulled Bobby out into the hallway. They hurried down the short hallway, past the prep kitchen and giant walk-in freezer.

Commotion from out in the restaurant. Roger's voice, over the din, orchestrating like the pro he was. "Okay, gents," he was saying above moans and groans. "Looks as though we're all dining by candlelight."

A candle already glowed butter-warm from the center of each table. Roger scurried about, lighting the rows of votive candles that lined the waist-high wooden shelf along the walls. Sam lit candles in the kitchen to give himself light while he cooked. Two skillets sizzled above the stove's gas flames.

"A little blackout, my dears," Sam announced as he heard David and Bobby approach. His jaw dropped when he caught sight of their white faces. "Good heavens! What's wrong?"

A second thump upon the roof: the scritch-scratch of animal claws.

All three glanced with alarm toward the ceiling.

"What in the hell...?" The spatula in Sam's right hand dropped to his side.

A shriek from the front of the restaurant: a man. "Did you see that!"

Bobby recoiled, yanking David's hand.

Sam glanced toward the restaurant's entrance. "Jesus Christ!"

Their one table of customers had sprung to their feet, the startled scrape of chairs loud and ugly.

A shower of shattering glass.

Above the shouts and gasps, Roger:

"Get the fuck out of my—"

And then he was screaming.

4

David lunged forward, releasing Bobby. He had to get a better look, had to see what was happening. But he was unprepared for what greeted him. Sticking a finger into an electrical socket could not have given him a more hair-raising jolt.

The plate-glass window to Uncle Charlie's lay in ruins. Its jagged-toothed outline was a Halloween pumpkin caricature. Pieces of glass shook loose from the frame and fell, tinkling, onto the carpet of glass already on the floor.

Standing before the opening stood something that looked like it was straight from hell. This man-creature surveyed the restaurant. It was naked, its body only partly recognizable as human. Mulish snout, pinned-back ears, slitted eyes. A tangle of hair floated above the head as though the thing lay in a pool of water. His inner workings were visible, siren red. The heart hung suspended in folds of gristly tissue that must have been its lungs.

The being glowed with its own phosphorescence; the energy that fueled it escaped in a gaseous steam. In that endless moment as David stared at it — and caught sight of other shapes moving toward the gouged window — he thought he understood what it was he saw:

They're like bodies caught in midtransformation between phantom and flesh...

"Get the fuck out of my—"

And then Roger was screaming as the creature bellowed a blood-curdling cry and hurled itself upon him. He staggered back, hands thrown protectively in front of his face, and smashed into a table. Plates of half-eaten food and glasses of wine overturned in the melee. The two men who had been dining together lurched away from the table and fell into each other's arms.

With jaws fully extended, serpent fangs bared, the creature fastened upon Roger's neck.

The two customers scattered in panic.

Roger grabbed the creature by its shoulders, intent to wrestle it off — and his hands sank into the gelatinous shoulders like two hands thrust into a bowl of pudding.

"Oh god that hurts!" Roger screamed.

Sam began to push his way past David.

"Stay away," David ordered.

"But it's killing him!" Sam shot back.

"It's too late."

Amorphous tissue seethed up and over Roger's hands, racing up his arms with a burning fire. Where teeth had clasped onto his neck he felt a gnawing vibrating pain, and a spray of something wet and boiling. He could no longer hear his own pitiful cries — or anything at all — as the being surrendered its physical shape and bubbled all around him. They fell onto the floor, flopping around like something sinking into a tar pit.

(You're coming back with me—)

Roger heard the man-creature chuckle into his ear, and then all was dark, he must have passed out, must be dreaming still—

—for he fell onto a thin mattress inside a tiny square room, music thumping overhead, screams and wailing echoing like a madhouse nightmare, and if he wasn't dreaming then he must be dead, for this sounded like a purgatory for the damned...

5

All David and the others saw was the creature dissolving, giving up its shape as it enveloped Roger. Hot air gushed off the floor with a liquid spray, and they disappeared. A sticky residue bubbled on the floor like the dance of grease upon a hot skillet.

Sam had bleached as white as his apron.

Stunned silence.

Everything began to happen very fast.

Three more of the steaming creatures hopped through the shattered window and landed in the center of the room. Vaporous wings folded into the fleshy mire of their backs, and their stubby red sex organs stuck out at attention.

The two customers stepped forward as if mesmerized. They held hands, and faced the demons. "Take us! We want to go! Take us!"

In that moment before the creatures happily complied with their request, David noticed how the men were dressed: skin-tight 501 jeans, colored handkerchiefs stuffed into back pockets like miniflags, key chains dangling; one wore a gaily flowered polyester shirt unbuttoned to the navel while the other wore a blue tank top bearing the inscription "Sit and Spin."

One of the men reached into his pants pocket and waved a ticket in his hand. "See? We were invited. We—"

The creatures swarmed over them. Their ecstatic death cries filled the restaurant. Absorbed in the same bizarre fashion as Roger, they vanished into a whirl of spinning matter and steaming air, as though the heat was a door they could step through with unlimited ease.

Now only one of the three creatures remained, and he fixed his lizardy face upon them, snarling.

"Oh, Christ," Sam muttered.

David pushed the burly cook behind him. "Stay with us," he instructed. His heart galloped within his chest. He couldn't swallow.

The man-thing slid toward them, a look of twisted amusement upon its face. He slapped his hands upon his glowing chest.

(Come on, Boy Wonder. Show me what you've got)

"Let's run," Bobby whispered. "Is there a back way out?"

Sam shook his head. "It dead-ends into a backyard fence. We'd be trapped."

The creature was gloating.

(I have a message, Davie ole boy. From the Big Guy himself)

All could hear the creature's words, which scalded the insides of their heads.

David stepped back, inadvertently retreating into the kitchen's interior. An awful truth was coming to him, triggered by the creature's raspy voice.

(I'm the guinea pig, Davie. He wants to see how much of a man you are. So go ahead: Give me your best shot)

Now David trembled uncontrollably, and not even Bobby's reassuring hand upon his shoulder could subdue it. He stared wild-eyed at the Hollywood monster in front of him and watched as its features began to liquefy, to rearrange. The snake's nest of hair settled upon its head while snout and protruding jaw sank back into human proportions. Slitted, insectile eyes widened and returned to their appropriate color: brown. The translucent crust of skin smoothed and softened like hot wax, pale but human. In this afterlife condition the broomstick arms were fleshed out, certainly strong enough to pump iron again, oh, yes. No purple lesions pockmarked the luminous skin. No needle marks attested to months of blood monitoring and IVs. In death, he had gained his wish.

"Eddie," David whispered. Something broke inside him to address this monstrosity before him with his best friend's name.

A chuckle.

(The one and only)

"Look what's happened to you."

(Yes)

Eddie gloated.

(Look at me! Good as new! Better!)

He slid toward the three of them, the soles of his misshapen feet making a squishy suctioning sound on the tiled floor.

God, it would have been easier not knowing the true identity, to fight monster, not former friend. Now he was robbed of all the farewell words he'd held like precious coins to his chest.

(Aren't you gonna fight me, Boy Wonder?)

"Stop it, Eddie—"

(Stop it, Eddie!)

the thing mimicked. A self-satisfied smile. Eddie's new canines flashed.

(What do you know. I get to take you back with me, after all. He promised to reward me if I did...)

Another liquid step. Another.

"Stay away from us!" Pasty faced, in shock: David was afraid to look away from him for help, afraid that after one sideways glance Eddie would be ripping his throat apart.

The Eddie-thing wrinkled his face in disgust.

(You're no match at all—)

Something hot sizzled past David's right side and splashed onto Eddie. It caught him across his upper torso and neck. Smoke and steam spurted out, like a balloon punctured by needles. Anguished screams tore the air. He began to spin in all directions, flapping at himself as though on fire.

Sam stepped forward, triumphant: "There, you son of a bitch! There!" In his right hand he held a black cast-iron skillet. Hot grease dribbled off its edge and splattered the floor.

David looked at this thing disguised as his former friend. The grease was chewing into it, dissolving its tenuous flesh like a highly corrosive acid.

And then Bobby appeared on his left side. In his hands were fistsful of ice cubes snatched from the ice machine. He flung them at Eddie in desperation, to keep the creature disoriented and confused — and was as surprised as the others when the cubes of ice pierced him with the same corrosive action as the hot grease. The ice cubes embedded themselves in Eddie's fake skin, ice and heat merging into gasps of escaping steam. It was as if the steam was the thing's lifeblood. In front of their eyes, he began to deflate.

"The freezer!" Bobby was shouting. "Back him into the freezer!"

Sam hurled the cast-iron skillet. It struck the impostor's right shoulder, slicing through the exposed tendons and foaming muscles like a knife slicing warm butter. Eddie shrieked and howled. He snatched at his right arm, grabbing hold of it in his pain — and it came loose in his grip like pulled-apart taffy. His shoulder socket contracted and tried to rearrange itself, flooding the gaping wound with yellowish fluid.

The ghoul tossed away his useless arm. It fell to the floor, fingers grasping and ungrasping air with the twitching of a spider, before the entire appendage boiled and puddled away.

Eddie turned on them, savage. With fangs bared he swayed toward them, his one good arm pawing the air with his clawed fist.

"You want more?" Sam roared. He darted over to the stove, pot holder in his hand, and scooped up a skillet of burning Alfredo sauce. "Come and get it!"

The Eddie-thing threw up its one good arm, backing away. Sam drove it back and to the left, skillet aimed.

Bobby ran to the walk-in freezer and yanked open its massive door. He sheltered behind it, listening to Sam bully the creature into it.

(No! No!)

Sam chucked the contents of the skillet. White Alfredo sauce flew through the air. The creature jerked to its left, heaving itself out of the line of fire, so that only a portion of the sauce struck home. It splashed onto its thighs and legs, sizzling. It lost its balance and smacked against the freezer door with a wet spongy sound. The thing's legs gave out beneath it and it collapsed, good arm waving, into the walk-in freezer.

"Now!" David shouted in a voice he did not recognize.

Bobby shoved the heavy steel door closed. Sam appeared at his side, broomstick in hand, which he slid through the latch handle to hold the door in place.

But such measures were not necessary. Inside the storage locker, the frigid cold ate at what remained of the Eddie-impostor, twisting it this way and that. Its death rattles seared into David's brain, sunlight-bright, its agony a tortuous farewell. David shut his eyes against it. Clasped hands over his ears. Mercifully, their psychic connection died, like a cluster of light bulbs exploding in their sockets. But out of the flickering rubble an image flared briefly: his best friend in his hospital bed, a smile of gratitude on his narrow face as eyelids drooped toward sleep.

David sagged, aching to sit, to rest. His legs wobbled beneath him.

Bobby rushed to his side, eager to comfort. David took his arm and they stared into each other's eyes, Bobby's face aglow in orange light, starkly painted by yellow and red—

Oh, my god. He whirled to his right, staring across counters and salad bar into the interior of Uncle Charlie's. None of them had noticed, in the commotion. Each had taken the coppery light for granted, misinterpreted the cloudy bank rising from the floor as steam.

The restaurant was on fire.

6

Two more creatures capered outside the gouged front window, unable to enter.

"Look," David said above the steadily rising crackle, "they won't come in. They're afraid."

"Fire and ice," Bobby said, almost as though confirming the fact for himself.

Sam approached the salad bar, heart-stricken at the wreckage before him.

Tablecloths and hanging draperies fueled a fire that ate at the wood-paneled walls. All about the room, fallen votive candles fed miniblazes. In another five minutes the entire restaurant would be ablaze, thick smoke a blinding, deadly curtain.

"Come on," David shouted, and he hurried out of the kitchen, past Sam. He picked up a wooden chair from the floor, where it had fallen onto its side.

"What are you doing?" Bobby cried.

"Getting us out of here." He hoisted the chair by one of its legs, ignoring the spasm of protest from his sore back muscles, and aimed the chair at the rounded edge of an overturned table. He brought it down with a heavy swing.

"Hey! Stop that!" Sam, distraught at the idea of any more destruction.

By the third swing David had pried a chair leg loose from the truncated chair. Smoke burned his eyes. His lungs ached from exertion. He yanked a white tablecloth from a nearby table, heedless of the crashing spray of wineglasses and china plates. With the tablecloth wrapped about the stick's end, he motioned for Bobby and Sam to come stand behind him.

Fire crackled at their feet, their sides. Smoke stung their throats and nostrils.

David dipped the cloth-draped end of his stick into flames, holding it there until the tablecloth caught fire. He raised his homemade torch.

Above the snap and pop of hungry flames, a siren pierced the night.

"Let's go." He led them through the rubble of smashed china and overturned tables. Glass crunched beneath their feet. He zigzagged a path the others followed, aiming for the front door. David pulled it open. He stepped through to the outside, his homemade torch a waved flag, intent to thrust it into any creature that might dare attack. Bobby and Sam hurried out the door, hands over their mouths, hacking and coughing.

A crowd was gathering, men and women drawn by the flames and commotion. Some regarded David oddly, glancing between the torch and his sooty face. He didn't care; he was just relieved Victor's gang had retreated.

"Come with us," Bobby said to Sam. "We have a car up the street. We can escape."

But Sam startled them both by shaking his head. He stared at David. "It's *you* they want, not me. Go on, get away while you can. The police and fire trucks will be here any second."

David nodded. Extending a hand, he shook Sam's hand with gratitude. Bobby followed suit, a frown of disappointment plain on his face.

The lines of Sam's cherubic face hardened. "Is Roger dead?"

"I don't know," David answered.

"But you know who's responsible for this?"

"Yes."

Sam stood silent for a moment. Their eyes locked. "Good luck," he nodded curtly.

They bid farewell and stepped away from the burning restaurant. David lifted his gaze to Uncle Charlie's rooftop and there they were, Victor's two remaining henchmen, buzzing the air on a pair of wings, just behind the billowing smoke, hidden from the gathering crowd.

David took Bobby's hand and they bolted up Castro Street, up toward Nineteenth, where they'd earlier parked the taxicab.

A police car swerved around the corner of Eighteenth and Castro, colored lights spinning the night air. It screeched to a halt in front of the restaurant.

David threw down the torch. Since no creature flew after them, he did not want to draw undue attention by waving it in the air. He unlocked the passenger's side and slid across into the driver's seat. Bobby quickly followed.

Neither said a word. David started the engine and drove past the burning restaurant as two fire trucks joined the police car.

36

Déjà vu

1

A furious pounding of fists upon the door.

From deep inside the shop: "We're closed! Go away!"

David stepped up to the door, angling his head to peer through diagonal slats of glass set into the wood. The interior was dark. "Mrs. Black?"

"I said go away!"

Bobby tugged David's arm. "You sure this is a good idea?"

"Got any better ones?" he volleyed back. It came out sharper than he had expected; Bobby's face stung with the slap. "Sorry. I'm sorry—"

"S'okay."

"It's just — I don't know how much time—"

Bobby nodded. They'd driven like madmen the long city blocks to the Déjà Vu, convinced that at any moment one of those horrors would swoop down out of the dark and fasten itself to the speeding car. Now they stood at the front door to the shop, bathed in a pool of yellow light from a street lamp. Living dark hungered outside their lighted sanctuary. Yes. Bobby understood. Time was of the essence.

David rapped the solid door with his knuckles. "Mrs. Black? Please. My friend and I — we're in trouble. If you'll give us five minutes—"

"I said go away!" Rachael called back.

But he noted her voice was closer, softer. He squinted through the glass slats and could just make out her shape, hugging a six-foot bookcase. He tried again.

"Please! You're our only hope now! A truce — it's all we ask."

"Look here," her voice rang out, like an irritated parent to misbehaving child. "I can't help you. Whatever trouble you've gotten yourselves into should be handled by the police, not me. Now if you don't go away and leave me alone I'll have my son come out there and get rid of you for me."

Bobby glanced at David, none too excited about the possibility of seeing Red in action, after what he'd heard. But David was shaking his head, and held a finger to his lips.

"She's bluffing," he whispered. "Red's not here. If he was, we'd have thrown punches long before now."

"So what do we do?" Bobby countered with his own whisper.

David shrugged. "Tell the truth." He regarded the shadowy shape within the bookstore. "Look, Mrs. Black, I don't mean to frighten you. Bobby and I were attacked just now. We believe the ... people responsible may be on their way here, to finish the job."

"That's even a *better* reason to keep the hell away!"

"We need the crystal! You have it." Sensing her rising anxiety, David hastily added: "We're not here to take the stone from you. Keep it. It's yours. But without its protection, we're going to be killed. We've nowhere else to go."

As he waited for her response, his thoughts circled back to the front steps of the Caverns, and the evil, giant face scrabbling as he and Bobby had joined hands. Out of their unity some primal energy had caught fire, creating a shimmering shield. If they could get the woman and her crystal on their side, did they stand a chance of protection against Victor's minions? Was this the final piece needed to complete the circle of their power?

Her voice was quiet, without inflection, on the opposite side of the door.

"How do I know you're telling the truth?"

David took a gamble. "Look inside me, if you can. Inside both of us."

Suddenly, they could feel her probing.

Unsettling, to be rifled through, pillaged. David opened himself to her, brought as much of the recent events as possible to the forefront of his thoughts, where she could see them. But Rachael wasn't reading his exact memories so much as gleaning their color and mood. Fright and desperation: These colors were already familiar to her, so she dug beyond them to what mattered closest to her heart, the crystal. As she rooted around in his head she saw his search for the stone as a quest for answers, not profit. And she saw something he hadn't meant to show her: her own reflection of cowardice and greed.

She let go; she'd seen enough. David's scalp tingled from her phantom touch. She skimmed Bobby's thoughts. Earnest and loyal, the reins of leadership willingly handed to David; she was struck by this show of loyalty, because she saw they'd only met that afternoon. She felt the strong connection between them.

Suddenly Rachael recoiled from an image of a man's hands grasping for a knife shoved between shoulder blades.

—*Oh my god he* killed *a man, stabbed him in the back, look at the* blood—

At that moment Bobby felt something rake across his scalp, like a sharp instrument slipping and cutting too deep. *She knows,* he thought, hot with shame and guilt. *She saw what I did—*

David and Bobby shared an anxious glance. The terrors of the day were sharply etched in their expressions, brutal cuts and shadows marring their sturdy good looks.

Bobby jerked his head, indicating Rachael on the other side of the door. He whispered, "I've blown it, David. She saw—"

David held up a hand for quiet; he felt a distinct change, a shift. One word blazoned in his head, movie-marquee bright: *Inevitable.*

A latch thrown.

Rachael opened the door.

2

They were inside all of five minutes before Red stumbled in, his pink face flushed with drink. He drew back as though the tableau in the kitchen had reached up and slapped his face: Mom, tea cup in hand, chatting ever so how-do-you-please with that asshole and another punk with a crew cut. Red's eyes narrowed with consternation, yet his pressed lips hinted at amusement.

"Well, I'll be damned," he said. "The little voice was right."

"What voice?" Rachael asked, anxious to diffuse the electric tension.

"I'm having my beers, blowing off steam, talking with the guys, and all the while this little niggly voice says to come back home. I could've stayed another half hour, easy, but my gut's telling me to get the hell home." He offered a crooked smile to his mom. "Maybe some of your whatdoyacallit's rubbing off on me at last. How about that, huh?"

David peered anxiously at Red, then Bobby. He scooted from the table but did not get up from his seat. If there was to be a fight, he wanted his ally safely out of harm's way.

"Red—" he began.

"Shut up," Red spat. "I don't want my name coming out of your mouth. Got that?"

David sat where he was, high color rouging his cheeks.

"I invited them in," Rachael announced.

He turned on her. "Why the fuck did you do that?"

"Don't use that tone on me," Rachael snapped. Instantly, her son wilted a little, cowed. "I offered them ten minutes, no more. Now sit down and join us, if you like; otherwise, you're out of line."

"He kicked me in the balls," Red sullenly reminded her.

Rachael fixed David with a reproving look. "You see? There's nothing but antagonism here. Why do you persist in coming where you clearly are not welcome?"

"Our backs are to the wall," Bobby said. He could sit through this exchange no longer without tossing in his two cents.

"Who are *you?*" Red demanded. He seemed to be looking at him for the first time.

"Bobby."

"Bob-*by,*" Red smirked in singsong. "Well, isn't that cute. A cute name for a cutsie pair."

"That's enough, Red—"

"How long you two been girl — oops, I mean *boy*—friends? That *is* what you call yourselves, isn't it? I never know which pronoun you guys prefer." He crossed his arms across his chest. He was enjoying himself.

Bobby scowled. "It's no wonder you deserved a kick in the balls."

Red's jaw dropped a little, then snapped shut. Cords stood in relief against his throat.

"Now, stop it, all of you," Rachael said. "Or I'll throw you out, and the hell with it."

"But, Mom," Red whined, "these guys want your crystal. That's what you told me."

"They need my help."

"So let them come back at a decent hour and *charge* them, like everyone else!" Red exploded. His hands sawed the air with agitation. "Jesus, *every*one wants a piece of you. What are you, a carpet? Gonna let every Tom, Dick, and Harry walk all over you? We haven't had a moment's peace since I brought you that fucking stone!"

"You brought it to her?" asked David.

"Yeah. A birthday present."

Something rippled beneath the glossy flush of Red's cheeks; David could see an image of a slatted box being broken into, straw and shredded paper hurriedly pushed to one side.

"That's right," Rachael said. "Red gave it to me in June. That's why the stone means so much to me."

"That — and knowing what it can do," David pointed out.

Rachael's expression was immutable. "What do you mean?"

He sighed noisily; weary, too weary, for this prevaricating. "It's the powers of that stone that brought us together in the first place."

She shook her head. "A crystal is only as powerful as its owner."

"Maybe with other crystals, yes," David countered. "But this is no ordinary stone. Is it."

"What are you insinuating?" Red smirked.

"This gemstone fine-tunes psychic energy, isn't that right?" He stared directly into Rachael's stoic face. "I think it must act as a magnifier. I think it was once used as a weapon against evil — this evil that's now pursuing us. Victor's intent on keeping us separated and fighting, because he doesn't want us to join forces against him."

"Why should a grown man be afraid of a chunk of stone?" Red asked.

David bit his lower lip. "Because Victor is not a man."

Red put a hand over his mouth, his giggles unsuppressed.

"Ask your mother how crazy it sounds," David retorted. His cheeks stung from Red's laughter. Getting this creature taken seriously as a real threat was always going to be a problem. There would always be ridicule, disbelief — and he felt powerless in the face of it.

Bobby piped up. "It's *not* a man. It's a monster. He kidnapped my lover last night. He killed David's roommate. Snatched a friend of ours this very afternoon. He's kidnapped people all across the city — and it's only going to get worse if we don't stop him right away!"

Red shrugged. "Why haven't I heard anything on the news? You can't keep something like that secret."

"You'd be surprised," Bobby said.

"No: The only surprise is what bad bullshitters you guys are. 'Cause I sure as shit would have come here with a better story. Monsters, for Christ's sake—"

"That's enough, Red," Rachael quietly reprimanded.

"But Mom—"

"They're telling the truth."

Red stared at his mother with disbelief.

David also stared. This was his first indication that his message had penetrated her armor. He pressed his advantage.

"You know it's true, because you've seen what's been happening through me," he pointed out. "The crystal called me to it. And you." He looked at both of them, mother and son, and implored: "So now that we're here, please, help us. You can have the stone back when we're finished."

"—Oh sure—" A sneer, from Red.

"It's true. I swear. We were attacked tonight—"

"What, someone call you a pansy—?"

Bobby jerked away from the table, hot with indignation. "Shut up!"

Red's eyes glittered with the challenge. "You gonna make me, Bob-*by?*"

"Yeah!"

"Ohh! I'm *so* scared!"

That did it. Bobby twisted away from the table, his chair kicked out of the way. David sprang to his feet and grabbed for Bobby, but his efforts gave him a fistful of air. Bobby circled the formica table and marched right up to Red, undaunted by his towering height and the vengeful look in his eyes.

"Get out of my face," Red snarled. He gave Bobby a rough shove.

Bobby dove into him. The two of them slammed into each other, spinning madly.

David and Rachael were two steps behind. The room erupted into noisy confusion as each tried to pry Red and Bobby apart. They knocked against the kitchen table, overturning cups of tea and saucers. Tea splashed across the table and dribbled onto the floor.

"Stop it!" Rachael ordered. "Look what you're doing!"

David grabbed Bobby by the biceps; Rachael snagged Red and tugged him to her. Noisy exhalations filled the room.

"He started it," Red spat.

"And I'll finish it," Bobby panted.

"Like hell you will," David said — who was not about to have Bobby fight his fights.

Rachael threw up her hands in disgust. "You see? This isn't going to work. We just flat out cannot help you."

David was about to respond when all heard it, the clapping of hands, like spectators at a boxing match.

It took a moment to locate the source of this applause. Four heads turned toward the sound, their movements comically synchronized. Bewilderment gave way to startled gasps.

Red was the first to speak, a slack expression on his face. "What the fuck—?"

They beheld their guests.

3

Three pairs of hands applauded from outside the den window, which directly faced the kitchen. An underwater, truncated sound.

Three figures pressed wet noses against the glass. The largest of them was a man, square chinned, square shouldered, chest molded like a Roman sculpture. Dark hair hung wetly into his liquid eyes. His alabaster skin positively glowed, as though the drizzly mist falling around him acted as a polish. He wore a leather harness across his chest, and a neck collar with silver studs; otherwise, he was naked. He towered over the two figures at his side. He unclasped his hands and dropped them to pat the heads of his towheaded companions: two boys.

It required only a perfunctory glance to recognize them; after all, David had watched them cavorting upon his fire escape just hours earlier. The darker of the two boys — Miggy — flickered between boy and beast, as though he could not maintain either shape: One moment, he was a boy, tousle haired and dark eyed. The next, he was a Halloween ghoul, with misshapen ears and snout, Bela Lugosi fangs, and eyes so black they might have been chips of charcoal sunk into putty flesh. His little hands clapped together like wet sponges. His companion was less substantial, translucent, but a child's delight (or a grotesque parody of it) clear upon his tiny face. He too clapped his hands, his mouth forming a goldfish O.

It took a moment, no more, to take in this lunacy floating outside the window. One minute, the four of them fighting, Red and Bobby anxious to test fists — the next second, this spongy applause.

Rachael recoiled from the sight, crimson faced as though physically slapped.

(Don't stop)

came the chiding voice of the naked man, though his lips did not move. He raised himself higher into the air so that they could plainly see his erection bobbing between marble thighs.

(See how you excite me? Show us your blood)

The darker of the boys reached up and fondled the man's testicles; the man sighed his pleasure.

"Stop that!"

David turned. Rachael was a mask of disgust and indignation. Her red hair shook with her trembling, as though she could no longer contain herself.

"Stop that this instant!" She threw her hands up to her face, wishing the vision gone.

The man chuckled. Both boys giggled. The sounds were chilling. The other, paler boy reached up and grasped the upward bow of cock, which he jerked up and down in his tiny hand.

Anger mixed with fear ripened in Red. "What is this shit..." His pink face colored with disgust, and he directed his pent-up emotions toward this new target. He started to wriggle free of his mother's grasp.

"Don't," David whispered. He caught Red's intentions out of the corner of his eye; he would not take his gaze away from the window. In a calm, steady voice that belied his fright he asked, "Mrs. Black, where is the crystal?"

Rachael opened her mouth to speak but couldn't answer.

"Listen to me," David whispered. "Any minute now they're going to come through that window. I think I can stop them, but I *have* to have the crystal."

"Don't do it, Mom," Red cautioned. "It's a trick."

"What: You think we're responsible for *them?*" Bobby hissed under his breath.

"Yeah, fuckface: I do."

Bobby bunched his fists. Oh, what a pleasure it would be to sock that stupid face. But David squeezed his shoulder. *Don't do it,* his pressure seemed to say.

More clapping.

Everyone stared at their guests outside the window.

(Punch him!)

said the man to no one in particular; he didn't care who threw the first punch.

(Rip his eyes out. Bleed! Go on: Give us a show)

"Go to hell!" David shouted at them.

(Give us a show!)

the man insisted, pleasure stripped from his expression now, lips curled tight across his teeth.

(Give us a show, or we'll come inside and do it ourselves!)

The pale boy bounced with excitement. He withdrew his hand from the man's erection and suddenly clawed at his own cheek. He dug ugly canals into his flesh.

A sob escaped Rachael's lips. "Kids," she said in a broken voice. "Innocent kids..."

"Where is the crystal?" David insisted. He hated to do it, but he would use the hurt and upset so plain in her voice to convince her. She had never anticipated that kids were caught in this tragedy, and her shock at this discovery was turning the tide in his favor.

"Where is it!" he pressed. "If not for me, then for those boys. We can stop them. Maybe even put them to rest!"

"It's a trick," Red stated flatly. He could not take his eyes from these figures outside his window. They were certainly nothing human.

The dark-haired boy scraped his nails against the glass. His gaze implored Rachael. His little chin quivered with undisguised pleading.

(You want to help us? Open the window. Let us in)

"Go away," Rachael sputtered. Concern creased the lines of her face. Her hazel eyes dampened with uncertainty, torn between the human suffering she saw and the horror of the phantom vision.

The younger boy shook himself like a wet dog and slapped his palms against the windowpane. His hands made smeary imprints.

(Mommy? Are you my mommy?)

"Oh, god!" Rachael jerked away from their display, her heart stabbed by their cries, her mind horrified by the rawness of their thoughts. She turned upon David, distressed. "Who's responsible for this?"

"It's Victor!" answered David. "The thing we're fighting!"

(Let us in! Mommy? Help me!)

Stage cries; yet their pleas demanded compassion. For who knew how much of their childhood selves remained?

Rachael's need to help battled with her loathing; her expression pulled and twitched. She glanced at the window, at David, and back again to the mock-pleading faces of the children. Her conflict subsided. "For *them*," she said, resigned at last, and dug into the pocket of her blue bathrobe. "Because of *them*, will I help."

"You have the crystal?" David asked, eagerly stepping toward her.

Red stayed him with a palm upon his chest. "No funny stuff, tough guy," he warned. "You and I aren't finished."

David sloughed off the hand. "Hurry! This is no time for personalities!"

She riffled through the pocket, her fingers caressing the silk that encased the gemstone. Still reticent and protective of the stone, she withdrew her hand.

They waited, impatiently watching. Even Red stopped glaring at David and chewed the inside of his cheek with anticipation.

Suddenly the glass was rapped so hard it seemed an improbability that it had not shattered. An ugly growl dug into their brains as the naked man at the window shoved the little boys out of his way.

(Do not help them)

he snarled, his threat directed toward Rachael. His eyes leap-frogged between the silk handkerchief in her hands and her face.

"Quickly!" David insisted, for he saw how she was numbing, chilling back into indecision. For all he knew, while they stared at the three outside the window, others were stealing in through the front, hooked claws ready to slice flesh, fangs extended.

Her hands played at the folds of handkerchief.

(Put that away! This isn't your fight!)

Rachael jerked: to hear those very words come out of the stranger's mouth!

(This isn't your fight)

She grasped the crystal with her right hand, its pyramid top pointing parallel with the palm of her hand.

(Give them to me)

the man ordered, and indicated David and Bobby with a flick of his hand.

(Do not make the Master angry)

"Or what?" Rachael surprised everyone by shouting. She pushed past the others, around the kitchen table.

"What are you doing!" Red cried in alarm.

"Get away!" Rachael demanded. She strode into the small den and stopped about four feet from the window. She struggled to maintain a poker face. Up this close, the three outside her window seemed nothing short of insectile; mutant bugs out of some 1950s science fiction movie she and her brother had watched in Tucson at the picture show. In a way, this horrible vision gave her strength; seeing them as human only robbed her of spine and guts.

David came up beside her. His feet danced as though he stood upon a hot griddle. Bobby followed, and Red, not wanting to be left out, came closer but hugged one of the arms of the sofa, anxious to retreat.

"Go, I say!" Rachael commanded. She thrust the crystal before her, arm outstretched. Her worn blue bathrobe rode up her freckled arm like a sorcerer's robe.

The creatures only laughed and pointed.

(Silly cunt! What good is a piece of stone? Now give them to us!)

"Nothing's happening!" She stole a glance at David. "You said this would scare them off!"

The two boys twittered.

"Let me try." David held out his hand.

Rachael hesitated.

(It's worthless, your stone! Worthless!)

"If it's so worthless, then why haven't you broken through that window!" And before doubt could overwhelm her, she made her decision and transferred the crystal into David's palm.

No time to savor the contact, though in that instant something profound tingled through his body. His fingers wrapped around the gemstone, and he felt its temperature jump several degrees. "Give me your hands. Everyone."

Bobby immediately came forward and took the same hand that held the crystal. David offered his left hand to Rachael. She motioned to her son. "Come on, Red."

But he shook his head, and clung to his perch beside the den sofa. Beneath the copper beard his skin was bleached.

No time to argue; Rachael moved in and clasped hands with David, and then Bobby.

Click: The sharp tang of ozone filled the room. An electrical charge filled the air. With their triangle union, something was unleashed. The blue flame of the crystal's center seemed to sputter with increasing phosphorescence. The power of their trinity was a hundredfold what it had been when just he and Bobby had defiantly stood their ground against Victor. This power vibrated through his limbs. But how to control it? Use it? He lifted his face to the window.

"You cannot trespass here!" he intoned. His voice boomed with authority. "This place is off-limits!"

The dark-haired boy swiped at the wet glass, and instantly shrieked: A spark of electricity zapped his fist.

(Stop it!)

the man shouted. He made to smash through the glass, his patience gone. But something caught his fist before it could shatter glass and flung him backward into the air with a shower of blue sparks. The man righted himself and buzzed next to the window, furious. He gnashed his teeth.

The crystal warmed David's hand with its vibrating heat, but he clung to it. He imagined a wall surrounding the apartment and store, a wall of sparking blue energy. "Tell Victor this place is off-limits, now and forever!" David shouted. "You'll only hurt yourselves if you come any closer!"

The man fumed with rage. Suddenly, he snatched the pale monkey-boy and lifted him in front of his chest as though he weighed nothing.

(Hurt? You want to see hurt? This is your fate — all of you — if you defy him! This!)

Snarling, he grabbed hold of each tiny hand and began to pull.

Rachael's mouth dropped open. "No—"

The boy wriggled and kicked against the man's chest, stretched taut in his unyielding grasp. His giggles became squeals of pain.

"No!" Rachael gasped. She tried to break free of their triangle, to stop this abuse. David and Bobby held her firm. "Leave him alone—!"

(*This* is what the Master will do!)

And with a sudden zippering explosion, the boy split apart. A maroon spray tattooed the window. Steamy lifeblood gushed into the air. Skin tore apart like paper ripped from a notebook. Wads of sticky, unrecognizable tissue struck the electric shield and sizzled before dropping out of sight.

Rachael burst into tears. The others were stony, stunned into silence.

The steam withdrew a bit, dissolved by cooling mist. The man reappeared, speckled with phlegmy matter, a ghastly, satisfied expression animating his smile. All that remained of the pale boy were his small hands, which the man held within his own palms. He ran his tongue across his lips, wiping clean the flecked remains splattered there. He fixed them with a final stare.

(Your fate)

he whispered so softly they unconsciously leaned forward to hear. He scooped the other boy into his arms, the two of them smirking at their stricken faces.

(Your fate)

A laugh like grinding shards of broken glass, and they were gone, swallowed by a night that rushed in to embrace them.

37

Bedbugs bite

D avid woke up. His eyes searched the unfamiliar room for a clock, and found one above the fireplace. Ten to two, it said. He frowned. The dawn was hours away. Despite the dragging heaviness of his tired muscles, he doubted that sleep would come to his aid tonight.

Bobby lay at his side. The glowing embers of the fire had softened his narrow face, turned it boyish. His crew cut heightened this effect, as did the curling ash of his eyelashes. For not the first time, David experienced a welling of love and admiration for Bobby far beyond what should have been appropriate for one day's worth of knowing. His earlier frown eased into a smile. If he was doomed to wakefulness this night, then watching Bobby sleep would help pass the time.

He sat up from his makeshift bed. A twinge in his back pinched a hello. God Almighty, he was really overtaxing his muscles, pushing himself to the limit. His body had just never healed properly from his fall, despite all the months of physical therapy and gym work and stretching. Tonight, it seemed that every tendon and sore muscle had decided to wake up and announce their presence. Of course, sleeping on the floor in front of the fireplace wasn't helping things either. He'd given Bobby the one sleeping bag Red had grudgingly provided because it offered a thicker mattress for the floor.

David groaned, getting to his feet. The apartment was silent all about him, yet he tilted his head and listened so intently the very molecules of the air whispered in reply. A faint ozone residue lingered in the apartment from the crystal's fantastic display. Was a shield protecting them from harm? Were they safe? Or were Victor's pals even now alighting on the roof, murderous revenge their intent?

No wonder he found sleep impossible.

He padded over to the fireplace and as quietly as possible added another log to the dying embers. Bobby moaned in his sleep, and rolled over onto his stomach, but did not wake from the noise. The embers licked hungrily at the dry log, and liking what it tasted, began to make a meal of the offering. The dark retreated from the flickering firelight and stitched the corners of the den. David drew comfort from this display of burning wood; if nothing else, he'd happily ram a burning stick into one of the creatures, should they now dare to attack.

The additional firelight reminded him of his own nakedness, and he stooped to retrieve his baggy pants from the communal pile of clothes. He slipped them on and went into the bathroom, where he relieved his bladder. In the medicine cabinet he discovered a bottle of Tylenol; he washed down two of the pills. Perhaps they would quiet the tense ache of his bones.

He came out of the bathroom and stood in the doorway, allowing his eyes the opportunity to readjust to the dimmer light. He felt like a prowler.

Walking back toward the den, a noise cut through the night's tranquility like the sharp teeth of a razor; David froze into a statue. Where? Where'd it come from?

Again he heard it: a soft scrape from the other side of the curtained partition. Icy goose bumps speckled his naked upper torso. Someone — or some*thing* — was in the bookshop.

He crossed the distance until he stood between den and kitchen. Bobby was a curled lump in his sleeping bag, unmoving. *Okay,* David challenged himself. *Go take a look.*

But he felt truly naked, weaponless. Rachael had taken back the crystal, once they'd determined the creatures' absolute departure. Could he use anything else to protect himself? His glance fell upon the pile of wood by the fireplace. Then he noticed the stand of black iron tools to the right of the hearth. Creeping stealthily forward, determined not to rouse anyone, he took a poker from the stand. Its cool metal and solid weight reassured him.

Again the scrape, like a dragged chair.

David's flesh tingled with apprehension. He tiptoed around the kitchen table, iron poker in hand, and stepped up to the curtained partition. He tucked his fingers around its fabric edge and drew it back for a peek.

Shuddering relief.

Rachael Black was sitting down at an expansive desk, her hands adjusting a reading lamp. She looked up with alarm at his entrance through the draperies, her mouth open in preparation of a scream. Her eyes surrendered their moony circles of fright for narrowed scrutiny. She indicated the poker in his hand.

"Come to beat me senseless, is that it?" she asked in a mock-serious whisper.

David was flummoxed. "I thought they'd — you know — returned."

"Not that *that* would have protected you."

"No. Probably not."

She waved him into the room. "Obviously, it must have been you in the bathroom," she said.

David nodded. "I couldn't sleep."

"Nor I. Not after that tale you spun." She offered him a wry smile, then hooked a thumb toward a chair. "Have a seat."

"Thanks." He felt self-conscious in her presence, acutely aware of his naked chest. Not to mention the fact that he was practically an intruder in her house. Still, this invitation was yet another indication of a truce between them, and David would not jeopardize that cease-fire. He pulled up an oak chair and sat across from her. He lay the poker against the desk, and when he straightened he saw her eyes giving him the once-over. He felt himself color slightly. "Maybe I should get my shirt..."

"No need."

He looked at her. She was swaddled in her blue robe. No makeup adorned her face, which, curiously, added to the vibrancy of her hazel eyes. Her freckled cheeks were unremarkable in comparison, her disheveled red hair almost brown in the light of the reading lamp. She seemed to share his weariness. He felt compelled to speak.

"Mrs. Black—"

"Isn't it rather late for such formalities? Call me Rachael."

"Okay — Rachael—" He cleared his throat. His eyes strayed to the front window of the shop. Its surface glistened with running water. He hadn't even been aware of the rain drumming down until that moment. "I just wanted to let you know — to say thanks — for helping us out. Especially now that you see what's involved."

She nodded curtly, but didn't answer right away, as if she sensed — rightly — that her answer wouldn't please him. "I still don't approve of all that you've done. I know you want me to say otherwise, but it's the truth. I can't help but feel you've brought some of this upon yourself—"

"Never in my wildest dreams," David interrupted, "could I — or would I — have imagined anything so terrible as this." His tone remained even, despite a barely suppressed anger at her words.

"Yes. Well..." And here she gave him that strange wry smile. "Apparently this Victor conjured *you* in his wildest dreams. And now we sit here and think of plotting battle in the dead of night."

David was silent.

"Up until tonight, I didn't want to believe such things could exist." She waved her hand. "Then again, plenty of people routinely dismiss the very powers you and I exhibit as preposterous. So who's to say what's out there in the world?" She indicated three books upon her desk. "I thought a bit of research was in order."

David glanced at the books, all on various forms of demonology.

Interesting, to see her like this. She'd been quiet during his explanations hours earlier, as his and Bobby's story twined together with its separate, fantastic threads. Poor Red (well — actually — he couldn't bring himself to call Red "poor"): He'd listened to the proceedings like someone locked outside a back door, straining to hear the conversation inside. Red had been oblivious to it all, to his mother's growing anxiety over the past weeks, her visions of David and that bathhouse, her sense of doom. David had expected snickers and guffaws throughout the telling, but Red surprised them all by remaining sullenly cooperative. Only once had he broken his silence to say:

"Why didn't you tell me, Mom? Aren't we pals?"

"I didn't want to worry you" was Rachael's reply.

"So I have to find out now, in front of these guys." And with a final shake of his head he'd lapsed back into stewing silence, the fingers clasping his mug of tea bone-white, as though he meant to crush the very cup from which he drank.

It had skirted David's thought then how shut out Red must feel — Red, who by all indications, had always been his mother's confidant. Perhaps the sting he undoubtedly felt accounted for his acquiescence to his mother's decision that they be allowed to spend the night. Not one mutter of protest had escaped Red's mouth. But his eyes, always busy, darting, had met David's across the kitchen table, and he didn't have to read minds to register the resentment and naked hostility.

David was stirred out of this contemplation with the sudden appearance of the crystal. Rachael had pulled it from her robe pocket and set it before them on the desk. For a moment, neither said a word.

"It's beautiful," David breathed.

Rachael concurred. "Yes. It is."

They stared at it.

"Great good," she suddenly said, "sometimes attracts a greater evil."

David knit his brow. "You think the crystal may have ... called him?"

A shrug. "Let me ask you a question. These people you saw in your vision, these apparent first owners of this stone: Whatever trouble they encountered with this 'Kahmaal' — you believe they used the crystal to drive him away, am I right?"

"Yes."

"But obviously, they didn't kill him."

"No. I guess not."

"Which makes our 'Victor' hundreds of years old."

"He's not a man," David asserted. "That much I know — can feel — but I don't know *what* he is, exactly."

Rachael nodded. Her eyes gleamed as though a complicated algebra formula suddenly revealed itself. "If he's not human, then he must be a sort of ... energy able to take on these forms. And since energy can only be *changed,* not destroyed, that may be our task: not to destroy, but to alter."

David frowned. "*No.* I want him gone. Dead. Not something that bides its time through the years, waiting for another chance to strike."

"If that were possible, perhaps the crystal's original owners would have accomplished that task when they had the chance."

"Maybe they didn't know how. Maybe they just ... struck back, utilizing the crystal's energy. Perhaps the best they could do was ... deflect him away."

Rachael met his gaze. "Doesn't bode well for *our* chances."

"What other options do we have?"

Rachael picked up the crystal, rubbing it between her fingers. A shudder suddenly ran through her. "You know — it must have been this creature's voice I heard in my dreams, warning me to keep my distance from you. But I wonder what other motives were also at work."

"What do you mean?"

"As much as this thing may fear the crystal — perhaps he yearns for it as well."

David only stared at her.

"As I said: Great good sometimes attracts great evil. Who knows what powers the stone is capable of — and what it could do in this creature's grasp..." She trailed off, allowing her words to sink in.

David bit his lower lip. Oh, how that prospect sent chills down his spine! But a question nagged at him.

"If Victor wants the crystal, why attack me and my friends? Why didn't he go after you right away?"

The prospect obviously horrified her, but her expression remained as puzzled as his. Finally, she answered the only way she knew how. "Maybe it was easier to keep me denying my premonitions, even though deep down I knew that something terrible was afoot. Waiting until he grew strong enough to take the stone himself."

David nodded. He saw the pieces fit together. "And now that we've met, and his fear tactics no longer work—"

"—he'll be after blood. He'll try to get the stone. By any means, now."

They stared at each other, neither one managing another word, as rainy night lashed against the glass windows of the shop.

2

"David? Is everything okay?"

"Fine, Bobby. Go back to sleep."

"Where were you? I woke up and you were gone." Childlike fright was clear in his voice. Bobby rolled over onto his back, one fist digging sleep from his eye.

"Rachael and I — we had a little chat."

An arched eyebrow. "*Ra*chael? Does this mean we're making progress?"

"Hope so."

David slid out of his pants, the glow from the fire buttering his naked skin. He glanced down and saw Bobby watching him. He felt himself flush a little, not so much out of embarrassment as his own sudden enjoyment in seeing Bobby's furry chest displayed before him.

"Do you think she'll be able to help us?" Bobby asked as David sat down onto his bedding. His eyes were anxious, imploring. "I mean — *really* help us?"

On impulse he reached out and patted Bobby's thigh through the sleeping bag, the need to reassure by touch strong in him. He thought of Mrs. Black, books under her arms as she had retreated to her bedroom only moments before. "She's more willing to help, if that's any consolation. I think she regrets that she stayed in the dark so long, denying what she saw — and felt — was going on around her." Bobby's expression was grave, waiting for the punchline both knew would come. David took a breath. "Whether she'll find an answer for us, I simply don't know." His hand remained on Bobby's thigh, and he gave it another squeeze. "No matter what happens, we have to rely on our*selves*. No one else."

Bobby nodded. He reached out with his own hand to circle David's ankle with a reassuring — and thankful — touch of his own.

They stayed like that for a moment, listening to the crackle of fire, the howl of wind and rain at the window. Eyes fluttering closed.

"David?"

"Ummm?"

"Can I ask you something?"

"Sure."

"Were you and Alex just friends, or...?"

He peered at Bobby through narrowed eyes, surprised, but not upset by the question. His companion turned away, watching the intricacies of the flames. "Just friends."

"Oh."

"He liked me, and wanted to help—" And here David smiled sadly. "—But the truth is, the crush I felt for him was one-sided."

After a moment, Bobby softly said, "Hard to lose someone, isn't it?"

"Come'ere." David snuggled closer, his heart close to breaking.

"You know what the worst part is?"

"What?"

"There isn't even time to mourn."

David massaged his friend with his hand. He understood exactly.

"Victor wants to take everything away from us. Lovers. Friends. Our way of life. Sometimes: I don't know whether I want to be left behind, or..."

"Shh—" He couldn't bear this kind of talk, the way Bobby's voice cracked with emotion. He spun around, twisting on his butt so that they lay in the same direction, their faces lit by the fire.

They looked at each other, so alike in so many ways, with their dark features and piercing eyes. David reached out with his hand and curled Bobby's fingers into his own.

Bobby whispered, "Would you mind — holding me?"

Without saying a word, David rolled back the fold of sleeping bag and slipped in beside him. Their cocks were hard, pressed against each other's bellies, a source of both pleasure and sticky embarrassment.

"I'm so afraid," Bobby whispered.

"So am I," David answered, then felt compelled to add: "But he can't rob us of love. Everything but love."

And they held each other late into the night, as though either one would bruise if they moved too much, and the sleep David was sure would elude him gently tugged his eyes into slumber.

3

It hurt to draw near. The atmosphere was charged, and it repelled his probing thoughts with blue fire. But it was worth the pain, if he could achieve his task. He had withstood all manner of attack over the many long years of shifting existence, and he would not allow a little pain to stop him now. Besides, his workers were very busy this night, the rooms within his palace filling very nicely indeed, fresh agony, fright, desire — ahh, they drugged him, their raw vitality an infusion of strength.

He returned his attention to the task at hand. It had been folly to simply allow the woman her denial, as if denial in and of itself was enough to keep the man at bay. He loved the hypocrisy within her: her desire to use her feeble gifts to help others while secretly being disgusted by her clients' sexual appetites. He'd used that, too, an effective means of keeping her callous and untouched by their pleas.

Yet the healer had broken through. He'd stolen into her very house, and shielded himself within its walls. Him and the other one.

Victor reached out with his tentacle thoughts. Ahh: as he suspected. No need to dig deep into subconscious murk for this one; he wore his intent as an armor, but it was easily pierced, sitting as it did upon a puffed chest. The young man's contempt was clear, unsullied by guilt or past expectations. He wanted only to please his mother.

So Victor steeled himself and plunged a tentacle into that blue-charged atmosphere, into the black bedroom where Red slept comforted by his grand dreams of retribution. The lights of the Caverns flickered dim, the cassette tape slowed with the expended energy. Costly, this enterprise, but well worth the pain.

He pierced Red's dreams, and whispered:

(Don't let the faggots take your mom away. This trouble doesn't concern you. It's a trick, it will hurt your mother unless you stop them. It's all up to you, my boy. If you listen to me, I'll teach you how to cover your thoughts, throw up a wall, so that no one can spoil our secrets. This is your mother's life at stake here — so what do you say?)

And Victor pulled back, singed but triumphant, as Red clenched and unclenched his fists in his sleep.

38

Seashell whispers, part two

1

How mischievous, these creatures of the night:

2

Walter had to admit: This was the best blow job of his life.

"You're gorgeous," the naked young man said to him as he sank in front of Walter. "Come on; give me a taste of you."

Gorgeous? Him? Twenty years ago maybe, but even that stretched the truth. Walter had never been one of the "in" crowd, the pretty boys, even in his youth. Only in his most secret fantasies did he dream of their worshipful stares, their adoration. Like this boy, who had appeared at his door as though materialized from a genie's bottle; summoned, he claimed, because of the disco music playing on Walter's stereo.

"Incredible," the young man whispered, pale hand at the cotton twill of Walter's pants, searching for the zipper.

"Are you sure?" Not daring to believe. Too many scotch-rocks muddled his thinking. Walter had been all set to investigate a commotion in David Walker's apartment down below when he'd opened his front door and there he stood, this boy with the flashing eyes.

The boy nodded. The zipper, undone, revealed boxers and a wink of swollen flesh.

"I'm the best. You'll see." And the young man, his preppie face simply glowing, pulled open the pants and allowed them to gather around Walter's pudgy calves.

Annoying questions buzzed in Walter's mind. Was there a party going on in David's apartment? But the feeling in his cock pushed away these distractions. He swelled against his white boxer shorts at an indolent right angle, anxious for this youth's liquid touch.

"Gorgeous." Whispered as an incantation, a prayer to Bacchus and Pan, who surely would approve of such delights.

Down came the boxers. Walter's erection bounced like a coiled spring, its mushroom top tinged pink.

"Delicious." And he lapped it up, a cat to milk.

Oh, but this boy knew his trade! No teasing lick to tantalize him; he was swallowed whole. The man's tongue felt a tad too sandpapery, but the very dryness added to the delight, the indescribable rush of sensations. He launched an attack upon Walter's dick, forcing him up against the hallway wall. Dry lips sank around his entire shaft and milked him. Never had he experienced such a ... a ... ferocious *eager*ness. This deliberate assault was wildly arousing. Another few minutes of this and he'd pop his cork.

Strange, tittering laughter filtered up through the floor from David's apartment. The laughter struck him as somehow wrong, as inappropriate and hollow as a giggle at a car crash. It pulled him away from the pleasures at hand. Some sort of celebration was taking place downstairs, yet his gut told him he wouldn't want to be down there, no way. His erection sagged in the young man's mouth like a deflating balloon.

He glanced at himself. The boy was all dogged determination. The sandpapery tongue continued to lap over him, encouraging his penis to grow, and he felt himself bloom again. Jesus, how this boy took to this! No spittle formed at the creases of his mouth from his exertions. No wheezing of breath through his nostrils. Only this silent impaling.

Walter anchored himself against the wall and shut his eyes. He listened to the Abba tune playing on his stereo in the den. He thought absently of the ticket he'd found yesterday evening beside the stereo. Admit One, it had said. To where? And where had the ticket come from?

As the fullness gathered again in his balls, his climax imminent, he had a sudden sneaking suspicion that after he popped, he'd just open his eyes and find himself somewhere else.

So he opened his eyes, and gazed down upon the tireless boy.

No sound, as he ate Walter's cock.

The nostrils were flat, unmoving.

No sound at all.

Walter thought: *He's not breathing*.

He reached down to touch the boy's head. His hands made contact, and the flesh came away on his fingers. He began to scream.

Yes, it truly was the best blow job of his life.

Right up until he realized he was getting head from a corpse.

3

"Ummm," Sugar cooed, the horse galloping through her veins. Its trail was hot, tingling. She loved this rush that was like no other, amen and *halle*lujah. She handed the syringe to Dobbs, who smiled his broken-toothed silly grin and prepared his own dose. Dobbs always let Sugar go first. He was sweet that way.

She lay back against the pillows and shut her eyes. They sat cross-legged on the single bed, and that was a shame. No room to stretch out. No room. It was the story of her life.

Outside the window of their tiny room — but, hey, at least this dump *had* a window, unlike the last two they'd shared — traffic tooted and honked, busy even for a Saturday night in the Tenderloin. Might have to work the wee hours of the night, make a few bucks, but Sugar didn't want to think about that right now. She didn't want to think about anything at all. The horse galloped, and she let it roam free.

Beside her, Dobbs smacked his arm with little slaps. "Shit," he muttered. "Got no veins." He chuckled at his predicament.

Sugar tugged open her eyelids. She got them up about halfway and looked at Dobbs as he positioned the needle. Something vague and half-remembered crossed her thoughts. "Aren't ya supposed to wash that first?" she asked.

Dobbs scowled. "Jus' you and me," he said, injecting himself. The vein was a poor one; the horse stung going in. He gritted his teeth, knowing that soon enough he'd be jumping over mountains, the sting forgotten.

Sugar's eyelids gave up, and closed. She sighed contentedly and drifted. Dobbs let out a sigh of his own. They listened to the traffic six stories below. Neither one liked to talk much during the first part. They drifted together, and that was just fine.

Besides, that place was filling up her head again, and jawing with Dobbs would have spoiled the mood. Sugar wore a red, low-cut dress. It sparkled like that sprinkle stuff Mom used to put onto her birthday cakes, glittery like a thousand mirrors. Her nails were not chewed-off stubs but long and red, cherry red. And her hair looked exactly like the models she saw on the covers of magazines, sassy and smart.

Yes, sir, she was dressed to kill, one hell of a hot dish. Smoke puffed up from the click of her high heels as she crossed the crowded dance floor in this club. Men and women turned to watch her (though, funny enough, most wore towels draped around their middles. Ain't that odd?).

And the music: not her first choice, but every time she dreamed about this club this was the only music they played. When Sugar had been a teenager and disco ruled the airwaves she'd hated it, dubbed it god's scourge on music. Those fairy Bee Gees deserved to have their pricks cut off; they *sang* like their pricks were cut off, might as well make it god's truth. Disco lacked soul, rhythm: It was all bass. But in this whatever this was, this dream fantasy, disco sounded okay, sounded just right. Kinda nice to remember being a teenager before she got all tangled up in detours and dead ends.

Dobbs nudged her. "Sugar?"

"Yeah, honey?"

"I'm havin' the nicest dream."

"Me too."

"We dancin'."

"Me too."

He fumbled for her hand, found it. "Let's wish it real."

"Okay."

There came a scratch at the window, the scrape of fingernails. And the music, like the tide, rushed in.

4

The phone call ripped through the silence of the bedroom, jarring its occupants.

Harry rolled away from his wife, Kate, with whom he had been hugging quite agreeably, to snatch the receiver in midring. "Hello?" he asked with rankled concern.

A voice on the other end whispered: "I have the answers, Harry."

Harry elbowed onto his side. "Who is this?"

"Can't you tell?" came the chiding reply.

"No—" But it came to him then, as the drawl revealed itself. "Alex?"

Silence. Well, not silence in the usual sense. Silence like a malfunction, like a moment of recognition of forces set into motion.

Harry searched for the electric glow of his bedside clock, and the late hour showed itself. He let loose his petty arsenal of curses. "Do you have any idea what time it is?" he demanded. "Can't this wait until morning?"

"Not if you want to know who's behind all the disappearances."

It was bait, dangling there on a hook, waiting for his nibble.

"What are you talking about, Alex?"

"I found out who's behind it all. I know who's doing it."

"Doing — what?"

"It's ... unspeakable." Said with shivery mock horror.

"Why are you telling me this?"

"Can I come over?"

"Now?" Barked out, incredulous. Kate's hand moved to his shoulder, concerned.

The response was an urgent whisper. "They're after me, Harry. They'll never find me at your place. And Harry: We'll solve this, you and I." The final bait. "Quite a feather in your cap, if you catch my drift."

Harry raked a hand across his face. "Why me?"

Mild astonishment. "I owe you one. And I *always* pay back my debts, you know that. So what do ya say? Can I come inside?"

Tomorrow's front-page headline dazzled enticingly across his cinema thoughts. Sleepiness dropped away. What was an hour's lack of sleep compared to fame and glory?

"Sure, Alex. Okay. Come on over."

"What's going on?" Kate asked as Harry placed the receiver back onto its cradle. She was a handsome woman, beautiful in a solid outdoorsy sort of way, chestnut haired and sleek limbed. "Is Alex in trouble?"

"No, honey." Harry bent low, kissed his wife on her cheek. No need to worry her. "He's got some information he wants to pass on. He's coming over."

Kate read between the lines of that, and guessed at the importance of this midnight visit. She swung her feet over the side of the bed. "I'll make coffee—"

He pulled her back. "Don't bother; go back to sleep. I'll take care of this."

She bit down her protest and rolled into his arms, enjoying the comfort of her Papa Bear, as she liked to call him. He stroked her hair and nuzzled against her neck. "Better be careful," she chided. "Don't start what you can't finish..."

"Wait until I get rid of Alex," he whispered back.

She smiled sleepily at that, the late hour and his wonderful caresses pulling her down, down, into dreamland, hostess obligations be damned.

A sharp noise woke her some time later, startling her. Kate opened her eyes and squinted, as though sight and not hearing was the proper sense to use to read the dark. There it was again: a muffled, mewling sound, coming from downstairs. Instinctively she reached across the bed for her husband, and patted empty sheets.

She raised herself to a sitting position. It came back to her, by degrees, where her husband was, and why he was holding this late-hour meeting. It must be awfully important. She thought of going downstairs and saying hello. Alex Webster was no stranger to her; they'd met on many occasions. She'd even noticed him giving her the eye, though she never admitted that to her husband. Alex told her once she reminded him of his ex-wife.

On the stairs: footsteps. A heavy, dragging sound. It made the hairs at the nape of her neck stand on end. Her breathing grew shallow. *What in the world* is *that? Like a ... a sack of flour hoisting itself up the stairs*. It thumped onto each step as though sagging, winded with exertion. Kate drew her knees to her chin, covers up around her neck. Thump-drag, thump-drag. She prided herself on her courage, her "ballsiness," as Harry called it, but this didn't sound like her husband returning to bed, his familiar clomp of feet upon the carpeted stairs. This was the sort of unnatural noise she remembered from the monster movies of her adolescence. This was the part where she'd sit in the theater with fingers splayed across her eyes while her boyfriend threw popcorn at the screen, anxious for the kill. Time for minor characters to go bye-bye.

"H-Honey?" Her voice tremulous, so low the dark of the bedroom snatched it away.

She heard a wet, sucking thump outside the door, as if the floor on the other side had turned to mud. Kate stared at the rectangular patch of hall light seeping under the door. A shadow moved into the light. And something odd: Was that water dribbling onto the carpet? A dark puddle pooled on the tan rug. Like colored melted wax.

Abrupt darkness. The hallway light switched off.

"Harry!"

"Shh," came his reply, as he slipped into the bedroom.

Relief flooded Kate. She let out a gasp and drank in her first real breath of air. "What in the world are you doing?" she asked. "You gave me such a fright."

A chuckle of apology, deep in his throat. "Sorry."

"Has Alex left? What was your meeting about?"

The strange fright had left her as quickly as it had appeared. Curiosity filled her now.

"That's what I want to talk to you about," her husband said. He was moving toward the bed, navigating the familiar dark. "We've made a gentleman's agreement."

A *what?* This didn't sound like Harry at all.

He neared the bed. And Kate distinctly heard it, a squishy, watery sound. Another soft chuckle, sly. "I'm ready to finish what we started before Alex interrupted..."

"Oh, you." She sank into the sheets with a grin on her face, waiting for her husband's arms. He could be such a romantic fool.

"Papa Bear has a surprise tonight," Harry whispered. He pulled back a corner of the sheets and blankets. "All the better to love you, my dear..."

Kate reached for him in the dark, welcoming his return. After her little fright she needed the reassurance of his familiar touch. He slid into bed and she reached out, her hand caressing slippery skin. He was slick, and slightly tacky to the touch. She recoiled with a startled little yelp, rolling away from him—

—and rolled into a body on the other side of the bed. She was about to scream when a soiled hand clamped over her mouth, and a naked body thrust against her.

"Hello, Kate," Alex Webster said.

5

She wished she hadn't pulled the night shift. This was a night for the heebie-jeebies, as Grandma used to say. A night when the hairs on her arms stood on end and wouldn't go down.

Perfect for Halloween, Bessie Watson thought with a little laugh, 'cept it's days too early.

Her chortle sounded unwelcome in the graveyard-silent hallway. Her white sneakers squeaked along the polished floor of the hospital. Time to peek into the rooms and listen for any irregularities of breathing, any labored signs of trouble from her patients. It was so sad; rarely did any of her boys pass a full night of sound sleep, despite weariness and a need for rest. Only two weeks ago she'd discovered one of her patients just in time. He'd been near death, exhausted from the effort to breathe, his left lung all collapsed from the pneumonia. Such was the nature of this rotten disease: You had to be watched twenty-four hours a day.

John Matthews was first on her rounds. She pushed open the door and slipped inside the room, one hand holding the door in place. A sound sleeper, tonight; Bessie listened for telltale rustling of sheets, but the room was still. She smiled in the dark. His medication must be helping his congestion. This was the best he'd slept all week.

Bessie quietly slipped out, blinking in the glare of fluorescent lights. She walked over to the next room and consulted the chart on her clipboard. Bart Powell. In for some tests and x-rays. She eased inside the room, the dark an opaque curtain cut only by the rectangle of light spilling from the doorway. She cocked her head and listened.

Again, no rustle of sheets, no snoring or other normal sounds of breathing. She frowned. Her ears rang with the effort to hear. She continued to stall, her abundant frame balanced on one foot. Impatience gave way to a warning that sneaked up and knocked on her door with the message:

He ain't here. He's gone, just like that John Matthews. That's why there ain't no sound of life, of living. And if you don't get your ass out of here you're going to join them, whether you like it or not—

Funny how the most irrational thoughts can crowd your mind at three a.m. Funny how childlike panic takes over in the blink of an eye, despite years of training, of living, of common sense. Bessie tried to dismiss these ungrounded worries, but they kept bobbing in her thoughts like red flags. The longer she stood in this room, the more convinced she became that it was empty. She remembered Eddie Blake. Eddie, gone.

But that can't be. He's too weak to go anywhere.

So turn on the light. It made sense, and yet she hesitated. If Bart Powell was in this room, it'd be unforgivable to wake him. Was he in the bathroom? No sounds from there, either.

Bessie retreated back toward the hallway, her hand creeping along the wall in search of the light switch. It was warm in the room, and a trickle of perspiration ran out of her Afro hairdo. She found the switch. Prayed she wasn't making a mistake. And turned on the light.

Fluorescent light lit up the ice-cream-colored wallpaper. The bed was partially hidden by the L-shape of the room. All she could see was the foot of the bed. Its blankets were smooth, unrumpled. She forced herself to approach. Her heart beat Congo drums as she peeked around the corner, and looked.

Empty! A large wet stain ruined the sheets, as though someone had dumped a bucket of water onto the pillow and upper half of the bed. A human outline in blood, an ominous red warning.

Bessie slapped a hand over her mouth. Her eyes bugged out.

Lord Jesus not again!

She bolted from the room and stood in the open hallway, panting with fright. She had to tell Maxine. And Larry, if he was back from his break.

I'll just go tell Maxine, that's what I'll—

Laughter broke the cemetery stillness of the morning. Muffled, coming from one door down. Bessie spun around in shock, her mouth popping open. The hallway: empty. She backtracked, edging toward the door. Glanced up to read the number on the door. One of her feet stepped back in involuntary reflex. A shudder ran through her.

Room 203.

The room had been ready for occupation two days ago, yet it remained empty. It had been scrubbed with every conceivable detergent and cleanser. Deodorized, to get rid of the foul smell. Yet Edward Blake's nasty disappearance still fueled the gossip mill, encouraging wild tales and speculation. Just the other day one of Bessie's co-workers had insisted with delicious horror that the room was haunted.

Sure, sure, they had all said — before the shadow fell over their faces.

And now:

Shushed laughter, like schoolboys planning a prank.

Professional duty rubbed against ballooning fear. No one should be in that room. No one should make that kind of laugh, like giggling through layers of dirt. It was too broken a sound, too like a squeaky hinge.

Look inside, she instructed herself. *Only right I see who's there. It's the professional thing to do...*

She clutched the clipboard to her bosom as though it were a shield. Her free hand flattened against the door, and pushed. It opened onto darkness.

She choked out: "Who's in here?"

Impish laughter. Tittering.

A reply, so soft it seemed to come inside her own head:

(All of us, Bessie. And now you, too—)

The dark whirlpooled in front of her, shimmering. Flashing red and yellow lights chased blue strobe lights upon a cavernous dance floor. In the center, all her patients, hospital gowned: John Matthews. Bart Powell. Paul Scott. Henry Learner. They waved her inside, intravenous tubes dangling from the crook of their arms.

(Come join us, Bessie. Room for all—)

The clipboard clattered to the floor. Bessie stumbled out the door and flew down the hallway, tennis shoes squeaking. Screaming to wake the dead.

6

Listen:

Not just the baying of wind.

Nor the shriek of wind-driven rain against a roof.

Like a ripple upon a lake, moving out and away in a perfect, ever-widening circle: the cries of a city.

Shutters drawn against the foggy night, the better not to see. Rain washes the red pavements, but they do not come clean.

The many hands in the darkness. Feeding the monster.

39

Insurance

1

David, his arm draped around Bobby, swimming up from sleep:
Kahmaal.
The crackle of fire. Dark faces lit by its glow.
A story:

2

Once, a tiny village sat upon the wild untamed coasts of Africa. For many years, its people prospered as fishermen and hunters in the nearby savannah and jungles. For as long as they could remember, and as far back as their mothers and fathers could remember, there had always been game and wildlife aplenty to support them. The people of the remote village ruled themselves, but were watched over by a shaman and his brother, who governed wisely and without prejudice.

One year, the rains did not come. Nor the next. Nor the year after that. Drought gripped their beautiful land, and with it, disease and famine. The animals of the forests either died or disappeared, having moved on in search of better lands. The grasslands shriveled. Mother Earth broke open in her misery, baking under the sun's unmerciful glare.

In desperation, the shaman traveled into the sacred caves by the sea and prayed. Should they move on? Here, they could at least count upon the sea to help feed them, but lately, even its waters had turned green and foul.

Down into the longest, darkest cave he traveled, and there he retrieved the sacred stone. It had been handed down to him by his father, and by his father's father. It was only to be used in the greatest of emergencies. The shaman climbed back out of the cave, and with the ocean breeze upon his face, he called upon the spirits of the sky. "Bring us rain and heal our land," he begged, "and I will give you anything you ask."

He was wise, this medicine man, but too desperate to recognize the foolishness of such a tempting offer. His prayers flew across the heavens and then sank into the deepest cracks in the earth, down to where creatures who hide from the light live out all their days.

For two weeks, the man prayed.

And then, one starless night as he emerged from the cave, he saw a bank of thunderclouds moving across the ocean toward him. Like a thief, it approached. The shaman gazed upon his own folly as he stared at the spirit who had answered his call: the Eater of Souls.

There on the cliffs, they faced each other.

"Rains for Mother Earth," the shaman announced. "Food for my people."

"And in return?" asked the Eater of Souls. "What of my side of the bargain?"

"I'll give you the finest hides in my land," he offered.

"What good is animal hide to me? It cannot cloak me, for I have no shape."

The medicine man rubbed his chin. "I'll give you our best elephant tusks."

"For what? Weapons? My teeth are the only weapons I need."

"Then I — I have nothing."

"No," the Eater of Souls said with a sly grin. "You have the stone."

The man was afraid of this. He put up a brave front. "What good is it to you?"

The demon's eyes gleamed. "The stone can make me flesh. Do this for me, and I will open my clouds and give you rain. Your land will grow abundant again."

Here the shaman trembled, for he understood he could not grant the demon its wish. These Hungry Ghosts were tricksters used to taking what they wanted, and should not have. To make one into flesh would guarantee ruin for all.

"No. I cannot make this bargain," he said to the spirit.

The Eater of Souls bristled. The clouds thundered his disapproval. "You promised anything, for rain. You cannot call me for no reason: It's against the sacred law. Give me what I want, or I'll eat you and your people, bite by bite. I'll steal their souls and leave nothing but empty husks."

But the medicine man knew this was their fate whether he helped the Eater of Souls or not. This was a creature of destruction, a worm in Mother Earth, and since he had summoned it, he had to be the one to send it away.

"You are right," he said to the Hungry Ghost. "Since I called you, and you came, I will fulfill my side of the bargain. Appear on these cliffs at this same time tomorrow night. I will bring someone in sacrifice, someone who will give you shape."

And the Eater of Souls stormed over the wide dark ocean, waiting for the moon of the next night. Meanwhile, the shaman returned to his village. For many hours into the night and the following day, he conferred with his brother, who could draw magic shapes. How could they save themselves, and their village?

Finally, they settled upon a plan.

The next night the shaman and his brother returned to the windy cliffs. A sour wind blew off the ocean, and the Eater of Souls appeared before them.

"I will give you my brother," the man announced, "if you promise to replenish our land."

"But of course," answered the Hungry Ghost, who twitched with excitement of having a physical body at last.

The medicine man held out the precious stone. He chanted the sacred words and shouted, "Into this vessel, I decree!" He pointed toward his brother.

The very air rumbled and shook. The Eater of Souls flew toward its new shape, letting go of its hold upon the clouds.

But the brother held before him a drawing he had completed that very afternoon. Onto the smooth inside of a tree's bark, he had sketched a picture of a boat.

And the Eater of Souls, powered by the forces within the stone, and the shaman's words, could not halt himself. He flew into the picture of the boat, his angry spirit locked inside its new home.

"Now be gone from us, and never return!" cried the shaman. He cast the drawing down into the churning ocean, where it drifted away from their land and out, out, into seas of gray and blue, never to harm them again.

Or so they thought.

Weeks, and then months, passed, and still no rain. They grew weak from the terrible famine, and many died. Even so, the shaman preferred this fate to what had been in store for them had the Eater of Souls gotten its wish.

But many miles out into the ocean, the Hungry Ghost buzzed in its locked shape, his long empty days spent plotting horrible revenge upon the shaman and his brother. He used what limited powers he had left to steer himself with the wind.

One day, a real ship appeared upon the horizon.

And the Eater of Souls grinned his wicked grin and began to float himself toward the boat, and his vengeance.

3

Anxious, fearful: "David? What's happening? Wake up!"

A gray curtain fell away, and with it, a long expanse of ocean. David opened his eyes as if lead weights were attached to each lid.

Bobby was shaking him awake.

He sighed and gave a little gesture to indicate he was okay, just needed a moment to pull himself together. His tongue felt heavy and dry in his throat.

"You were thrashing about," Bobby said with concern. "Sweating up a storm."

He was indeed sweat-grimed, hair plastered against his head. None of it mattered: He took Bobby's hand into his own, keenly excited. "I dreamt about the Africans," he said, and Bobby's eyes widened with surprise.

"Yes...?"

David gave it to him straight. "It's like I wasn't dreaming at all, but sitting around a fire as a story, a ... a legend ... was passed on to me." He told it in quick, broad strokes. Already the dream was growing fuzzy around the edges, wakefulness pushing it aside.

"But what happens?" asked Bobby.

"I don't know. You woke me up."

They looked up as Rachael strode into the room, blue robe draped about her, hair every which way. Her glance at them was less a greeting than a swift appraisal of their proximity to each other.

"I'll make coffee" was her good-morning salutation. She busied herself at the Mr. Coffee machine on the kitchen counter.

Bobby whispered, "I thought we had reached a cease-fire."

David shrugged. "Maybe we look too chummy."

That got a rise out of both of them, a slight coloring of the cheeks.

David caught Bobby's happiness like warm sunshine directed onto his face, a flattering mixture of love and admiration. An image of Mick cooled some of this sunlight's warmth, guilt like a shadowy chill. His feelings were raw, confused.

"Hey," David soothed. "We're pals. Brothers in arms. Don't be embarrassed."

There was a pause, and a stillness came into Bobby's face, inescapable knowledge. The eyes that looked at him were wise beyond their years.

"Today's the day," he intoned. "Can you feel it?"

David nodded. And thought, *We have killed the people we were. The men we might have been, had this evil not come into our lives.* Would this fight somehow ennoble them? Or would blood always dirty their hands?

4

They took turns cleaning up. David was careful to keep the shower water cool, hopping out quickly before any steam had the chance to fill up the tiny bathroom. One by one they assembled around the kitchen table to a late breakfast of bagels, toasted English muffins, and lots of coffee.

Red pointed to the Sunday paper, which David had picked up from a newsstand half a block down the street. "Nothing," he declared, and dismissed the paper with a wave of his hand. "Nothing in there at all about this Victor guy."

True, but David found an article on page twelve about the fire at Uncle Charlie's.

Bobby hovered behind David's shoulders. His mouth was set, grim. "Life as usual," he muttered.

"Maybe 'cause it ain't so bad as you say," Red piped in.

"Take a look outside," David said, and jerked his thumb toward the den windows.

Red already knew what lay outside the windows, but instinctively he looked again.

Dense fog, thunderstorm dark, patted the den windows. Occasionally a sort of scoured aluminum light peeked through whenever the fog pulled back. The sight was unrelentingly dreary, like staring out into a day in February, the cemetery of the year. The wintery pall suggested biting cold, but David had learned otherwise when he'd dashed outside for a paper.

This was no winter fog; the air was humid, steamy. Every day more darkness, every day the outer world began to match that world within the Caverns' mildewed walls. Soon, only unending night. What then? A trip to Victor's funhouse for everyone?

He shuddered. His teeth chattered. Not even this second cup of coffee could chase this cold that lay upon his soul.

"No one can take away daylight," Red asserted. He took a noisy slurp of his coffee. "It's not possible."

"What you saw last night: Would you have thought *that* possible?" Bobby asked. There was certainly no love lost between the two of them.

"Enough," Rachael interrupted, her frown of displeasure immediately silencing further taunts from either party. "Time is too precious to waste arguing. We have to move, and quickly."

"Did those books tell you anything?" asked David.

Bobby and Red looked up as though they'd missed out on something.

"I did a little research late last night," Rachael explained to their puzzled faces. "And the sad truth is, I came up with nothing."

David opened his mouth to speak, couldn't find words, and snapped it shut again.

"Oh, I found all kinds of information," she added hastily. "Seems every culture in the world has their special monsters and demons, just as, I might add, every culture has their stories of gods, creation myths, and devils." She shook her head with exasperation.

"Monsters," Red breathed. "Oh, brother."

"That's it exactly," she agreed. "I didn't believe a word of it."

David just stared at her.

She held up a hand. "I *know* what we saw last night. But searching for answers inside those books is like rummaging through comic books for scientific information. None of them cast a glimmer of insight into how this Victor has apparently survived throughout several centuries. Or why my crystal is powerful against it."

The room fell silent. Without full awareness they were jerking at outside noises, at sudden gusts of wind which moaned a hello, or the cat-soft pat of fog against the window. The hands of the kitchen clock moved toward noon, but they huddled around the table like cavemen around a fire, wishing for dawn.

Then David spoke, breaking the uneasy silence.

"Whatever he is, he's entangled himself into that place — the Caverns — and we should use that to our advantage."

"What do you propose?" asked Rachael.

He gripped his coffee mug. "Last night, Bobby and I uncovered a weakness with these creatures. Not counting your crystal, of course."

Everyone leaned in, waiting.

"Fire," he whispered with talismanic reverence.

"Fire?" Red scowled with uncertainty, and pouted. He massaged the side of his neck, working on a kink that refused to unknot.

David glanced at Bobby. This was the first time he'd aired this suggestion, and he needed his unguarded reaction. "We've no time for delay. We have to strike back, while we have the chance." He drew a breath. "I think we should torch the Caverns."

Two reactions played across Bobby's face, one after the other. The first: Yes. Fire. Just torch it, burn it up, good riddance to all. The second reaction wiped off the first, a queasy doubt that set his lips trembling and clouded his brown eyes. This was the reaction that had to be voiced.

"What about Mick? And Alex?"

David said nothing, eyes downcast.

"Do we burn them up as well?"

"I don't know," he answered in a small voice. He implored Bobby. "What other choice do we have?"

"How do you know we won't be attacked?" Red asked.

He shrugged. "I don't."

Red shook his head with derision. "Sounds pretty half-baked to me..."

David ignored the remark and made a point of staring at Bobby eye to eye. "If we can find Mick and Alex, and can rescue them, great. But if not..." His words wilted under that hurt expression.

"What do you think the fire will do to Victor?" Bobby managed.

"He's connected to the place. My god, you saw that face appear on the front of the building. The more enmeshed he is with the bathhouse, the better, because if we break in and set it on fire..."

"What if it doesn't hurt him?" Red interjected. "What if it just pisses him off?"

No one answered.

Bobby remembered a thought that had crossed his mind yesterday afternoon: how even something such as this beast had to have a place to call home. And the way the shadowy men had retreated from the flames at the restaurant ... Perhaps David's scheme would work.

"The bastard's ripped us from *our* homes," David said. His hands balled into fists. "I want to return the favor."

Silence.

Bobby nodded. "Let's do it. If nothing else, it'll be worth the risk to see Victor get a dose of his own medicine." But in his heart, he secretly feared for his lover. Was Mick safe — or already lost to him?

David reached out with gratitude and squeezed Bobby's arm.

Red grunted with disgust at this display of affection.

David focused his attention upon Rachael. "Thank you for letting us stay the night, and helping us as you did. I have one more favor to ask, and then we'll be out of the way."

She regarded him with curiosity.

"I can't ask you to involve yourselves any more than you already have. This is our fight. Whatever's going to happen is between us and Victor. All we need now is—"

"No," Red interrupted, anticipating the punchline. "Don't let them take it, Mom."

"Mrs. Black, without the crystal we're too vulnerable. Finished. If we can borrow it for a few hours—"

"—No—" Red, once again.

"—it might protect us. We need every weapon at our disposal."

Red fumed in his seat. "Don't let them, Mom. Not your present. Don't let—"

"Hush, Randall," Rachael admonished. Her cheeks were blotchy beneath her splash of freckles, lips compressed into a firm line. Agitation fumed her eyes dark green.

David, watching, suddenly thought: *She won't let go of it. Look at her: as hooked to that stone as an alcoholic is to the bottle.*

"What about us?" Red charged. "What's to protect us if you're off with the crystal and those ... those *things* ... come calling again? We're fucked."

"I don't think that'll happen," David stammered.

"So *you* say."

"Look," Bobby jumped in. "Why are you complaining? We're offering you a way out. Isn't that all you've wanted? To be left alone, and have us handle this ourselves?"

"You can't have the crystal." Red was adamant.

Rachael scoured her son with a blistering stare. "That's *my* decision, not yours."

Red's lips pursed together.

"I'm the one who's used to the crystal," she said. "It came to *me,* not you. I've made it work. So if anyone should accompany you—"

"No." David and Red, simultaneously.

"If anyone goes with them, it's me," Red asserted. Something clicked in his face, the illumination of an irrevocable decision. For one of the few times that morning he faced David with an expression free of contempt and anger. "Mom stays here. I'm coming with you."

David and Bobby exchanged looks.

He slapped both hands onto his chest. "Look: What I do best is fight. If there's going to be any trouble I'm the person to have on your side."

"Why should you help us now?" asked Bobby suspiciously.

"Because when this is all over, that crystal comes back to my mother." He smiled wickedly. "Think of me as ... insurance."

Everyone was quiet. An undeniable logic threaded Red's reasoning, yet David remained uneasy. Was this the same guy who'd cowered last night?

Red was waiting. "So what do you say?"

What a funny alliance we are, David thought. *A psychic who involves herself only because she wants to help those children, and a man with a grudge against queers. This is the best we can hope for?*

He caught Bobby watching him. A smile toyed at his mouth, as though he, too, asked himself, *These are the only people who can help us?*

What else could they do?

5

They trudged around the back of the building to where Red's Nissan truck was parked. Wedged into a corner of the truck bed was a five-gallon gasoline can from the Black's storage and a one-gallon can David had discovered in the trunk of the taxicab. Stuffed into their jacket pockets were half a dozen books of matches and two Zippo lighters.

Rachael embraced her son. "You be careful," she admonished. Her eyes were shiny in the dull light.

Red nodded. "Don't worry about me. I can take care of myself."

She patted his chest and forced herself to turn away. She came up to David. A myriad of expressions played the muscles of her face. Her eyes dug into his. She held the stone as though it were a fragile bird about to take wing.

"With my life," David broke the silence by saying. "I'll guard it with my life."

Red muttered something under his breath.

"Just come back. All of you." She pushed the crystal into David's palm, wrapped his fingers around its cool shape. "Remember: It's the user who wields true power, not the stone."

David nodded with gratitude.

Red climbed into the cab of the truck. The ignition kicked over. He revved the engine. Bobby slid into the middle seat. David lingered at the passenger door. "Thank you for doing this—"

"Oh, go on, go, before I change my mind." Rachael stepped back from the truck, eyes full and moist. She shivered, despite the warm drizzle. "Hurry," she said in a voice as soft as the rain about her. "Hurry."

And when they were gone, when the truck disappeared out of the alley and onto the adjoining street, a thought rose in her, vibrating uneasily:

So: I'm alone now. Just like you wanted.

Rachael fled back into the shop.

40

Strike two

W¹
ithin five minutes of their departure she was trembling, her skin
clammy and slick, a spray of perspiration ungraciously wetting her
upper lip. One minute hot, the next minute so cold she debated
throwing on a sweater over her blouse and slacks.

Stop this, Rachael commanded herself as she set about opening
the bookstore for business. *Stop feeling this way.*

How easy the words, how difficult their execution. Simpler to give
advice to others. Yes, how simple, when the wind slamming against
the building did not sound like the rattle of skeleton bones.

She flipped the "Closed" sign on the door to "Open," then went
to the desk, lifting out the metal box containing petty cash, and tried
to count a hundred-dollar bank for the cash register. Her sweaty fingers
greased the money; she had to count it twice. She waited for the
comfort of routine to take away the ache of missing her crystal. And
waited. And waited.

Was this addiction? Was this the process she saw so often on
television, drug addicts writhing in padded cells as the drugs of their
choice departed in these waves of little deaths? Such a recipe of
ailments: Dizziness. Nausea. Clammy skin.

She sat in her big mahogany chair and stared into the empty
bookstore, not wanting customers any more but open out of stubborn
habit. She had to stay busy.

For it wasn't all attributable to the loss of her crystal, this
trembling and fight-or-flight panic. Yes, she felt vulnerable without
her precious jewel, naked. But right now her real concern centered
on Red. Something odd was going on. He hadn't acted like himself
this morning. She'd caught him giving her funny wounded glances,
like a child confused by his punishment, and she knew why he was
upset with her. They were confidants, after all, and yet she had kept
him in the dark, denying him access to her feelings even as she had

denied the soggy dark truth of the menace seeping into her heart.

She had to admit it was a stroke of genius on Red's part to insist he accompany David and Bobby to the Caverns. This David seemed sincere, but was there a hidden agenda to steal the crystal? She remembered the high it had given her when the stone reawakened her own special talents. How long in David's hands before he'd hear its siren call?

Minutes passed. The unease would not go away. Her thoughts kept circling back to her son, and the odd expression on his face. The way he kept rubbing his neck. And offering to *help*. So ... unlike him. Yet surely she could take some pride in that, couldn't she? Her business was in helping people. Maybe this change in attitude signaled a new maturity in her son.

Attitude. It governs everything, doesn't it?

She paused, a truth swimming up, something half-remembered. Rooted within the sappy cliché was a kernel of knowledge.

Attitude. Power of thought.

She scooted away from the desk. Ideas sparked in her head. A book: There was a book she'd breezed through once, hadn't deemed it important at the time. Something from Africa...

An unaccountable excitement tingled her limbs.

Where is it?

She went to the back bookshelf, her fingers skimming leather bindings. That's right; certain tribes held a curious position on the power of thought and what it could create.

She froze, her breath caught, as she plucked the book from the shelf.

Myth and Magic: A Look at Shamanism in Ancient Cultures.

She gave only a passing notice to the front door swinging open, and the young blond man who walked into the store.

2

Thump-thump. Thump-thump. Thump-thump.

Windshield wipers sliced the drizzle neatly to each side as Red piloted the truck down South Van Ness in search of an open gas station.

"Quiet," Bobby observed.

"Yeah," David agreed.

On a typical Sunday afternoon this part of the Mission would have been explosive with color and action: packs of families swarming out church doors, the homeless scrounging through garbage cans for lunch, fruit and vegetable stands busy with customers picking up last-minute items for Sunday dinner.

Today the Mission was a ghost town, utterly deserted. The empty streets were portraits in blue and gray, reflective like the sleek black skin of a seal.

"Do you think people know?" Bobby asked.

David shook his head. "Not in so many words, not in any tangible way. But they must feel it. A ... moodiness in the air. Don't you?"

"Stop it," Red gruffed good-naturedly. "You guys are giving me the spooks."

"We should be psyching ourselves up, not hiking our own fears," David agreed.

Red pointed off to the right. "Here we go." He pulled the Nissan into the Arco station and drew up to one of the pumps. This was the first station they'd spotted that was open.

David fumbled for his wallet.

"I'll take care of the gas," Red said.

David waved a ten-dollar bill. "Let me give you the cash, at least."

Red grinned. "Fine by me." He took the money and hopped out of the cab.

As soon as he was out of earshot, Bobby turned to David. "What do you think he's up to?"

David shrugged.

"I don't trust him," Bobby flatly announced. "Can you read anything from him?"

"No. He's a blank slate."

Bobby lowered his voice. "Maybe you should use the crystal."

He gave a partial nod of consideration, then shook his head. "Let's give him a little rope before we go and hang him. Remember: He wants the crystal back—" and here he patted his chest, the stone safely tucked into his left breast pocket. "I'm not so fond of him myself. You know that. But what else can we do?"

Bobby was silent, his eyes full.

Look at them, Red thought as he stood back around the rear of the truck, gasoline nozzle stuck into the five-gallon can. *I'll bet they're whispering about me, sure as shit.*

He shook his head and reached up to massage the stubborn crick in his neck. He'd awakened with it, and despite massage and a couple of Tylenols it still ached like all hell. Probably just hung over, even though he'd consumed half his usual allotment of beers.

Truth was, he'd felt out of joint all morning. Hard to put into words exactly. Aside from the crick in his neck, he was otherwise okay. Yet he felt as if he were ... slipping. Yeah; that was it. Like he was getting pushed to the side, even while he remained inside himself. Crowded by some ... something...

Red licked his lips. *Boy, listen to me. Getting to sound like those two fruitcakes.*

He wiped sweat out of his eyes and pumped gas into the cans, finishing with the first one and moving on to the other. Hard to believe the task before him, it seemed so unreal. Christ Almighty, look at what he was doing! Helping two queers burn down some old bathhouse that they said wasn't so abandoned any more. Well, at least he'd get his own pleasure in watching it burn; places like that, like that bathhouse, didn't deserve to stick around. Burning was just what the doctor ordered.

Despite what he'd witnessed the night before, despite the fantastic story he'd heard, he still didn't believe it. Not one hundred percent, anyway. Maybe if he'd inherited some of his mother's gift, if he'd felt more included and less like a third wheel, his attitude would be different. But this: This was like saying the UFOs had landed, follow me while we go burn 'em up. Hell, that made no sense, did it? To burn something up just cause they didn't fully understand it? And Mom said *he* was the hothead, the irresponsible one. Shit. Far as he could see, this thing was doing everybody a favor. No great loss to get rid of a few perverts. Now the *kids:* That was a different story, that was a crying shame. On that point he sided with Mom.

Shit. The gas can overflowed, an oily stream spurting down the side of the red can. *Pay attention.* He removed the nozzle, hooked it back to the tank, and went up to the glass booth to have his money snatched away by some oily-haired guy who could barely speak English. Christ; sometimes it seemed there weren't any decent folks left in the world. On this account he was old-fashioned, a throwback. Mom could take a few lessons from him on picking and choosing some of her clients.

He hopped back into the cab and passed David his change. They were grinning at him, scared little pasted-on smiles. As if he couldn't see the nervousness underneath. As if they were all just hunky-dory pals. Jeeze, what impostors, these two. But he wasn't going to let on, no way. He pulled his face into a matching smile. "So do I get directions, or should we sit here all day?" He kneaded the sore muscles of his neck.

David indicated they should follow South Van Ness to the overpass, then cut down Folsom and hang a left.

They merged onto Van Ness. Traffic was still light, with few cars maneuvering the slippery streets.

Red flipped on the windshield wipers and turned up the defrost. Hot in here. His sweatshirt was glued to his skin.

Thump-thump. Thump-thump.

Like a metronome. Calming. He enjoyed the sound, and found himself concentrating on it. Sure as hell beat listening to his passengers cough into their hands as nerves wired them up. There seemed to be a voice riding the wipers, melodic, encouraging him to listen.

Like water sprinkled onto hot coals:

Raaanndalll...

Raaanndalll...

He felt himself pushed to the side again, as though his inside self wore ice skates and he was being directed away from the center of the rink to the edge.

The other two were talking.

"Can you feel it?" Bobby asked.

David nodded. "It's like someone's squeezing my lungs. Look how dark it is."

Red looked. And for just a moment, to see this darkness coiled around this part of town — it quickened his pulse, made him dizzy with fright. Dear god, what was happening down here? And why did he feel so ... strange...

They lapsed into silence. They had to: Their bodies were talking to them, nerves sending out flares of alarm. Tremors danced in their clenched muscles.

Thump-thump. Thump-thump.

Ahh, that was better. Just drive. Don't think about it. Sure, it looked terrible outside, the industrial buildings and bars and dilapidated Victorians peeking out of fog like the thrust of a jagged cliff. As if this place they were headed for were the evil castle perched high atop the mountain, theatrical storm clouds forming a halo about its walls.

Red's neck ached when these thoughts intruded; a hot, spiked pain like a pinched nerve.

Just get to the bathhouse and take them inside, then everything will be just fine.

Red scowled. Wait a minute. They weren't supposed to go inside; they were just going to burn it down.

Again the snake voice:

No, Randall. Bring them inside. Bring them to meee...

The voice was followed by that sensation of being pushed to the side, like a bully elbowing onto his turf. For a moment he felt as though he were floating, as though a hand had swept beneath him and cut the cords of gravity. It was extremely pleasant, this feeling, like the high he got after a few tokes of killer weed.

"Hey? You driving or what?"

Red came back into himself, dropped into reality by David's voice. He'd forgotten where he was, forgotten the wheel to the truck beneath his hands. He'd been gliding into the oncoming lane of traffic.

"Sorry," he said shakily.

"You feeling okay?" the cutsie one, Bobby, asked.

Red nodded, and said what he knew they wanted to hear. "It's really spooky down here. We must be close."

David agreed. "Roberts Alley is two blocks away. We'll make a left." He patted Bobby's knee. "You ready for this?" he asked, his voice low, affectionate.

Red looked with repugnance at David's hand upon Bobby's knee.

I'm ready, he thought. *Wait until I get you cutsie boys inside—*

Everyone sat at attention now, stiffly erect with necks craned, like weary passengers sensing the end to a long journey. Red slowed the truck, found the sign for Roberts Alley in the fog, and hung a left.

The rain had slacked off down here; it was calm, close to the building, as though they were entering the eye of a hurricane. Swirling eddies of blue mist made the air almost three-dimensional. Impossible to imagine sunlight ever touching this place. Impossible to imagine children ever playing on the street, or families living out their lives behind those Victorian doors. The idea was as repulsive as playing in a graveyard.

They pulled to a stop.

Red felt his lungs contract. He couldn't take a deep breath. "Holy shit."

They stared. Madness stared back at them.

On one hand the building was perfectly ordinary, typical of any city building that had once flourished and was now bereft of life and attention. Weary. Mournful, like something passed over.

But a photographic effect was upon it, a Polaroid in the process of developing. Yes, a building, wood and brick and concrete; but seemingly alive too, somehow alive, powered by the forces hiding within its walls. Red couldn't stare at it, couldn't get a proper fix on its dimensions and structure. It shifted, it seethed, it blurred around the edges with an unholy aura, fog wisping its sides and roof.

It only looked asleep, this place. Its idiot blank stare was a ruse, a trick. They knew it, in that contemplative silence that rang their ears with singing blood and accelerated their heartbeat.

Red's mouth dried up.

David fumbled with his shirt pocket. Even as he pulled it into view, even as the stone remained webbed within his fingers, blue light seeped through, spilling into the truck's interior. "Look," he said, and opened his hand. Light against true darkness, flaring in recognition of evil.

The blue light reached out, filling the cab. As some of it spilled onto Red a spark seemed to go off inside his head, a sudden combustion of understanding and unmitigated fear. It *was* real, this villain — and *it* was the owner of the voice coiling inside his head. A gagged, closed-mouth sound stalled in his throat.

"Red? What's wrong?"

He started to reply, the words on the tip of his tongue, when the snake voice bit down inside his head.

Hussshhh, Redddd—

Not pushed out of the center this time: *thrown.*

Physically Red didn't move a muscle, but inside he felt himself hurtled. He cried out in alarm and heard his own voice bounce back at him — he'd fallen too deep, and his scream couldn't reach his mouth. He tumbled into a dark abyss. Something bullied over him, scrabbling into the space from which conscious thought was piloted. He opened his mouth to scream and fluid stuffed his mouth. His eyes bugged. He thrashed and kicked. From the bottom of this prison, Red looked up to see a reptilian shape holding him down.

David reached across Bobby and gently shook Red's shoulders. "Don't be afraid."

Red flexed his hand. He stared at it as though the simple ability to move it gave him great pleasure. "I'm fine," he said in a flat voice, knowing he had to speak.

David nodded. "Let's do it, then."

A smile hinted Red's lips. *Yes. Let's do it.*

3

Rachael heard movement. She jerked out of her revelry and glanced up, her expression softening. Nothing to worry about. Only that boy again, still in the store. A browser. He was methodically moving along row after row of bookshelves, one hand tracing titles as he went.

Her store attracted all kinds, from the upscale set in Pacific Heights who had recently discovered (much to their chagrin) that money and two BMWs in the garage did not constitute happiness, to the down-and-out, the graspers, all curiosity and desperation. Certainly this young man belonged to the poor end of the scale. His clothes were disheveled and smudged in the back, as though he'd slept in them for several days running. He carried himself stiffly, and walked as if his tennis shoes hurt his feet. She couldn't swear he did this on purpose, but he kept his back to her, eyes averted. When she'd asked if he needed any help, he'd waved a hand to indicate his intention to browse. Not once did he give her the courtesy of a simple direct look.

Rachael watched him for a few more minutes and then went back to her book. A light rain tattooed the roof.

She glanced up to catch him staring at her. No cursory glance, this: a no-holds-barred stare of reproach. He quickly averted his eyes and darted around a bookshelf.

But Rachael had seen. Oh yes.

Even without the power of the crystal to aid her, she saw what lay behind the young man's blue eyes: jumbled, black thoughts. Crazy, confused thoughts that ricocheted against the walls of his skull like a speeding train shooting out of control. And worst of all, caught with just that moment's glance, the terror of a sane man looking out, out, unable to tame or control these wildly flashing impulses.

All this was instantly relayed to Rachael. Now that she had seen into his eyes, she literally felt buffeted by the waves of confusion and seething anger that percolated inside him.

"Hey," she called out. "What do you want in my store?"

The chime over the front door tinkled, and two women swept inside with a gust of wind. Rachael's connection to the disturbing young man was broken as he darted back among the bookshelves. She was forced to turn her attention to her two customers.

"Do you have anything on reincarnation?" the shorter, mannish woman asked.

She motioned them over to one of the bookshelves. "Any of the Seth books are good. And Edward Cayce. *Why We've Been Here Before* is pretty informative."

"Where is that one?"

She scooted around the desk to show them. Her gaze wandered the shop, but the young man remained hidden by the bookshelves. As soon as she took care of these women she was going to throw him out, period.

But she didn't have to throw him out. While she was standing with the women, her back to the front door, the door opened and closed with a swish of warm, wet air. She spun around so fast both women uttered gasps of surprise.

"Did he leave?" she asked breathlessly. Without waiting for a reply, Rachael peered out the front window for a retreating figure. The glass was fogged over, outside shapes just blurs across the glass.

"I guess he did," one of the women said. "I heard the front door."

With her best shopkeeper's smile frozen onto her face, Rachael tentatively reached out with her mind. She wasn't sure if she could do this without her crystal, but to her amazement she picked up the man's psychic residue over everything. It was oily and tart, like a tangy spray of salad dressing. But she no longer detected his presence in the shop. She went limp with relief.

The women eventually settled upon a couple of books and had them gift-wrapped for a birthday party. Rachael fairly gritted her teeth by the time she escorted them to the front door.

"Good-bye," she called brightly. "Come again." *In a year or two,* she added to herself. She wiped her forehead with the back of her hand. What an ordeal. Red off on god-only-knew-what kind of mission. Street lunatics giving her a fright. On a day like today, maybe she *should* just close up shop. If any of her regulars came by she'd let them in. Otherwise, she'd just as soon wait for Red's return in her own private way.

She peered out onto Eighteenth Street. Cars zipped by with their headlights on and windshield wipers flapping. The day seemed to tremble at its edge, and yet it was only midafternoon. Her free-floating anxiety returned with a vengeance.

Rachael wrenched away from the front door and returned to her desk. She scooped up the book on mysticism and crossed the floor to the curtain leading into her apartment. Perhaps a cup of tea would settle her nerves. She was two steps into her kitchen when she saw him there, grinning like an apparition from her worst nightmare.

"Raaachael," he rasped. A snake's hiss.

Her book tumbled to the floor. One hand flew to her throat. "God help me."

She saw that he was sweating. No, not just sweating; something more grotesque. Fetid water ran from the young man in rivulets. It started at the crown of his head, dripping out of his shaggy blond hair as though he stood underneath the spray of a shower nozzle. The water made his once-handsome features tallow soft and malleable, like someone simultaneously melting and drowning.

The voice again, cutting her to the bone: "*Raaachaelll...*"

"Get out of my apartment," she sputtered. "You have no business here."

Her words brought a chuckle of amusement, as though it were the silliest statement the man had ever heard. Then his lips pressed together, his scowl fierce and not to be dissuaded. "Where is it?" he asked.

Rachael blinked, flummoxed. "Where is what?"

"The crystal."

Whatever fright she felt, whatever she assumed this confrontation to be about, paled in the dawning horror of that moment. This was no street urchin, no bum looking for a dry warm spot before braving the elements one more time. He was one of *them.* "Who are you?" she gasped.

The man stared at her, giving her a glimpse at the dark behind his eyes. Suddenly a double exposure rippled across the man's face. Something slithered around the man's brain, turning to stare out at her, and she saw him for the first time, the Being behind this man. But worse — worse — she heard a faraway voice at the bottom of a deep tunnel, hoarse with pleading, frantic to be heard: "Help me! Somebody help me *pleassseee!"*

"Get out of my head, woman," the man said. Water gurgled from the corners of his mouth. He shambled toward her, his wet tennis shoes squish-squishing across the floor. His head twitched as if in response to commands from within.

Rachael stumbled backward.

"Give me the stone," he insisted.

"But I don't have it!" she spat at him. And a subsequent flash of understanding. Wait a minute. This being was weak. He *had* to be weak, sending a mere boy in his place; didn't he know David had the stone? Maybe this creature was not all-powerful, after all. Maybe he had spread himself too thin. Perhaps she could reach down with her mind and touch this man, the true self, and shake him out of his trance—

"Your power's no good here!" she shouted at him. "Let this boy go!"

Then she saw the steak knife the man had stolen from the dishpan beside the sink. He brought it from behind his back and raised it before him. It was grasped tight in one wet hand.

"For the lasssttt time," he hissed, "give me the stone."

"Please," she begged, backing away, "don't you know I don't have it?"

He lurched toward her.

"Don't—!"

But the blade cut a path of savage pain, catching her just below her right shoulder.

He withdrew the knife. Slammed her against the kitchen table with a loud crash. And raised the blade above his head.

41

Fire games

1

They climbed out of the truck. Red picked up the five-gallon can of gasoline, Bobby the one-gallon can. Instinctively, they turned to David.

"Let's go around the building," he said in a low voice. He blinked against the mist, his head slightly bowed like the others. "There must be a fire exit back there."

"Why not the front doors?" asked Bobby.

David shook his head. "Probably locked tight. Besides, do you want to go inside after what we saw yesterday?"

His friend blanched with the memory of that face clinging onto the front of the bathhouse, a spider and its web. He shuddered his reply.

"Hey," Red called out to them. "Look at this." He stood off to the right by a chain-link fence. He pointed across the parking lot to where the building met the ground. "I think I see a basement window over here."

David and Bobby came up beside him and looked. Sure enough, partially hidden by a pile of boxes and assorted garbage, a low rectangular window peeked through.

"Perfect," Bobby said. "A fire down there will burn through the whole place."

True; yet David hesitated, appraising their odds. Besides involving a climb over the fence, lugging the gas cans, that would put them squarely on Victor's territory. It would be hard to make a fast getaway. But Bobby was right: A fire in the basement stood a good chance of thoroughly spreading.

He glanced at the Caverns, his skin crawling. Every moment in its presence was an abomination. Every moment the danger multiplied geometrically. "Let's do it."

Red, the tallest of the three, clambered over first. Navigating the spiked top proved more difficult than first appearances credited. His height and long legs worked against him. Still, up and over he went, dropping to the asphalt parking lot on the other side.

"My turn," Bobby said. He climbed to the top, his tennis shoes digging into the rusty chain links for holds. While he balanced at the top, David hoisted the five-gallon can of gasoline up to him. Grunting, Bobby lifted it over to the other side and handed it to Red, who stretched up to receive it.

The one-gallon can was a breeze compared to the first, quickly dispatched and onto Red's side in moments. With the task done Bobby swung his leg over and scrambled down the other side.

David followed suit, though this bit of gymnastics pained his back as he went over the top. A curious image revealed itself as he dropped down to join the others: that of a boy climbing over this very fence. He'd scraped himself on one of the wire teeth, the boy; a piece of his sweatshirt had gotten caught in the chain link. No face accompanied this fleeting vision: just the sensation of the boy's movement, up and down the fence.

"So far so good," Bobby whispered.

"Yeah," David agreed, "but a SWAT team we aren't. Come on."

They raced across the parking lot, mindful of the clumps of weeds shooting through the broken asphalt and the dozens of shattered bottles and sparkling glass. Their rough footsteps were loud, surely a giveaway to whatever forces lurked inside the building. As they neared the discarded pile of boxes and trash, David voiced his suspicion.

"This is too easy," he said in hushed undertones. "It's too quiet. It feels like we're being set up."

"Oh, come on," Red sighed. He looked away from them and stared at the brick building. "Let's take advantage of this quiet while we've got the chance."

Bobby set down the one-gallon can he'd carried and boldly stepped forward to inspect the low, rectangular window.

"Careful," David warned.

Bobby pushed past some of the boxes and dropped to one knee. The window was dirt grimed, almost opaque. "I can't see inside," he reported. "No telling where this window leads."

"Is it locked?" David asked.

"Not sure."

"Keep watch," he instructed Red, and bent to join Bobby by the window. The latch was obviously on the inside. Then again, the window could be false, never meant to open in the first place.

"Should I kick it in?" Bobby wondered.

"No," David answered. He reached out to touch it, and again a curious image flashed through his skull of the boy snatched through this very window, pulled inside because it opened all right, a Venus's-flytrap—

He laid his hand against the glass and pushed. Nothing happened. He twisted his body closer and placed both hands against the window's metal frame. Again, he pushed. The window made a juddering sound and squealed open.

They gaped at each other. "Yes," David whooped. "Yes!"

His pleasure was interrupted by something oily being splashed onto his back and shoulders. He swiveled around to look and was rewarded with a smelly splash across the side of his face and neck. "What the hell...?"

Bobby raised an arm across his eyes; he too was being hit with the liquid. He started to raise himself when Red's voice stalled him with its implicit warning.

"Stay where you are."

"Red," David gasped. "What are you doing?"

"What's it look like I'm doing, shithead?"

And he continued to splatter them with gasoline, the five-gallon can breathing metallically with each splash.

2

David started to break out of his kneeling position when Red thumbed back the lid to his lighter. One tiny yellow flame had never looked so deadly. "I told you to stay put."

His face looked alarmingly different in the foggy, gunmetal light. The eyes were all pupils, encased by a thin ring of white. Tufts of shaggy orange hair puffed with the damp breeze, the curls writhing like a restless nest of snakes. Even the closely cropped beard seemed to move, each wiry hair alive unto itself. But the most ominous sight was his nose — blood dribbled out of each nostril, only to be licked up by Red's roving tongue with a catlike gesture. Each little shake and tilt of his head spurred on the flow of blood.

"Red? What's wrong? What is happening to you?"

"The real question at hand is: What's going to happen *to you?*" This amused Red. He thought that was just too rich. His wheezy laughter let loose another liquid spray from his nostrils. It painted his chin as it streamed down both sides of his neck. "My wants are very simple. And what I want is for you to give me the crystal."

Silence.

He held up the lighter and once again flicked a yellow flame. "A simple choice, wouldn't you say?"

"Don't do it," Bobby said to David.

"That could prove a painful decision." Red motioned with his free hand. "Now give it to me."

David slowly reached into his breast pocket.

Bobby grabbed his arm. "Don't do it," he insisted once again.

"What other choice do we have?" David answered, but out of the corner of his eye he winked.

Bobby's grip on David's arm loosened. Warily, he looked at Red.

The crystal was ominously silent in David's hand, dead, as though it understood the transaction about to take place.

"What have you done with Red?" he demanded.

Red cocked his bloodied head, amused. "He's in safekeeping," the voice rasped, and to their amazement Red lifted up his sweatshirt to reveal his white stomach. As they watched, the skin began to undulate as though under great pressure. Incredibly, a face no more than five inches high squeezed against the flesh of his stomach. Tiny eyes bulged behind shut lids, mouth open with a tormented, sucking-for-air scream. It was Red's face jutting out like a baseball; a tiny hand punched at the stomach cell wall.

"He'll stay there until we're finished," the thing mastering Red's body said. He slapped the face and tiny hand down, down, the stomach going smooth again as the sweatshirt dropped back over it.

It was a mercy, covering that horrible sight. Both of them were unsettled far more than either one cared to admit. But it also roused in David a necessary anger, and he let these instincts carry him.

Outraged, he thrust the crystal toward Red.

"Get out of him, you son of a bitch! Leave him alone!"

Red only threw back his head and howled with chilling laughter. "That won't work on me," he cackled, immensely pleased with himself. "You have to be *dead* first."

"You're lying," David sputtered. He stole an uncertain glance at the crystal. It had not powered into life.

"Now give it to me. The big bad wolf wants it." Red's face jumped and twitched, showing utter blankness and vulpine cunning.

"You want it?" David screamed. "Then go fucking get it!" And he pitched the gemstone far across the parking lot.

Red's jaw dropped. He was enraged, torn with a desire to rip these two apart with his bare hands, and to run after the crystal. With a warning snarl, he galloped after the stone.

Quickly, they scrambled to their feet. Bobby was after Red like a shot, sprinting across the parking lot even before David had straightened his aching legs. Red was about twenty yards away, hunkered down in a frantic sweep for the crystal. The fog-dimmed light and the shattered glass strewn across the lot conspired against an easy search.

Bobby jumped onto Red's back, plowing into him from behind. They tumbled to the dirty asphalt with mingled cries of protest. He struck out blindly, furiously, pummeling this bloody creature with his fists. But Red was strong with his new power. He snatched at Bobby's jacket, hands hooked into talons, and wrestled him off of his back. Bobby smacked against the concrete. Red pounced onto his stomach, holding him in a wrestler's grip. Bobby turned his head, steeling himself for punches. And then he saw the crystal, like a forgotten chunk of glass, resting amongst a clump of weeds. The thing on top of him followed his gaze. "No—!"

Red scrabbled forward on his hands and knees, blood foaming across his chin, and snatched the stone into a grubby paw.

"Mine!" Red bellowed. He rolled onto his ass, the gemstone held aloft like the torch on the statue of liberty. Blood gushed copiously from his nostrils.

Bobby scooted away, trying to sit up. Terrified.

"Now watch!" Red shouted. "Now watch my powers multiply—"

His screech was interrupted by his own gargling sound as liquid splashed across his face. Triumph turned into startled protests. "Stop! Stop!"

Bobby looked to his left. A few feet away stood David, gas can grasped with both hands as he shook gasoline onto Red's prone body. His eyes were huge silver dollars, his teeth clamped tight. He advanced with deliberation, soaking Red head to foot with the gasoline. "There, you fucker! Take this!" When the one-gallon can emptied he threw it aside, where it clanged to the ground. He dug into his trousers and produced his own lighter. "It's a simple choice, wouldn't you say? Now give me the crystal."

Red broke into a bloody grin. "You wouldn't dare. There's gasoline over both of you. You'll burn yourselves as well."

A flicker of doubt crossed David's face before determination righted itself. "Then we'll all burn, if it means getting rid of you."

Bobby came to his feet and brushed himself off. He pulled books of matches from his pocket, but held them at arm's length. It was true, he stank of gasoline, and despite the mist dampening him he'd probably all too easily go up in flames.

The thing that had stolen control of Red's body held up a hand, fingers spread in a gesture approximating an inch. "That's how much of me is in this boy. Burn me and all you succeed in doing is killing your precious Red."

"Give me the stone."

"Never."

The bloodied creature was on his knees, starting to stand up. "It's too late! I'm coming alive all around you—"

The earth shook. The Caverns wailed with a grinding of gears. A light flipped on in the basement window.

Bobby tossed a lighted match. It fell short, extinguishing during its short arc in the air. But Red jerked his head in Bobby's direction, furious.

"You," he hissed. "I have a special room for you."

With a cry, David jumped forward as though playing a game of tag, a plastic lighter clenched between his fingers. His right hand dipped to touch Red's shoulder. And he sprang back as flames coughed into ferocious life.

The fire flashed across Red's chest and shoulders, catching his lower neck and chin. Briefly, he looked like one of those martyrs who sit in protest and set themselves on fire. The flames ate at the carrot-colored hairs of his beard, exploding up the left side of his face to singe the mop of hair above his face. He flapped at it with his hands — and both hands burst into yellow orbs of flames. These he beat against his torso and legs in an attempt to put out the fire, but instead he ignited his gasoline-soaked clothes.

It was unbearable to watch. The stench of cooking flesh gagged David and made him throw a hand over his nose and mouth.

Bobby stumbled toward David and fell against him, anguished. He could not watch.

David did. He didn't want to, but Red still clutched the crystal. It was imperative they get it back.

What was left of Red writhed on the pavement, thrashing against the flames. But something else: the way he slammed his fists against his stomach, his chest, and then higher to his throat, as if something were moving up, up, into his charred face. His throat worked, his mouth yawned opened, and a terrible scream gushed out, a sound like a man who had just discovered he was on fire. Red's eyes popped open.

"No!" David muttered, not wanting to believe.

An anguished cry: *"Get him out of meee!"*

And Red tossed the crystal toward David, the blackened flesh of his hand curled into a claw.

David let go of Bobby and bent to one knee, where he scooped the crystal into his hand. It was warm.

"Get him!" Red gasped. "Please, before—"

He had no opportunity to finish.

A dark shadow swarmed out of Red's mouth and nostrils. It rose like a genie out of Aladdin's lamp, smoking the air. David and Bobby stepped back as this charcoal cloud wrapped itself around Red. The air quickened, spun clockwise. Flames no longer ate at him, but were doused by this saturating wind. He curled into a fetal position, chin tucked almost touching his knees, and the dark swarm devoured him.

"Run, cowards," they heard Red say — though which one was speaking, they did not know. "Run home, and see my work."

The air plumbed with smoke and steam. Bits of pebbles were hoisted with the tornado wind. When all had settled, Red was gone, the asphalt black with his image.

3

They clambered back over the fence, dropping to the other side. All they wanted was to get away from this loathsome place. Their legs were so wobbly they could barely stand without holding on to each other.

They dashed across the street to Red's truck. Keys dangled from the ignition. With grateful sighs of relief, they both slid into their seats. On the third try the engine kicked over.

They glanced at each other. The shame and sheer terror over the outcome of their fiasco weighed heavily upon them. In the confined space of the car, they stank of gasoline. To David, they stank of miserable failure. Victor was winning, winning; and soon his time would once again fall upon the city.

There seemed nothing to say. David backed the car up, then shot forward with a squeal of tires. He was determined to put as much distance from him and this nightmare as possible.

And drove headlong toward an even greater nightmare waiting for them at the shop.

42

Victor returns the favor

1

"**L**ook," David said. It came out a sandpaper whisper.

They pulled up in front of the shop.

The front door to the Déjà Vu bookstore banged desolately in the wind.

2

Rachael was in the kitchen.

On the floor. A bloodied knife beside her.

"Oh no!" David cried as he burst into the kitchen. "Bobby!"

But Bobby had taken up the rear, his eyes taking in the vandalism to the shop. Books lay in bulky piles on the floor. Entire shelves had been knocked to the floor or pushed into each other, where they rested uncertainly.

And now David shouted from the kitchen.

He tore himself away from the damage and elbowed through the curtained partition. David was kneeling beside Rachael. Her eyes were closed, her face ashen against her red hair. It was impossible to determine the color of the blouse she wore, it was so blood soaked.

More blood. Would they ever again be free of its sight, its coppery smell?

Bobby summoned the courage to ask: "Is she—?"

"Alive," David sighed with infinite relief. He lay her hand back down by her side. "She still has a pulse." Leaning closer, he reached out with his hand and lightly feathered the rips in her blouse. His voice choked. "She's been stabbed!"

Bobby shook his head and cursed. "How can that goddamned thing be everywhere? I just don't understand."

"Call 911. Get an ambulance over here. Fast!"

Bobby scooted away and stumbled toward the telephone in the living room. He picked up the receiver and punched in 911. Then: tap tap. The jiggle for a dial tone.

Breathless, he held out the receiver. "Listen."

David heard. Even across the space of the room he heard it, pouring out of the phone.

Which one is it now? he thought bitterly. *"Devil's Gun"? "Love Hangover"? "Don't Leave Me This Way"? What old song ripe with nostalgia has been plucked from our minds?* Ahh, he recognized it, as he knew he would, an old ditty from 1976. Victor's macabre humor strikes again.

> *There just ain't enough angels*
> *To walk upon the earth*
> *Bathe me in that heavenly glow, baby*
> *Show me what you're worth*

Bobby slammed down the receiver. He'd gone white. "Now what?"

David shook his head.

"I'll go next door," he offered.

"No. I don't want us separated."

"We can't let her die!"

David was adamant. "We won't. But we have to stay here and defend ourselves. Rachael—"

He froze in midsentence, eyes bugging out in surprise. He glanced at Mrs. Black's hand cradled within his own.

David, softly: "Look."

She was summoning herself up from unconsciousness, willing herself awake. She squeezed his hand.

"Mrs. Black?" he whispered. "Rachael?"

Her eyelids rolled back. The hazel eyes, once so piercing and clear, were clouded by a skein of white. Her shallow breathing was phlegmy and labored.

"What is it?"

She motioned him closer.

"He's coming," Rachael said.

3

She wanted to be moved to the couch in the living room. With reservations they obliged, wincing as every movement racked her with new pain. They brought fresh hand towels from the kitchen and pressed them against her wounds to stem the flow of blood. Most of the knife sticks, they discovered, were superficial. One or two they eyed ominously.

And they waited for the inevitable question, which finally came after Rachael was fairly comfortable and more alert.

"Where is Red?"

Silence. Each passing moment a pointed finger of accusation.

David crouched beside her. It was hard to meet her stare, to look at her with this news. He cleared his throat. "I don't know how to tell you this," he began, and took her hand into his own.

Abruptly her expression changed. Puzzled concern dropped away. Shock and anger lit her face. She yanked her hand away as though it had been scalded.

"He's dead — Oh, my god — You!" she spat. "You killed him?"

"No, Rachael—"

"Don't lie! You burned him up. I saw. I saw what you did to my son!"

David, distraught, turned to Bobby for consolation. His friend's face was pinched with shame and concern. He turned back to Rachael.

"Victor killed him, not me," he insisted breathlessly. "Look inside me if you can, and you'll see. That monster got into him somehow. Got into his *head,* and took over. He was going to burn us up unless we gave him the stone. I'm sorry. I — I had to stop him."

Rachael shook her head back and forth; she was having none of this. Exhaustion and dismay sank into her. "See what you've done? What you've brought to our house? Death for my son. And for me."

"No," David insisted. "Not you. We'll get help."

A tight smile, grim. "That blond didn't have good aim, but he still managed to give me a few good sticks." As if to punctuate the seriousness of her words she broke into a phlegmy coughing jag.

Bobby raised his head with an almost premonitional fear. "A ... blond man did this to you?"

Rachael nodded, her coughing jag back under control. Her hand fluttered in the air. "Longish blond hair. Blue eyes. He snuck into the kitchen and surprised me."

Bobby collapsed heavily into a nearby chair. He buried his face in his hands.

"It doesn't mean it was Mick," David said stubbornly.

Bobby would not answer. He knew. They both knew.

"I got the knife away from him," Rachael continued. "Gave him a good stick myself. He fled, tearing up the shop as he went." She was breathing easier now, in this new position.

"I'm sorry," David apologized. He looked at her and let her see the naked truth on his face. "I'm so sorry this happened."

"Yeah. Me too." She licked her dry lips. "But I think I found something. About Victor. Before I was interrupted."

Hope brightened David's face.

"Trouble," she said. "That's all he is. Trouble and death." Her eyes closed, then rolled slowly back open. "Who knows what he is, or where he came from? Maybe we'll never know. Some questions just don't have answers."

"Tell us," he begged, excitement in his voice. "Hurry."

Hurry. Yes, she would hurry. For she alone felt the wind on her face. She alone heard the tick tick tick of escaping time. And she alone felt the creature, like a blast of warm air rushing ahead of a subway train, expanding out of his home, coming for them.

4

"Our thoughts," she gasped. "He's our thoughts."

David looked blankly at her.

Bobby scratched his head.

"Thoughts are like blueprints," she explained. She paused, taking a breath. "They have their own power. Their own energy. What we send out shapes the world. Energy is never destroyed, you know. Only changed into another form. So what we send out stays with us."

David's face remained frozen in confusion. Bobby shared this confusion; when Rachael wasn't looking, he rolled his eyes at David.

She continued. "Negative energy is particularly powerful. It feeds upon itself, and gains strength, the way a magnet attracts metal. Over hundreds of years this energy can literally manifest into its own personality. It can become what some cultures call a Hungry Ghost."

"A Hungry Ghost?" Bobby frowned. It was a name out of a comic book.

But David felt a chill across his face. Something half-remembered bobbed near the surface of his thoughts. He heard a crackling fire and a voice: *We called it the Eater of Souls.*

"Where did you learn this?" David asked.

She waved vaguely toward the kitchen. "A book. I was reading. Then—" Rachael closed her eyes. This was wearing her out, but still she pressed ahead. "Listen to me. This type of demon roams the world in constant states of hunger and thirst. Their agitation can disrupt nature, causing natural disasters."

Bobby's eyes widened. "The storm," he breathed. He stole a glance at David.

"This creature can change its shape to fit any requirements. It strikes, and feeds, wherever there is despair and indifference. All it cares about is getting a foothold into our world." She fell into another agitated fit of coughing. "Got to ... rest," she gasped. Her body shook.

Bobby drew closer, kneeling beside David. "Mrs. Black, if Victor is one of these ghosts or whatever you call it — does the book say how to kill it?"

Her face fell into shadow. Perhaps it was a trick of late-afternoon light. Her hazel eyes rolled in their sockets. "He can't be killed."

Bobby looked at her, stricken.

"You can't kill a thing of pure energy."

"Maybe not," David conceded. "But you can shut off the power at its source."

Rachael grasped at her chest and moaned, her hands twisting the towels with her pain. She was at the bottom of her reserves, worn out. Her jaw worked but no sound was coming out.

Bobby touched David's shoulder. "We've got to get her to a hospital. It's worth the risk of our separating."

He was right, and David knew it. Besides, his conscience weighed with remorse over Red's death; he couldn't bear adding Rachael to their growing list of casualties. "Okay. Go next door and see if you can find a phone."

An agitated moan from Rachael. Bobby stopped in his tracks.

And David felt it then, a pressure against his skull, a pushing through. Rachael's voice spilled into his head.

Stay. It's too late.

Incredibly, David reached out with his mind in the same fashion.

Hold on, Rachael. We'll get you help.

Too late. It's too late—

No! Don't say that! Feeling in her a surge of unparalleled terror.

Suddenly, shockingly:

Run! RUN!

What? Misinterpreting her panic. Confused by this turn of events.

HIDE!

A dark wet wind slapped his face. Gaseous. Revolting. It was directed at Rachael, but because their minds were connected he experienced it through her.

Bobby was backing away from the wall. "Jesus," he moaned. "Not again. Oh Christ! Not again...!"

Suddenly, David knew.

He knew even before he glanced up and away from Mrs. Black's face. Even before he saw brackish water dribbling along the ceiling and spilling down the wall directly behind the couch where Rachael lay.

They had paid Victor a call.

And now he was returning the favor.

5

The temperature in the apartment jumped ten degrees. Waves of moist heat fanned out from the wall. Droplets of water danced on the ceiling and began to merge into small rivers. The water thickened as it trickled down the wall, bubbling like hot jelly. It darkened into an algae green, the color of scum on stagnant water.

The entire wall began to ooze. Melt. Sizzle.

Runners of water took on the tangled shape of underbrush. Gelatinous branches slithered across the wall in search of a final shape. A network of veins and nerves began to appear.

"God, no!"

With a cry of disgust David lunged forward and hooked his hands underneath the sofa, intent on pulling Rachael away from the wall. But before he could budge her an inch, one of the mossy green cords whipped away from the wall and smacked him backwards. He crashed onto his rear end with a tumble of hands and legs.

The livery cords slithered across the face of the wall with lightning speed, braiding together into the viscous frame of a giant head. The bubbling stew puffed away from the wall, which was no longer a wall.

And began to outline the face of a devil.

The face seemed to borrow its features from every Halloween ghoulie mask that mothers buy their children in grocery stores, to low-budget horror movie schlock. It was a compilation of everything familiar, everything that had ever frightened them as children: It was the boogieman and the devil, and yet utterly unique unto itself. A pointed chin. A protruding nose. Wickedly pointed ears. The eye sockets deepened, darkened, and sputtered into red life, the eyes of a furnace. Hair churned above the eyes like Medusa's crown of snakes.

Yet no flesh appeared. Only this animated, three-dimensional outline formed by the mucusy strands of moss and mold. An overripe smell swallowed all the fresh air out of the room. It was bacterial and spongy, the underbelly of things that grow in the dark.

No more than minutes had passed.

Minutes, and here was the monster with his demon face and furnace-lit eyes.

The apartment rattled down to its foundation. Glasses and dishes fell from heaving cabinets, exploding onto countertops and the tile floor.

Victor's face was fleshing in — and yet still not flesh — as the viscous cords shaded in the cartoon outline of his features. His breath wheezed with the mechanical hiss and suction of steamroom apparatus. He growled his welcome and looked about the room.

Rachael, in the extremity of pain and terror, began to moan.

The paralysis broke. David scrambled to his feet, fists thrust out ahead of him.

Vulpine lips parted, revealing shockingly huge fangs and yellow teeth. The inside of the thing's mouth, unlike the rest of his features, was completely formed. They glimpsed a raw, cavernous mouth as the lips opened. A mottled tongue snaked and darted. And the warning snarl that issued out of that mouth was spine shattering.

"One step closer," Victor growled at David, "and the woman is mine." He punctuated his threat by snapping together his huge jaws, teeth grinding against teeth. He was inches from Rachael's prone body.

David recoiled with a yelp of frustration. He stood his ground, sweating.

Bobby sidled up beside him.

"Well, well," Victor chuckled. "The fearless monster-killers, all gathered into one room. How extraordinarily convenient."

His voice seemed to go right through their heads, through their bodies, jabbing with icy fingers.

"Why are you here?" David demanded.

"To finish what *you* started," Victor answered.

Bobby was trembling with fury. "I've never hated anything so much as I do you," he said with disgust.

The thing on the wall laughed.

David dug into his pants pocket and grasped the crystal. It tingled with that mysterious energy. He was about to pull it out of his pants when Victor growled his disapproval.

"Bring out that toy and I'll snap off the woman's head," he warned, and dipped his snout low against Rachael, who twisted away from his touch.

Perspiration blurred David's vision. He felt sick with panic. He looked at the sinewy cords that made up Victor's face. Was this thing really here? Or was this just another vehicle for that demonic life force?

The distinction somehow mattered. Mattered a great deal.

He pointed at the giant face. "Go away," he ordered, though his voice wavered with fright. "You're just an image. A mirage. Because you can't leave the Caverns any more. Isn't that right?"

"I'm here now," Victor answered. "And soon you will all be with me."

"Leave Rachael out of this," David said. "It's Bobby and me you want, not her."

The creepshow face glanced down at Rachael, his eyes narrowing. "You weren't supposed to help. You were supposed to turn them away. Now, we have our own score to settle."

Rachael summoned her strength. "You've already taken my son."

Victor snorted. "Willingly, my dear. He came to me with open arms."

That blasphemy rankled her; she squirmed with anger.

Bobby lay a hand on David's back, the pressure seeming to say *Do something*. Yes — but what? Should he risk using the crystal, and possibly hurt Rachael by his own ineptitude?

"All your friends are with me," Victor continued. He clearly enjoyed the terror this bit of news caused them. "This 'life' of yours has nothing to offer now."

David's skin crawled at the image of Alex and Mick in this creature's hellish home. He was about to respond when he felt a probing against his head, and he sensed Rachael touching his mind.

Use the crystal.

She was weak, her thought frequency little more than a whisper. Yet it was fantastic, this communication. As if, nearing death, her abilities were blooming open in a final display.

Seconds ticked off loud in David's ears. *How? How do I use it?* He threw the question out at her, even though he was terrified that Victor could somehow intercept their secret messages.

And she answered, simply:

Send it away. Together—

A charge ran through him. He and Bobby at the Caverns. Joining hands. Combining this energy between them. And last night, in this very room.

"What are you doing?" the beast demanded. He eyed them suspiciously, his steamroom growl hesitant.

David groped for Bobby's hand.

"Be still," Victor cautioned. "Move away—"

"Leave us alone!" David shouted, and advanced. He thrust the gemstone at the giant face. The crystal, freed from his pocket, sputtered into fiery blue light.

The monster reared back in surprise.

Rachael, her face the color of pizza dough, watched through her haze of pain.

David and Bobby pushed forward. "Get out of here! This place is off-limits!"

Victor's shock at David's sudden move gave way to fury. His nostrils flared; his breath snorted like an angry bull. The spongy face lifted with predatory swiftness.

"This is what I think of your weapon!" Victor shouted.

The ghastly mouth opened. Wide. Wider. The raw throat, the yellow fangs surrounded by rows of pointed teeth: David and Bobby stared with incredulity.

Before they could stop him — before either of them knew what was happening — the creature lunged, jaws snapping.

And bit Rachael in half.

6

An explosion of blood.

Anguished screams.

Like some great white shark, Victor dipped his head and swallowed Rachael to her waist. She was yanked up and off the couch, legs kicking the air. His face whipped side to side with the frenzied feeding. They heard an obscene crunch of bones snapping and rending flesh as the woman sank deeper into the monster's foaming mouth.

David's mind was still connected with Rachael. A high-pitched wail

Aieeee—

roared through his brain and then — mercifully — an explosion, the light bulb of her consciousness shattered beyond repair. He staggered backward in revulsion and fell to his knees. He was too overcome with grief to leap upon that face, to pull apart the lips frothing with blood and somehow save her.

Screams rent the air — David and Bobby adding their voices to the wailing.

Victor's mossy eyes rolled in ecstasy. A noise escaped his throat — a high-pitched keening of sweet revenge. Rachael's rag-doll legs slapped against this gargoyle's snout. Her blood sprayed the couch.

Bobby had turned away, retching his guts out.

Victor raised his throat to swallow, and the last of Rachael's legs slid out of sight. The spongy face convulsed and gulped as he swallowed. A tongue snaked out to wipe the lips clean.

David raised a fist, his eyes blinded by tears.

"How many, Victor? How many are you going to kill!"

Fiery eyes leveled David with a stare.

"All," the thing gloated in triumph. *"I shall have you all!"*

Followed by a dragon's roar, its breath the reek of a charnel house.

The furnace eyes closed.

The mossy face collapsed, giving up its animation.

The wall sizzled and churned.

Neither Bobby nor David watched. They had fallen together, holding onto each other in the extremity of their grief and horror.

Steam hissed the air. And Victor was gone.

7

David was the first to raise his tear-stained face. He choked on the sight that greeted him, and nudged Bobby.

They stared.

Where the creature's face had been, there appeared a door.

It was slimy green. Comprised of the same viscous strands that had formed Victor's face.

No choice, now.

This was it.

Their one-way ticket into the Caverns.

3

Disco inferno

Burn baby burn
It's a disco inferno
Burn baby burn
Burning down the house y'all

—Trammps

43

Inside

1

They faced each other, stunned, unable to move, in the center of Rachael's den. The phantom doorway shimmered and pulsed with invitation. Slowly, David extended his hands, and Bobby took them, the two forming a circle. A whistling wind shrieked outside the apartment. At the window, milky faces with snapping fangs pressed against the glass. The sentries watched with ridicule and contempt.

"For Eddie," David said urgently.

"For Mick," Bobby echoed. "And all the others."

David nodded. "Yes. All the others."

The two men, their faces white from what they had seen, gazed into each other. They felt the bond cementing them together, giving them strength to face the horror that they knew lay before them. Years of friendship in ordinary times could never have matched its depth.

"You know," David broke the spell by saying, "no one would call us cowards if we ran."

"It's gone beyond a question of courage," Bobby said. A fire shone within his dark pupils. "I just know we're the only ones who can do this. I *have* to do it."

David bowed his head. He could not voice his worst fear: that at the moment of confrontation he would be unable to find this creature's Achilles' heel, even with the stone. That they might yet be doomed to failure — and death.

Bobby clasped him on the shoulder. "Don't worry," he soothed, reading David's despair. "You'll know what to do when the time comes."

"I hope so."

"Just trust your instincts. I do."

David's heart swelled. Taking strength from their connection, his voice brimmed with emotion. "Whatever happens," he stammered, "I want you to know you're the most courageous friend I've ever had."

Fiercely, they embraced. It felt good, this contact; comfortable and right. For a moment, the terrors fell away. Suddenly they were forced apart by unearthly sounds at the window. Cheshire Cat faces snickered at their display. A man with half his neck torn out clicked dirty fingernails against the rain-splattered glass. A youngish black woman pawed her breasts with delight and stuck out her tongue, laughing with a dark-red mouth and yellow teeth grown razor-sharp.

The sight made Bobby tremble. "I hate them."

"Yes. I hate what they've become. But ignore them. It's Victor's fault. He steals the good and leaves behind something twisted."

A terrible vision filled Bobby's head. "What if they're *all* growing as powerful as that monster! What then? How do we fight so many?"

David could see Bobby's resolve begin to waver. He grasped his friend's forearm and exerted firm pressure. "Stop it!" *Don't panic,* he thought wildly. *Don't panic, or we'll be lost.* So he blurted out the first words that popped into his head, words he hoped would give courage to them both — and was pleased to hear their rightness:

"I love you Bobby. We can't fail now."

Bobby met his gaze. His eyes showed his love — yet the image of Mick and the peril he must be facing was there, clouding everything.

David pulled him into an embrace. They were too caught up in the moment to notice that their union had unleashed the crackle of electricity in the room, and that the man and woman at the window had suddenly retreated, laughing no longer.

David turned his face to the hateful door. It perched above the couch, stretching almost to the ceiling. It undulated as though it sat at the bottom of a lake, currents rolling over it. A sort of jelly ooze dribbled down its length and puddled onto the back of the couch. They would have to step onto the blood-splattered sofa, exactly where Rachael had been killed, to step through the doorway. He imagined touching that doorknob, and sensed that it would feel like thrusting his hand into an algae-slick pool of stagnant water.

And when they opened the door — what would they be stepping into? Perhaps the very heart of the Caverns, and its horrible occupant?

The steel edge of revenge rose in him. He began to move, his arms still around Bobby. "For love," he said, guiding them toward the door. "And justice."

2

His tennis shoes sank into the stained splotch on the couch with a muddy sigh. David balanced himself, one foot on the upper lip of the couch, and reached out his hand.

The doorknob moved under his fingertips, bits of green tissue surging around his fingers. He jerked his hand away. Strands of living moss wriggled wormlike and fell to the couch, where, like leeches, they supped on the blood-soaked material. David's face contorted in disgust. He gritted his teeth. With a burst of courage he reached for the doorknob and yanked open the living door.

He gasped — but with relief. He raised himself and walked through, one foot on the couch, the other landing on wet pavement.

Bobby squinted after him, tense and anxious.

David surveyed his surroundings. He stood in the middle of the street, twenty feet from the Caverns' front steps. A strong wind tugged at his blood-splattered clothes and blew his hair. The doorway back into Rachael's apartment looked like a portal into another dimension, as if a giant pair of scissors had cut a rectangle out of the fabric of reality. Even now he could see it telescoping away.

Back through that opening, Bobby watched him with mounting alarm.

"Hurry!" David shouted against the wind. "Come on through!"

Bobby glanced back to the den window. Victor's sentinels watched him with leering smirks on their faces. Satisfied that their job was now complete, they eddied into the darkness, and were gone.

He steadied himself on the top rim of the couch. He kicked at one of the leechlike bits of green tissue and it burst open with its stolen blood. Struggling to keep his nausea in check, he propelled himself through the door. He fearfully avoided touching the jamb.

"You okay?" David asked, as he helped his friend through the door.

He nodded, and looked around.

"At least we aren't inside that place," he said.

"No. Not yet, anyway."

A bubbling sound caught their attention. They turned simultaneously to look behind them. The door frame quivered and sagged, the veinlike strands giving up its shape. They could still see into Rachael and Red's apartment, but only for a second more; the door collapsed into a sizzling heap, a stewing puddle upon the black pavement.

Flickering light, like heat lightning before a storm, strobed the foggy sky. They faced the bathhouse. Beams of neon-colored light pierced the top floor's boarded-up windows.

Underneath it all, the roll of distant thunder: music. An old Bonnie Pointer song, "Heaven Must Have Sent You."

David began to march toward the Caverns' front doors.

Bobby scrambled after him, tugging on David's sleeve. "We can't just walk in through the front," he said, aghast.

"That is *exactly* what I intend to do," David announced. His voice was hard, determined. "We're expected. We're his *guests.*"

He walked up the three steps to the front door. He meant to just yank it open, to just bully his way inside, but he was stopped by an overwhelming fright.

He knew in that moment that his whole adult life had come to this — gathering enough courage to open doors that might be better off closed. It began back in New York, when he had startled the burglar in his apartment. Despite all his efforts at re-establishing a normal life, he had not been able to shake the feeling of menace that had stalked him, always waiting for him just on the other side of a door, around a corner, hidden in the darkness.

This was the final door. Now to confront the menace at last.

"God help us," David murmured.

Expecting claws, teeth — any unspeakable horror — he drew air between his teeth and pulled the metal door. It swung open on squealing hinges.

He went inside, Bobby very close, his trailing shadow.

3

Warm air breathed over them, eucalyptus-scented. Surprisingly comforting, after the chilling winds. The heavy black door screeched shut, cutting them off from the outside. Both jumped at the finality of that closure. Nervously, standing close, they looked around them.

They stood in a small, spare foyer. Durable industrial gray carpeting on the floor. Bobby noticed the dark stain on the carpet but thought better of mentioning it to David. Movie posters decorated the walls. Scantily clad gladiators. Cinema Hercules Steve Reeves, in *Hercules and the Minotaur*. Stills from the same movie, of damsels chained to rocks in an ominous cavern, were everywhere.

"I thought this place was condemned," David whispered, puzzled by how this entry looked so ... ready to receive guests.

"Not condemned," a man's voice startled them by saying. "Temporarily shut down, in preparation for its new owner."

They whirled in the direction of the strange voice.

Directly in front of them was a glassed-in counter, like a movie ticket booth. A broad-shouldered black man addressed them. His smile was all teeth. He was naked (at least from the waist up; the counter hid the rest). Tight curls of black hair were flecked gray at the temples.

"Can't go inside without a ticket," the man admonished. The dreamy expression on his face never wavered. He turned to a machine just out of sight and depressed a button. A ticket popped onto the counter. He repeated the process, and another ticket joined the first.

They drew closer.

Admit One, each ticket read. Underneath, in red ink: a drawing of each of their faces.

David bit his lower lip. Bobby clapped a hand over his mouth.

On each ticket, their faces appeared horribly mutilated. David's had no eyes; maggots swarmed in the sockets. His head was split open, as though it had been crushed between two powerful hands. Bobby's face was partially eaten, his right cheek a gaping hole where his skeleton glistened through sinewy cartilage.

The man pushed the gruesome tickets under the bowl slot of the glass partition.

David waved a hand. "No!"

"Oh, but I must insist," the man said in that dreamy monotone. He jerked a thumb at a hallway entrance, and a turnstile. "Can't get through without them." At each of his wrists was a gaping slash, each long past bleeding.

David peered through the glass. Tiny irregular markings — almost hidden by the man's dark skin — completely covered the man's body. Scar tissue, pink in the low light. Scratches? No. Deeper. Puncture marks, like

teeth.

He shuddered. Yes. Teeth. This man with the faraway smile looked like he had been sewn back together. Regenerated, the teeth marks making it obvious he had been a meal for the voracious appetite of many mouths. David's teeth clattered together. "Who are you?" he managed to say.

An idiot smile. "I'm the *old* proprietor," the man answered. "Flint Stone's the name, har har." His dark eyes swirled galaxies of madness. "The new owner wants me to extend his pleasure at your arrival, tonight. He's reserved some of the best rooms of the house just for you." As he spoke, saliva dribbled from the corner of his cracked lips. He pushed two room keys with rubber bands on them next to the two tickets. Beside them he lay their towels, folded neatly, and soaked in blood.

David shoved the keys away. "We don't want rooms," he said.

Pink lips peeled back with mirth. "You may not *want* rooms," the Flint-thing said, "but He has them waiting for you anyway. Oh, *yes,* indeedy." His neck muscles bulged with suppressed mirth. A deep-throated laugh strained the stitches holding the cartoon face together. Wide. Wider. Stitches plinked undone. The laugh sobbed out.

"Oh, yes, in*deedy,*" he repeated, and his face split open.

His cheeks flapped apart and rolled back like scraps of quilted fabric. His chin dropped free and dangled several inches from his face by a bluish thread. Even as he fell apart, he laughed.

They retreated in horror. David grabbed Bobby and propelled him toward the turnstile. He pushed him against the metal bar. It would not budge.

"The tickets," Bobby pointed, but could not look at the ruined man behind the counter.

David cursed under his breath. He returned to the booth and grabbed the tickets into his hands, not wanting to look at the thing heaving with laughter behind the glass booth.

"Sign in first, gentlemen," the voice gurgling out of the jawless head ordered. A registration card appeared on the counter. The thing held out a pen.

Unable to control himself, David took it. As he began to sign their names, the card in front of his eyes turned to flesh; the pen, a scalpel; his signature, blood. He jumped away, crying out, the tickets clutched in his hand. Returning to the turnstile, he heard a fly-buzzing squeal: high-pitched, helium voices. David looked down at the tickets and saw that their faces had come alive, screaming beneath his thumb and fingers.

"What is it?" Bobby asked above the din.

"Come on," he answered, and inserted Bobby's ticket first, then his own, into the turnstile. The tinny voices screamed their suffering as they were swallowed into the machine.

Both heard Flint speak one last time.

"A room as black as night!" the thing crooned. "That's where you'll be chained. They'll come to you. *He'll* come to you. Oh god! Eternity! The FEEDING!"

They hurled through to the other side.

44

Chutes and ladders

1

"**Y**ou okay?"

"Yes. Where's the crystal?"

"In my pocket."

Now they stood in a hallway, a locker room changing area off to their immediate left. Music flowed over them, loud and yet echoey, dreamlike. The disco segued seamlessly from one song to the next without skipping a beat.

They were rooted to the spot, unwilling to take another step until they could get their bearings.

Colored lights of reds and blues and greens reflected off the glint of metal lockers, though David could discern no source for them. The walls themselves seeped color, as though the music itself pushed the neon lights through layers of plaster and board and wooden beams. Somewhere an energy source governed this place. Controlled everything: the music, the lights, the temperature.

A frosty chill: Could it all go, on a whim? Could their host plunge them into total darkness at any moment?

Bobby held out a hand. "Listen."

After a moment, David heard it. Voices. Disquieting laughter, like the sudden cough of exploding glass. These voices, too, seemed to emanate from the very walls. Shrieks of pain. Pleasure. Sobs and moans. As if the building itself cried.

"Where are they?" Bobby whispered. Despite the warm air, he shivered.

David shook his head. *Everywhere,* he thought. *They're the new ghosts haunting these halls.*

Beyond the rows of benches and lockers, the walls surrendered their smooth painted gloss and transformed into the narrowing tunnel of a deep underground cave. Imitation rock boulders jutted from the walls. Stalactites festooned the ceiling. At one point the hallway branched off into several directions.

"A maze," David whistled under his breath. "Christ Almighty."

Where the cave entrance began, a sign: BEWARE THE MINOTAUR!

"I don't suppose you know the geography of this place?" Bobby asked.

David shrugged.

"No."

"Neither do I."

"They must be similar, don't you think?"

"How do you mean?"

"Well," David frowned, his forehead squinting up. "All the baths were built about the same, weren't they? I mean, the private rooms are usually up on the top floors. Lots of hallways for cruising. The middle floor is a diversion: A snack bar, maybe a dance floor. TV room. Down below, in the basement—"

"Showers," Bobby whispered.

David remembered his tumble down a flight of stairs, and landing at the foot of the steamroom. "That's where we go. Down."

"But which tunnel?"

They chose the middle one for no reason except that it lay before them. Electric lamps in the shape of torches were mounted to the walls. This artificial light lit their way. Almost immediately the tunnel veered to the right, then swung around in a corkscrew. David took Bobby by the hand.

They followed the incline, unsure of their footing. Huge spider-webs stitched the corners of the rocky walls. Closer inspection revealed the webs were artificial. Most of them, that is.

"Thank god," Bobby breathed. "Giant spiders: I don't think I could handle that."

David nodded his agreement. He was preoccupied with mapping out this tunnel. They needed to go *down,* not up. Should they retrace their steps? The cave had branched off into several more passages, confusing their sense of direction. Better they just stick together and forge ahead.

An orange-red light painted the corridor a few steps in front of them. They rounded the corner and skidded to a stop.

"The crystal, quick!" Bobby encouraged.

David needed no urging; he had already rooted for the gemstone within his pocket. But even before his hand clamped over it he saw the stone was unnecessary.

The tunnel had flattened out into a straight hallway. Men stood around in all manner of undress, flicking glances their way with practiced boredom.

If they had expected screeching caws of alarm, hands fashioned into talons, the rushing of many feet, they were surprised. These men with hospital-white towels wrapped provocatively around their middles ignored them, looks of bored indifference on their faces. Here, a man wearing only a jockstrap leaned against the cavern wall, smoking a cigarette. There, a man in leather chaps and harness, both hands idly tugging on his nipples. Showing off, should anyone care to watch.

"They look real!" David whispered. He was reminded of the men he'd seen in the steamroom: beautiful Adonises lifted from the pages of magazines.

"No — no — they're ghosts," Bobby said, grabbing David's arm. "Look!"

Indeed: The men seemed speared by the orange fire-glow light, as though too much illumination would reduce them to angles and lines in the air: stick figures, empty shells and nothing more.

And this indifference: as though time had narrowed down into a corkscrew trail of smoke wafting from a cigarette. As though this hallway, this music thudding through the floor was immune to the erosion of time. A captured moment, a living photograph that looked as if it would never change, but instead would play itself out, over and over again.

David looked to the end of the hallway. A group of men gathered three-quarters of the way down but did not talk to each other. Beyond, the hallway speared off into tunnels again. "Come on."

They began to walk through this sea of statues. Only their eyes moved, these statues, watching as David led the way.

There were rooms in these walls, open doors that looked upon tiny cubicles furnished with beds. Reposing upon the mattresses, more men.

One man lay on his stomach, butt wiggling invitingly in the air, a can of Crisco at his side.

Another held his legs spread wide, showcasing his droop of balls and richly veined cock, motioning with his free hand to enter, enter.

In yet another room two men busily sucked each other. Their worshipful devotion to each other's manhood left no room for breathing; in fact, each was red faced, cheeks puffed and eyes wild with the agony of slow choking.

Just beyond, where a group of men gathered by an entrance, they heard prolonged moans and the slap of skin against skin.

Bobby chilled at the sound. His grip on David's hand tightened so much David winced. "What do you think's in there?" he asked. He had a sudden vision of his lover inside this room, Mick being taken, abused, broken. He remembered being trapped inside the phone booth, and Mick's accusatory screams.

The pale men fell away and allowed them to enter. Once inside, they saw a huge projection TV and a tiered lounge area adorned with pillows. Men were sprawled across these pillows, jacking off to a grainy black-and-white porno film on the screen. In the movie two men were busy taking turns fucking a third, doggie style. They were sweat drenched, surrounded by columns of cloudy steam. The voices of the men in the room were rough, whispered, as a chantlike unity encouraged the group to become one. But there was no pleasure in this group, only an air of desperation. As David looked around, he could see their glazed expressions, hands wrapped around flaccid cocks, arms pumping. Their motions became more and more violent as they performed their hopeless masturbation.

Bobby tugged on David's arm. "Let's get out of here." This chanting mantra unnerved him, set his teeth on edge.

They turned to leave.

"Pick a room," a man cackled. "Any room."

David whirled to face the voice. It belonged to the man in the porno film, getting fucked. Only now he was being fisted by one of the others. His gaze flashed out from the screen, smote them. "You can check in any time you like," he singsonged, "but you can never leave." His lips foamed red. Blood spilled down the corners of his mouth. He was literally being torn apart by the other man's fist thrusting inside his rectum. The watching crowd grunted its approval, moaning in empathetic pain. Their cries turned to screams.

"Let's go!" Bobby said again, "or I'm going to be sick!"

The two of them staggered out, the men in towels snickering at their squeamishness. They squinted their faces and licked red tongues across yellow teeth. It appeared as if some wind ruffled their features, the way they flickered like candlelight under siege. This wind stripped away the outer shell of normality, revealing the glistening sinew of something half-born.

David nudged Bobby and they scurried away. Though the men made no move to follow, they trembled from the confrontation, hearts wild and untamed.

"What now?" asked Bobby. He held a hand to his chest as though its pressure would calm his racing heart.

"We must find the steamroom," David answered. He frowned. "But I'm not sure how to get to it. Meanwhile we're to have this tour, it seems. A little cat-and-mouse inside the maze. Be careful!"

They progressed down the hallway until it dead-ended into a rocky wall. A staircase spiraled up to another floor.

"I thought we were already on the third floor," Bobby said in a small voice. "Where could that possibly go?"

David shook his head. Suspicions buzzed. He was beginning to realize just how little rooted to reality the inside of this bathhouse was to the old Caverns. Which were the true hallways, and which ones false? How many were nothing more than corridors created by the monster, great depthless chambers of smothering dark designed to confuse and frighten them? They were blind men in a maze of Victor's making.

Another staircase on their right descended about twenty steps into impenetrable gloom. He crossed to it, perched at its top step, and held himself very still. His nostrils flared. Humid air, moisture-laden and eucalyptus-scented, wafted up the stairs and caressed his face. Though it frightened him to contemplate that darkness, he hooked a thumb in its direction.

"This way."

This time he would take the stairs — *down*.

2

Off-limits, this staircase, or it should have been, for its stone lip crumbled beneath their feet, not wanting to support their weight. Predatory dark nipped at their clothes. No electric torches to light their way, not on these steps. David held the crystal before them and summoned its power to cast forth light. A blue glow, like the inside of a photographer's darkroom, pooled around them.

They tested the steps, the slippery crunch of pebbles skimming ahead of them. A crazy image filled David's head: These were the steps to some medieval castle's dungeon, and they two, the frightened villagers come to do battle.

How many times over the great haul of centuries has this creature played out this confrontation, and won?

Down they went, the air growing steadily more humid, walls thudding as though massive speakers blared just behind them. Suddenly the staircase ended, emptying into another hallway similar to the one they had just left. Empty, though a short distance away came the bark of men's laughter, and the roar of music. Electric torches blazed.

Halfway down the hall David recognized it as the other place he had found himself during his "trespass." There were rooms in these walls too, he remembered, though their entryways were better hidden, obscured by the confusion of rock. A short distance ahead, if memory and present auditory senses served him, lay the dance floor.

"Let's go see," Bobby said, suddenly eager. For the music spilling out behind the massive doors tugged on him, stirring deep emotions. A promise of light, and laughter, and good times such as he had not seen in ages. It called to him, as they stood that short distance away.

David hesitated, wary. "I'm not sure..." But a dusty part of himself wanted to look, to peek back into the past. For wasn't that what this creature was recreating, if not in substance then in trappings? He'd wanted to take a look the last time he was here, but his presence then was an intrusion, a secret. But now — Victor was allowing them this little tour, encouraging them to view his handiwork. What else could explain their not being attacked?

Bobby floated toward the doors. David couldn't see his face but he knew a smile was planted there, an ear-to-ear grin of Christmas anticipation.

"Wait—"

Bobby stood at the doors. Beams of neon light slipped through its central crack, slicing the air like laser beams.

"We'll only be a minute," he said, waving David's caution away. He leaned his weight against the door, and pushed.

Pick a room. Any room.

"No!" David screamed. He pitched forward to try and grasp Bobby's shirttail.

Inside Bobby went, the music a sudden loud caress.

David lunged after him, rushing through the doors—

3

—and his momentum hurled him halfway across the gravel roof of a building. He skidded to a halt, and gulped for air. A New York City skyline stared at him with soulless eyes. Warm summertime night breezed the air, cooling his perspiration.

David spun around, sick with dread, waiting to see if that horror from his past would come banging through the rooftop door.

45

Dreamers, all

1

An illusion. This must be an illusion. A dream.

But could a summer breeze whisper hello in a dream? Could a hallucination duplicate the stink of garbage piled into overflowing trash bins from four stories down? The smell of soot and grime and tar grown soft by summertime heat?

Or the heartbeat of a city: congested streets, tooting horns; voices spilling out of countless open windows thrown open to catch the evening breeze.

David was dizzy with it all, the hallucination so complete it took him a moment to remember how he'd gotten here. The Caverns, the dance floor — *they* were the illusion now, the memory. He'd reached out for Bobby, and missed. Disco echoed magically in his head, as though its source was very near. Then it, too, faded under the siege of honking horns and the distant symphony of a late-night television movie blaring from an open window.

He walked to the edge of the roof, his feet singsonging on the gravel, and peered over the edge. His heart stalled. In the luminescent light of a fat moon he saw it, the concrete four stories down that had so cruelly broken his body. He relived that plunge — for he could never forget, never in a million years, the instant his fingers gave up their grasp of stone ledge. His scream, exploding out of him. The claw of gravity, yanking him downward.

No, he had never forgotten. Could never forget.

And now, with horrible sureness, he knew he was doomed to repeat it.

He turned around and faced the hinged door that shot out of the flat roof like a swollen deformity. His limbs were loose, wobbly. There was a taste of vodka on his lips. His clothes smelled of cigarette smoke and beer. He'd been out with his buddies, out hitting a few dance bars—

No No No! I'm in the Caverns, I'm still in the Caverns, where's Bobby—

He squeezed his eyes shut, opened them. The rooftop, the city, never wavered.

The door. Maybe if I go back through the door I'll be ... wherever I was ... before this...

David started across the roof, hurrying to beat whatever was about to happen next, he had to get downstairs, that was it, he should have gone *down—*

—Thought he'd gone down—

From the other side of the steel-plated door, footsteps clanged up the stairwell. A machine-gun sound. A killing sound. David panicked, halted so quickly he might have been balancing on a high wire, the way his arms cut the air. He reversed his direction, and backed away. A funny stone was clutched between the fingers of his right hand. The logic of it escaped him for the moment, but he held on to it, grateful for the weapon. He could always hurl it upon his pursuer.

The door crashed open, and — history repeating itself — the burglar advanced. He was as David remembered: a punk, a teenager; but a teenager with a knife. The kid waved the knife, slashing a jagged path.

"Shut up!" the boy cried. "I'm warning you!"

Don't make me do this again, David thought, stumbling backward, ever backward, until his feet struck the ledge. It waited for him, this ledge. Waited for him to swing over its side, popping buttons on his shirt, feet kicking empty air.

"Don't," he gibbered, hands in front of him, pleading, desperate. "Don't make me. Not again..."

"Don't make me! Don't make me!" the punk mimicked, and he shimmered slightly, as though caught in a trick of moonlight. David had a quick impression of a much younger boy standing in his place, a boy with tangled black hair and feral eyes. The moonlight corrected itself, and the double image was gone.

The teenager cocked his head. Grinned. "You don't want to go over?" He stole two steps.

"No!"

He pointed with the knife. "Give me the stone."

Confusion. Past and present, jiggling. David held up the stone. "This? You want this?"

A vigorous nod. Lips smacked with the anticipation of a holiday meal.

David glanced over the rim of building. Down below: the sidewalk, a gray sea in the moonlight. He looked at the boy, who had crept closer. The clouds obscuring his thoughts lifted just a little, and he squeezed the stone tightly between his fingers.

"No," he said, this time with refusal, not entreaty. It must be very important, this stone, for the burglar to want it so much.

The kid glared, his body trembling with outrage. He hadn't expected such an answer. His lips curled into a snarl. "Then die!" He jumped at David, the blue teeth of the knife cutting the distance between them.

David reared back, hands raised to ward off the inevitable kiss of steel, and he was rolling backward, somersaulting over the ledge.

No! No! No! Not again!

Twinkling lights of New York skyscrapers. Slate-gray sky. Ball of moon. He saw it all as he flipped backward, headfirst this time, falling headfirst toward broken bones and cracked ribs, toward—

—a mouth.

Giant lips slid back, muscles taut with the rictus of a smile. Bits of shredded clothing and stringy flesh were caught between the gaps of pointy teeth. The warm stink of a slaughterhouse rose to greet him.

David shut his eyes, curled into a flying ball. *I'm going to die.*

He felt himself slam into a surface so hard it snatched his breath away. He flopped about like a fish thrown onto dry land, bits of gravel digging into his back and shoulders.

He reeled into a sitting position, and had he the breath he would have screamed and screamed, shouting until the air in his lungs — or luck — ran out.

He was back on the roof.

Cars honked their horns. A television blared a late-night movie. A breeze whispered across his tear-stained face with delicate fingers.

A voice filled David's head, indecipherable:

(I have a room prepared for you)

It made no sense to him, seemed to come from some future self, some part of him that was never going to happen.

For on the stairwell, once again, forever and ever, world without end: footsteps.

A machine-gun sound. A killing sound.

2

It blew away the intervening years, these lights, music, dancing. Like feeling himself drawn up, up, onto a cresting wave where everyone was happy, everyone had smiles for one another, and love could be had for a night — or a lifetime.

The dance floor lay before him, packed with dancers of all descriptions. Peppered among the mostly male sea were a few women, heads tossed back, arms flung to the ceiling. The sharp odor of amyl nitrate teased Bobby's nostrils.

He was laughing. When was the last time he'd experienced such easy happiness? He felt twenty-one again, like the kid he had been when he'd first ventured into the world of gay bars.

The sky above the dance floor was a glittering galaxy. Laser beams and strobing neon lights challenged each other with meteorite trails zinging across the ceiling. Mirrors caught the beams and ricochetted them into wild patterns. Dry-ice steam squirted out of hidden pipes, floating down over the crowd, and a whooping cheer rose from the dancers.

Bobby bobbed on the toes of his feet. It was all he could do to keep from rushing out onto the dance floor and insinuating himself into the crowd. Where was David?

He looked behind him, and his grin faltered just a bit when he saw he was alone. The swinging black door had closed. Why hadn't David followed? This room appeared to be the one haven inside this monstrous place, the one room where, seemingly, joy was not a confectionery icing covering something dank and spoiled underneath.

He took a few steps closer to the dance floor. No one else stood on this wide strip of floor fronting it. Everyone crowded under the spray of lights, gyrating to the music.

And the clothes they wore: That had Bobby laughing too. Some were draped only in towels, though how in god's name they managed to dance and keep their modesty was anyone's guess. Others wore basic clone attire: 501 jeans and a painted-on t-shirt (or shirtless, the cloth stuffed into a back pocket during a particularly wild burst of music, where it dangled like a rubber tail). And yet others wore bright polyester shirts, collars wide enough to fly a 747, sleeves rolled up and buttons undone to the navel. Women clomped in high platform shoes and seductive low-cut dresses, a Mary Richards hairdo bouncing at their shoulders.

He had never dreamed such an expansive dance floor and sophisticated lights and sound system had existed within these walls. Men didn't drop good money here with the intention of dancing all night. Too many better-equipped bars vied for that competition.

Yet here it was, as splendid as any of the very best dance clubs he'd ever stepped foot in. The room stretched on and on and on, filled with dancers. Lights flashed from every direction. Strobe lights caught the dancers in a thousand photographs: the quirk of mirrors doubling the effect.

A new song caught the crowd's approval. Bobby recognized the lyrics.

> *I'm puttin' on those dancing shoes*
> *Gonna shake and shimmy all night*
> *Forget what waits outside these doors*
> *In here we're all right, all right!*

I want to be out there! His fingers snapped to the beat. He bopped. He swayed. What the hell. One dance. He stepped up to the dance floor, where some of the nearest dancers encouraged him with their hands. He glanced behind one last time.

Where was David? It soured the pleasure of this moment, got in the way of riding this cresting wave. Fishy. They were supposed to be ... doing something ... fighting?... Fighting what, when there was all this great music?

> *Is there more than dancing*
> *Is there more to life?*

No — and Bobby plowed through the crowd, threading his way to the center of the floor. Men gave him room, egging him on with cheerful grins. He was a great dancer, could move with the best of them when the mood struck, and now he let loose. The crowd was his partner, and welcomed him. Sweat began to pour from him almost immediately; the heat of many bodies crammed together. Someone shoved a bottle of poppers at him and he took a sniff in each nostril.

Now he was one with the music. Everything intensified: the lights, song, his liquid movements. The amyl rushed through his blood, numbing his limbs and gonging his heart. He rode the wave, surfing its magical crest until he was utterly sweat drenched. A pleasant weariness slowed his frenetic steps as one song gave way to the next, and the next. A dull ache settled into the back of his neck. He'd forgotten that inevitable headache that always accompanied his use of poppers.

Enough, Bobby thought to himself as Donna Summer sang that love was unkind. *Time to find David. Time to ... do...* He couldn't quite remember *what* it was he and David had planned. Maybe it would come to him when he got off the dance floor. He turned to leave.

His feet danced. He wanted to walk off the floor, but he danced.

Stop it, Bobby scolded himself. *Time to go.*

He raised a foot, and the floor gummed up with him. He raised the other sneaker and the taffy floor sucked at his foot, held it with the sticky grip of a roach motel trap.

Bobby's chest heaved with his effort to free himself. He stared at the mob of dancers. A curtain parted from his eyes, a curtain that revealed the backstage of these theatrics. He saw the terrible expressions on their faces, could feel their aching weariness.

No one stamping with such profound exhaustion could possibly keep moving, but they did. They had to. Otherwise the floor gathered around their ankles, a quicksand mire that threatened to pull them under. There were men in hospital gowns around him, scarecrows with tubes dangling from their arms. The bright colors of the polyester shirts were not whimsical designs, but *blood,* blood that had sprayed out of gaping throats and ripped-out hearts.

Living corpses. That's who shuffled their feet to the disco beat, yeah yeah: men and women at the bottom of this spectral hierarchy. Dancing to hold back true death, true oblivion, faces blank and drawn with utter exhaustion.

Dry-ice steam showered the dancers. Only it wasn't ice at all: It stung Bobby's nostrils, choked his throat raw. What he'd earlier mistaken as whoops of joy were pathetic cries for mercy.

His feet were sinking. He began to dance again. Several dancers away a woman with needle tracks up and down her arms shook her head despite her male partner's pleading; he watched as the woman slumped still and allowed the floor to slurp over her, eating her up.

Someone nudged Bobby. Thrust a bottle of poppers under his nose.

"No—?" Too late, inhaled.

The man beside him said, "How do you like your room, Bobby? How do you like your room?"

It was Roger, the manager of Uncle Charlie's.

All around, from the speakers, once again:

> *Is there more than dancing*
> *Is there more to life?*

"Yes!" Bobby screamed. "Yes! There is!"

But you'd never know it, from the way he boogied to beat the devil.

3

Alex.

It was Alex who walked through the steel-plated door. His clothing hung in loose tatters around his wide shoulders and midsection. Jeans in Robinson Crusoe ribbons. His face was contorted in such an expression of hatred that for a moment David was confused by the incongruity of this man who stood before him with the policeman he knew.

Only the knife seemed real, gleaming there in his fist.

David coughed out the name: "Alex?" Suddenly knowing this thing was *not* Alex. A blinding flash: This snatched bit of his history in which he stood was only a room somewhere within the Caverns' walls! He must hold on to that — remember that!

Alex jerked toward him. His legs were wooden, as if unused to the task of walking. "It's not so bad," he rasped through a mouthful of marbles. The voice, in death, had lost its soft cotton, its bourbon quality. "Whatever you've always wanted, you get. Like this." To David's surprise he dug into his 501s and pulled out his penis. It began to inflate under the machinations of his hand. He winked at him. "Aww, come on. I know you've wanted this from the very first time we met. I did too." A ghost of a smile. "Or a part of me, anyway. So be a good boy and take care of my buddy, huh?" He wagged the erection at David.

A stabbing pain at this display; to have this Alex so brazenly revealed soured his mouth with distaste. He shook his head.

"Do yourself a favor and give in," Alex encouraged. He motioned at their surroundings, and his voice, and expression, grew serious. "How many times can you fall off this roof, David? How many times can you break every bone in your body, before you beg to have it end? For you'll feel it, this time: no passing out either. And when you open your eyes, it'll start all over again." A shudder racked him. "So come on. Behave yourself. You'll only make things worse if you don't."

"Worse?" David's mouth was utterly dry.

"He has many rooms he can unlock. Bits and pieces of your past; whatever you haven't let go. He can freeze you into a moment. Make you relive your worst nightmares — or take even a good moment and stretch it out so far you'd rather die than have it go on."

"What about *you?*" he challenged. "Why aren't you in one of those rooms?"

A wry smile. "But I am," he answered softly, and David trembled. Yes: To pit friend against friend must be a special torture. To work against the very people and situations that had been cherished in life.

He shook his head. "Go away, Alex. Leave me to this. And Victor."

"Not until you give me the stone."

"No."

"If I fail, he'll put me back in my room. You won't subject your old pal to that, will you?" His expression hardened. "Will you?" A flash of incisors.

"You know what I have to do."

"No," Alex said, tucking himself back into his blue jeans, "what you have to do is get by me. And *this.*" He jabbed the knife. "Now give me the fucking stone."

David retreated, and tightened his grip on the crystal. He chanced a look behind him at the building's ledge. God: not again. If only he'd run *down* the steps, all those years ago. If only. If only. A person could die from these if-onlys. Or spend eternity awash in his regrets.

"What do you say, partner? This?" Alex brandished the knife, and pantomimed sticking it through David's heart. "Or do you save yourself by giving me the stone?"

"Over my dead body."

Alex's face twitched; the cliché, blurted out, made him chuckle. "With pleasure." Any trace of the policeman that had recognized a friendship between them vanished with that chuckle. He hungered for violence, now. He filleted the air in front of him with the knife, advancing across the roof.

David prepared to duck off to the side, to dodge this Alex-shell and dash for the door, but his shoes were sinking into the tar and gravel. He lifted a foot and the motion teetered him backward, back toward the ledge.

—No!—

He saw it clearly. Saw how this script could not alter. The sticky roof sucked at his feet. Only when he moved toward the ledge would his tennis shoes pop free. Any other direction and the roof held him fast.

Alex was drooling out of the corners of his mouth. One hand wiggled in front of him, encouraging David to drop the crystal into it.

With no time to think about what he was doing or what would happen next, David straddled the ledge. What other avenue was open to him? He kicked a leg over, and rolled onto his stomach. Buttons popped off his shirt as he slid down the ledge. Once again he gripped the brick as his fingers strained to support his hanging weight. Only this time, the crystal was buried within his left palm.

Into that square of sky above the ledge, Alex appeared. He swallowed the sky with his shape. Huge. He raised the knife point-end down with almost casual indifference. Making ready to thrust it into one of David's hands, if necessary.

"Wait," David gasped. "Help me, and I'll give you the stone."

Triumph. But a wariness. A flash of light across those soulless eyes.

David held himself very still, not wanting to lose his grip. Seconds ticked off, hours of them. His hands ached.

Alex stared down. "The stone."

"Yes! I'll give it to you! Just help me up!"

The blade lowered to the policeman's side, away from David's hand. "Give it to me," he demanded.

"Help me up. Please."

A thin smile of amusement. "That's what friends are for." He thrust out a hand.

David caught it. Dared himself for the task. And pulled. Hard.

"Hey!"

The scream was high-pitched, rough with shock. Caught off balance, his knees smacking against the ledge, Alex tumbled over him. In an attempt to catch himself he let go of David's hand — and a good thing, too; otherwise David would have tumbled after. As it was, Alex flew over him like a bird shorn of wings. His cry speared the night.

But David had no time to think of him; he scrabbled to keep his balance, to keep himself from falling. His fingers dug into the ledge, both hands now firmly grasping brick. Alex's startled cry receded as though somehow swallowed up. Before the strength in his fingers gave out, David hauled himself up and over, collapsing in a sweaty heap back on the roof. Only after he was breathing again did he force himself to sit up and peer over the edge.

The sidewalk down below had vanished. Only black remained, a whirlpooling black nothingness.

I'm sorry, Alex. If I've sent you back to some horror — forgive me.

Now heat waves began to shimmer off the rooftop. Neighboring buildings softened and dissolved, like drops of rain smearing a painting. So: They were finished with this place, then. At least for now. Soon, would some other room take its place? Where would he find himself this time? In a New York hospital, every bone broken, unable to move from his bed, eyes swollen to slits?

Or would his head fill with a favorite song until it burst his eardrums — or he'd wish to god that it would, if it shut out the confounding racket?

Whatever moments he held close, whatever events he had not forgiven himself for — wasn't that what Alex had said? He looked at the roof. At the door, so silent and implacable. Almost expecting footsteps to bang up the stairwell even now.

Yes. If only he had rushed down the stairs on that summer night so long ago. If only he'd run down into the lobby and out into the street, and escaped.

A sudden thought paralyzed him.

True. If only. Yet so much of his recent life would be different, wouldn't it? Would he have moved back to San Francisco? Taken care of Eddie?

He shut his eyes. He felt he had to do this, right *now,* before this bit of his history reassigned itself into another room. Had he ever truly forgiven himself for running up the stairs, instead of down?

He discovered in that moment that his life was exactly as it should be. *Where* it should be. There were no accidents: Hadn't he said that to Bobby? His fall from the roof had somehow prepared him for this fight against Victor. A part of him had had to die to make room for the special gifts.

The landscape shifted and whirled about him. As the wind died down, music took its place. With trepidation, David opened his eyes.

He was back in the hallway of the Caverns, sitting on his haunches. Before him stood the entrance to the dance floor, where Bobby had disappeared. Vast relief went through him.

But where was Bobby?

46

Alone

How did he like his room? 1

He hated it.

Time, and his energy, were running out. There had to be a way to disconnect himself from this dance floor. And he had to do it before he joined this pack of weary dancers who gave up, and allowed the floor to swallow them whole. For they did not go easily, these others. They ranted and swung their arms about in futile hope another dancer might save them. Where did they go, after the floor entombed them? He had no wish to find out.

Bobby looked at the ceiling. A glitter ball spun colored points of light. The dry-ice vents spurted out another dose of steam. No help from anywhere up there.

He glanced beyond the pack of dancers to the rim of the dance floor. Of course; while he'd stood on the sidelines the floor had beguiled him, encouraging him to step onto its lighted squares. If only he could thread his way toward the lip of the floor...

There was a commotion behind him.

"Well, well," graveled a voice. "Look who's here."

Bobby spun around.

Weaving through the crowd was Will Garter. Bits of dirt and pebbles still lodged in his torn-apart face. His greasy, waxen features glowed as though he were somehow lit from the inside. Caked blood speckled his t-shirt. He armed aside dancers as he plowed toward Bobby.

"Get away from me!" Bobby shouted. In his fright, he'd stopped dancing. The floor bubbled around his shoes, hungry for this appetizer. He suddenly realized what was happening and hopped foot to foot in odd imitation of dancing. Oh, this was impossible: How could he dance and retreat at the same time? Would he have to pick between the lesser of two evils?

Will Garter pushed through the crowd, delighted with Bobby's predicament. His own feet were submerged as though the floor were a shallow pool of water. His hands wiggled before him.

"Come'ere, boy," he said above the driving disco. "I got plans for you. Big fucking plans."

Bobby retreated, edging toward the lip of the dance floor, his feet bopping to the music all the while. He spotted Roger in the throng. "Help me," he begged. But David's boss only pulled another bottle of poppers from his pocket, inhaled deeply with both nostrils, and languidly stretched the bottle toward him.

Bobby knocked the vial out of the man's hands, disgusted.

"Come'ere, baby," the thing behind him said, his voice hot needles cutting through a Diana Ross song. "You're gonna take care of me. Take care of me *real* good," he chuckled. "No use running."

Bobby brushed his way past two dancing women and saw the edge of the floor. With a whoop of joy he raised his leg and made to hop off.

But it was like smacking into an invisible wall, a force field out of some science fiction movie. He kicked at the air but could not push through. Trapped. He spun around.

"See?" Will grinned. The laser lights seared his face in a sickly purple light. He looked like someone who had been strangled. "Give yourself up to the floor, baby. You and me. Let it make you over."

"Get the hell away from me," Bobby snarled.

"You're only gonna have eyes for *me*, sweetheart. Me and my new face, thanks to you. Those pretty little lips of yours are gonna kiss it and make it all better. Kiss me *all* over. So come'ere." The hands wriggled, encouraged. "You're *mine*, boy. All mine."

He flattened against the edge. He had nowhere to go, except into this tattered thing's outstretched arms. The music crescendoed inside his head as though in finale. No, no! To have it all come down to this...!

Will swiped the air, his fingers clawing the sleeve of Bobby's flannel shirt.

Out of reflex Bobby grabbed the thing's arm and yanked. His fingers sank into the tallow skin with a burning sensation. Had he held on for long, who knew what damage may have happened. But the tug threw Will off balance, as he had hoped. The zombie stumbled. Bobby twisted out of the way. Will collapsed onto his knees, his hands thrown out to protect his face. They grasped the edge of floor that bordered the dance floor.

With a shriek Bobby leapfrogged over Will, his hands pushing Will's head down toward the floor as he hopped over him. With both his feet airborne, he sailed off the dance floor.

A hand snatched at his ankle.

Bobby spilled to the ground and turned to look. He had escaped the treacherous floor, but not Will Garter. The madman had him by his ankle, dragging him toward the dancing crowd.

"Get back here!" the zombie clamored. "Get back here and take it like a man!"

He kicked at its hands. One of Will's fingers popped free with a branch-snapping crack of bone. He batted against the hand with his right heel and the thing's fingers flattened like something made out of Play-Dough.

"You little shit! Stop that—!"

His left tennis shoe slipped off into its hands. Bobby retracted his leg after a final kick, and scooted away. But Will Garter had no chance to come after him. The floor, as though angry at this escape, boiled over the madman like molten lava.

"Hey! *Stop!* Nooo!"

He was swallowed up to his waist. He waved Bobby's tennis shoe like a white flag of surrender. The dancers nearest to him simply moved out of the way, allowing the floor to finish its meal. Looney-tune eyes glowered at Bobby, full of revenge.

"Just you wait—"

But the floor yanked him under, and he was gone.

As Bobby watched not two feet from the dance floor, the multitude of dancers began to fade, disappearing as the dry-ice steam sprayed the crowd. Lights strobed a now-empty floor, and sparkled the mirrors. The people were gone.

But, no, he knew with certainty. They may cast no reflection upon the mirrors, but they were there, all right. Caught in their eternal dance.

He turned away, exhausted, and felt the floor he was sprawled upon tilt beneath him. On hands and knees he scrambled back toward the door, his only exit. Like a ship rolling onto its side, the floor tilted higher and higher, with one purpose: to have him slide back onto that dance floor.

He flew up its side, a mountain climber squashed flat against a sheer cliff, hurrying toward the door before the angle would grow so steep he'd be unable to keep himself from falling. He threw himself at the doorknob. The door squealed open. Bobby held fast to the knob and swung to the other side — for now the floor was almost completely vertical. His arms revolted under this new agony, his sweaty fingers greasing the knob.

Hold on, hold on, he pleaded with himself.

Swinging the door as close as he could to the edge of the door frame, he hooked one hand, and then the next, on the frame, and hauled himself over. With a grateful cry he tumbled into the hallway.

2

He lay still for a long time, waiting for the throbbing in his arms and legs to diminish.

And waiting, his numbed mind realized, for help. For David.

But his friend was nowhere to be found. Something had happened to David, he was sure. Something similar, but different. Otherwise he would have been trapped on the dance floor right along beside him. No; David had been taken elsewhere — maybe to his own particular hell, and he would have to use his own wits to get himself out.

Bobby sat up. The doors leading to the room he had just left were complacently shut, their perpendicular angle now correct for the hallway. If he pushed through that entrance once again, would it still be a straight drop onto that terrible dance floor?

He took a quick inventory. David, gone. The crystal, gone. But he had outsmarted the creature without aid of the stone, and if he kept his courage about him, he could do it again. He thought of the promise he and David had made in the Blacks' apartment before stepping through that door. The vow, to all their friends.

He rose to his feet. He kicked off his remaining tennis shoe and stood in his socks.

Yes, he was alone. But he had a job to do. Vows to keep. Inside the creature's domain, but still alive. And while he lived, he had but one goal: to find this Victor, and save Mick.

He started down the hall, which quickly turned left and then right. Again, lost in this cavernous maze. His fists bunched at his sides, prepared for anything.

"Bobby."

He whirled, an open room in front of him.

An olive-skinned man sat upon his thin mattress. Naked. Inviting. Slim and hairless.

Attached to each nipple was a set of teeth. They were gnawing at the flesh, chewing twin holes into his chest. His chest and stomach were covered with a foam of blood and speckled matter.

The man held out his hand, palm open. Two sets of teeth chattered and snapped, like a child's toy. "How about a pair of tit clamps, huh, Bobby? Want those tits worked over?"

He backed away and fled.

A row of rooms revealed themselves, doors open.

"Help me," one man gasped. He lay curled on his back across his mattress in an impossibly tight ball. His eyes beseeched Bobby before he returned to matters at hand: sucking himself off. Only he couldn't quite reach, and he strained and grunted with effort. Bobby could almost hear the tension in the man's spine, the snap of muscle and bone wanting to give way.

Another room, another misery.

A portly man in boxer shorts. In his hands, a tattoo needle gun. Fresh tattoos had been scrawled across his thighs and arms. He stood up and displayed himself. Tattoos of nets. Trees. Two men standing upon a high cliff, facing a cloud. He peered out at Bobby. "Come'ere, son," the man said, all butter and cream. He slapped a hand against his hairy chest. "All that's missing is a boat. You draw boats, don't you?"

"What are you talking about?"

A smile with no warmth.

"You're the one who draws. Come on. It's easy. I'll get you started."

The tattoo needle hummed into life. The man drew it toward his bare chest.

Bobby had seen enough. He groped almost blindly down the hall, not wanting to peer into any more of these rooms. These were the real chambers of horror; the ghosts he and David had seen up on the higher floor had been mere reflections of this terror. The geometry of this bathhouse no longer seemed to be following a logical path. As he sank deeper and deeper into its halls, he knew he could lose himself completely inside this labyrinth of Victor's making.

He rounded a corner. A few men loitered about the entrance to a room. A confusion of noises poured out, the din of many voices. Bobby tried to pass, but a man draped in a blood-soaked towel stood in his path and gestured toward the room. Each time he attempted to escape, the man moved to block his way. Unable to do anything else, he reluctantly entered.

It was a bar.

Men and women in various stages of visibility stood everywhere, their bodies torn and mutilated. They lounged on bar stools and clustered together at tables, braying laughter. Some wore t-shirts, polyester suits, jeans. Others wore towels or underwear or gym shorts. Men that looked almost perfectly normal sat grouped with men who were no more than lines drawn into the air, ghosts of the newest order. One man tilted back his beer mug filled with a frothy red concoction and it spilled out through a gaping hole in his throat.

Screams from a TV set fastened to the far wall. A monster movie—

Bobby cringed.

No. Not a movie. Real life. Scenes from all across town as the creatures tapped at windows to be let inside darkened bedrooms. Men who waited with tickets bunched in their hands. The channel changed abruptly, and there they were, he and David facing that huge monstrous head hovering over Rachael Black.

"This is what I think of your weapon!" the giant bellowed, and bent to bite Rachael in half.

The bar erupted into catcalls and whistles of pleasure. Spongy hands slapped against the tables, upsetting their drinks.

"What can I get you, Bobby?" a voice near him asked.

Bobby looked away from that horrible scene on the TV. A black man, the bartender, watched him with a smile. He was busy drying a glass. The man wore nothing but a jockstrap. Pinned to his bare chest was a gold name tag: RALPH. "How do you know my name?" he asked.

A dry laugh. "We all know who *you* are. So what'll it be? Red or white?" He took a pilsner glass and tilted it underneath one of the spigots. A white, viscous fluid plopped out, slopping down the side of the glass. A faint ammonia smell drifted out from it.

Bobby knew what it was, though he had never seen it in such quantity.

"Here you go," Ralph said, smacking his lips. "No other taste in the world quite like it, eh?" He pushed the glass across the bar. "The specialty of the house: a sloe jism fizz. Now put that frown away. This one's on the house."

Gore rose in his throat. He turned and ran, pushing past the men in towels who gathered around the doorway. His ears burned with their echoing laughter.

Immediately, he stood at the entrance to another staircase. He took a few moments to gather himself, to push that grotesque room out of his mind.

Out of his mind. Yes. Stark raving mad, if he didn't get out of this place soon. But the worst was yet to come, he knew. Facing Victor alone would be the ultimate test of his sanity.

Endless music piped through the hall. As he strained his ears, he thought he heard a noise below the music. Running water. Showers. They were down past this final staircase, which was cloaked in shadow.

He started down.

The steps were warm beneath his stockinged feet. Tendrils of wet smoke whispered against his face. He groped for a handrail in this dark, and his fingers touched something sleek and hard. A liquid splashed onto his flannel shirt from the thing he held in his hand. It burned a hole, stinging like acid.

Holy shit—

A row of bobbing erections. Anxious for his touch, anxious to release their burning white liquid.

Bobby shuddered in revulsion and drew his arms around him, not wanting to risk touching anything else. He was halfway down the staircase when two men stepped out of the shadows and blocked his way. They wore green hospital gowns. Tubes dangled from the crooks of their arms.

"That's far enough," one of the men said, his voice like shaved ice.

Bobby froze. He sensed movement behind him, and he turned to look. Three other men jostled for room at the top of the staircase. Scarecrows, also dressed in flimsy gowns. Their hair was matted, plastered against their heads. Eyes, the hard glint of coal.

The man who had talked began to climb the stairs. He raised his hand. A hypodermic needle stuck out between his fingers. "Look what I got? This is good shit," he grinned. "You'll *liiikkee* it. You'll just float on cloud nine."

He thought he'd been prepared for anything, but seeing that needle ... knowing it was meant for him...

They came for him, swooping down the staircase in a sudden tackle.

Bobby screamed.

He charged down the stairs, intending to bulldoze his way past these wraiths.

Hands grabbed him from all sides and pitched him to the floor. He sprawled on his face and stomach. Before he could turn over they were upon him, yanking at his shirt, pulling it up to expose the crook of his elbow. They flipped him over, their waxy faces inches from his own, bright with victory.

Bobby's cries undulated out of him.

Too fast, it was all happening too fast—

A terrible sting, at his arm.

"Sweet dreams," the scarecrow in front of him said.

47

At the bottom of the well

1

Davic's eyes dropped to the floor. A tennis shoe. Abandoned. A streak of blood on one side. He picked it up. Bobby. This was Bobby's.

He stood up and tossed the shoe back onto the floor. Had his friend somehow escaped the room, or was this all that remained?

He couldn't leave Bobby inside, if that's where he was. But it took all his courage to grip that door handle once again, and push.

Only it wouldn't budge. Locked. The room was sealed off.

He stood for he didn't know how long until the debate inside his head quieted, and gave him his answer.

I'm sorry, Bobby. If you're still inside there, forgive me.

For he knew what had to be done, despite all costs.

2

His groping journey took him down a winding tunnel, following a new path in the maze. He needed no metaphors to tell him he was in the intestines of the beast. This new decline took him into rougher country. All semblance of a hallway, of being inside a building, ended. The ceiling lowered, and he had to wind through stalactites and stalagmites that lined floor and ceiling like the bars to a private cell. Disco echoed far, far away. The rocky walls practically writhed with living moss and scummy blue-green foliage. He reached out a hand and recoiled when his fingers touched slippery damp rock. Real. No plaster of Paris, this.

The electric torches gave way and were replaced by real candles. Fitful pools of light flickered in their homes within the rock. Tunnels branched off in all directions, bottomless holes of black from which he heard the rattle of chains and indescribable moans of anguish. The grunting chants had a hushed, sexual nature to them, though to David's cars the groans were hollow, lacking any real pleasure. It was sex like dirty laundry in a basement, secretive and unclean.

He paused, and selected his direction by sheer instinct. He glanced behind him and saw that where earlier there had been tunnels shooting off into darkness there was now solid wall. The real and the imagined, coexisting.

He pressed ahead. A strange calm settled over him. His breath was determined and steady. Odd, because in so many ways he felt that he could be walking toward his death. It ought to have frightened him, but he'd been numbed by all that had preceded this walk in darkness. Besides, his other life was already dead. There was nothing to do but continue.

Suddenly, a figure swam toward him.

David reared back.

The figure was his own, entombed within a mirror. There were mirrors all up and down this particular path.

His reflection had the face from his ticket into this bathhouse. Maggots rolled out of his empty eye sockets. His skull, cracked open and lopsided, as though he'd been run over by a truck. Between his legs, a bloody stump revealing his castration.

Here was Bobby in another mirror, torn and twisted almost beyond recognition.

In another mirror, Victor's snarling mouth, the tattered remains of Rachael Black smeared across jagged teeth. Stringy bits of her blouse dangled between the teeth.

In yet another, a naked man clawed at the inside of the glass, trying to scratch his way out.

They're nothing more than carnival fun-house mirrors, he told himself. *They can't hurt me. Don't look at them.*

He hurried past, the crystal clenched in his fist. Out of the gloom a door appeared, smooth against the rocky surface of the tunnel. A dead end. He turned around.

The mirrors were gone, but so too all the other hallways. There was nowhere else to go — all avenues of retreat had dissolved into blackness. This was the end of the road. He turned to face the door. But as he reached out for the handle he experienced a sure and powerful premonition: No man should see what he was about to see. What lay behind this door sweated despair, heartache. The only way he'd survive this was to seal up his heart.

The door was cool, its skin oily with condensation. He pushed through.

An eye-watering stink assailed him. His hands flew to cover his mouth and nostrils against the dark vinegary smell. Breathing through his mouth didn't help; it just let in more of the fouled air. He coughed as though being asphyxiated.

Even the crystal seemed reluctant to share its light in this room, hugging close to him, wrapping him in phosphorescent blue.

One sound broke the silence and chilled his heart with a terrible familiarity: the constant drip of water striking water.

He hugged a blue-green wall, afraid of this watery sound from the center of the room — a sound so like the echoes at the bottom of a well. For this was it, that imagined hole in the ground, that place best unseen by human eyes.

As he walked through the expanse, the crystal's light caught the cold glint of two hoops sticking out of the earth. David stretched out his arm, using the crystal as a torch, and relaxed a little as the shape revealed itself — and the mystery of this room.

A diving board. The hoops on either side of the board were hand hoists.

Briefly, he thought of the chlorine he'd smelled so often, usually right before a premonition or an attack. It was here in this place, only slightly obscured by this riper, darker smell.

He stepped boldly forward, the blue glow of the stone illuminating scummy tile and the concrete lip of a pool. He chanced two more steps, curious for a glance into the heart of this place. He held out the crystal. His arm thrummed as though he held an electric razor in his hand. This electric current had ignited a switch inside the stone.

Blue light touched water. Its surface, a frozen calm.

But underneath, shapes moved in the still water. Shapes like huge stalks of seaweed massed together, yet alone. Each shape separate in all that crowded togetherness.

What no man should ever see...

3

Down, down into darkness.

Carried in many arms.

Bobby's eyes rolled open and he saw men standing under scalding showers, screaming their agony. Oppressive heat and vapor were everywhere, like the spray from Niagara Falls. Then — back into his own darkness.

He plummeted back down into his cottony world, back to where the walls were supposed to soothe and caress. Only he felt no welcome here. The landscape was barren. Uninviting. He couldn't understand. It had been such a happy union, the last time. The last time he had escaped ... whatever it was...

He was about to set foot into this place when the dark man with the crooked teeth stepped out of the cotton and shooed with his hands:
Go back! Go back!

Why?

Fight it! the anxious hands seemed to say. *Go back! Fight!*

Protests died on his lips. He found himself staring at this thin black man. Staring, because there was a sudden familiarity about his gestures, his face, his gap-toothed smile. A familiarity that went much deeper than from their one other meeting.

As if hearing these thoughts, the man nodded, a grin of pleasure upon his lips. He raised a hand and lay two fingers upon a spot on his forehead just above his eyes and bridge of his nose. He reached out and lay these fingers against Bobby's own forehead.

And uttered three words:

"Go. To. Kahmaal."

Bobby wrenched awake. A little gasp escaped his lips as the man's words and touch tingled through him like an electric current. He blinked against the dark, momentarily confused because he could discern no difference between eyes open and eyes closed.

Where was he?

He tried to move his arms, but there were chains about his wrists. His hands were held on either side of his head. All around him in this dark he heard the rustle of chains, moans, and sobs. At his back, hard stone. He was fastened to a wall.

He wanted to drift in and out of consciousness. Vaguely, he remembered the attack by the men in hospital gowns, and the stinging burn of an injection. God knew what poison now worked through his veins, muddying his thoughts. Stay awake. He had to stay awake.

Music thumped from somewhere way, way up above. He tuned in to it, to keep himself awake.

Gradually, almost imperceptibly, a red light began to infuse this dungeon. Like the flames of some unseen fire, this orange-red glow revealed his surroundings.

It was better not to have known. The dark, he now realized, had been a kindness.

There were other men around him, down here in this pit. Alive, as he was alive. Some were chained to the rocky walls. Others hung on their backs in leather-and-chain slings, stripped of clothes, legs spread wide.

In the center of this room a naked man lay chained to a round table. Blond, probably in his late thirties. He lay perfectly still, arms and legs spread-eagled, vulnerable. Silent, as though already dead. Only his eyes moved, wild and huge with dread.

Somewhere in that darkness, a heavy latch was thrown back, and a door slid open on steel tracks.

The men whimpered their fright.

Bobby held his breath.

The shadowy men in hospital gowns fluttered in and surrounded the prisoner on the table. Their hands soothed and stroked as their fingers ran along his nakedness. They murmured kind words into his ear. So odd, this gentle sound among the chains. Bobby watched with distrust. A movement beyond the table caught his eye.

A figure moved toward the table. He was less recognizably human, his features singed by fire and rage. Bits of clothing hung in shreds. The skin on which hung shirt and pants was blackened charcoal. Smoke smoldered from him, as though somewhere in his center a flame still ate at him. The carrot beard was a forest of dark nubs on one side of his face. His eyes were pools of shocking white. The burnt rubber of his lips cracked open into a greeting.

"You may begin," Red said.

And Bobby shut his eyes to it, couldn't bear to watch how the gathering of scarecrows made a meal of the man upon the table. He could shut his eyes but he could not drown out the gnashing of teeth, the high-pitched wails of pain.

Perhaps, he blacked out. For when he opened his eyes, the men had stepped back from the table, away from the ruined carcass. Out of the chest of the man a ghostly light twirled up and out, then plopped to the floor, red and newborn. Like angles in the air, the stick figure came to his feet and looked at himself with pride.

The carcass of the blond was dragged off into the dark. A new man was brought to the table, and chained despite his frantic pleas.

Bobby was swallowed by a flash of terrible insight:

The spirit, corrupted by violent death, hungry to begin its journey back to the flesh...

He turned his eyes once more as the infant creature was given its first taste of its new life.

And knew it would soon be *his* turn upon the table.

4

What no man should ever see...

David's gasps choked the air. It should have been screams. Wails. A noise so loud in its sorrow it shook the very walls, and could have awakened the world.

He stood beside a floating graveyard.

The pool was crammed with bodies.

They were naked. In pajamas. Robes. Men in 501 jeans and leather vests and chaps, dressed for a night on the town. Women in gowns and negligees, their hair a nest of snakes about their heads. And there: Was that a boy, his white putty face staring up at him in a silent scream? And there: two teenagers, arms wrapped about each other in final embrace.

All the ruined carcasses of the hungering spirits who roamed the halls up above. The pool was crowded, yet seemed to have room for them all. Bodies at the edge of light became black motionless shapes. Who could comprehend their tangled number, there in that endless pool? All deserved accounting. All had families and friends and lovers, people left behind to grieve their unnecessary passing.

Yet it was left to David to see, and record, this underwater dumping ground.

He lowered the crystal. He'd seen too much, enough to haunt a thousand lifetimes. He thought of Eddie at his apartment, the sound of the squish of water between toes. How the hair on so many of Victor's creatures floated like seaweed above their heads. And preceding any attack: the bubbling brew of water and moss upon the walls.

He backed away. Away from decomposition and death. He looked across the expanse of darkness to something he had earlier missed: an exit sign. It glowed weakly, a red wound stapled to the wall of dark. But of course, there was no exit, there could be no real exit within the Caverns' walls, not until Victor had been driven away.

He made his way toward the door, anxious to be rid of this place.

As he pushed through, a voice jabbed the inside of his head:

(One more time healer! One more time!)

Underneath his feet: air.

Falling.

Darkness engulfed him. But darkness, this time, was not enough.

Death ship

H¹e lay on a splintery bunk bed. All around and above him men and women lay practically atop one another, inhumanly sandwiched on beds that were no more than shelves. All was dim, and hot, and foul: Down in the belly of this ship, where they were, the ocean's tossing was unmercifully cruel. The stench of vomit and excrement cloyed their cramped quarters.

He clung to his bed, rocked and battered. As he glanced upon himself he saw that holding on was unnecessary: His foot was shackled to the bed. An even greater shock: His skin was black, taut with emaciation.

"Kahmaal."

He jerked toward the voice whispering to him. Beside him lay another man. The black man touched his arm in consolation, wanting to soothe. The face that stared into his was familiar, though not immediately placeable. He was also terribly thin, this man, and when he opened his mouth a few crooked teeth winked through the shy smile.

Memories not of his own making shot through his mind: Villagers in starvation. A gathering of men. A hunt for food. Nets dropping down out of the trees, wild shouts. Being beaten by hard wooden sticks. Gunshots. And waking up here, chained to this very bed. These thoughts loomed hugely in his head, warrior cries that screamed his anguish. He'd never seen white men before. Never seen a boat this size.

From somewhere up above a door banged open, smacking wood. The women and men around him yelped with terror as heavy boots descended a staircase.

The man beside him tugged on his arm. "Soon," he whispered. "Soon, we will avenge."

The language was strange, unfamiliar, yet he recognized every word.

"Use it, Kahmaal. Free us." The man pointed at his hand.

He looked into his unfamiliar pink palm and saw the gemstone, cradled, precious. When he glanced at the man beside him it was as though a layer of onion skin peeled back.

Kuba. His brother. The artist of magic shapes.

A slurred voice boomed in the cramped quarters.

"Who shall it be, my pretties? Who deserves a taste of my wick?"

The man staggered about the cabin. This was not the ocean's tossing: The man was blind with drink. He wore an outfit of blouse and breeches, boots. A scarf looped loosely about a bearded neck, and another scarf tied back his hair. He spied a partially clad woman upon a bunk and reached for her, pulling her legs apart.

"Ahh," he chuckled. "You'll do very nicely indeed."

The woman lay as still as death, submitting to this assault. The man pulled himself out of his pants and clumsily mounted her.

The boat creaked and groaned.

Silence, as the drunken sod heaved upon her with little gasps of pleasure.

From his own bunk, he watched. His senses tingled. Kuba nodded at his questioning glance. This had happened other times before. But something in the air, now...

"That's good, my pretty one. So good..."

The woman's bunkmate, a man, raised above the wrestling shapes. He held out his hands; chains draped between them. Suddenly the woman pitched the guard to his side, and the bunkmate's chains swiftly bore home.

The cabin exploded in noise as the guard kicked and bucked, his protests a gargled cry. The shackles dug into his throat. He could not hook his fingers beneath the chain links. His tongue popped out like a sausage. The boots gave up their mad kicking dance.

The woman spat upon the dead man, and reached for his keys. She held them triumphantly in her clenched hand.

Like wildfire, the next chain of events.

In a silence crackling with tension, the men and women freed themselves of their shackles, the guard's keys passed from bunk to bunk. They had never seen keys and chains before this journey, but they had learned the purpose of the keys very swiftly indeed.

Kuba turned to him after they were freed. He pointed up above. "The captain," he said gravely.

The other men and women had gathered around them, their dark faces anxious and determined. A riot. They were going to storm the upper deck. They looked to him, pointing at the stone.

"Kill it," they urged. "Kill the Evil."

He raised the gemstone to his face, and again this onion skin of perception peeled back. The Evil. Yes. He should have recognized its insinuating stink. As though it had seeped into the very boards and planks of this ship.

They armed themselves with the chains that had bound them inside this hellhole. Climbed the stairs to the upper decks. It was night. How extraordinary, the breeze upon his face! It revived all of them, and fueled their courage. He raised his head to the heavens. The vast canopy of stars seemed to hold their breath. All fell calm: the ocean, the wind. The sea was black glass in the silvery moonlight.

Suddenly the immense silence was broken by cries of struggle. Pandemonium. Confusion. After enduring such terrible hardship, they took out their rage and frustration on the outnumbered crew. They had caught the men in the middle of the night, and despite the fire sticks, chains and surprise worked in their favor.

One pale shape moved off to the right, heading toward the ship's bow. Kuba tugged his arm and pointed. The captain.

They threaded through crowds of fighting men and women, navigating the unfamiliar deck. The crystal flashed in his palm, warm. When they could go no further they faced each other at last, the three of them once again.

The onion skin pulled back a final time.

A bearded, powerfully built man faced them. He wore breeches and vest, with a three-cornered hat perched upon his head. He bared his teeth at them, and then bellowed a laugh.

Even in this silvery moonlight he saw the sweat pouring off of this man, the sickly sheen he had come to recognize so well. Blood dribbled from the man's nose. Neither spirit nor man had full control of the captain's body, and the man's face jerked and twitched under this assault. For the spirit, while *in* the man, was not the man. Just as a smell may inhabit a room and not be the room. The ultimate merging could not take place without the stone.

"So," growled the Eater of Souls. "Time to keep your promise, shaman."

His lips spoke words of their own doing, words dredged from this living memory. "No," he said. "You stole my people from our lands. You brought only death with you."

"And you: a trickster as well. Breaking promises you had no intention of keeping. But I held a promise to *my* heart: revenge upon you and your people. After many days and nights afloat in the sea, I came upon this ship. Ship to ship, you could say. I broke my bonds and merged with this vessel."

He stepped forward, stone in hand. "Yes, but your grasp is that of rain. I still have the power to send you away." And a chant sprang to his lips. The sacred stone glowed blue, its light pouring out to squelch the dark, to rip the spirit from its physical home.

The Hungry Ghost roared in fury. A storm seemed to hang above their heads. Winds blew and waves lashed the boat. The creature stabbed an accusing finger and spoke with words that branded, iron hot: "Mark my words, Kahmaal. *We shall face each other again.*"

The captain hauled himself to the ledge of the boat.

Suddenly, he knew: The stone was loosing the evil spirit from the man, yes, but it would not kill the Eater of Souls. It would only release it back into the night. Yet while it lived within the man—

He thrust the crystal into Kuba's hands and sprinted for the man on the bow. The captain had been facing skyward, arms outstretched, in preparation for the spirit's departure. Blood poured copiously from his nostrils.

With a cry he lunged upon the captain and knocked them both backward.

"No!" the thing inside the captain screamed — and then they were all tumbling overboard in a tangle of arms and legs. Down they fell, into the churning ocean.

Down—

2

David slammed awake. Sweat-drenched, with the briny taste of ocean upon his lips. He shut his eyes against a glare of bright lights and waited for his equilibrium to return. His thoughts swirled.

The fall into the ocean.

So like the fall from the building in New York.

The African. Kahmaal.

The gesture in the hut: Kahmaal pointing to himself, the stone, and David hovering in the air. *I. You. We.* As though Kahmaal knew he had summoned his future self.

They were one and the same. He, as Kahmaal, reborn.

And Kuba, his brother. The link to these incredible gifts and powers — alive in Bobby. Their connection unleashing again the power of the crystal.

A gigantic growl rumbled across David. Wheezy, air-filled; a sound like the disturbed slumber of some huge creature out of a Tolkein nightmare. The hissing of jets. It was a sound he knew well, a sound that telegraphed his location long before his eyes adjusted to the naked bulbs hanging from the basement ceiling.

Across the scummy tiled floor: the steamroom. Water glistened off its walls. The stone bricks sweated. No: breathed. The glass window of its center was patted white with steam. Funny how his eyes trained to it, even before David saw the man guarding its entrance. Perhaps because the guard was nearly unrecognizable, standing there as though he had never known any other kind of life.

The blond hair, once preened and fussed over before gym-steamed mirrors, was a tangled knot of curls. The high Nordic cheekbones were pink with heat, shiny as a Washington apple. He was naked. His chest bore an ugly scar where a long knife wound had been sewn back together. His penis hung semierect between his thighs. His feet stamped in anticipation — his poor, misshapen feet, mutilated and squashed into something not quite man nor beast.

"Promises to keep," Mick said, and grinned.

49

Promises to keep

1

Two others had been to the table, suffering the same appalling fate. Now, it was Bobby's turn. One of the scarecrow men in a hospital gown approached him. He fought against his chains, desperate to escape this thing coming for him. No, he would not go easily into this night. They'd have to drag him all the way.

"Wait!" Bobby said frantically into this fiery darkness. "I have a proposition. Where are you, Red?"

The scarecrow still moved toward him. Bobby twisted against his chains. A funny double image came to him, a feeling of déjà vu. Chained in darkness, and a room that rocked and pitched as though tossed by waves. What did it mean?

A charred figure slid out of the womb of darkness. Wisps of smoke circled his head. His blackened face twitched with irritation. "Shut up," Red said, his voice the scrape of fingernails against a blackboard.

"Wait, Red—"

"I said shut up."

"Don't you know who I am?"

Red slumped toward him. A smear of white teeth set in burned rubber lips.

"Yeah, fuckface," he said. "I've been waiting for you. This is going to be a grade-A pleasure. You've had this coming since the moment we met." He snapped a burned stump of fingers. The scarecrow descended upon Bobby.

Bobby clawed at the air. His fingers dug against a greasy mound of shoulder. Like a clump of moist clay, it pulled free in his hand. He dropped the chunk of flesh in disgust, where it flopped about.

"You want another dose, fuckface?" Red held up a hypodermic needle.

Instantly, Bobby stopped squirming against his chains. "Please," he begged. "Listen to me, Red." He grasped for strategies, his thoughts zooming at hundreds of miles an hour.

Red folded his arms across his chest. "You got ten seconds."

"Don't — don't do this to me here. Don't you realize how special I am to Victor?"

Red hesitated, sensing a trick. "Of course. I'm following his orders."

"But you're special to him too, aren't you, Red?" Bobby's eyes gleamed in the hellish light. "Why sacrifice me here, where I'm just one of many? Where he can't watch? Take me to him. Prove your ultimate worthiness."

"He sees everything in here," Red sneered. "He's watching, even now."

"*Is* he?" Bobby challenged.

Doubt flashed across the burned face.

"Victor wants me dead. Take me to him. Kill me there, where he can watch."

Oh, but it was a desperate gamble. If he could buy just a little more time. Was he putting off the inevitable? Or dear god — was he going to get his wish?

2

This is my death, David thought as he raised himself to his feet. It would be a comfort, in its own way. Everyone he had ever known or loved, taken from him. Yes, it would be a special comfort, to be reunited with them all.

Mick stepped away from the steamroom door.

David held his breath.

Silently, the door glided open. A fog bank of steam rolled out, a seething cloud that tumbled across the expanse of floor to gather around David's feet. It moved in time with the dreamy disco music wafting from above. Out of that slashed mouth a dark shape sculpted the steam. It swirled the currents of the air, whipping up the mist in its path.

Shadow flowed into substance, and then the Eater of Souls emerged. The front of the steamroom shimmered like oozing black oil.

David's teeth snapped down so fast and hard he bit the tip of his tongue.

(What's the matter?)

snickered a baritone voice.

(Am I not ... *familiar,* healer?)

It was a stew of stolen life, and dreams. A gaseous shape of all shapes, human and monster. The demon's huge face sat upon its bed of steam.

Weakly, David held out the crystal.

The creature reared back in mock gesture of fright: a vampire whimpering before the shape of the cross. The charade broke. His wheezy laughter, like the shooting jets of the steamroom, rushed through the basement. His eyes flared, giant red lanterns.

(Ahh. The stone. How *good* of you to bring it to me)

Even Mick, dwarfed by the huge face, stared at it with naked longing.

"Why?" David croaked. "Why did you show me that ship?"

Fangs bared.

(Revenge holds no sweetness without full knowledge of the deeds. I swore we would face each other again)

Revenge. The word cannon-blasted through David's head. Up until that moment he had never contemplated how so much energy could be corralled behind such a word. It was the push behind those hurricane winds. The seed whose fruit was murder and destruction. And it was the force that had brought all of them together, after so many years, into this future time and place.

(You know what I want. What you promised me, so many years ago. Only *you* can do it)

David stared at the crystal sparkling within his fingertips. All the mysteries came clear. The triangle shape of the stone. The mystical power of three, the trinity: earth, body, and spirit. He swallowed, his mouth an arid desert.

"I won't do it."

(You *will*)

"No. I wouldn't do it then and I won't do it now. Kill me if you like. Chase me across another century if you must. But I'll never make you flesh."

Mick bristled. He turned to Victor. "You said—"

(Silence)

They glowered at each other, all three of them.

A noise off to the side of the basement, rising out of a shadowed hall. Muffled shouts of protest.

David turned to look.

(No)

Victor chuckled.

(I won't kill ... *you*)

As Bobby was dragged into the room, Red hauling him under his arm.

3

"Bobby!"

"David!"

A warm relief flooded through him, to see Bobby alive. How he wanted to lay his fingers upon his friend's cheek. *Brothers. We were brothers...*

And then his gaze shifted to the burned corpse dragging Bobby into the room. The sweet smell of cooked meat, the crisped skin and stubbled, singed hair. Alive, but simultaneously dead, too. For surely Red could not suffer that kind of abuse, and still live.

It was an awkward moment, as each eyed the other.

Bobby looked away from David. His face lit up when he saw Mick, as though a flashlight had been suddenly trained upon him. But pleasure gave way to wary concern as his eyes traveled up and down Mick's body, resting upon those misshapen feet. Swiveling further still, he recoiled at the sight of the gargoyle face clinging to the steamroom. His happiness in seeing his lover caved in with the sight of the monster.

In a strangled whisper he asked of Mick, "Tell me you're dead. Tell me you can't possibly be alive, and look like that."

Mick cracked a smile. "I look pretty good, don't you think? Look how strong he's made me." He flexed his arms and thumped his chest.

"Yes," Bobby croaked, near tears. "I see."

"Come on, come on," Red snapped, impatient with this sappy dribble. He yanked on Bobby's chains and pulled him into the center of the basement. They stood near the bubbling jacuzzi.

"David?" Bobby asked. "What's going on?"

The Eater of Souls turned his attention to Red.

(Hold him)

With surprising agility Red slipped behind Bobby and pulled him into a wrestler's hold. To keep him from jerking away, Red stamped on the chain swinging between both stockinged feet and held it to the tiled floor. One arm wrapped across the stomach; the other dug into Bobby's neck.

"What's the matter?" the charred being whispered into his ear. "Don't you like the way I smell, up this close? Don't I turn you on?"

"Let him go," David demanded.

"Or what?"

A rumbling growl shook the room. They all turned to stare at Victor, but the creature's eyes were fastened upon David.

(No ship's bow to throw me off, eh? Nor your brother's magical drawings to get in the way. Do as you promised, shaman. I'm more powerful now than at any other time in my long life. *Do what I demand*)

David trembled, holding his ground. "No."

(Once, you promised me your brother. By all rights he is mine. But I have picked my own vessel. Do as I say, without tricks, or I swear by all that is unholy your precious brother will be dead before he strikes the floor!)

In counterpoint to that warning, Red yanked his arm beneath Bobby's throat, squeezing with enough pressure to choke.

"Stop! Leave him alone!"

Bobby twisted in Red's grip, his face a mask of confusion and pain.

David clutched the stone to his chest. He glanced at the seething, crablike face and the beauty that was Mick, standing by its side in worshipful adoration. Yes. So that was it. Easy to imagine eternity within such a beautiful body.

"Let Bobby go," David said with resignation. "I'll do it."

Red loosened his grasp but did not let his prisoner go. Bobby hitched in gulps of air.

Mick turned to Victor. His eyes swam, unfocused. "Everlasting life. That's what you promised. You promised!"

(Yes, my pet)

Victor cooed.

(My beautiful one. You've served me well. Look how you've transformed, as our desire to be one brings us together. Come close, and we shall finish what we started)

The Hungry Ghost leered at David.

(Now, healer. *Do it now*)

4

The hairs at the nape of David's neck stood on end. The air was sodden with the foul stench of corruption. He glanced behind and watched as all the lost souls within the bathhouse literally seeped out of the walls, like droplets of water squeezed from a sponge.

There was Jack, who stood arm in arm with the same old woman he'd cavorted with on David's balcony.

Alex, with the boy, Miggy, in his arms. A chestnut-haired woman stood at his side, and beside her a chubby, balding man.

Flint, the man who had given them entrance into this place, his features regenerated and put back together — though still not human in their completeness. A man in a jockstrap with a name tag pinned to his chest. The taxi driver, Will Garter.

Roger, his manager from Uncle Charlie's, and the two men in clone attire who had been eating at the restaurant.

There were men in hospital gowns.

Walter, his upstairs neighbor, wearing a pair of boxer shorts while hand in hand with a young, slim man.

A black couple, male and female, their arms scarred with needle tracks.

In horror he watched them — each familiar face a knife wound to his heart. And so many others, he could not count their number. They gathered as silent witnesses, these ghosts. Some had shape; others were no more than a stirring in the thick air, as ethereal as the wisps of steam rising to the ceiling.

David turned back around to face the Eater of Souls. Over. It was all over. They'd fought the beast, and failed.

Kahmaal, he beseeched, *what else can I do? Help me now. Come to my aid.*

He closed his eyes and mentally cleared his head. The gate within him opened.

Bobby could not hold still. "Don't," he begged. He ignored the extra pressure under his chin, as Red held him. "Don't do it."

"Together?" Mick's eyes shone: the fulfillment of the dream.

The Hungry Ghost's lips curled into a smile.

(Together ... forever...)

A force gathered in the basement.

The sacred stone hummed in David's hand. Its current vibrated up his arms. Blue light whirled out between his fingers in an ever-widening spray. Words tumbled out of his mouth in a language he did not know, words that rang loud and strong. At that instant he was merely a channel enabling the past to burst through into the present.

The air was charged with electricity, hot, like sparks against his skin.

Earth. Body. Spirit. The crystal did its bidding.

The giant face of the monster surrendered its hold upon the steamroom's walls. It peeled itself free and began to disintegrate like black drops of oily tar.

Mick began to scream.

The dark cloud swarmed over him, a whirlpool of vapor and spinning matter. A sound like air escaping from a tire. Mick screamed in agony as the evil force flew into him. He shook and sputtered with convulsions, like someone being electrocuted. Only the swirling cloud held him on his feet. His skin was pierced by a thousand needles as each drop of Victor's unholy vapor sought entrance through the pores of his skin.

The lights in the basement flickered.

The pounding disco slowed as though losing its power source, then revved up again.

The terrible exchange climaxed, and was complete.

The crystal's vibrant light dimmed in David's hand. He blinked, throwing off the hypnotic trance that had gripped him.

An exclamation of joy bellowed through the basement. Mick threw back his head. "At last! AT LAST!" It was Victor's voice, amplified as though through a dozen speakers.

Red picked up the cry. The ghosts exulted in this triumph.

"Look at what you've done!" Bobby screamed at David.

David could not manage a reply. He was too stung by the enormity of his deed.

Mick raised an arm, studied himself. He slapped hands against his chest, then cupped his erection into a hand. His pleasure, supreme. He lifted his eyes, which burned with fiery light, and leveled David with a searing look. A contemptuous leer stretched his face.

David broke his silence. "I've given you want you wanted. Now let us go. You promised."

"I promised nothing," the creature spat. Sweat sluiced down his body, sweat that was pink with blood.

The lights in the basement flickered again. The building groaned. The spirits glanced at each other with sudden unease.

Red let go of Bobby. He looked at his arms, which were smoking. His face twisted with confusion. He stepped toward his new master. "What's happening to me? Why do I hurt?"

"It will pass," Mick said with Victor's voice. He waved an arm to take in the crowd. "For all of us, a new beginning. You hurt because you need to feed, to gain your own strength." He jabbed a finger. "Here is my offering. Take these two, that you may grow strong again. Eat of their dreams, their flesh, and live. Like me."

David ran over to Bobby and stood by his side. The ghosts watched with interest, their eyes turned from Victor. But some of them began to moan as pain and a new awareness of their situation seeped into them. David seized the moment. "He's lying!" he shouted to the restless crowd. "He has what he's wanted all along. Look: All the power running this place is fading. It's all inside him. He needs you no longer!"

Red's face was pinched with pain. He stepped forward. "Is it true?" he demanded. But he knew the answer as his ruined body suddenly became aware of its condition.

And the creature housed within Mick looked frightened as the spirits broke into spontaneous wails and chanted among themselves: "Is it true? Is it true?"

David grasped Bobby's hand. Together, they held the crystal between tightly clenched fingers. Its watery luminescence was only a shadow of its former strength, as though it had been broken by its own handiwork. But then each felt it, and they stared into each other's eyes, a connection that was beyond the stone and its powers, beyond the astonishing truth of their past lives: the love and respect they felt for each other for having fought the good fight. This connection gave David the strength to address the ghosts one last time.

"He stole your lives," David told them. "Don't you understand? Don't you remember? And now he means to sneak off and leave you to your fate."

The air was thick with hatred. They began to close in, this crowd of half-souls hovering in a purgatory between life and death: Alex and Jack and Flint and Will. Men and women and children. They slid across the floor.

"Nonsense!" Victor snapped. "I won't leave—!"

There was a sudden stirring in his chest. Victor glanced upon his new body — and screeched with horror.

The stitching that held Mick's knife wounds together began to stretch and pull, bulging to its limits. His chest was ballooning, pushing out under extraordinary pressure. His skin puffed taut, each muscle a grotesque parody of itself, inflating to a bodybuilder's nightmare. He became a lesson in extremes, every feature too large, too exaggerated.

As he watched the scene being played out before him, David recalled a hot summer day on Fire Island, and an air mattress he'd accidentally left to bake in the sun. The scorching heat had been too much. The mattress had abruptly popped at the seams, zippering along its length, mushrooming into a bloated shape as the heated air of its guts pushed out. Mick's body now began to do this as David and Bobby gripped each other, watching, frozen with wonder. They did not notice the crystal's heat within their hands.

"Yes," Red rasped, closing in. "You've fed well. Perhaps it's time we had a taste of *you*. Shared in the wealth." Smoke gushed out of his pores.

The creatures rubbed their misshapen hands together in anticipation.

Mick's chest heaved. He pushed down with his hands. His stomach responded by stretching as though pregnant. Now his left shoulder ballooned out, throwing him into a hunchback pose. His eyes were wild with startled surprise, his mouth opening and closing. He began to spin in a mad circle, whirling as individual sections of his precious body retaliated against the enormous strain of the pressure of a spirit packaged within too small a frame.

"No!" he screeched at them. "No! No! No! *You tricked me!*" His cheeks puffed like popcorn popped in a microwave bag. Blood spurted from his ears, his eyes, his nose. His expanded chest was a sea of red.

David shook his head, and shouted, "No! I gave you what you've always wanted!" He backed away, pulling Bobby with him. And thought, *But to live within a body is to pay the price of being human, mortal—*

The crystal flashed within their entwined hands.

The ghosts advanced, circling, their screams of revenge rising to a deafening roar.

The Eater of Souls danced his mad dance. He no longer had control of his body. Blood and steam squirted out of his body everywhere. His skin could not hold, under that impossible pressure. Every inch of him inflated to the breaking point.

The ghosts flew upon him, a great swarm of buzzing anger and gnashing teeth.

David went cold with sudden alarm. *Oh my god.* He threw himself upon Bobby, knocking them both to the tiled floor.

The stretched flesh holding Mick together gave way with a tremendous wet explosion.

50

Disco inferno

1

The explosion thundered over them.

Mick's body blasted apart. It ripped under the tremendous force, splattering the walls and ceiling of the basement with a grizzly red spray. A wave of pure energy screamed though the building, mushrooming up and out like a nuclear cloud.

All the windows to the Caverns' three floors shattered with a glass cough. Shards of glass and wood rained twenty feet away from the building and tinkled onto the street. Splintered fingers of two-by-fours jutted out along row after row of the windows.

Every light aimed upon the dance floor ruptured with the cacophony of bombs. Klieg lights twisted off hooks and hinges, tumbling to the wooden floor. Neon snapped. Laser beam lights shattered.

Pipes split and burst open like veins slit with a razor.

The television in the snack bar crashed to the floor.

The tape player in the front office began to smoke. "On and On and On" distorted into unrecognizable groans as the tape seared onto the gears. Movie marquee posters curled and fluttered to the carpet.

2

David raised his head. Dust and reddish powder showered the air. He looked at where Mick had stood and saw a spaghetti clump of bones and tissue. The walls above and on both sides were painted dark maroon. The steamroom door had wrenched off its hinges and collapsed inward.

Bobby raised himself onto his arms. David tried to prevent him from seeing, but Bobby brushed him away. His determined expression crumbled as the truth sank into him. "Mick," he sighed, lingering over the sound of his lover's name, a mourner over a grave.

David pulled himself to his feet and glanced about the basement. A broken shape slumped against a far wall. He ran to it, and knelt.

Red twitched and spasmed, a profound trembling racking his poor shattered body. Dying at last. His eyes slid open, and recognized David.

"Red?" David cradled one of the burned stumps into his hand. The barely recognizable shape in front of him stank of blistered flesh, but the need to give comfort moved him deeply. It seemed the least he could do.

"Thank god," Red croaked through his misshapen mouth. "Thank god."

He shuddered a final time, and lay still.

David laid the man's hands across his chest. He took the keys from Red's waist and rushed back over to Bobby, who had staggered to his feet. They embraced.

"Where are the others?" Bobby asked.

David shook his head. "Gone. All of them — gone."

The warped ceiling groaned above them with a splintering scrape of nails and sagging floorboards.

"We have to get out of here," David said as he freed Bobby from his chains. "It sounds like the building's going to collapse."

Bobby nodded. His brown eyes were very white in his face, which was sooted with reddish grime. "Do you hear that?"

"What?"

Then he heard. Like a swarm of angry hornets, buzzing. David forced himself to stare at that still-smoldering clump that was all that remained of Mick's body and saw the cloud rise, a smoky tornado that hummed the air. He held his breath.

The Eater of Souls. The distilled essence of pure energy. Mutable, but never destroyed. Wasn't that what Rachael had said? The black shape shimmered as though it were heat waves rising off a fire. Defiantly, it mocked them. A voice on gossamer wings, faint and unforgiving, a litany:

(I cannot die I cannot die I *win*—)

Making ready to fly off in all directions, ready to hitch another ride on the dark clouds of the night. Off in search of another gateway.

Bobby backed away.

"No!" David cried under his breath. "No!"

3

What happened next they held to themselves always.

Pinpoints of light — the winking of hundreds of stars — rushed to contain and surround this spirit's darkness. A humming filled the basement, like a multitude of prayers.

There were bodies in the spectral light. The shadow, the darkness of Victor's corruption, had burned off them. Now they were of glass, illuminated by the unending power of their own being. No special-effects wizard out of Hollywood could have captured it, could have come close to the astonishing purity of light that was the total absence of dark.

David pulled Bobby to him, and they watched.

The spirits of all who had walked the Caverns' halls surrounded this angry cloud, and contained it. The basement ceiling vanished with a cyclone swirl of white light. A figure was descending, a robed figure with flowing angel-glass hair and beatific smile. Mother to them all.

Rachael.

Rachael, who gathered the men and women and children together. Up and up the starlight spiraled, small lights vanishing into one grand shining. The black cloud that was the Hungry Ghost's truest self struggled, but could not break free.

Suddenly Victor's voice insinuated itself into their heads with a final ice-pick jab of doom:

(There are worse creatures than me who make their home in the night! We'll get you all!)

David blanched, and gripped Bobby in terror.

Up and up, light and dark, a galaxy of flashing stars. Individual lights were swallowed by a light so all-encompassing they could not lift their faces to gaze upon it. This was not their time; it wasn't right for them to glimpse that bridge to the other world.

The white light began to fade. The ceiling reasserted itself.

Around them, pulling them away from this spectacle: the flickering of lost power. Thunderous crashes ripped through the entire building as floors sagged under their own weight. The psychic blast had loosened all joints and supports, softening steel and wood into putty.

The Caverns was about to collapse into itself.

4

David grabbed Bobby's hand. "Hurry!"

They made their way across the basement floor, moving toward the staircase. Light bulbs shattered behind them. They made their way blindly, pounding up stairs that had now become ordinary, all of the traps of Victor's making gone. Chunks of plaster — the imitation rock walls — broke off in huge pieces and sprayed the hallway. The electric torches sputtered and died.

They rushed through this darkness of dust and falling plaster, screaming in blind terror. Convinced that at any moment they would meet their end within these doomed walls, they ran along the twisting corridors. David held the crystal before them, but its blue light was exhausted, of no use to them.

Down past the dance floor.

Past the snack bar, bar stools knocking to the floor. The whole place shook as though gripped in a major earthquake.

The maze gave way to a wall of lockers. They scrambled over the turnstile. A fusillade of explosions encouraged them forward, terrible squeals of twisting metal grinding against foundation boards and concrete.

They swung onto the other side of the turnstile. Sensing freedom just a scant few feet in front of them, they dashed through the foyer and slammed against the front doors.

They spilled outside, hurrying down the front steps and onto the street. Each drank in the clean air — great gulps of it, as though they'd been inside a box that now had its lid ripped off.

"Are you all right?" David gasped.

Bobby nodded.

As they began to leave, neither could resist a final parting glance.

5

When they turned to look, a shock awaited them.

From the outside, the bathhouse appeared untouched. Only its windows had been touched, gutted open, glass and wood strewn across the sidewalk and street. Now they were like empty sockets, a skeleton's eyes. No sign of the evil that had been stamped upon the place. It was just a building. A plain ordinary building, a relic to be condemned and forgotten.

But inside they could still hear the bathhouse continue to collapse in on itself. The Titanic might have sounded a little like this, sinking finally into an infinite deep.

The earth stopped shaking.

Silence.

A silence belying the destruction that had gone on before it. The empty quiet of a building finally dead and abandoned.

David raised his eyes to the heavens. Off to the east, dawn glowed orange upon the rooftops. Long fingers of fog ran across the velvet sky, disintegrating with this first touch of morning's light.

The night had not completely surrendered its domain, not yet, anyway. But this predawn darkness was friendly, and protected them as they walked arm in arm to Bobby's apartment.

After

Oh no not I; I will survive...
—Gloria Gaynor

After words

1

David's journal: November

The nights are the worst. And that's all there is to a month like November, short gray days and endless nights. Even though we finally enjoyed our Indian summer, with several weeks of brilliant sunshine, fall has given way to winter.

Sometimes Bobby jolts awake in my bed and cries out Mick's name. I hold him. Let the tears fall. I'm not jealous. How can I be? We've all lost so many. Funny. Out of our losses, he and I found each other.

I have my own nights of wakefulness. Victor's last words burn my ears: *There are worse creatures than me who make their home in the night! We'll get you all!*

I want to say he lies, that it's his attempt at a grand, final trick. And then I stand at the sliding glass doors of my apartment and watch the fog roll in over Twin Peaks and I know there is much work to do, much to understand. There are forces in the night. The only way to protect ourselves is to band together, hold strong.

And in a box, secreted away, I keep the crystal. My guardian.

2

David's journal: March

Spring trembles in the wings. Hard blue skies. Air cool, and clear. The smell of growing things, of rain-saturated earth. The redbuds on Noe Street are in full bloom.

I still can't get over this turn of events. Eddie should have told me. But, as he said in his will, this was his final way of saying thanks. Bobby and I have had long talks, trying to make sure we do what's right. There was never any question of *not* doing it — more a concern as to whether or not we could pull it off.

We sign the last of the contracts tomorrow. Thanks to Eddie's money, the Déjà Vu will be ours. Out of respect for the Blacks, we're not going to change the name of the bookstore. We still have some legal finagling to plow through. The police never found Rachael's body, of course, nor Red's. It's slowed up the process considerably. I think most everyone wants to forget.

I can't forget — for the fog still hangs on the hills. Waiting.

The newspapers had a few whispered reports in the beginning. Suspicions, with no motives, no bodies, no evidence. Soon enough, the articles disappeared. Just like the people.

Bobby wants me to write about what happened. I laugh. I haven't been able to put *any* words to paper, except in this diary. My days of writing porno stories are over. Still, Bobby insists. But how can I write about something as terrible as that creature without having it sound like fiction? I tell him I'll think about it. One day, I just might gather enough courage to write about it, to make sure there's a true record of what happened. Memory is short. As years go by it'll all seem a fantastic nightmare, unreal. But someone may need to know, one day.

In case Victor — or something like him — comes back.

3

David's journal: June

Business is slow. I don't mind, even though we have a stack of bills waiting to be paid. Rachael had a good eye, a smart taste in books. One by one I'm going through them all. I have so much to learn. So much to understand about my own gifts. One lifetime may not be enough to figure it all out.

Bobby smiles indulgently at all this. He's taken up drawing, but it's frustrating to him. He feels like someone in kindergarten. A beginner. But like me, he searches for his own answers. So we put up with each other.

I must jot down what happened just now. I was sitting at the kitchen table, writing in this notebook, when Bobby startled me by going to the record player and putting on an old Abba tune, "Lay All Your Love on Me."

I sprang up from the table, my heart going ninety miles an hour. He stood in the living room, motioning for me to join him. It was the first time we'd dare play that music again.

Without a word he came into the kitchen. He took my hand, and led me into the living room. Before the fireplace, where we had held each other in our arms that very first time, last October.

And danced.

Old bones creaked and groaned. The music thawed us — music I thought I'd never be able to listen to again. In my ears I heard ice breaking. We shook off the ice, the deadweight of grief that up until that moment I hadn't realized we still carried, and laughed. Really, truly laughed. For that moment, at least, we climbed out of the fog of mourning which hangs over our city still, and breathed clear sweet air. Threw our arms around each other. And marveled that after so much grief, so much joy could come from remembering.

Alyson Publications publishes a wide variety of books with gay and lesbian themes. For a free catalog, or to be placed on our mailing list, please write to:
Alyson Publications
40 Plympton St.
Boston, Mass. 02118
Indicate whether you are interested in books for gay men, for lesbians, or both.